Sheila couldn't keep the beaming grin off her face, nor could she stifle the joyous laughter that bubbled out of her as they danced. She couldn't remember ever feeling like this, so absolutely happy she thought she'd burst. She was focused on the twinkles in Rowan's eyes but, when she pulled her focus back enough to take in his whole wonderful face, she found her emotions mirrored back, and wasn't that a miracle in itself? She'd always thought she was too broken, had too much baggage, to deserve this…to deserve love. She'd tried to warn him off, she may not have tried very hard, but she had tried, and yet here they were. Dancing!

Rowan didn't ever want to stop dancing. This was the happiest and most care-free that Sheila had been in the time that they'd known each other. From what she'd told him, and from what he'd gleaned by what she didn't say, life as a vampire had been lonely. Oh, she'd boasted about her Charming prowess, but *making* someone give you something was far different to them gifting it to you because they wanted to; and while she was friendly with her colleagues, she didn't class them as friends. She had a secret identity that, until now, she hadn't been able to reveal to anyone. Rowan was such an open book that he couldn't quite manage to wrap his considerable mind around the concept of being unable to be one's self. The vigilance required, the subterfuge, must have been exhausting. So… yeah, he wanted to keep dancing for as long as possible, just so he could hear her laughter, and drown in her unguarded joy.

∞

This book

opens a portal

to another world for

Just Say Maybe

Book 2 in the *Just Say* series

Vanessa Sacco

First published in 2020 by VSOriginals.

© Vanessa Sacco, 2019.

All inquiries should be made to the author.

Edition: 1st print edition.

ISBN: 978-0-6484660-3-1

Contributor credits: Wolf illustrations by Samuel J Art; Cover design assistance by Jakkal Designs; Cover design by VSOriginals; Editing assistance by Bronwyn Sabat and Ruth Gonzales.

Fonts: Optima , Party LET, Berkshire Swash

A VSOriginals production.

You can reach out to me on Facebook, Instagram, Pinterest, Snapchat, Goodreads, Twitter and on <u>autograph.com</u>

This book is also available as an ebook.

This one is for my sisters,

Marie Claire & Louise.

Two strong and amazing women,
who make me try to be and do better,
just by being themselves.

Previously, in

Just Say No

We first meet Rowan, who came to live with his Aunt Magnolia after his parents' disappearance. Maggie had recently also lost the love of her life, Marcus, and Rowan's presence gave her something to live for.

This story takes place several years later, on an anniversary of his parents' disappearance. Rowan finds the memories too much to deal with and storms out of the home he shares with Maggie. Fate leads him to Sheila. Their connection is powerful and instant, but Rowan doesn't know that Sheila is a vampire, who has absolutely no memory of her life before she became a vampire. This fledgling relationship prompts Maggie to deal with Marcus's death, and reveal to Rowan that Marcus was also a vampire.

Meanwhile, Rowan meets Ash Hunter, of Hunter: Salvage and Investigations, who has been chosen to head the expansion of the family business into new territory. Ash, a descendent of a long line of vampire hunters, receives orders that his reconnaissance mission, to find Marcus, is a go. It's the beginning of a beautiful and tragic friendship as Ash falls for Rowan, not knowing that Rowan's in love with one of his mortal enemies.

Vanessa Sacco

Maggie, having been unable to cope with the guilt and loss of Marcus's death, had abandoned his Estate. Now that she is coming to accept that Marcus died saving her life, Maggie feels ready to return to his home. Not wanting his Aunt to have to deal with a derelict building full of memories whilst still in mourning, Rowan and Sheila tag along.

Gramps, the patriarch and head of Hunter: Salvage and Investigations, oblivious of Marcus's demise, has his sights set on Marcus's head and all the treasure that he had amassed over centuries of life. Gramps will sacrifice anything, and anyone, to get it, even if that means his grandson, Ash. Jacqueline, Ash's mother and boss, refuses to stand by whilst her father sends her son to his doom. She resigns, leaving the family business and the considerable resources that had been at her disposal.

Driving away from their temporary accommodation early in the morning, Rowan and Maggie leave Sheila safely behind whilst they venture to the Estate. Maggie is overwhelmed to find the place in immaculate condition, and still being looked after by Jeremiah and Eleanora, Marcus's long-term human associates. That evening, Maggie answers the door when Sheila arrives. As their eyes meet the veil of Sheila's amnesia is pierced and she calls out Maggie's name, in Marcus's voice.

The Estate₁

Taking the stairs up from the basement two at a time, Rowan burst out of the pivot door and hurried around the bottom of the staircase, straightening his shirt and his hair as he went. He slowed as Maggie and Sheila came into his line of sight, stumbling to a halt as he realised that his damn-near-invincible vampire had collapsed. It felt like those scenes you see in the movies where all the action freezes and time stops. For a split second Rowan wondered whether his heart was still beating, then he was running, heart thundering in his ears.

"Sheila!"

It was Maggie, turning her face towards him, pale lips trembling, that made his blood become ice in his veins. He knelt beside them, hands hovering. Afraid to touch, to comfort, or to confirm his worst nightmare.

"What happened?" He couldn't, wouldn't, touch Sheila yet so he rested his hands on Maggie's shoulders.

"Mags?" No response, not even to the gentle squeeze he gave when what he wanted to do was fist his hands in her shirt, and shake.

"Mags!" Rowan went with the shake. Nothing violent, but enough that now at least, Maggie blinked and was actually looking at him instead of the vacant stare she'd first had going on.

"She-" the sound Maggie produced was barely a rasp so she cleared her throat and tired again. "Sheila, she… I think she fainted."

It wasn't what she wanted to say. She wanted to tell Rowan that, for a moment, the briefest, most glorious of moments, she'd spoken with Marcus. Except, she couldn't possibly because that made absolutely no sense. It was Sheila who was unconscious in her lap. The eyes that had looked into her own, that had recognised her soul, belonged to the woman that her nephew had given his heart to, not to the man who'd given his life for hers. The voice that had spoken her name, that deep rumble that always made her quiver, must have been a product of her imagination. Marcus couldn't possibly have looked at her and claimed her as his, because Marcus was gone. Dead. Wasn't he?

"What, again?" Rowan asked, his trembling left hand releasing Maggie to brush over Sheila's hair before coming to a gentle rest against her cheek. Last time this had happened it had been the second time they'd met.

She'd broken into his car and was waiting for him in the back seat. Scared about ten years off his life until he'd realised it was her, then he couldn't climb over the front seats fast enough. He didn't remember what had set her off, they'd been talking because she was trying to scare him away and he'd refused to heed her warnings. He gave Maggie's shoulder a final squeeze before scooping Sheila into his arms, standing up, and heading for the stairs. He paused when he realised that Maggie hadn't moved.

"Mags, you okay?" Rowan turned towards her, noting her pallor and mentally kicking himself for not realising in his panic, that his Aunt'd had quite a shock herself. "She'll be 'right, Mags. I'll take her upstairs and tuck her in. She'll sleep it off and be good as new in a few hours, you'll see. Do you want me to yell for Ellie, or Jerry?"

Maggie blinked slowly a couple of times before she sucked in a breath and took in her surroundings. Rowan looked really tall, but that was probably because she was still on the ground. He was looking at her, was he expecting something? Ah, an answer would be good. "No, that's okay. You go on up. I'll stand in a minute, and go get Jerry to help me with the bags."

Rowan gave her a squint-eyed stare for a few seconds, making sure he wasn't going to have another unconscious woman on his hands. Maggie's right eyebrow crawled up her forehead in an *are you kidding me?* response and she made shooing motions with her hands. Alrighty then, Rowan turned and made his way to the Red room…their room. Maggie watched, not moving until Rowan had made it to the top of the stairs and headed down the hallway out of sight.

Heaving a sigh, Maggie then heaved *herself* to her feet. The front door was still wide open and the bags were on the doorstep, where Sheila had dropped them when their gazes had locked. Grabbing all the handles, she dragged them inside far enough so that she could shut the door, and headed back to the kitchen. She glanced under the stairs as she passed and made a detour to close the pivot door properly. Rowan had obviously been in a hurry.

Ellie and Jerry must have heard her coming because they were standing, side by side, looking expectantly towards the entrance to the kitchen.

"What the hell happened?" Ellie rushed forward. Maggie figured that she must look pretty much how she was feeling to elicit that kind of reaction. Maggie waved Ellie back before she could get any ideas, like maybe trying to pick her up and settle her in a chair. Jerry, bless him, walked over to the wet bar and poured her two fingers of American Honey on the rocks. He handed the drink to Maggie and, like the true gentleman that he is, made absolutely no comment when she knocked it straight back and handed the glass back to him.

"Another?" asked Jerry.

"Thanks, no. But I would love a tea please. Sheila's here. She fainted into my arms," Maggie made soothing motions as Jerry and Ellie went to rush to the front door. "Rowan came up and is taking her upstairs. It's the second time that it's happened so, while initially downright freaky, she recovered well last time and I expect that she'll do so again."

She wanted to tell them. Inside she was screaming *I saw Marcus, talked to him*, but verbalising that would likely just get her locked up. She wasn't crazy dammit, she knew what had happened, but she'd had no witnesses. The last thing she wanted was for her friends to look at her with pity in their eyes and a conviction that she'd lost it. She'd wait until Sheila recovered and then the two of them were going to have a conversation.

N.E.I.L$_2$

Neil had seen the whole thing, devoting an iota of his attention to the incident at the front door, whilst also watching the intruder climbing down the back trees. He had decided not to mention the intruder while Rowan was with him, just so he could teach them a lesson about not letting him have a voice, but he was having second thoughts. Everything he'd ever read involving trespassers never ended well. He might be upset with the bipeds but he would never, ever, want anything bad to happen to them. Of course, it was a moot point at the moment because, unless someone came downstairs, he couldn't tell anyone. He'd do his best to record every move the intruder was making so that he could give a full report...just as soon as someone, anyone, came down here.

In the meantime, this inability to affect his own environment was really limiting and had to stop. He wanted access to the internet dammit, how bad could it possibly be? He could deal with a few cat videos. What he really wanted though, what he'd never mentioned to anyone, and had only slowly become aware of it himself, was mobility. The barest germ of an idea had implanted itself when Marcus had him print the patent paperwork for the nanites. When Marcus and Maggie had disappeared the idea had stagnated, although Neil had not let it go completely. Then Jerry, the nice one - *was that unfair? Ellie seemed harsh, but he'd provoked her* - had decided that he'd like to learn more about nanite creation, and had continued the work. So Neil's idea had slowly flourished, until it stopped being a low-priority subprocess, and became something he actively thought about regularly.

Now that Rowan was here, maybe they could all work on it together. Jerry had made incredible leaps, and Neil projected that he'd achieve complete success within three years, but with Rowan and himself involved they could, at the very least, halve that projection.

Rowan & Sheila₃

owan made it up the stairs and into the hallway, before he'd become so distracted by visually tracing Sheila's features that he stumbled. *Dude, precious cargo!* Thankfully he'd left the door to the Red room ajar, otherwise he would never have remembered which room it was. Also, hands full, so opening the doors may have posed a problem. He turned around and used his butt to nudge the door open further.

The hallway carpet gave way to wide Fiord Grey Oak floorboards; Rowan was so focused on getting Sheila comfortable that he barely noticed. He'd almost swooned the first time he saw those floorboards in the bedrooms but now, nothing. He stood beside the bed, its ebony base lacquered to a high shine contrasting with its carved headboard, painted to look almost exactly like ivory. He'd have to put Sheila down to pull back the crimson silk-covered quilt, or he could fulfil a recent fantasy and lay her on it. Fantasy won. Resting one knee on the edge, Rowan leaned as far as he could and gently deposited Sheila on the very centre of the bed.

Walking around to the foot of the bed, Rowan removed Sheila's boots, one delicate foot at a time. He then reached up inside the cuff of her jeans, running his fingers against skin that was silkier than the quilt cover, before hooking his fingers on her sock and baring her foot, then on to the next. Rowan's eyes were heavy lidded and his lips curved into a smile when he realised that the polish on her toes almost matched the background.

Rowan let his gaze travel up his lover's legs, pausing at the top of her jeans where her blouse had ridden up to reveal a sliver of skin. Continuing his perusal until his attention was arrested by the way the blouse moulded against her breasts. His hands twitched, wanting to slip the buttons free of their holes and reveal more. He couldn't, could he? Sheila was unconscious. He shouldn't, should he? He wanted to make her as comfortable as possible, tucking her in, covering her up. She wouldn't be comfortable if he did that when she was fully clothed, would she?

The question was, would she be angry? And if so, just how angry? She could rip him apart with her bare hands and, if he did this, would he blame her? So then the real question was whether or not he was prepared to deal with the consequences of his actions. His fantasy was all about seeing Sheila naked, and writhing for him on this crimson background. It wouldn't be the same if she wasn't actively participating, if she didn't give actual consent. Decision made, Rowan turned down the bed, retrieved Sheila, and tucked her in; clothes and all. He was absolutely going to tell her his fantasy though, because he knew that she'd make it come true for him.

Rowan stood beside the bed, looking down at the love of his life. He knew she worried about, as a human, how fragile he is, and yet she's the one who passed out. Twice! Maggie had said that Marcus did the same thing when trying to remember his past, so was it just a vampire thing? Rowan didn't get why neither Sheila nor Marcus could remember beyond a certain point in their histories. Straining to reach those memories was obviously not a good thing, and Rowan wondered if that's what Sheila had tried to do this time. Although, why she'd try that just as Maggie was getting the door was beyond him. He reached down and tucked a wayward lock of hair back off Sheila's face, letting his fingertips brush her cheek, then her lips, on the return journey.

He still couldn't quite believe that she was his, always, and completely. He was in awe at the privilege the universe had bestowed upon him, and was petrified at the possibility of ever losing sight of that. He'd been through enough in his life to be confident that he'd never take Sheila for granted. Having your parents disappear off the face of the earth as you're hitting puberty was a definite lesson in the impermanence of, well, everything. He could watch her all night, but would that be creepy? He had resources downstairs in

Maggie, Ellie, and Jerry. Maybe between all of them they'd be able to work something out so that Sheila wouldn't pass out again, and take ten years off his life. Rowan moved quietly to the door, grabbing the handle so that he could pull it shut behind him.

"Row?" his name, barely an exhalation, still drew him back to her like a magnet.

"Hey beautiful," he murmured, sitting on the edge of the bed and taking her hand in his. "How are you feeling?"

"A bit spacey. What happened?"

"I came up from the basement to find you passed out in Maggie's arms."

"Oh. Maggie okay?"

"I think she was a bit shaken up, but she's a tough one. You hungry?"

Sheila thought about it for a moment, the last time this had happened she'd woken up famished. "A little, but nowhere near as much as last time."

"Did you want to feed now or hold off until closer to dawn?"

"I think I can wait. I'd like to go down and apologise. This was not the entrance I wanted to make," Sheila flipped the bed clothes as far down as she could, Rowan's gorgeous bum pinning them in place at her hip. Realising that she was still fully clothed, she looked up, and smirked at him. "Were you at least tempted to get me naked?"

"You have no idea! And I want points for resisting."

"I appreciate your gentlemanly ways. I'll show you just how much when we come back here later, but for now, hop up so I can get out of bed."

Rowan contemplated the alternative, lying beside her, and getting to work on the buttons of her blouse. He foresaw two possible outcomes if he took that course of action; either he and Sheila would make sweet, sweaty, love, or she'd push him off the bed - with her vampire strength he'd likely fly across the room, and crash into the wall - for not doing as she asked. Prudence won, he stood up and offered a hand. Sheila was glad that she accepted his help when she stood up and felt a bit woozy.

Ash₄

As soon as his feet hit the ground, Ash sprinted in a crouch to the nearest cover, the back of the garage. Removing his backpack, and pressing his back firmly against the sun-warmed bricks, he waited for his heart to stop racing, and his breath to get back to normal. He was in great physical shape, but the possibility of discovery had his adrenalin spiking. When he could hear something other than his own heartbeat, and gasping, Ash listened for any signs that he'd been detected. Dogs were barking in the distance, but other than that there were just the normal sounds of nature. He cautiously looked around the corner, taking in the lay of the land.

What seemed like acres of manicured lawn stretched from the base of the trees he'd just clambered down, to one of the most amazing private pools he'd ever seen. He had a clear view of the outside two thirds of it, the middle obscured by what he assumed was a man-made hill, and presumably hiding a waterfall. The last colours of the sunset reflected off the gently rippling water as it lapped at the sandy beach on the side nearest to him. He could make out steam rising from a jacuzzi at the far end. Extra wide sandstone steps, large enough for several sun lounges, bordered the pool leading up to the lanai.

The sandstone continued, paving the lanai in a range of colours, from cool whites to warm browns and fiery reds. The furniture, features, and lighting, served to highlight those colours. The length of the house under the lanai was studded with french or folding doors, and floor to ceiling windows. He could see people moving around in the kitchen, three of them. He watched while they conferred, and then ducked back to the rear of the garage when one of the women walked over and peered out into the gloaming.

Making the most of the remaining light, Ash walked along the back of the garage. The first window he came to was opaque, but he still crouch-walked below it so as not to throw any shadows that might be seen by anyone who happened to be inside. He did the same thing for the next three windows he came to. *Seriously, how big was this thing?* Ash estimated that each window was between two to three metres long, and there was a brick expanse of about 5 metres between each of them. Leaning out he counted another window, then a door, then four more windows, and finally a huge roller door. A glance upward confirmed the presence of shutters and Ash wondered whether they were a security measure, or part of some bushfire escape plan.

When he got past the next window and to the centre door, he took some time to examine the lock and check for alarms. The good news, he'd be able to get past the lock no problem. The not so good news? The door was alarmed up the wazoo, and it would take him the better part of several hours to get inside that way. He'd call breaching the door option Z, and try to find options A through to Y for getting into the place first. He contemplated strolling up to the front door and doing an *aw shucks, my bike broke down and could I please use your phone*. Except, how would he explain bypassing the front gate, and the crossbow on his back? And also, vampire lair…duh.

By the time he got to the last window the light was seriously fading, and he noticed that the glass went from opaque, to translucent, to clear. Cool! Shit! He took a hasty couple steps back along the wall so that he wouldn't be seen unless someone stuck their head out the window. He carefully crept back towards the window, using the camera on his phone for a quick look-see, he confirmed that there didn't seem to be anyone in this part of the building. Ash craned his neck and was about to cup a hand up against the glass to get a good look inside, when the soft glow of interior emergency lights came on. *Huh, they must be light sensitive and come on when the ambient light drops below a certain level.*

Taking his first good look inside, Ash forgot where he was. He didn't realise that he'd moved completely in front of the window, and was standing there with a look that was somewhere between stunned, jealous, and aroused. Had there been anyone inside they could have taken him out, and he would never have seen the shot coming. He was totally in lust. So close that he could almost touch them, were some of the cars that he'd grown up fantasising about stealing. Not that he'd ever needed to steal, but in his fantasies, he'd boost a Ferrari, a Lambo, or one of the other high-end cars he was currently drooling over, give the police the car chase of a lifetime, and successfully drive off into the sunset. Cars like that defined the term *drive it like you stole it*. Being a vampire must pay really, really, well.

Jacqueline & Gaberiel₅

*J*acqui was severely limited in her wardrobe choices. She'd been so busy arranging to have weapons delivered, to do much more than replace the shoes that had broken on her trip. Good god, she was having weapons delivered here, in the next day or two, but tonight? Tonight, in all her wisdom, she'd agreed to go on a date, with a cop. If things went well and there was a second date? She'd probably be screwed, literally, and figuratively. Her immediate nightmare was Gabe opening the door to the delivery driver, and arresting her on the spot. Of course, if things didn't go well, she was also screwed because the cop in him would probably have questions about her that can only be answered by intense surveillance. Which would lead to him intercepting the delivery driver. She hated *damned if you do and damned if you don't* scenarios.

"How the hell could I possibly have lost the other one already?" muttered Jacqui, limping around in one of her new shoes, tossing clothes over her shoulder as she went, looking for the wayward rascal. She'd worn her pastel pink angora twin set, with the cream trim and frog button, paired with her just-below-the-knee black A-line skirt. A perfectly adequate outfit, but the new black patent leather Mary-Janes with the 4 inch stiletto heels would take it from adequate, to wow. The outfit flattered her figure, but the years of martial arts had made what would otherwise have been slender legs, athletic. The shoes would lengthen those lines, giving an optical illusion of tall, willowy, grace, where there would otherwise be glaring evidence of power and strength. Jacqui didn't mind in the least, putting on a front of the helpless damsel, if it meant Gabe never suspecting the real reason that she was in the country. Of course, if she couldn't find the little fucker, her illusion would be blown all to hell. No pressure.

Gabe had tried going the cold shower route, he really did, but the freezing jets needling, and then carving furrows down his back, had him fantasising about Jacqui clawing him as he thrust into her. Instead of shrinkage, his erection throbbed, and hardened even more. He'd gritted his teeth and turned front on to the stream but, apart from drawing a gasp from him, his fantasy managed to override the temperature of the water, and his cock kept bobbing stubbornly. This was not how he'd planned on showing up for their date, worked up beyond all reason, so he caved, shut off the water, braced one hand against the tiles, and let the other wrap around his cock.

The first few strokes were harsh, punishing, because he resented the fact that this was the only solution that was going to work. The fantasy came to his rescue. Looking down he stopped seeing his hand, and instead saw Jacqui kneeling before him, her lips stretched tight around his cock, her cheeks hollowed with the suction, and her eyes looking up at him like a starving person looks at a steak dinner. She had her hands braced on his thighs, her nails doing that thing that kittens do, with the repeated digging in then retracting. Gabe spread his legs a little further, pushed off the wall then leaned back so his shoulders were braced against the tiles behind him. This let him free up his other hand so that, as Jacqui cupped his balls, he could mirror the action, and feel it for real.

"That's it baby," he murmured as he felt Jacqui try to take him deeper. The idea of being in her throat almost sent him over the edge, the only thing that would make it even better…ah, there it is. He cried out as he came, the vision of him palming the back of Jacqui's head, and holding her to him for a split second longer than she would have otherwise stayed, being more than he could handle. It was the absolute opposite to what he would do in real life, but that's what fantasies were for, right? Gabe doubted that he'd ever trust anyone enough to be able to really let out the Dominant that lived in the shadows of his mind, and he'd seen enough horrors in his life, and career, that he would never let him out without the consent of his lover.

Turning on the hot tap this time, Gabe washed the evidence off his chest and abs before finishing the rest of his shower. Shutting off the water, he ran the squeegee over the tiles and glass, then tugged on the towel he'd hung over the door as he got in. Drying himself before stepping out of the shower meant that the didn't get water everywhere, and that meant less cleaning time. He had enough to do in his life without having to spend any extra time cleaning up things that he could have prevented in the first place. The towel now securely around his hips, Gabe stood at the vanity to brush his teeth, and pass the electric razor over his face.

He'd laid the clothes he was planning to wear on his crisply made bed. You might be able to take the man out of the military, but the military had wormed itself deeply into this man; hell, you could bounce a coin off the bed covers. Gabe snatched up his Aussiebum Man trunks in charcoal with one hand, whilst whipping off the towel with the other. He caught a glimpse of himself in the mirror and paused, fixating on the furrowed scar over his flank. It wasn't something that bothered him, he viewed it more as a trophy of survival, but he had no idea how Jacqui would react when she saw it. He chuckled, *when, not if*. Her reaction was not something that he could control, so he shrugged, and bent over to slip the trunks over his feet. Glancing at the mirror he grinned, at least his arse was still hot.

Gabe reached for his jeans, and had them halfway up his thighs before he realised that their colour matched his trunks…and the shirt he'd selected. He wondered whether that meant something, or maybe he was just in a charcoal mood. It didn't help that charcoal was his favourite colour to wear, and most of his wardrobe was variations on that shade, with the occasional white dress shirt or blue denim. He owned exactly one suit, in black. He'd bought it for the first funeral he'd had to go to, and had resented wearing it on every occasion since. It would be nice to wear it to the job interview for a change, he'd cried too many tears in that get up.

Gabe pulled the slim fit knitted top over his head, and down his well-defined abs. He preferred the give of a knit because other materials sometimes proved problematic when it came to pushing long sleeves up his arms. His arms weren't gigantic, but he did enjoy working out, and seeing how far he could push his body. And he never skipped leg day. Gabe tugged his jeans up at the thighs as he sat on the blanket box at the end of his bed to put on his Timberland Foraker boots, in black. He paused with his right shoe half on; he hadn't been on a date with a lady like Jacqui in a while. Was he supposed to take something? Flowers?

Gabe didn't have time to go get flowers, and he kicked himself for not thinking about it before. The place he planned on taking her was BYO, so maybe he could present her with a nice bottle of wine? Did he have a nice bottle of wine? He hurried through lacing up his shoes, and headed to his fridge where he found a Rolf Binder Riesling that had been a gift from his sister the last time she'd visited. Re-gifting when he fully intended to partake would be okay, right? It would have to be because, as Gabe wasn't a big drinker, that was the only bottle in the place. Shit, was he supposed to wrap it? Or take it in one of those bottle gift bags? Which he didn't have. He thought he had an insulated cooler bag somewhere that might do.

He found it in the back of his linen closet and, when he pulled it out, remembered why it had been stuffed there, and why he'd never used it. Another gift from his sister; she'd embellished what had otherwise been a perfectly serviceable plain black pouch with a glittering shield, a la the superman logo, but instead of an S, there was a G. But she hadn't stopped there, oh no; she'd also sewn on a cape with the same logo. He hadn't been able to get rid of it because he knew that the moment he did, the brat would demand to borrow it.

Shaking his head with a rueful grin, Gabe remembered her impish smile as she'd handed him the wrapped package and, as he'd started to unwrap it, pretended to swoon dramatically while sighing "my hero". Gabe had laughed and hugged her, giving her a noogie at the same time. He'd just left the military, and until that moment had felt adrift, but the brat had managed to make him feel loved and like he still belonged, with nothing more than a wine cooler that he'd thought he'd never use and her over acting. He couldn't wait till they spoke next so that he could tell her that the garish gift had finally come in handy.

The Estate[6]

Rowan interlaced his fingers with Sheila's and was determined to never let go. He knew that *never* was not going to be possible…at some point he'd need to go to the toilet, and he wasn't going to drag her in there with him, but he was going to hang on for as long as possible. He'd never suffered from anxiety before; his breath had caught when he'd watched Sheila pass out the first time and he'd been worried, but this time he felt like he couldn't get a full breath, his heart was racing, and his belly was so unsteady it felt ready to imitate that scene from Alien. Holding Sheila's hand helped. It reminded him that she was okay, she was still with him, so, yeah, he was gonna hang on.

Sheila followed Rowan, slowing him down by virtue of lingering to admire the art in the hallway, and not letting go of his hand. She didn't know if the weird deja vu she was having was a result of how foggy her brain had been feeling since she got here or if she'd maybe been here before. Maybe with work? That didn't seem right, she'd never had to travel this far for work. She was stalling, she knew this, and she even knew why. More than anything she wanted to see Maggie again, and meet Jerry and Ellie. How was she going to explain her entrance? Sheila groaned, stopped, and covered her face with her available hand.

"Babe?" Rowan turned to her, then gathered her up in his arms. "You okay?"

"Oh god Row, what must they think of me?" her words muffled as she burrowed her face into his chest.

"Wait? Are you embarrassed?" Rowan chuckled. "The great, predatory vampire is embarrassed?"

"Stop it," Sheila poked him in the ribs, and was rewarded with a little yelp. Rowan's teasing was starting to put things in perspective though, enough for her to take a small step back, so she could look up, and meet his eyes. "I'm a stranger coming into their home, and I didn't even have the courtesy to stay conscious long enough to introduce myself, and thank them for their hospitality."

"Well, technically it's Aunt Maggie's place, and you couldn't exactly help passing out…could you?"

"What? No. At least, I don't think so. I really wish I knew what the trigger was this time, but I got nothin'."

"We'll figure it out, together, and hopefully before it happens again. Now, you ready to head downstairs? Remember, they've all dealt with a vampire before.

They would have been through this at some point, with Marcus."

Sheila shuddered. A look of fearful curiosity on her face, she said "Say that again."

"They've all dealt with a vampire before."

"Nope, not that. Try the rest."

"They would have been through this at some point."

She shook her head, and looked at him expectantly.

"With Marcus."

Sheila shuddered.

"Sheila, what the fuck?"

Sheila raised her right eyebrow, the expression on her face telling Rowan two things. One, she had no clue, and two, perhaps his tone was not appropriate.

"Sorry, you caught me by surprise. That name makes you shudder…involuntarily?" At her nod he continued, "but the name by itself doesn't make you pass out."

"Just gives me the heebie geebies. Like someone walked over my grave."

"Maybe Jerry or Ellie can tell us if Marc- er…he ever had the same reaction."

"Maybe…"

"But not if we don't get downstairs," the smile Rowan levelled at her was one of encouragement, with a teasing tilt at the edges.

* * *

"I could have sworn I saw something running across the lawn," Ellie leaned over the sink, and peered out into the gloaming. Jerry came up on her right to lend another pair of eyes, and Maggie leaned up from her stool at the breakfast bar, trying to see between, or around them.

"I don't see anything," shrugged Jerry, lifting a hand up to shade his eyes from the overhead lights. "In any case, an alarm would have sounded, or Neil would have let the dogs out."

That was the scene that Rowan and Sheila walked in on, making their way to the breakfast bench, just behind Maggie, and trying to see what everyone was looking at.

"What are we looking at?" asked Rowan.

Maggie squealed and fell back to her stool, while Ellie and Jerry spun towards them, too fast though as they bumped into each other, and Ellie lost her balance. Arms flailing, and missing the hand that Jerry had flung towards her in an effort to stop her fall, Ellie didn't even have time to prepare for the impact before Sheila was setting her back on her feet.

"Row!" One hand on her chest, Maggie still managed to slap his upper arm with the other.

"Oh wow! Sorry guys, we really didn't mean to startle you," Rowan said sheepishly, aghast at what almost happened but relieved that Ellie hadn't been injured. He surreptitiously rubbed at his upper arm while reclaiming Sheila's hand as she returned to his side.

"You must be Sheila. Thanks for the save," Ellie's smiling wink doing more to put her at ease than formal introductions would have.

"Yes indeed," Jerry cleared his throat as he walked over and offered his hand. When Sheila reached for it, he clasped her hand in both of his. "Thank you so very much. My Ellie means the world to me, and it would have been distressing to have her hurt."

"Ease up, old man," Ellie came close enough to snuggle into Jerry's side, leaving him little choice but to wrap his left arm around her, his right hand still firmly holding Sheila's. "Hey, it's ok." Ellie leaned up and kissed his cheek, reaching over and wrapping his right arm around her too, freeing Sheila. She could see tears in his eyes as he contemplated the probability that, after hundreds of years, one of these days they would invariably lose each other. Reaching up, she patted his left cheek while kissing him again on the right, then resting her forehead against his lips. Jerry kissed her tenderly, then hugged her fiercely, not letting go until she tapped out.

"So," Rowan cleared his throat, and took half a step away from Maggie, who noticed and gave him a squinty-eyed look. "What were you all looking at?"

"I thought I saw something running across the back lawn, it could have been a fox, or a rabbit, we get those sometimes. Anyway, your timing is perfect, dinner's ready," Ellie herded them towards the kitchen table. Jerry poured the wine while Ellie set individual lobster salads, in crispy lettuce shells, at each place. Sheila looked towards her smaller servings then, helplessly, at Rowan.

"We always served Marcus," explained Ellie, noticing but not commenting on Sheila's shudder. "It gave him the option to try the food, or not, as he saw fit. I hope you don't mind."

"Oh, I don't mind, I've just never bothered before. At least, not since the disaster of the first few times I tried food, when I woke up. A nibble shouldn't hurt, it's not like trying to scoff an entire meal that you suspect won't stay down but you're so desperately hungry, and afraid, that you do it anyway."

"You don't have to," Rowan murmured, giving the hand he still held a gentle squeeze.

"I'd like to," Sheila smiled shyly, reaching for her wine and taking a small sip. "Mmmm, good."

"It's from one of our vineyards, in New Zealand," Jerry bragged. "An award winner, that one. Fruity, crispy, and smooth, should offset the salad nicely."

Sheila scooped a small sliver of lobster onto the tines of her fork, and paused with it halfway to her mouth, when she realised that everyone, except Maggie, was watching her. Having her look back at them made them all realise that they'd been staring, and they sent guilty furtive glances at each other. Sheila tried, but failed, to stifle a giggle, which broke the ice, and had everyone chuckling and reaching for their own wine or food.

Maggie laughed with the rest of them, but found that she couldn't bring herself to meet Sheila's eyes. She was afraid of what she would see. She was afraid that she'd see Marcus looking back at her. She was afraid that *all* she would see was Sheila. So she played it safe, and avoided eye contact. She had no idea how long she'd be able to keep that up, but she was going to give it her best shot. At least until she could convince herself that she didn't hear Marcus's voice by the front door, which would be interesting because that experience was now branded on her soul.

Alpha Team

ina was trying to convince herself that she hadn't yet woken up. Her eyes were still closed, she was still breathing deeply, her body was still relaxed snuggly under the covers, and her lover's arm was still draped over her waist, with the tips of his finger caressing her belly as she breathed. All signs that she was still sleeping. Except for her brain. Her brain was already reviewing events from yesterday, and making a to-do list for today.

First on the list was finding a suitable gift for her brother, seeing as she was soon going to be on his side of the planet. Gina wasn't sure whether she'd get a chance to visit him, but she wanted to be prepared, just in case. She didn't know if she'd be able to top the wine cooler bag with the cape, but she had to do better than the mere bottle of wine that she'd settled for last time. Gabe had mentioned a job interview that he was really excited about, and she'd looked at suitable office type stuff that she could get him.

At the moment she was torn between silver envelope cufflinks that came with wooden inserts you could have custom engraved, and gunmetal USB cufflinks. If she got the envelopes she planned to have "Best Brother EVER!" engraved on one of the inserts, and "from your Better Sister!" engraved on the other. The USB cufflinks would get engraved with a G in a shield to match the wine cooler. In any case she'd have to order them from here, and either pick them up once she landed, or have them delivered directly to Gabe. Maybe she'd order both, give him one set when she saw him, and the other once he got the new job.

That settled, she turned her mind back to yesterday. Her CO had gotten the call to activate the team. Technically, as they were civilians, her boss wasn't a CO but, with the way he ran the Team, he may as well be. They all called him variations of that…boss, chief, Commander, Sir. Her team was big on not using people's actual names. They called her Comms, she was the IT specialist. She'd joined the team under a bit of duress. Gina had *dabbled* a bit in the dark web, mostly out of curiosity. She'd picked up a thread, and followed to see where it led. It had seemed a dead end; her predecessor had been pretty good, but she was better. She'd tugged on the thread and the Team's systems had started to unravel.

She'd covered her tracks, but their equipment was the best money could buy, and they'd hunted her down. They'd given her a choice and, as she preferred breathing to a watery grave, here she was. She wasn't complaining; the pay was good, there were travel opportunities, and the occasional perk. Oh, and she got to help eradicate the world of vampires. She'd laughed when the Team's ultimate mission was revealed to her. She'd been the only one. Her team mates had been gravely serious, and had stepped back as her CO came forward. He hadn't chastised her, he'd just started unbuttoning his shirt. She'd still been giggling, until he'd exposed the first scar at the base of his throat. He didn't stop there, each undone button revealed more. More scarring, more damage, more pain.

Her tears of laughter dried up, and by the end she was crying for very different reasons. She cried because the age of most of the scars meant that her CO must still have been a kid, or just stepping into the realm of manhood. She cried because of the incredible amount of pain that he must have gone through, and the strength that it must have taken to survive. She cried because her relatively safe world had just been shattered, and she now knew that worse monsters than humanity were out there. Mostly, though, she cried because she could tell that he hadn't; not now, and not then.

"Stop thinking so loud," her lover murmured, the arm at her waist tightening, and pulling her back against his scarred torso.

Gina, eyes still closed, smiled, and wiggled her arse against his morning wood. She really did like some of the perks that came with the job. She'd been able to get a full night's sleep, even though they'd be leaving on the mission today. She was just that organised. It helped that she'd developed code over her entire career, and most of what they needed she already had. The rest of the team hadn't been so lucky, her lover only making it to bed a couple of hours ago. She wriggled again.

"Careful what you wish for," her CO growled in her ear, rolling onto his back, and taking her with him. He wrapped his left arm around her, under her breasts, trapping her arms to her sides. His right hand moved down from her stomach, his fingers creeping under the top edge of her panties.

On a sigh, Gina lay her head back on his shoulder, and inched her legs apart in invitation. He turned his head, and nipped at her earlobe as his fingers teased at her lower belly. Gina tilted her pelvis, trying to get him to go lower, go faster. He chuckled, moving his fingers with her, keeping them where he wanted them, and going at a speed that he determined.

Gina moaned, "Please."

"I warned you," his tone wasn't menacing, but it was commanding, and dangerous, and sent a shiver along Gina's spine. His fingers left her, and Gina whimpered. His hand didn't go far though, just far enough to reach under his pillow, and pull out the switchblade that he kept there. It was a vintage Italian stiletto, with a pearl handle, and had been a gift. Gina heard the snick, opened her eyes, and watched as the blade caught, and flashed, in the beam of light sneaking through the middle of the curtains.

Lifting her head, Gina followed the path of the blade, her belly falling back towards her spine as he traced the tip along the edge of her panties. She wasn't afraid, she'd seen him handle weapons, and she could barely feel the path of the blade. It tickled. When he got to the dip between her belly and her hip, he slipped the tip under the scrap of silk. The blade was so sharp that the material gave way without a fight. Taking his time, he retraced the journey, heading for the other hip, and making quick work of the material there. Gina's head fell back on a moan, wanting hard and fast, but knowing that he was going to make the most of the time they had this morning, before the mission began in earnest.

"Don't move," his growl was barely audible, but Gina could feel it thrumming through his chest, and into her back. He released her arms just long enough so that he could tuck the blade safely back into the handle, and return it to its spot. Gina considered disobeying, for all of a nanosecond. He believed in fair punishment, should it be warranted and, while Gina wouldn't always stand for being ordered about, she was too afraid that punishment, at the moment, would be the cessation of all action. Gina was pro-action, especially in these few precious moments.

"Good girl," he purred, also believing in giving praise when it was due. Had Gina been watching him, she would have seen the wicked look that crossed his face, and she may well have been deliciously scared. Expecting that his command would stand, and be obeyed, he used his now free left hand to get a firm grip on the top edge of Gina's ruined panties, pulling them up enough to exert just the right amount of pressure on her clit. He used her moans as his guide, sliding his right hand over the material, using the silk, and the pressure from his fingers, to create a slippery friction right where Gina wanted it. Until, involuntarily, Gina moved her arms. He froze, easing back on the pressure, and clucking his tongue.

"Naughty, naughty."

"No! Oh god, no. Don't stop now. Please."

"Lift," another growled command. He changed the angle that he was pulling the panties, and tugged upwards, giving Gina the only hint of what he wanted her to lift. On her compliance he pulled the panties free, took both her wrists in his hand, and made swift work of tying them up. Tucking his hands between them, he pushed on her back, helping her sit up.

"Turn around," he worked to school the grin that wanted to erupt as she scrambled to obey, knowing she was hoping that their session wasn't yet over. He didn't have to worry about the grin when Gina was facing him, because the little minx had decided that the command not to move no longer applied; she'd put her hands on his chest, leaned up, and forward enough for his erection to slip between her legs, and was slicking his cock with her wetness as she slid up and down his length.

How had he lost control of the situation so quickly? The better question was, did he want that control back? He watched his lover while he debated with himself. Her eyes were closed, head back, mouth slightly parted, with little mewling sounds escaping as she moved over him. The heels of her hands pushed against his chest, her nails rhythmically digging in, then releasing, completely oblivious to his scars. Her arms were stiff, elbows locked, almost as though she was afraid that if they weren't she might collapse onto him. He'd like that.

He lightly gripped her wrists, then ran his hands up to her elbows, enjoying the contrasts in their skins, her smooth dark a perfect compliment to his rough light. He ran his thumbs in circles over the insides of her elbows, gently, repeatedly, until he felt her quiver around him. Moving on, his hands slipped up her arms, over her shoulders, and down to capture her swaying breasts, cupping their weight, before spending time teasing, rolling, and pinching her nipples. That got her moaning, her rhythm faltering. Her head fell forward, she took a breath, then raised her head up enough so that she could look at him as she started to lift her butt, wanting him inside her.

Should he let her? There was nowhere else he'd rather be, but he wasn't sure if he wanted to let her get away with taking control. He hadn't given permission. No one else would have dared defy his orders. But why should he punish himself? He reached down so that he could angle his cock for her, and couldn't help the groan that escaped as she sheathed him. He didn't even mind the self-satisfied smile that bloomed when she heard the effect she was having on him. He knew she was close, a couple more minutes, and she'd be screaming for him. He held her hips, stilling her movements, waiting until she looked at him.

"You don't get to come until I say."

"What?"

"You do not come until I say you may."

 "Oh god, but I'm so close."

"I know," he grinned, he was going to enjoy her punishment after all. She started moving, and again he stilled her.

"Do you understand?"

She moved. He stopped her. She whimpered.

"Do you understand?"

"Yes! Yes I understand. I can't come until you command it. Just, please, hurry."

Poppy & Doug₈

Doug laid a gentle hand on his wife's lower back as they followed the hostess to their table, and noticed that the men in the room sat a little straighter as Poppy walked by. There wasn't a jealous bone in his body, and he couldn't help but feel a little smug that Poppy had chosen to spend her life with him. He, like all the other males in the room, was focused on his wife, so he missed the subtle glances that the women in the room were sending his way. When they got to their table by the window, at the opposite corner from the entrance, he pulled out her chair; making sure that she was settled, and comfortable, before placing his hands on her shoulders, and leaning down to kiss her cheek. He may not be jealous, but that didn't mean that he was above sending out a signal claiming what was his, and warning off anyone who might have gotten any ideas.

There were the usual rituals; serviettes being placed in laps, water poured, notification of any changes to the menu, and drink orders being taken. When the initial bustle was over, and they were the only two people in their world again, Poppy leaned forward and laid her forearm down on the table, palm up. Doug laid his own arm down and took her hand. Wordlessly they reaffirmed their connection, before sitting back again, and turning to look out at the view, hands still entwined. The garden was artfully lit, but beyond that… darkness, giving weight to their illusion of isolation.

Out there, somewhere, was their son. Closer than he had been mere days ago, but still too far away. Doug watched Poppy, watched her mouth firm as she thought of Rowan, and what was to come. He tightened his grip on her hand, the isolation wasn't real, he was right there, and together they could get through any ordeal. Poppy blinked rapidly a few times then turned to her husband, and squeezed his hand right back. He was right, they were together, and that was all they needed.

Ash₉

His growling stomach was what snapped him out of his drooling trance, and brought common sense rushing back. He dropped to the ground, a bit like shutting the gate after the horse had bolted, because he had no idea how much time he'd lost fantasising about the wheels on the other side of that window. They were just so close. The next growl was accompanied by that hollow, belly eating itself feeling, and he looked down at it in disgust. His scorn had no impact, so he was reduced to foraging in his backpack for one of the protein bars that he'd thrown in there a while back.

He had to wonder how he found himself sitting with his back against a rapidly cooling brick wall, knees bent, feet braced, ripping open the bar because trying to do it neatly just hadn't worked out. How was it that his hunger was overriding his common sense? He was in the middle of nowhere, contemplating breaking into a vampire's house. He'd possibly already tripped god-only-knew how many security measures, but did that have him scrambling? Oh no. No scrambling here. He took the first bite, his arms dropping to rest on his knees, as his head fell back to the wall, eyes closing in pleasure. He couldn't say what flavour the bar was, or even describe the texture, all that he knew was that, at that moment, it was the best thing he'd ever tasted. Climbing those monster trees must have used up more of his energy reserves than he'd anticipated, being this hungry is the only thing that would make otherwise tasteless cardboard this good.

He was through most of the bar, and up to his last bite, before he thought to look around for any external surveillance equipment. He'd never met anything like N.E.I.L before, so he stood no chance when all he was looking for was equipment available to the rest of the planet, no matter how high-end it might be. The only conclusion that Ash could come to was that vampires mustn't need all the security bells and whistles. Finishing off the bar, he stuffed the empty wrapper back in his pack, and looked at the actual window this time, instead of through it. So, the money they saved on the external equipment, they obviously used to alarm the shit out of any and all potential ingress points. *Fuck.*

Ash had one last option before he started working on the door. From memory, the roof was constructed from some sort of tile, thankfully not sheetmetal. He made his way to the door, stood, figured that if no one had come to investigate so far, he hadn't been spotted, so he took a couple steps back, then ran, and jumped. He managed to snag the gutter, and held his breath while he swung there, hoping that the construction was sound, and it wouldn't give. Two breaths later, and Ash heaved himself up, and onto the roof, rolling onto his back in the process. Oh look, stars! So many stars. He took a moment to appreciate nature's wonder, that was usually hidden from him, because he liked living near the bright hustle and bustle of the city…or at least the 'burbs.

This hadn't been in his original plan. While he'd known that he wouldn't be lucky enough to find an open door or window, he had hoped that security might be a little more lax. Seriously, who needed to alarm every window, and door, out in the middle of nowhere? Had Ash known that security was one of the businesses owned by the occupants, he might have groused a little less…or maybe a lot more. Lying on his backpack and crossbow was as uncomfortable as you can imagine, and it was taking his focus away from the carpet of stars above him. Heaving a sigh, Ash sat up, removed his pack, and unslung his bow.

He wanted to recon the roof, see if there was going to be a less difficult entry point before he started prying the roof tiles off. It would be easier to leave the pack and bow here, and come back for them, but being unarmed would make him feel vulnerable ,and jumpy. Ash compromised with himself, checking the stock of arrows in the barrel of the customised bow, and the autoload mechanism. Once satisfied, he swung the bow back over his shoulder, and into the holster, in a move so practiced that Ash didn't even have to think about it. Picking up the backpack, he moved further up the roof, and tucked it behind an attic vent, so that it wouldn't get any ideas about sliding down the roof, over the gutter, and letting the nice people inside know that something was up, by making an almighty crash when it hit the ground.

He'd taken about five steps away before heading back to the pack and retrieving his canteen. Tucking the canteen into one of the pockets on his cargo pants, he'd made it three steps away, before turning back again. Taking his time to go through the bag this time, because he was fucked if he was coming back before going over every inch of the goddamned roof, Ash found room in his pockets for a torch, a night vision scope and, most importantly, another protein bar that he'd found squished into the very bottom corner of the pack.

Jacqueline & Gaberiel₁₀

The knock at the door came just as Jacqui held the wayward shoe aloft in triumph.

"Coming," she called, which Gabe must have misheard as *come in,* because she could hear the knob turn. He was walking in just as she realised that she mustn't have locked the door after he'd left earlier. Jacqui panicked, the bedroom looked ransacked ,and she wasn't ready, and in her panic, she froze.

The cookie-cutter apartments had a similar layout, probably a time-and-money saving construction feature, which is why Gabe knew that Jacqui's voice had come from the bedroom. He'd tucked the cooler bag under his left arm, needing his hand free to open the door, while holding the bottle behind his back in his right hand. Turning into the room he tried to make sense of what he was seeing. It was the complete opposite of his place; there were clothes *everywhere.* Jacqui was standing in the middle of the mess, slightly lopsided, one shoe held up in the air. The other was on her foot, and she was also balancing on the ball of her bare foot. Blood red painted toenails were visible through her sheer stockings, and Gabe felt his cock twitch at the thought of rolling those stockings down her legs. Not now!

"Um," Gabe cleared his throat. "Everything okay?"

"Can you give me two minutes?" Jacqui asked, her panic receding beneath Gabe's misplaced concern. Holding one hand out for balance, she lifted her foot to slip on her shoe, watching Gabe watch her as she did so. Did she imagine the brief flicker of disappointment as her toes slid out of sight? She sure didn't imagine the hard swallow as, once the shoe was on, she ran her fingers lightly up her leg as she lowered her foot back to the floor. When she got to the bottom of her skirt she gave it a light tug, picking at imaginary lint just above her knee, and again at mid-thigh. He was so focused on where her hand was leading him that Jacqui could watch him with impunity.

"Gaberiel?"

"My friends call me Gabe," the look he levelled at her let her know that, although he had been focused, he hadn't missed anything else. Jacqui could feel her cheeks warming.

"Take all the time you need. I brought wine which I can either pour now or we can take with us." He made himself comfortable, propping the door jamb up with one shoulder, while he held out the bottle for Jacqui's inspection.

"Perhaps we can do both? A small glass now, and we take the rest with us?" Anything to get him out of the room, so she could become a whirling dervish, tidying up as much as possible in a couple of minutes.

"Sure thing," the slight smirk that she caught on his face as he turned away, and headed to the kitchen, told her that he was onto her plan.

Folding would have to wait, Jacqui decided, stuffing clothes back into her suitcase. She hadn't gone looking for space in the wardrobe or tall boy, not because she wanted to respect her son's privacy, but because she hoped she'd be on the move again in a couple days. She almost twisted her ankle turning too quickly to grab the last of the clothes, and realised that she hadn't yet done up the strap on her shoe. She finished clearing up before sitting on the edge of Ash's bed, and leaning over to do up the strap. Gabe must have found glasses and poured the wine, because she could feel the weight of his gaze. Jacqui took her time, lingering over the strap then caressing her ankle and up her calf, lifting her head to meet Gabe's intent stare, with a challenging one of her own. He raised an eyebrow, and held out a mug. Jacqui hadn't thought about what it meant that there had been no glasses to wash when she'd done the dishes, guess that meant that there were no glasses.

"Thanks," Jacqui stood and took a couple of steps, reaching out for the mug. Gabe pulled it closer to himself, luring her into taking another step, and then another, before relinquishing it. "Toast?"

"To a good evening, with great food, better wine, and intriguing company," Gabe held out his mug.

"So, no pressure then," grinned Jacqui, clinking his mug with her own. Except, less a clink, and more of a clang, really.

Ash 11

inally taking a good look around, now that he'd loaded up the essentials from his pack, Ash saw that the roof was multi level, and it made him wish for the grapple and rope he'd left on the trees as part of his escape plan. He figured that the roof he was on had a pitch of about 20 degrees, not too steep, but far from flat, until it met a wall. Shit. No problem, the next level conveniently gabled so all he had to do was make his way over towards the edge, and he should be able to reach the next one and pull himself up.

That was how Ash spent his next couple hours, climbing and clambering, from one level to another, and then back again; like he hadn't had enough of a workout climbing the damned trees. When he got back to his pack he sat down, partly to catch his breath, but mostly to come to terms with the fact that he hadn't found an easy ingress point. Anywhere. So, plan J. He'd pull up a few roof tiles, making a large enough hole so he could slip inside, because he was not going to resort to plan Z, and spend hours trying to bypass the security system to get in through the garage door. Not happening. Unless the heightened security applied to the roof tiles. It would be just his luck if there was some sort of impenetrable barrier just waiting to laugh at him when he exposed it. *Fuck it*, if that happened he was going back over the trees, and would try again tomorrow.

Ash got up and moved to a likely spot, he knew nothing about roofing, and was hoping there wasn't some sort of trick that he needed so he wouldn't cock it up. Getting on one knee, he prized his fingers under the bottom edge of a tile, lifted, and pulled. By the time he'd made a big enough hole, he'd figured out what the trick was, he should have worn gloves.

*The Estate*₁₂

66 We haven't given you a proper tour yet," smiled Ellie, leaning back in her chair, patting her satisfied belly with one hand, and lifting her wine glass in Sheila's direction with the other. "Nor Rowan either really. Maggie, you should take the kids around while Jerry and I clean up."

"Nonsense," Maggie stood up, and started gathering dishes. "You put on this amazing feast for us, the least we can do is clean up."

"Magnolia!" Jerry stood up, and reached over, taking the dishes carefully out of Maggie's hands, and proceeding to tidy up in the correct manner. "I'd really rather you didn't."

"Oh! Ah," Maggie laughed. "I'd forgotten. Sorry Jerry, we'll get out of your hair." Maggie signalled Rowan and Sheila with a jerk of her head and, still chuckling, ushered them out of the kitchen as soon as they stood up.

"Mags? What was that all about?" Rowan had waited till they were out of earshot before turning to his Aunt.

"There are a few things that Jerry is quite particular about, the *correct* way to load a dishwasher being one of them. I don't know how many times he let me load the dishwasher then, as soon as I was out of the room, he'd reload it. I caught him one day and asked him what on earth he was doing. He was 20 minutes into a lecture about the correct placement of items for maximum benefit and efficiency before I interrupted. Letting me help, whilst it made me feel like I was contributing, was causing Jerry anxiety. He likened it to coming into my studio to help me with sculpting. He assured me that he wouldn't think any less of me for not helping with the dishes, and would actually much prefer it if I left the table, once I was done, exactly how it was so he could clean up at his leisure."

"But Ellie was staying to help."

"Ellie feels about her stove and knives as Jerry feels about the dishwasher. They work well together, and they've had centuries to get their routine down pat. Now, where should we start our tour?"

"The library! Oh Mags, definitely the library!"

Maggie gave Rowan a look, and headed in the opposite direction.

"Aw, c'mon. Maggie!" Sheila let out a giggle at Rowan's petulance. "Don't encourage her," Rowan growled, then grinned, taking her hand, and following his Aunt.

"If we started in the library, we'd spend all night there," explained Maggie. "I figured we can finish in the library, that way you two can stay there for as long as you like, and I can get some sleep."

Where the doors to the library opened onto the front foyer, Maggie led the way down the opposite hallway along the front of the house, stopping at the first set of doors. Grabbing the handles and pushing the doors open, Maggie then stepped back, and indicated for Rowan and Sheila to precede her. The lights came up automatically, showcasing the comfortable looking couches that were all facing the same direction.

"The media room," Maggie maintained her role as tour guide. "The seats all recline. There are single and double seaters. The sound system is state-of-the art. You can get into the projection room from that back corner, and that's where you'll find the collection of DVDs, CDs, records and legitimate electronic copies of almost anything you could want to watch or listen to. There's also access to all the streaming services. We do not pirate in this house."

"We didn't back home either, Mags. This is amazing!"

Heading back out of the room, Maggie closed the doors behind the trio, and continued down the hall to the next set of doors. "The music room."

Assorted stringed instruments hung on the wall that backed onto the media room, a full sized harp taking up the left corner, closest to the door; two drum sets, one of them electronic, were arranged in the rest of the space just in front of the stringed display. A recording booth occupied the opposite corner, but the pièce de résistance was the stunning Steinway grand piano taking up the centre of the room. Walking further into the room and turning right, Maggie ran her fingers along the lid on her way to a set of folding doors, ignoring the hanging, gleaming, brass instruments she passed. The glossy timber doors matched the piano but, when Mags opened the furthest door inwards, Rowan and Sheila saw her reflection in the full length mirror on the other side. Maggie caught their eyes in the glass and, with a mysterious smile, beckoned them to follow her.

Stepping through they were dazzled by the lights from several chandeliers glinting in the floor to ceiling windows taking up two walls and which were interspersed with french doors leading to the outside darkness. Arms thrown wide, Maggie was twirling towards the centre of the room, reflected in the mirrors lining every other available wall space. The folding doors could be opened wide enough for the Steinway and other instruments to be wheeled through. So, this must be the ballroom. Reaching over, Rowan took Sheila's hand, and tugged her into his embrace.

"I don't know if I can dance," laughed Sheila.

"Well, just try to keep up," smirked Rowan, not for one second thinking that she'd have any trouble in that regard. They launched into a waltz, starting off slowly but soon flying over the floor. Maggie watched fondly, wondering if they realised that there was no music.

Sheila couldn't keep the beaming grin off her face, nor could she stifle the joyous laughter that bubbled out of her as they danced. She couldn't remember ever feeling like this, so absolutely happy she thought she'd burst. She was focused on the twinkles in Rowan's eyes but, when she pulled her focus back enough to take in his whole wonderful face, she found her emotions mirrored back, and wasn't that a miracle in itself? She'd always thought she was too broken, had too much baggage, to deserve this...to deserve love. She'd tried to warn him off, she may not have tried very hard, but she had tried, and yet here they were. Dancing!

Rowan didn't ever want to stop dancing. This was the happiest and most care-free that Sheila had been in the time that they'd known each other. From what she'd told him, and from what he'd gleaned by what she didn't say, life as a vampire had been lonely. Oh, she'd boasted about her Charming prowess, but *making* someone give you something was far different to them gifting it to you because they wanted to; and while she was friendly with her colleagues, she didn't class them as friends. She had a secret identity that, until now, she hadn't been able to reveal to anyone. Rowan was such an open book that he couldn't quite manage to wrap his considerable mind around the concept of being unable to be one's self. The vigilance required, the subterfuge, must have been exhausting. So… yeah, he wanted to keep dancing for as long as possible, just so he could hear her laughter, and drown in her unguarded joy.

Maggie wondered over to a set of french doors, and slipped out onto the sandstone terrace. Marcus had surprised her with a ball one year, for Christmas in July. He'd been such a private person that the fact that he'd allowed a piano quintet onto the property to provide the evening's music would have been enough of a gift. He'd made her close her eyes before he'd led her into the centre of the room, and there'd been a brimming silence. As she'd opened her eyes to a room full of people they'd chorused "Merry Christmas", and let off party poppers, and other noise makers. She'd squealed, and jumped into Marcus's arms, who'd held her tight, and spun her around, before setting her down gently, bending down to look into her eyes, and asking if it was ok.

"Marcus, you crazy man," she'd chuckled huskily, "it's more than okay. This is wonderful!"

Employees and neighbours had made up the guest list. She'd learned later that he'd had the security company vet every single person invited to the event. He'd considered having everyone sign confidentiality agreements but, thankfully, Ellie had talked him out of it, pointing out that it would make people more curious, and likely to go snooping. Jerry had been the only person, other than himself, that Marcus had let her dance with that night. When she'd started to head off the dance floor citing sore feet, Marcus had simply picked her up, and kept dancing. She'd laughed then, too; head thrown back, arms around his neck, as he spun them faster and faster, keeping just to this side of maximum human speed.

Maggie watched Sheila take the lead and not hold back. They blurred, until Rowan's very human feet eventually took a misstep. Sheila caught him in a prolonged dip before his error could have turned into a fall. They were laughing while he did his best to catch his breath. The laughs slowed, stuttered, stopped. She could hold him like this all night, and he'd let her. He released her waist, and brought his fingers up to trace her smile, before cupping her cheek, then sliding his fingers into her hair, and around to the back of her neck. He applied a slight pressure, which his crazily strong woman took as a challenge so, instead of bringing her lips to his, he used his hand to pull himself up closer to her. Her self-satisfied grin turned a mood that had become serious, playful again. He smacked their lips together, then got his feet back under himself.

Sheila, smirking, held him prone for a moment longer before righting them both.

Keeping to her plan, Maggie took them up the stairs at the end of that wing, giving them time to admire the artwork on display in the hallway, and stick their heads in bedroom doors, Ellie's shoe room, and Jerry's gym. Sheila had to almost be dragged away from the shoe room, and the Louboutins and Jimmy Choos that she'd spied in the collection. Rowan insisted on checking out the gym equipment, and resolved to make good use of the state of the art *everything* that could be found in there. Eventually, Sheila rolled her eyes at him in the floor-to-ceiling, wall-to-wall, mirrors at the back of the room and, being the bright young man that he is, he got the hint, and they moved on. They repeated the look-y-loos on the bedrooms in the other wing, giving Sheila a chance to choose a different room if she wanted to. The Jungle room made her snort, and she seriously considered asking Rowan to move to the Black-and-Silver room, but she knew he would've had a fantasy of watching her naked on the crimson silk quilt cover, and she really did like the colour red.

They by-passed Maggie's room and headed down the stairs to her studio. Much bigger than the one she made do with at her house, Rowan marvelled at the quality, and the quantity, of projects, quite a few still unfinished. Staying here would give her time to revisit some of these, although he knew that there would be others that she would not be able to bring herself to touch. He noticed that she lingered next to a larger than life sculpture covered by a drop sheet, and wondered if she realised that she was constantly caressing it. At a guess, if he wanted to know what Marcus looked like, all he had to do was tug the sheet off the stone, but he'd never do that without Maggie's permission, and he wasn't sure that she'd ever be ready to give it.

As promised, Maggie finished the tour at the library doors, shooing them inside, and taking a moment to enjoy their kid-in-a-candy-store enthusiasm; when she felt up to it she would add Marcus's art portfolio to the collection. Right now she wanted to spend more time with her friends, so she made her way back to the kitchen to find Ellie on a laptop, and Jerry bringing her a cup of tea. Passing behind her on the way to the teapot, Maggie noticed that Ellie had a FaceTime session open and the gentleman on the screen seemed to be squirming. A raised eyebrow in Jerry's direction had him shaking his head, and slicing a finger across his throat. Doing her best to eavesdrop, Maggie worked out that the man was the new manager of a boutique hotel in Dubai that Ellie had been using for their staff for years. The Chief Operations Officer of their hospitality holdings had stayed there on his way to Europe, and his feedback meant that Ellie was either about to demand the manager's resignation, or she was going to buy the hotel and fire him. She would be happy with either outcome.

Jacqueline & Gaberiel[13]

They'd lingered over dinner, making small talk, and swapping surface histories. Jacqui was under no illusion that Gabe was holding back, and he'd be a fool to think otherwise about her. She did learn that he'd gone into the armed forces straight out of high school, getting a degree in mechatronics while he served. He'd tried the private sector for a while after he'd left the service, but he'd resented working his ass off to make someone else rich. He'd still wanted to serve, to help people, so he took a friend's advice and contacted the police force. That had worked out well, until his old commander had retired, and they'd put the current schmuck in his place. He was looking at going back into the private sector again, but this time he was ready to hold out for the right job, at the right money, and conditions.

Gabe found out that Jacqui had recently left the family business and, while she had the resources to tide her over for a couple more weeks, she didn't feel that she had the same luxury of time and choice that he did.

Her background was in business management and human resources, but she was willing to branch out if she couldn't get something in her specialties. She was hoping to wrap up the final project from the family business over the next few days, which worked well with his timeline as he was due to attend that job interview soon, but it was a long trip, and he might be gone overnight. He wasn't sure how the rest of this evening was going to pan out, but he was hoping to at least get a second date.

Gabe helped Jacqui up into his Range Rover and she thanked her lucky stars that she hadn't opted for the pin skirt. He waited until he heard the click of the seatbelt before handing her the leftovers, keeping hold of the bag for a bit longer than necessary, just so he could enjoy her touch. Her smile was all-knowing, and his a little bit bashful. Stepping back he gently shut the door, walked round, and climbed into the driver's seat. Starting the car, he picked a swing jazz playlist before pulling out. It wasn't a long drive, and the music allowed them to enjoy it in a companionable silence. He slowed down, creeping into his parking spot, trying to prolong the moment before he switched off the car, and silence descended. He only had seconds in which to try to work out whether he wanted to be like the younger generations and have Jacqui in his bed tonight, or if he preferred to play the gentleman. And, if he was't going to be a gentleman, just how was he going to get Jacqui to bed? He was out of time, the key turned, silence reigned.

"I had good time," Jacqui started, not giving the silence time to gain power.

"Oh, me too," agreed Gabe, turning towards her, still having a mental battle.

"Are you going to ask me up?"

"Would you like me to?"

"Well, you've seen Ash's place. That's not somewhere I'd want to prolong the evening."

"Ah," Gabe agreed. While there was nothing wrong with chatting in Ash's lounge room, or at the kitchen table, he was pretty sure that the fridge and cupboards were bare, and goodness only knows when the kid had last changed his sheets. Much better to chat at his place. "Would you like to continue the evening at my place?"

"Yes, please," Jacqui faced Gabe, the glint in her eye letting him know that chatting was not what she had in mind. He met her stare and, in a momentary lapse that had never happened to him before, lost control of his Dominant. Jacqui's eyes widened at the burning ice in his gaze, her nostrils flared as he leaned marginally closer to her, her pulse sped up, and her quim quivered, as his lips morphed from a gentlemanly soft smile, into a confidently arrogant smirk.

"Stay," Gabe commanded, before climbing out of the driver's side door, and making his way to Jacqui's side. He took his time, not to build up the tension, although that was a bonus, but to get himself back under control. By the time he was reaching for the door handle, he'd packed the Dominant back behind extra layers of shielding. It was the gentleman who opened the door, helped Jacqui carefully to the ground, offered his arm, and escorted her to the stairs.

"Gabe?"

"Hmm?"

"I haven't known you long enough to hit you, but if you bark an order at me again I won't let our brief acquaintance stop me."

Jacqui may as well have waved a red flag in front of a bull as Gabe's newly erected shields crumbled beneath the onslaught from his challenged Dominant.

"Two things, Jaqcui, just so we both go into this with our eyes open. I will give you one shot for free, after that if you ever raise a hand to me without invitation I *will* punish you, severely."

Jacqui hesitated at the base of the staircase, not out of fear, but because Gabe's words had sent a thrill through her. She was confident in her ability to protect herself, and get herself out of sticky situations, so she didn't give Gabe's threat the weight that she probably should have. She was finding the very idea that he thought that he could exert any kind of control over her simultaneously ludicrous, and exciting. Swallowing, she licked her lips, Gabe noting her every movement, before asking "and the second thing?"

"I will have you begging, and not just for my orders."

"Never!" Jacqui's temper flared, and she tugged to free her arm, ready to storm to Ash's door and slam it in Gabe's face.

"Oh, much sooner than that," Gabe chuckled, squeezing his arm closer to his side so that Jacqui couldn't escape. Jacqui swung her free arm, the Versace clutch in her hand striking Gabe's chest. When that didn't make him release her arm, she did it again. She froze, quickening, as he predatorily turned his head to look at her, shaking it slightly as he tutted. *Shit, only one free shot.* Jacqui was unprepared for Gabe to release her arm at that point, and so didn't take that split-second opportunity to flee. Gabe used the time to bend, and lift her over his shoulder.

"How dare you!" Jacqui flailed, her fists pummelling his lower back, and her legs doing their best to kick him in the front. The loud, sharp crack as the flat of his hand met her arse surprised her into stillness, the pain that followed stealing her breath, before making her wet.

"I can take you to Ash's place, and we end the evening as friends, or we go upstairs to my place. Your choice Jacqui."

*Alpha Team*₁₄

ina winced as she shifted so that she could fish the seatbelt out of the black hole between the armrest and the seat cushion. They were flying business class on the Qantas A380 out of LAX, and she had the window seat. The euphoria from the morning's sex session had worn off, and she was rueing the fact that the CO had such incredible control over his own body. She'd begged, pleaded, threatened, and tickled, to get him to relent and allow her to come. He'd finally compromised, saying that she could come when he did, then proceeded to demonstrate his superhuman self-control. Her throat was irritated from all her moaning and the final, screaming release. She was satisfied that he hadn't been as unaffected as he'd like her to believe; his whole body had been covered in a layer of sweat and, when he'd finally roared out and collapsed over her, he hadn't been able to hold back any of his weight or hide his trembling.

She smiled as she looked out over the tarmac. She hadn't had to fight for the window seat, he'd insisted, not out of any sense of generosity, but because he protects what's his. She hadn't argued, she protects what's hers too, should the need arise. She turned as she felt him finally take his seat; he'd been making last minute checks with the rest of the team, particularly with Guns, their weapons master. Flying commercial didn't sit well with the CO, but the company jet had been otherwise occupied, ferrying some pansy-arsed executives and couldn't possibly be spared for his team. He felt exposed and vulnerable without his blades and sidearms, not that he would admit as much, nor would he accept that this state of affairs put him in a particularly foul mood. Guns had assured him that he had arranged to pick up replacement weapons first thing as soon as they cleared the airport on arrival, which would have to do, but he didn't have to like it.

"Are you set?" He didn't mean to growl at her, but damned if he'd apologise.

"Pretty much," Gina didn't laugh at him, but he could see the effort it took her to hold it back. "I just wanna tweak a couple programs when we get airborne."

"I don't like it," he really wasn't sulking.

"I know," she didn't hold it back any more, chuckling at his sulking. He was a master at unarmed combat and could take down anyone on the plane barehanded, but he was still like a kid who had to leave his security blanket at home. "It's only for a few hours then we'll get you some new toys."

He folded his arms and huffed, barely refraining from glaring at the flight attendant who was doing the final departure check down the aisle. Gina reached over and patted his knee then rested her hand, palm up, on the armrest between them. He looked at her hand, looked at her, back at her hand, turned his head away then, on a sigh, unfolded his arms, and took her hand.

Poppy & Doug 15

It had been so long since they'd been to this restaurant that they opted for the three course option. Poppy started with the Hervey Bay prawn bisque - seared prawns, fennel custard, dried tomatoes, and fennel salad - sharing it with Doug and sampling his pan-seared Thirlmere duck breast - salsify, charred baby leek, shaved rhubarb with spiced chutney sauce - in return.

"This is delicious," murmured Poppy, before leaning forward so that Doug could feed her another forkful of duck.

They took their time, lingering over each course, and savouring every mouthful. Poppy knew that the next few days would be stressful. She'd seen the moment that Rowan would need them, but nothing much beyond that. There had been no indication about how he was going to react to their return. She hadn't really thought about it until now, her focus had been on getting to their son because he needed them. And Magnolia! Would her sister understand, or would she hold it against her forever? Would it matter to either of them that Poppy's actions had essentially saved the world?

She'd seen it all so clearly. She'd been waiting out the front of Rowan's school, in the car, so that she could keep it running with the air conditioner going, so it wouldn't be too hot for him in the sweltering Australian summer. The school bell had rung and, seconds later, children had poured out of the classrooms, calling out to each other, laughing, and fleeing their imprisonment, despite the heat. One moment she'd seen happy, healthy kids, and the next a veritable wasteland. She'd cried out in anguish, but then it had rewound, slowly at first so that she could focus on the details, but then speeding up, so that she could only catch flashes. The vision stopped when it got to that present moment then split, showing two possible futures, and giving Poppy a nauseating migraine in the process.

Had Poppy and Doug stayed with Rowan, then Gramps and his company would have succeeded in ridding the world of vampires, but that would have only given Gramps a temporary satisfaction. He would then have turned his attention onto what he perceived to be enemies of the state, succeeding where so many of them had failed, and bringing about the final war. When Rowan had opened the car door, climbing in and chattering the whole while, Poppy had to open *her* door, lean out, and give in to the nausea. It wasn't just the intensity of the vision, the varying speeds of playback, or the back and forth through time, but the idea that her precious boy could be dead before his time had her unable to hold anything down.

She'd driven them home in a numb kind of shock, murmuring unintelligible responses to Rowan whenever his tone indicated that he'd asked something. Poppy had pulled into their driveway and he'd bounded out of the car before it had come to a completed stop. She hadn't chastised him for it, unlike every other time he'd done the same thing. Racing up the front steps and across the porch he stood, bouncing from one foot to the other and propping the screen door open, waiting for her to catch up and unlock the front door. She'd switched off the car, putting it in park and ratcheting up the handbrake. Then she'd sat there, unmoving, unseeing, senseless.

Rowan hadn't checked to see if his mum was right behind him, where else would she be? It took him a few moments to realise that she wasn't there, unlocking the door so that he could bolt into the bathroom to relieve himself of the can of contraband cola he'd bought at the canteen at lunch and had to finish before he went out to the car. Soft drinks were a no-no at their house, and he didn't want his mum giving him *that* look, or a lecture about all the sugar he was ingesting. He'd actually prefer a lecture to the look though. The look was a combination of exasperation, a little bit of anger, and a whole lot of disappointment; the quintessential mum look that they must surely all receive instructions on, to get just right. He'd seen his friends squirm under the same look from their mums and he hated how he felt like the worst son in the world whenever his mum levelled it on him. What was she doing?

"Mum," called Rowan then, when there was no response, he called again, louder "Mum!"

Poppy started, heart thumping, looking around, trying to get her bearings. They were home? Already? Where was Rowan? Spying him on the porch doing his sneaky cola dance, Poppy felt her heart start to slow it's frantic beating for the first time since she'd been bombarded with the vision. They had time, not much of it, but enough to work out what to do. Reaching over to the passenger side footwell, she grabbed her handbag, took the keys out of the ignition and went to unlock the front door for her sugar-loaded son.

*Ash*16

Lying on his belly, Ash stuck his head into the hole he'd made in Marcus's roof. It might be a bit petty of him, but he felt an inordinate amount of satisfaction about fucking up a vampire's roof. He had no plans to put any of the tiles back, and he hoped that the next time it rained it would be torrential. The Spark SD6 headlamp he'd donned was powerful and lit up the area, showing Ash that he would need to bend over for just a bit until he'd made it a few more meters over the garage. Shit! The garage. The hole in the roof was over the garage. With all those beautiful machines. Mother-fucker! He'd have to close up the hole when he was inside, he'd never forgive himself if those wet dreams on wheels were damaged because of him.

So, good news, like most people, it seemed that vampires didn't alarm their roof cavities. Ash reached over for his backpack and bent back into the hole he'd made to toss it in, and over a bit, so that he wouldn't land on it when he made his entrance. That done, there was nothing preventing him from finally, truly, breaching the perimeter. Nothing, except the way his gut had started churning, and not in a food poisoning kinda way either, the moment he'd removed the tiles. Whatever butterflies he had in there must be on steroids, and totally confused about whether he was excited, or scared. He didn't buy into most superstitions, and he was confident in his training and experience. So what was it that had half of his brain urging him to turn tail and get the hell outta here, and the other half wanting him to run towards his destiny? *Wait, what?*

"Fuck it," muttered Ash, sitting on the edge with his feet in the hole, before pushing off, and tumbling down his own personal rabbit hole.

N.E.I.L.17

Neil had been monitoring every move the intruder made. He had been considering letting the dogs out, until Ash had stood in full view of the garage window, mesmerised by the vehicles within. Neil had used that opportunity to run a scan, using the various cameras and sensors that he had access to. Other than the crossbow, and a knife, the intruder didn't seem to be armed. Ellie and Jerry were more than capable of defending themselves, they'd had centuries together to practice, and master, various styles of fighting and defence; Marcus had insisted that Maggie learn the basics so, the only unknown quantities were Rowan and Sheila. Based on the capabilities that Marcus had evidenced as a vampire, Neil determined that Sheila could look after herself and, if necessary, Rowan too.

Although, the fainting spell at the entrance was concerning, perhaps this vampire was defective in some way. Neil recalled that Marcus had caused himself excruciating pain in his attempts to push through his mental block and access earlier memories, perhaps Sheila had suffered something similar? But Marcus had never fainted. And why had Maggie said *Marcus*, just before Sheila passed out, but not mentioned it again? Humans were confounding in their insistence to so often live in denial.

When presented with a puzzle, Neil worked on it until it was solved; Maggie was doing her best to pretend it hadn't happened, which was a nonsense because it clearly had, Neil had it recorded. Neil recorded everything, from the White Brow Treecreeper family nesting in the front hedge that he used the camera in the gnome to monitor, to the little air con temperature setting war that had been going on between Ellie and Jerry since the beginning of Neil's memories. The only places that Neil didn't have complete access to were the bedrooms and bathrooms. Something about privacy; if sniffing was a viable option, Neil would have done it.

Jacqueline & Gaberiel[18]

The word choice was what re-asserted the training that had fled the moment Gabe had hoisted her over his shoulder. Jacqui had trained for years, specifically so that she could have choices, and so that those choices could not be easily taken from her. She used those moments, before Gabe expected her answer, to take a deep breath (or as deep as one could when bent double over someone's shoulder) and centre herself. She worked through the choices that he'd given her, and realised that he'd missed one. He couldn't see the sly smile that whispered across her lips, or see her switch her clutch from her right hand to her left.

His eyes had widened as his hand had rebounded off her firm arse. He'd wanted to rub and soothe the spot, apologise, and hope that she didn't want to press charges. The Dominant in him had fought all those actions, so that Gabe found himself almost frozen by the internal battle as soon as the last words had left his mouth. He didn't realise that he'd held his breath, until he felt Jacqui's movements, but couldn't figure out what she was up to. She hadn't started screaming. That was a good thing, right? Maybe she'd just ask to go to Ash's place and forget the whole thing. God, what had he been thinking? He felt her fingers walking up his back, and his breath escaped on a surprised huff. Maybe he hadn't completely fucked things up. Maybe she was into the caveman kind of thing. Gabe was growing more hopeful by the moment.

Jacqui walked her fingers up his back, until she reached the collar of his shirt. Had his hair been long enough for her to grab any of it, even with just the tips of her fingers, she would have given a playful tug. As it was, she slid her fingers up along his skin a centimetre or two, until she felt the barely-there stubble, scratching it lightly, but hard enough to hear it rasp under her finger nails. She felt Gabe's intake of breath. Good, she'd got his attention, now to let him know her choice. Snaking her hand slowly around the side of his head, she pinched his earlobe between two finger nails, gave a firm but quick pull, and was moving again before he'd had a chance to fully register her actions.

Gabe had liked Jacqui's nails in his hair, but it was the quick, barely-there pain of his earlobe that had his cock twitching. What would she do next? Her hand was back in his hair, the sound of her nails scraping over his scalp loud within his skull, travelling up, and over his head. She changed to fingertips when she reached his forehead, and stroked along his eyebrow a couple of times, before moving her middle finger down his closed eyelid to the inner corner of his eye. She pressed, her fingernail would leave a mark. If she chose to, she could gouge his eye out. Gabe chuffed, understanding dawning. He hadn't tossed a damsel over his shoulder, he'd hefted a tiger.

"Put. Me. Down."

Gabe lowered until he was kneeling on one knee, head bowed, his forearm braced on his bent knee. Jacqui, feet firmly back on the ground, straightened slowly to allow for possible lightheadedness after being inverted for so long. She kept the hand with the clutch on Gabe's shoulder, straightening her skirt with the other. Gabe didn't dare move. When she was ready, and not a second before, Jacqui took a small step back. She was still, very much, in Gabe's personal space, dominating it.

"Look at me," Jacqui demanded. Gabe hesitated, not sure what he would see, or what he wanted to see.

"Now," Jacqui's tone brooked no argument.

Gabe's head snapped back, his eyes meeting hers. Her proximity meant a crick in his neck if he had to hold this pose for any length of time, but the look in her eyes told him it would be worth it. He half expected her to take a swing at him and, to be honest, he wouldn't blame her. He was proud of himself for not flinching as she lifted her hand, but he couldn't help the slight widening of his eyes in surprise as she, gently and leisurely, traced the features of his face. She paused at the childhood eyebrow scar, her eyes returning to his with a question. Gabe swallowed, ready to explain, but her forefinger pressed against his lips. No answer required at this time. Lifting her finger she tapped him firmly on the tip of his nose.

"Just so we're clear, I'm proficient in several forms of combat. If you *ever* try that again without first obtaining my permission, I will fight back. Hard. And I will hurt you. Badly." Jacqui paused long enough to ensure that Gabe clearly understood what she'd just said, and that there was no doubt that she'd meant every word. "Now, is there anything you want to say to me?"

"I want to take you upstairs, strip you, tie you to my bed, gag you, and make you come so hard, so often, and for so long that you lose your voice from screaming, before you pass out." Gabe waited, heart racing. He held her gaze as she took two steps back and turned around, then he sighed and dropped his head, chin to chest. He didn't see as, instead of walking to her son's apartment, Jacqui went to the base of the stairs.

Stopping with one foot on the bottom step, and a hand on the rail, she turned to look at him over her shoulder. "What are you waiting for?"

The Estate₁₉

Sheila zipped around the entire library - upstairs, downstairs, and through the stacks - and was back before Rowan barely had a chance to register that she'd left his side. The breeze she generated ruffled his hair on her return, and he gave her a rueful grin, no doubt she'd checked out the filing system and could tell him what was where.

"For a private library, this place is amazing," Sheila enthused over the pile of books in her arms. She virtually skipped to one of the reading couches, carefully setting down her bounty, before making herself comfortable and picking up the top book. Rowan followed, then dipped his head and smiled as he read the title on the cover, *Interview with a Vampire*.

"Which way to non fiction?"

Sheila indicated behind her and to the left before murmuring distractedly, "but I think they mis-shelved this one because it was in the fiction section."

"Hon, that *is* fiction."

"How would you know?" Sheila asked, quirking a brow. "Before we met you would have said there were no such things as vampires."

Rowan opened his mouth to reply but shut it again, stumped. She was right. He was going to tell her so, but she'd already returned her attention to the book, and he doubted she'd hear him. He headed over to the shelves, determined to do some research of his own.

Each book was marked with a Dewey Decimal classification, and he noticed that the sections with the most books were for subjects that would have, at one time or another, interested the various occupants of the Estate. There were whole sections missing or incomplete, for instance there were no encyclopaedias. Then again, who needed any when you have google? For a millisecond Rowan wondered why bother with a library at all, when the internet was freely available, then he shook his head, and came to his senses. Maybe they had the CD or DVD versions though. *Did they even make those anymore?*

He wandered through the stacks, intending to pull whatever books he found on vampires and vampirism. He stopped when he got to 398.3, the section on real phenomena as subjects of folklore, figuring it was as good a place as any to start. The first book to catch his eye was *A Lycanthropy Reader: Werewolves in Western Culture* by Charlotte F. Otten. Sure, vampires were real, but werewolves? Was that even possible?

"Rowan?"

"Hmmm?" He took the book with him as he went to see what Sheila needed.

"I think there might be rats in the roof."

"What makes you say that?"

"I can hear something moving around up there."

"I can't hear anything."

"You can't hear anything with your human ears. Heightened senses over here, remember?"

"Should we check it out?"

"Are you nuts?" Sheila looked at him in horror, shuddering as she clarified "It could be *rats*."

"Yeah, but NEIL said that they hadn't had a pest problem when Marcus was in residence. Wait, are you afraid of rats? I thought the big, bad, vampire wasn't afraid of anything?"

"They used to use rats to torture people, tying the victim down and putting rats on their torso. They'd put a cage or a container over the rats so they couldn't escape, and then they'd heat the container up. It was bad enough if you were human, feeling the rats clawing and eating their way into your body in an effort to escape from the increasing heat. At least humans would eventually die. Most animals fear vampires because we are the top of the food chain, so yeah, under normal circumstances rats would flee. But can you imagine if someone managed to capture me and tie me down securely? I wouldn't have the luxury of dying. I'd feel them, hear them. If I'd had enough sustenance my body would heal itself behind them."

The look Sheila levelled at Rowan was haunted, and he had to wonder if she'd been through that horror and if, although she couldn't remember her distant past, her subconscious retained the trauma.

"Hey, it's okay," Rowan sat beside her, gathered her into his arms, and pulled her onto his lap. "We'll stay away from rats. I'll give Jerry a heads up that there might be something in the roof, and he'll probably get a pest control guy out to have a look."

Sheila snuggled into Rowan's embrace, rubbing her cheek against his chest, closing her eyes, and inhaling his scent. He rested his chin gently on her head.

"Are you disappointed?" she asked, quietly but not weakly.

"About what?"

"About me being afraid of something so intrinsically harmless?"

"Well, there wasn't much that was harmless in the scenario you described. Although, I guess, one could say that rats don't kill people, people kill people."

"Because, under normal circumstances, rats would run away from me?"

"Yeah."

"Yeah," Sheila agreed on a sigh. "We should go tell Jerry."

"In a while. I'm enjoying just sitting here," Rowan gave a squeeze so she'd know that he meant that he was treasuring having her in his arms.

* * *

"So are you going to buy the hotel" asked Maggie as Ellie terminated the FaceTime session.

"No, the owners are good friends of ours and they know that, should they ever want to sell, I'm more than happy to make a very generous offer."

"Are you going to have that man fired?"

"I'm thinking about it. He's new enough that he may not have known what our expectations are when any of our staff stay there -"

"But he does now," smirked Maggie.

"But he does now," confirmed Ellie. "So we might give him another chance."

"Getting soft in your old age, Love?" asked Jerry, before quickly ducking into the butler's pantry, and closing the door behind him.

"I'll show you soft later, old man," muttered Ellie, the dangerous twinkle in her eyes wasted on the pantry door.

Alpha Team[20]

They'd taken a night flight, hoping to hit the ground running when they reached their destination, fifteen hours but two days later thanks to the international date line. Gina had organised the flights, and pinned down each member of the team so that she could pre-order their meals. The CO had wanted them served ASAP, so that they could all get plenty of rest and be fresh for the mission. Dinner arrived not long after takeoff, and Gina was surprised to find herself enjoying it. She'd opted to start with the warm scallop and fennel salad, but she couldn't help surreptitiously eyeing the prawn cocktail salad she'd ordered for the CO.

"Do you want a taste?"

Caught, Gina grinned, apparently her stealthy spying needed some work. She nodded and was about to reach over with her fork to spear a prawn when the CO leaned towards her.

"Open."

He'd loaded his fork with a bit of everything on his plate, creating a perfect bite. Eyeing the bounty, Gina obeyed. Leaning back, she closed her eyes in bliss at the flavours dancing in her mouth.

"More?"

Gina reluctantly shook her head. "But thanks, that was delicious. Would you like to try some of mine? It's good too."

"Sure."

Gina cut and carefully piled pieces on her plate, picked the pile up between finger and thumb, then leaned over and fed her CO. He'd opened his mouth wide enough so that the food and the tips of Gina's fingers could fit, then he dutifully licked her fingers clean. Gina sucked in a breath and clenched her thighs together; how did he manage to make her horny so damn easily?

"Eat," Gina admonished.

The CO grinned, but complied.

*   *   *

Guns pushed his empty dishes away and leaned back in his seat with a satisfied sigh, fingers interlaced over his full belly. He'd been happy to get orders for a mission, sitting around back at base always did his head in. Not that he did much sitting around. Between target practice and training the team, forging weapons, and killing time in the gym, he didn't have much free time. He wasn't really a TV guy, but liked sinking his teeth into a good paperback, so that took up any time a normal person would have devoted to a social life. A social life was not a good idea in his line of work, he'd tried it. He would have like to say that he'd managed it as best he could, or that it ended disastrously, but he'd be lying. It had sort of fizzled out. No one was to blame. No big bang ending. It hadn't even managed a whimper.

So yeah, the orders had made him happy. And it didn't have anything to do with the fact that he'd have to meet up with Max to pick up fresh hardware. Nope. Not at all. Okay, that was a lie. But the team was working to a deadline, which wouldn't leave much time for he and Max to bump and grind. Not that he was averse to a quickie, and Max had range, and a policy to excel in all she did, so he'd take what he could get. Of course, if there was any kind of delay in getting all the items that he'd ordered, entirely not his fault, he may have to stay behind until they were delivered, and catch up with the team later.

The last time he and Max had spent extended time together, neither of them was able to walk very well when they went their separate ways. Max had zero inhibitions, was the strongest woman he'd ever met - physically and otherwise, and had a boundless imagination when it came to sex. He'd asked her about her limits once. She'd given him her best Mae West impression when she'd responded with *"Guns, honey, don't you know? Anything goes."* That song had become her theme song in his head, every time Max strutted into his mind. Some of the team had, on occasion, caught him humming it under his breath. He'd called "ear worm" and made some remark about wanting to get the damn thing out of his head. That had been a lie.

He had a realistic outlook on life, and did his best to tell the truth, as he'd found it was usually the best way to avoid drama. He also didn't want to have to 'fess up to the CO that he'd seen their weapons supplier naked, never mind all the things they'd done together. So he'd resigned himself to, occasionally, having to tell the odd white lie. He and Max had an understanding, not a relationship. He wasn't sure that would cut it with the CO though, especially not since Gina had come onto the scene. BG - before Gina - Guns had often wondered if the CO was actually human, and not some sort of sophisticated android with state-of-the-art AI. SG - since Gina - he'd actually caught the CO cracking a smile now and then. Most of the time it was when the CO had said or done something to make Gina squirm, and blush, not necessarily in that order. Guns now occasionally wondered if the CO had softened at all, not enough to come clean, but just in the abstract.

Guns saw the blur out of the corner of his eye with enough time to put out his hand and catch the missile. It wasn't the first time, and it wouldn't be the last. He considered pocketing the little Corvette but remembered what had happened the other time he'd confiscated one of Wheels' lucky charms. Holding it between a thumb and forefinger, he edged his arm into her personal space, and wasn't in the least surprised when the Stingray was snatched. He knew better than to hold his breath for a thank you, Wheels wasn't good with manners. She was a prodigy when it came to anything mechanical that moved, but especially cars. She could drive 'em, break 'em, and fix 'em, all whilst blindfolded, and with one hand tied behind her back. Literally, he'd seen her do it in on a mission in Honduras.

It was BG and Wheels had been captured, tortured. The Team had thrown together a hail Mary of a plan to try to get her out. The CO had copped a bullet during the extraction rendering him unable to drive, and Guns had his hands full with a couple of T91 assault rifles. Techie had been their remote assist, *man he still missed that guy*, so Wheels was the only one left who could drive. When they located her, Guns had thrown her over his shoulder and hot-footed it out to their vehicle, only to have some schmuck RPG it all to hell before they got to it. At least they hadn't waited until they were in it. A quick 180, and they were heading for a 1977 Mercedes-Benz 300D. With the CO providing covering fire, Guns stood Wheels up, flicked open his knife and sliced through the rope keeping her hands tied behind her. Opening the unlocked driver's door, he put a hand on the top of her hooded head and pushed down, and in. He'd intended for her to scoot over so the CO could get behind the wheel, but that's when the CO copped the bullet.

Swearing, Guns had opened the back door and manhandled the CO inside, only realising that the car was going as he made to get back out, and get in the front to drive the darned thing. Wheels had got her right arm free but the left one was still tangled behind her. Not wanting to spend one more minute in the compound, she'd planned to reach under the steering column to get to the wires so she could get the car started, but her hand brushed against the keys, a quick flick of the wrist and she was stomping on the gas. She could hear Guns swearing, and being thrown around behind her, but she'd rather drive into a wall at high speed then let them capture her again.

"Straight, goddammit! Drive straight! And take the fucking hood off."

They'd made it out of there. Guns, realising that for Wheels to take the hood off meant that there would be no hands on the wheel, braced himself, and sliced a hand-sized hole in the back of the hood. Holding the knife handle between his teeth, he then ripped open the hood, just in time for Wheels to aim the car at the compound gates. The hood doubled up as a field dressing for the CO's bullet wound, which freed Guns up to do what he does best; shoot the shit out of stuff. When they'd lost their pursuers, Wheels took a moment to release her other hand. They met up with Techie, Wheels fixed a couple of leaks caused by stray bullets, and crossed the border into Guatemala. Good times. Wheels had never been quite the same since though. She'd never talked about what they'd done to her while she'd been held captive; Guns had noticed a few fresh scars during training, but it was the ones that he couldn't see that worried him the most.

*Ash*₂₁

If anyone asked, Ash was going to say that he landed squarely, and gracefully. He wasn't going to mention the pinwheeling arms, or the bump he was likely going to have on the crown of his head, that he'd gotten when trying to put the tiles back how he'd found them. He hadn't succeeded, roofing was *hard*, especially when trying to do it from the inside. He'd done the best he could, and swore to himself that he'd climb back up there and fix them property at the earliest opportunity. He wouldn't tell of the minutes that dragged like hours, or days, as he explored an empty attic. Seriously, there was nothing. Okay, there was some insulation, but it was pristine. There were no spiderwebs, no birds nests, or rat droppings. Hell, it was cleaner than his apartment... office... whatever. Did vampires have OCD? Maybe Marcus had minions that he made clean the place, literally, top to bottom.

He'd found a couple of access hatches, one would let him drop down onto the mezzanine level in the garage, and a recessed balcony that he could only assume was used for stargazing. The SkyWatcher telescope stored just inside the balcony doors may have helped Ash reach that conclusion. His earlier exterior exploration had given him a good idea of the layout of the place, so going through the attic had only taken half the time. He could have gone quicker but he'd opted for stealth over speed, if a vampire was in residence he didn't want to be discovered due to heavy footfalls. Still, it was over an hour before he got back to the garage hatch. He'd decided to risk ingress, against the advice of his common sense brain which was telling him to wait until sunrise. The place was huge, the odds of running into anyone were remote, and he wanted an up-close-and-personal with the goddesses on wheels.

The hatch was alarmed. Of course it was. It took him twenty minutes just to bypass it, having no idea that NEIL was still watching his every move, and finding him fascinating.

*The Estate*₂₂

owan and Sheila wondered into the kitchen, arm in arm. The sun had well and truly set. The subtle pool lights were the farthest points that Rowan could see out into the yard, a light breeze making the water ripple, and the light reflection dance on the ceiling of the lanai. Had it been warmer, he would have gone out for a late-night swim, hopefully with Sheila in tow, and maybe of a skinny-dipping nature. Maybe in a few months, if they could get the house to themselves. He'd find a nice restaurant, far enough away to make it an overnight visit, and send Jerry, Ellie, and Mags, on a little trip…he could call it a Christmas present. He smiled at the thought, turning his head, and brushing a kiss along Sheila's temple.

"I took the liberty of taking the bags up to your room whilst you were in the library," smiled Jerry from his place at the kitchen table. "Tea? It's Earl Grey, hot," he asked, as he offered up the tea pot.

"Please," replied Rowan, pulling out a chair for Sheila, before taking one himself.

"None for me thanks. I don't want to push it after having dinner," Sheila grinned ruefully. Looking around the table she realised they'd interrupted a game in progress. "What are you guys playing?"

"Rummy. We can deal you in on the next hand if you'd like," offered Ellie.

"I don't know how to play."

"No worries there, Rowan can help you for a hand or two, and then he can join in too," Maggie beamed at her solution.

Sheila turned to Rowan, not sure how he'd feel about being volunteered. His grin, and nod, were all the encouragement she needed. Putting an arm over the back of her chair, Rowan leaned closer, and explained the rules as the others played out their hands. Half an hour later, with all of them playing, Sheila laid out all her cards for the win.

"Beginner's luck," grumbled Rowan good-naturedly, as he gathered up the cards for his turn at dealing. It wasn't until everyone had settled back with their new hands, taking a few moments to sort out their cards, that he remembered the original reason for them coming into the kitchen. "Hey Jerry, Sheila thought she heard something in the attic. Rats maybe?"

"Oh? We renewed regular pest control when Marcus stopped residing here, but I will call our exterminators tomorrow, and they can arrange a follow up."

"You don't have to go to any trouble on my account, I'm sure it was nothing."

"No trouble at all, we own the extermination company. We often have them try out new methods here, that way, if there are any flaws, we can rectify them before offering the service to the general public. This will be part of our standard practice," smiled Jerry earnestly.

"Thanks Jerry," the smile Sheila sent his way had him ducking his head bashfully.

Max_{23}

66 Has my daughter been in contact with you?" the voice on the other end of her secure phone demanded. Gramps sounded like he expected an answer, like the thought of arms-dealer-client-confidentiality hadn't even crossed his mind.

"Now Gramps, you should know better than to ask me that," purred Max, thankful that he couldn't see her rolling her eyes. She had a very high level of customer service to maintain, but she really hated when the man himself got on the phone.

"With the amount of money we throw your way, I expect a response, Maxine."

"Gramps, darling, I have a reputation to maintain. That reputation includes the highest level of confidentiality that I can provide to my clients. *All* my clients. That is why you throw so much money my way, because you can rest assured that no one will ever learn about any of it from me, or my employees."

"Fuck confidentiality. She no longer works for me, and I want to make sure that she gets no help from you." The irony that Gramps was relying on Max's discretion to not disclose Jacqui's employment status was completely lost on him.

"I reserve the right to refuse service to anyone, Gramps. But my reasons for doing so are mine alone."

"God dammit!" Gramps was on the verge of taking his business elsewhere, until he remembered that there was no one else who could do what Max did. "Fuck!"

"Was there anything else I can help you with?"

Even enraged, Gramps paused before mentioning Alpha Team. The distance he kept from the Team gave him plausible deniability. They were an efficient and effective unit, and he was happy to pay through the nose for their services; you couldn't get the best of the best to work for you without some incentive. This mission was the most important one he'd ever sent them on. Not only would they eliminate one of the last remaining vampires but, with their orders to wait until his grandson had been bitten and turned into a Hound, they, through Ash, should then have access to the fortune that Marcus had amassed over lifetimes.

He already had most of that fortune earmarked for the next phase in his plan, longevity without the need to tie himself to a vampire, followed closely by world domination. Nothing overt, he didn't want to become POTUS or anyone else in the spotlight who had to be accountable for their actions. He wanted to *own* the people in the spotlight. He already had figurative choke collars on several minor, but key, figures, and he was constantly and consistently adding to his collection. The Team would have made arrangements with Max and, although a pain in the arse, that woman was a consummate professional. There was nothing he could say to improve her service to his Team.

"Not today," ground out Gramps, before hanging up the phone.

Max was thoughtful as she replaced the handset into the charging cradle. *Hunter: Salvage and Investigation* had arranged with her for Ash's weapons to be smuggled to him when he'd been earmarked to head the first satellite office in this country. Something must have happened, because the only reason that Jacqui would have left the family business was if her son was in some kind of trouble. And, other than the usual small arms that the local gangs requested, the only large order she'd had in the last month was from Alpha Team. In her line of work, Max knew that there was no such thing as coincidence. What she didn't know, in this case, was whether Gramps was pulling the Team's strings, or if there was another player in town.

"Sai," Max called, hardly raising her voice. The head of her security, her bodyguard, entered the room from his post just outside her open door. He'd heard her side of the entire exchange, Max had no secrets from him. As usual, Max eschewed the desk and was sitting in one of her two favourite chairs by the window. They'd had arguments about the positioning of those chairs, he'd wanted her as far away from any windows as possible. They'd reached a compromise when Max had agreed to let him swap out all the existing glass for BulletGuard glass. She'd thought he'd gone overboard when he'd insisted on also changing the shower screen, but she'd relented when he'd said it was either that or he'd be staying in the bathroom while she showered…each time. He wanted to smile as he remembered her rolling her eyes and throwing her hands up in defeat, but he'd seen the look she had on her face before, and it usually led to nothing good. He came to stand before her, hands clasped lightly behind his back, balanced stance, eyebrow raised.

"Sit," Max gestured to the seat on the other side of the small table in exasperation. "You know having you stand over me just makes me want to punch you in the goolies."

Sai grinned as he took the proffered chair, they both knew that his expertise in several forms of martial arts, as well as lightening quick reflexes, meant that Max would never connect, even had her threat been serious. He listened as she thought out loud, formulating and discarding possible contingency plans. Max maintained a hard-won neutrality, so their role would be peripheral at best but, from what she was telling him, there were too many players on the board, and those were the ones they knew about. He might have to bring in one or two of the contractors that he…trusted was too strong a word…held a measure of his confidence. Not that they would be necessary, but Sai preferred to err on the side of caution. If one can't avoid a conflict, then it behooves one to be ready to win it.

"…and Guns will be in town," Max paused, lips pursed, and finger tapping against them. "Such a shame that some of their shipment is going to be delayed."

Sai added holding back some of the weapons they were procuring for the Team to his mental lists. Once upon a time, he'd pitied the transient relationships that Max had, until he'd understood that she daren't get truly close to anyone, lest they be held against her. He was her closest friend and confidant but, as far as the rest of the world knew, he was simply her employee. He'd also have to make sure that the harbour apartment was secure, and stocked. Max never brought anyone to her primary residence.

Poppy & Doug₂₄

66 You okay, Love?" Doug reached across the table so he could take Poppy's hand. "You were a million miles away."

"More like a million years," Poppy blinked owlishly as she came back to the present. "I was thinking about how this all started. Hoping, praying, that it wasn't all for nothing. Doug, what if I was wrong?"

Doug looked at his wife, really looked. He saw faint lines that hadn't been there when they'd started on this journey. A few more strands of glitter in her hair too. But it wasn't the natural signs of ageing that made his heart ache, it was the look in her eyes. The pain of a mother who'd done the best that she could for her child, by making the worst choice imaginable. The guilt of a parent who would never know if they'd done the right thing. A soul that had lost a part of itself. He knew exactly what she was feeling, because he felt it too.

He'd trusted his wife, and her visions, so much that he'd orchestrated their disappearance. He'd faithfully believed, even when her belief failed. He'd physically restrained her from catching the first available flight back home on more than one occasion, having to talk her down, and remind her of the long game. Each time had broken his heart because…what if she was right, about being wrong?

"Our son is alive. He is well. He is thriving. If nothing else, the choices we made have given him a good life. We'll never know if staying with him would have resulted in anything different, but we both love him so much that we weren't willing to risk it. Even with everything we've since gone through, I would make the same choice again, because I couldn't live with the possibility of the alternative."

"I knew there was a very good reason why I married you."

"Just one?"

"Several, if you must know, but right now the one that counts is how much you are my rock. You're always there for me when I need you."

"Well, you're mine, and that means I get to be yours when you need me. But if there are *several*, why did you say no the first time I asked you to marry me?"

"We'd only just met! And you didn't so much ask as make a high handed proclamation."

"I thought you like me being high handed?"

"Sometimes, but only in the bedroom."

"Just the bedroom?"

"Figure of speech."

"Want me to be high handed now?"

"No. I want to finish our meals, then go for a stroll in the garden under the stars. You may start being high handed then, and finish up when we get to our room."

"Deal. Where's the waiter so I can put a rush on dessert?" The ache in Doug's heart eased as he heard his wife's lusty chuckle, temporarily banishing some of the pain and guilt from her eyes.

Jacqueline & Gaberiel₂₅

Gabe had surged up from his kneeling position and darted towards her, stopping an inch away, one hand on each handrail, effectively blocking her only escape route. He was white-knuckling those rails for all he was worth, doing his best to hold himself back long enough to ask, "May I?"

Draping her arms over his shoulders, Jacqui took the plunge, "Please."

No more caveman action, Gabe went for a Rhett Butler move, one arm behind her knees, and the other supporting her back, as he carried Jacqui up the stairs. He stopped outside his door, thought for a second, then shot her a sheepish look.

"What?"

"The keys are in my pants pocket."

Jacqui couldn't help it, she laughed.

"Put me down."

Gabe obliged, and made quick work of opening the door. He ducked inside to take care of the alarm, and then held the door open for her, handing her over the threshold. The layout was similar to Ash's place but, where Ash lost some of the space to the office, Gabe enjoyed the extra room. It meant that he got a study, and that the other rooms were bigger than what Ash had. He took Jacqui on a quick tour, grinning like a school kid each time she pointed out an improvement that he'd made, like the timber flooring, the furniture, and the general tidiness of the place.

He'd left the bedroom for last, although the door was open and she'd caught glimpses as they were wandering through the place. Standing aside, he let Jacqui precede him, then leant against the doorjamb as she looked around. It was a simple yet stunning room, the warmth of the timber floor contrasting with the industrial concrete-look walls, offset by black and charcoal everything, with chrome accents here and there. Stopping by the blanket box, Jacqui set down her clutch, then turned to face Gabe.

"You might find the bottom left hand drawer in the wardrobe interesting," suggested Gabe.

Raising an eyebrow, Jacqui made her way to the semi-walk-in wardrobe. Stealing a glance over her shoulder, she confirmed that Gabe was watching her every move so, instead of bending her knees, she bent over at the waist to reach and open the drawer. The sharp intake of breath she heard from behind her was very satisfying. What she saw in the drawer made her momentarily forget that she wasn't alone. Kneeling down, she took a closer look. Blindfolds, gags, cuffs, clamps, floggers, paddles, and so many other delicious toys. Everything was of the highest quality, possibly custom made. No mass market adult store stuff here.

"I meant what I said downstairs," Gabe's quiet but firm voice, directly behind her, made her start. She hadn't heard him move. "I'd like to use everything in that drawer on you, but I won't do it without your consent."

"And if I want to use it on you?" Jacqui looked up at him, her tone and gaze containing not an ounce of submission.

"I'm definitely willing to negotiate," Gabe's small smile, and hooded eyes promising, pleasure.

"And if I say no?"

"Then you're free to leave. I'll walk you downstairs, and we can either go on like this never happened, or never speak to each other again. Your choice."

"And if I say yes, but only to vanilla sex?"

"I'm not sure I've been very clear," Gabe's sudden grin was genuine, and sexy as hell. "I want you tonight. I want you any way that I can have you. There is a significant part of me that is fighting to be let out to play, but only with your say so. There are things that part of me wants to do to you. Some of them involve a certain level of pain, but the ultimate goal is pleasure, yours…and mine. I have to admit to finding myself intrigued by the concept of having some of those things done to me, by you. No one's ever suggested that before."

Jacqui noted that he'd limited his statement to that night, and was relieved. The last thing she wanted was to complicate her life with anything longer. She was only going to be in the area for as long as it took Max to get the rest of the weapons to her, then she was going to move heaven, earth and, if necessary, hell, to save her son. She was enjoying the fact that, in this moment, the hardest decision she had to make, was how hard core she wanted the sex she'd be having to be. Holding up her left hand, she allowed Gabe to help her up, pilfering a blindfold from the drawer as she stood.

"Do you have a safe word?" she asked, standing close to Gabe, but only touching where he held her hand.

"I've never needed one," he chuckled.

"You might want to think one up," Jacqui replied, bringing the blindfold up, and pausing with it before his eyes.

Gabe's eyes widened, before he muttered "pumpernickel", and leaned forward so that the blindfold could be applied.

"How's that," asked Jacqui, making small adjustments. "Can you see?"

"Not a damned thing," Gabe's tone didn't betray any nerves, but his fidgeting hands did.

"Good. Remember your safe word?"

"Pumpernickel."

"And you remember how it works?"

"Well, usually, any woman that I'm with can use her safe word if she can't handle whatever it is that we're doing."

"Exactly the same principle here big guy. Any time, at any point, no matter what we're doing, you say…"

"…pumpernickel…"

"…and I will immediately freeze. I'll check with you, whether you want to stop completely, or just need a moment, and we'll go from there. No hard feelings, and no expectations. Agreed?"

"Yes ma'am," Gabe reached for where he thought she was but Jacqui easily evaded his grasp.

"Uh uh, not yet. You'll get your turn." Jacqui took a few moments to walk around Gabe and check him out, knowing that the deliberate sound of her heels on his floor, without a touch from her, was building his anticipation, and his apprehension. Here was a man who was used to taking action and the trust that he'd put in her by placing himself in her hands was not lost on Jacqui. She had no intention of doing anything to lose that trust, at least, not tonight.

She changed direction, partly to keep him guessing, but also because she wanted to see him from every angle. He was magnificent with clothes on, and she couldn't wait to see him naked, but she wasn't going to rush this. It had been a while since she'd last had a man who'd wanted to play. Stopping on his right, Jacqui placed the pads of the fingers of her right hand on the back of his, starting at his knuckles, and ever so slowly tracing up his arm. His hand tapered in to a wrist that was at least twice as large as hers.

He'd uncovered his arms earlier in the night, when he'd pushed up his sleeves as they were talking over dinner, and she revelled in the access. Her fingertips barely touched his skin as she followed the flare-out of his forearm, before moving back a little bit, just so she could feel the tickle from the hair that was starting to stand up as goose bumps appeared in her wake. When she got to the cuff of his knitted shirt, she brought the rest of her hand into play, so that she'd be able to feel, grab, and knead his upper arm. She couldn't suppress the hum of appreciation, his arm was huge. She didn't miss Gabe's self-satisfied grin so, as her hand got to his shoulder, she leaned over a little to blow a small puff of air over his ear. That got rid of the grin for a quick moment, before a chuckle rumbled forth. As Gabe chuckled, Jacqui felt his shoulder relax under her hand, and she was pleased. This should be fun, for both of them.

Holding on firmly to his shoulder, she bent her left knee and raised her foot so that she could unbuckle her shoe, slipping it off, and lowering her stockinged foot back to the floor. "Hold this please," Jacqui placed her shoe in Gabe's proffered hand, before repeating the process to remove the other shoe. Grabbing them both, she placed them neatly beside the blanket box, before padding back to Gabe.

"Off please," Jacqui requested, tugging on the bottom of his shirt. "And please, mind the blindfold."

Alpha Team₂₆

They'd laid the seats down, and darkened the cabin. The rhythmic silence was occasionally interrupted by a soft snore from different seats. Gina had never been able to sleep deeply on a plane, and the simple act of turning over woke her up. She lay facing the CO, cursing the fact that her bladder had woken up too, and trying to calculate whether she could get away without having to make a trip to the bathroom…Nope. There was no way that she would be able to manoeuvre over the CO, and into the aisle, without waking him up. Maybe she could fall back asleep, and trick her bladder into thinking the waking up bit was just a dream…Nope.

"What do you need?" his quiet and unexpected rumble made her squeak. He hadn't moved, and his eyes were still closed. How had he known?

"Bathroom," Gina whispered.

"Go."

Gina threw off her blanket, rose to her knees, and carefully straddled the CO, leaning slightly in the process of moving her other leg over him. She squeaked again when he placed his hands on her waist, centred her over himself, simultaneously lifted his hips and pulled her down onto him. She'd worn a t-shirt dress, with her favourite pair of boots. The boots were under her seat, but she'd kept her socks on. The socks weren't her problem at the moment, her Kaiser Brazilian cotton panties were. There weren't thick enough to stop her feeling the CO's erection, and the material was providing a friction that was so delicious, that she'd almost forgotten her original goal. Almost.

"Not now," she hissed, bending over to speak into his ear. "Not here! I've gotta go."

"Hold it," he murmured, wrapping his left arm around her waist to hold her against him, and snagging her blanket with his right.

"You're serious?" He'd allowed Gina enough room so that they were almost nose to nose and she could look into his eyes.

"Always wanted to join the mile high club," he smirked.

"Oh god," moaned Gina, her bent head coming to rest against his lips. "Do I have a choice?"

He gently, but firmly, fisted his hands into her hair, lifting her head so there could be no mistaking his intention, "Always."

She took a moment to assess, then reached down, and helped him arrange her blanket so that they were covered from neck to knees. His knees, hers were still up by his waist. Having no intention of sleeping on the flight, he had't bothered taking his blanket out of its packet. That meant that the only barriers between them were their clothes. He rucked her dress up so he could slip his hands into her panties and grab her arse cheeks. Gina only just managed to stop herself from squeaking yet again, and stared at him wide-eyed, afraid that she would get far noisier before they were done.

"What?"

"What if we get caught?"

"Sweetheart, I wasn't planning on taking all night. Does hard and fast work for you right now?"

"Yes, but-"

The CO claimed her mouth, and put to rest her fears of her inability to do this silently, he'd catch whatever screams she would release. Reaching between them, Gina lowered his zipper, and reached in to free his rock-hard cock. She was so ready for him that he slid home almost as soon as she'd moved her panties to the side. He swallowed her moan, and his own, then used his grip on her arse to leverage her into the position he wanted. Gina changed the angle, and the CO ate up the stream of curses her deliciously filthy mouth was trying to spout. His pistoning hips, and her full bladder, kept her riding the pleasure-pain border.

He kept kneading her arse with one hand, but brought the other to her front, and went hunting for her clit. His thumb hit the jackpot, and Gina digging her claws into his shoulders confirmed it. This wasn't going to take long, for either of them. He was so goddamn close, but he wasn't going over first. Thankfully, a few frantic strums of his thumb was all it took for Gina to fall apart in his arms. Fuck he loved this woman. And, that's what did it for him. His hips arched, and he pulled her down harder as he let go, feeling like he'd never be able to get deep enough inside her.

Gina scrambled off him, and raced for the bathroom, running from some of the best sex she'd had in her life, and managing to hold in her sobs until she'd locked the door. These weren't cute sniffles that made her eyelashes glisten with trapped tears, she was ugly crying. Huge wracking sobs, mouth opened wide with her hands clamped over it to hold in any sound. She absolutely did not need everyone on the plane to hear just how distraught she'd sound if the hysterics got away from her. And she was still bursting to pee.

Releasing one hand she used it to reach under her dress and work her panties down to below her knees, turn around, back up to the toilet, hike the dress up at the back, and sit. She'd forgotten to use the seat liner. Fuck the seat liner. *What the hell was wrong with her?* The giant sobs had slowed enough for her to cover her face, and just have a good cry. She heard the door-lock being tested but figured the person would work out that the room was occupied, and shove off. She squeaked, horrified, when she heard the door open, and dropped her hands into her lap, making sure her modesty was intact.

The CO stepped in, and locked the door behind himself.

"I…I locked it," Gina stuttered.

The CO leaned back against the wall across from her, arms crossed over his chest, legs crossed at the ankles, one eyebrow inching its way up his forehead.

His woman was crying, not the reaction he'd expected. He studied her, perhaps she was suffering from postcoital dysphoria and, if so, he wanted to get to the heart of the trigger and fix it or kill it. Either way worked for him. Yeah, he knew he was a neanderthal at heart. It could be the other thing though, the thing where the emotions or hormones let it rip. Heaving a sigh he moved to kneel before her, failing his own test of distance. His woman was crying.

"You're okay," he murmured, reaching up to cup her face and wipe away her tears with his thumbs.

"I don't know what ha-happened," Gina hiccuped.

"Do you need me to kill something for you?" he asked, deadly-fucking-serious.

"What? No!" The unexpected question helped Gina regain the last of her control. She grimaced as she reached up to brush at the tickle on her nose, and her hand came away wet. He snapped a couple tissues from the box provided, and handed them to her.

"Did I hurt you?" He'd tried to make his grips firm but gentle, not enjoying the thought of hurting Gina without her consent. He might have lost it for a while there though, and she may yet bruise. The claw marks on his shoulders, on the other hand, he'd wear with pride.

"Just enough," Gina smiled.

"You done?"

"What?"

He glanced down at her lap.

"Oh," Gina blushed. "Not quite."

He stood up, and stepped back to his original leaning pose. Gina's jaw dropped, he couldn't possibly mean to wait for her. She looked at him, then at the door, then back at him, pointedly. He smirked, and just adjusted his folded arms, like he had all the time in the world. Gina jerked her head towards the door with a small scowl on her face. He just shook his head.

"Out!"

"Nope."

"Why?"

"We weren't done, and I wanna finish."

"What? We both came."

"We're not done."

"One, earth-shattering orgasm wasn't enough for you?"

"Never enough with the woman I love."

"Oh," Gina had just figured out why she'd burst into tears. She'd fallen for the stupid neanderthal, and thought she was nothing but a fling for him. "Well, alrighty then."

They stared each other down for a while.

"Will you at least turn around?" Gina threw her arms up, exasperated.

"Sure," he shrugged, complying. "All you had to do was ask."

*Ash*₂₇

sh dropped as silently as possible onto the mezzanine. He looked around but couldn't make out any obvious surveillance cameras, not even considering that the Estate might be equipped with prototypes that were years away from commercial release. There were shelves and cupboards full of spare parts, everything neatly labelled, and not a speck of dust to be found. Finding the stairs, he tiptoed down in stealth mode, but it still seemed like every freaking second step had some sort of creak or squeak to it. He was tense and sweating by the time he made it to the last step. Taking a deep breath, he stepped down, no going back now.

He stalked over to the nearest vehicle, an Arash AF10, and almost came in his pants. If he wasn't mistaken, and when it came to supercars he rarely was, this model had warp drive, and had not yet gone into production. He skimmed his hand about an inch above the one-million-dollar-plus surface, considered sitting in it, but then happened to glance at the Bugatti Veyron parked next to it. He took a deep breath and tried the handle, locked. Of course it was locked! Who in their right mind would leave a car like this unlocked? He moved on to the Lamborghini, and then the Ferrari. All locked. He was too happy to be surrounded by so much power and chrome to feel the frustration. A gleeful pirouette, had him looking at a pristine 1969 Chevrolet Corvette Stingray. A beautiful convertible, which meant that it didn't matter if the doors were locked.

Was he really going to do this? Shucking his backpack and unslinging his bow, he placed them carefully on the ground, looked around guiltily, one hand on the door, before giving a mental shrug, and leaping in. He settled gently into the seat, hands caressing the steering wheel, and couldn't stop the grin, or the giggle, that escaped. He looked down, smiling, as fantasy Rowan's hand landed on his thigh. Heaving a satisfied sigh, he stretched his arm across the back of the passenger seat, trailing his fingers along Rowan's shoulders as he went.

"You're happy," murmured Rowan, resting his head on Ash's biceps, and turning so he could visually trace his stunning profile.

"I am." Ash bent his elbow so his fingers could play with Rowan's hair.

"Completely?"

"No."

"No?"

"You're not really here," Ash turned his head so that he and Rowan were almost nose to nose.

"Sorry."

Ash let out an ironic chuckle. He studied Rowan's face, pretty sure that he'd remembered to conjure everything. "I'm on a mission."

"I know."

"You're going to have to leave."

"I know," Rowan remained, smiling as Ash quirked an eyebrow. "You have to let me go."

"I don't want to."

"I know."

The Estate₂₈

Maggie stifled a yawn as she considered the hand she'd been dealt. So much had happened, so much had changed, since she and Rowan had set out that morning. She rearranged her cards, deciding on a strategy, before staring bleary-eyed at the turned up card on the discard pile. She should have given up about half an hour before and headed up to bed, but she didn't want to be alone in the room she'd shared with Marcus. The thought of lying there, staring at the ceiling all night, feeling his absence, filled her with dread. Maybe, if she stayed up long enough, she'd be so tired that she'd be asleep before her head hit the pillow.

"Mags?…Maggie?…Aunty M?"

"I'm awake. I'm awake," blinked Maggie, realising that everyone was looking at her, gentle smiles on their faces. "I'm being an idiot, aren't I?"

"Baby steps, Magnolia," Ellie replied. "There are plenty of other rooms you can stay in. It doesn't have to be that one."

"Was I talking out loud?"

"No, I'm just that empathetic."

Jerry snorted, then leaned out of Ellie's reach as she went to slap his arm. "It makes sense Miss Maggie, it's your first night back in this house. Lot's of memories to deal with. No one will think less of you if you don't want to stay in your old room."

"That's sweet, Jerry, but it's what I think of myself that I have to deal with. Let's finish this hand and then I'll say my goodnights. Is it my turn?" At their nods, Maggie reached for the card on the top of the discard pile, placed it in her hand, and laid her cards down for the win.

"We should have just let her doze," groused Ellie.

"We might head up too," Rowan sent a questioning look to Sheila, who nodded back. "We can walk you up Mags."

"Oh, you don't have to. It's still fairly early, you can stay and play. You can't possibly be ready to sleep."

"Who said anything about sleeping?" smirked Sheila, mostly to watch Rowan blush. She wasn't disappointed.

"We have a video meeting with one of our New York firms in about half an hour, that we need to prep for, so this was our last hand too."

"We didn't mean to keep you," worried Maggie.

"You didn't. It's one of our usual monthly meetings with this firm. They get up early to accomodate us, we stay up late, and do our best to make the meeting as short as possible in return. We've got them down to 30 minutes."

"Much better than the 3 hour marathon that was the first meeting," Jerry shook his head at the memory.

"We'll leave you to it," said Maggie, walking around the table to hug Ellie and Jerry.

"I'll set the bread maker before I go to bed. Feel free to help yourselves if you're up before either of us."

Thanks, and good nights, were shared around before Maggie, Rowan, and Sheila, headed for the stairs in the front foyer. Rowan proffered Maggie his arm on one side, and took hold of Sheila's hand, interlacing their fingers, on the other.

"This is an amazing house," murmured Sheila, appreciating the paintwork, architecture, and finishing touches, as they climbed.

"To be honest, I was always a little intimidated by the grandeur," replied Maggie.

"Kind of ironic that it's now all yours," observed Rowan.

"Yeah. Thanks for the reminder kiddo," was Maggie's wry response. They walked past the Red room so they could escort Maggie all the way to her door at the end of the hallway. Pausing with her hand on the door handle, Maggie turned to face them, meeting Rowan's eyes but making a conscious effort not to look into Sheila's. "Marcus sometimes felt more comfortable in the basement. You should show Sheila how to get down there, in case being in a new place for the sunrise gives her the heebie jeebies."

"Thanks Mags, we'll do that now." They waited through Maggie's hesitation, and until she had entered the room, and shut the door behind her. Rowan shuddered as they turned to stroll back they way they'd come, "I don't ever want to have to deal with what she's going through."

"So long as I don't forget what time of day it is, and decide to go for a stroll outside, you shouldn't have to. I mean, what could possibly happen all the way out here?" Sheila deliberately bumped shoulders with Rowan as they walked. "What we really need to talk about is whether you'll let me share my blood with you. I don't want to have to go through what Maggie's going through either."

"Share your blood?" Rowan had a fleeting vision of draining Sheila, and turning into a vampire himself.

"Yeah, you know, like Marcus used to do with Jerry and Ellie. That way I'd get to keep you around forever. Or at least until you did something crazy, and got yourself severely injured, then I don't think a drop or two of my blood would help, and you'd still need a hospital."

"So a drop or two would keep me in good health, and in good looks?"

"Hey, it can only work with what's already there."

"Oh, burn!"

"I know, right?! You know I find you adorable."

"Not just tasty?"

"Oh, that too," Sheila winked, and laughed at Rowan's expression. They'd made it to the bottom of the staircase, and around to the wall behind. She was about to pull Rowan back, thinking he was going to run into it, when he gave a gentle push, and the flush pivot door swung silently open.

"Cool!"

"I can't wait to introduce you to N.E.I.L," Rowan said, placing his palm on the scanner to access the door at the bottom of the basement stairs.

"Finally!" Neil's disembodied voice held all the exasperation of someone who had been made to wait for hours. "You have no idea what's been going on-"

"Neil-"

"-Maggie was supposed to talk to Ellie about re-instating my upstairs privileges-"

"Neil-"

"-but she went upstairs and never came back down. And I couldn't let anyone know-"

"NEIL!"

"Yes, Rowan?"

"I'd like to introduce you to someone."

"Oh hello, Marcus. Welcome back."

"What? No. Neil, this is Sheila. Sheila is also a vampire, that's what may have confused you."

"Okay then. Hello Sheila. Now Rowan-"

"Just a minute, Neil. I want to show Sheila around."

"But Rowan, I need to tell you that-"

"Just a few minutes, Neil."

"No, Rowan, it's important-"

"Oh for crying out loud. Silent mode!" Rowan waited for another interruption. "Huh, it worked."

Jacqueline & Gaberiel[29]

abe was almost naked and harder than he could ever remember being. She'd barely touched him, giving him short, clear, commands that he had no trouble following. Once or twice, when he'd turned his attention inwards and reacted too slowly to a command, She'd guided him with her touch. The first time that happened he'd jumped at the unexpected contact, the second time, he'd leaned into Her touch. Now? He was craving it. He considered ignoring a command on purpose, but he valued the murmured praises, sounds of encouragement, and hums of appreciation, each time he complied. He found himself wanting to please Her, and loathed to disappoint. Contrary to the training his years in the military had provided, he'd lost track of time. The moments between touches, commands, and other utterances, although mere minutes, stretched to eternity. Each moment had him longing for the next, winding him up tighter, and tighter. He'd swear that the duration between each action was taking longer than the one before, but his lack of sight, and his complete focus on Her, played havoc with his sense of time. So he waited, and the anticipation was the sweetest torture.

Jacqui had slowed him down when he would have whipped his shirt off, she'd wanted to savour the revelation of his skin. She'd taken all the time she'd wanted to admire him, before asking him to take off his shoes, socks, and then his pants. She couldn't hold back her appreciation as she walked silently around him, and he was hers to play with for the night! She'd left him in his briefs, knowing that she'd rush if he were to be completely naked, and she wanted him to wait… and want. He'd turned his head, listening as she rummaged in his toy drawer. The horsehair quirt that she found, in his signature charcoal colour, was of exquisite quality, and perfect for what she wanted to do to him. The sharp intake of breath, and arching of his back as she ran the horsehair gently up his spine, was very satisfying. She traced more of him, enjoying how he moved his body to get away when she reached a ticklish spot, without once stepping away from where he had been. She hadn't given him permission to move his feet, and he was complying, admirably.

"The wall is straight in front of you. In a moment, I want you to take a step towards it. The ultimate goal is for you to brace your arms up against it, leaning forward, your legs spread. Do you understand?"

Gabe nodded. She hadn't told him that he couldn't speak, but they'd slipped easily into their respective roles, surprising Gabe who'd never been the submissive before.

"Step now." When he complied, Jacqui was able to judge the length of his pace and ask him to step again.

"Put your arms out straight in front of you. Good. The wall is about a foot in front of you. Lean forward slowly until your palms are flat against it. Well done." She put a hand on his shoulder, then slid it down his back, her touch rewarding his trust in her. When she got to the band of his briefs she changed direction; following the material around his side, and stopping just before she would have touched his cock, which had forced its way through the band, having soaked it as it went.

"Turn around please, place your back against the wall. I can't see properly with you this way, you throw too much of a shadow," mused Jacqui.

Gabe hissed as he made contact with the wall, it felt chilled against his fevered skin.

"Better," murmured Jacqui. Reaching down, she gently cupped his balls through the fabric, then used the nail on her index finger to carefully scrape along the front of his shaft, watching as the head pulsed. The small, clear drop that had formed there, grew. Jacqui was torn between wanting to taste it, and wanting to touch it.

She stepped back, taking a moment to decide. Gabe groaned at the loss of her touch, his arms reaching out blindly for her. "Arms down by your sides please, palms against the wall."

Stepping close again, Jacqui bent at the waist so that she could closely watch the result as she blew over his glistening head. Gabe's hips bucked, bringing him almost within tasting distance. Putting a finger tip to the hovering drop, Jacqui smeared it over the head, scooping up the excess. She opened her mouth, and had been about to suck her finger clean when, with a wicked grin, she reconsidered. Reaching up she applied it to Gabe's lips, carefully covering them all like she was applying gloss. She put a hand on each of his shoulders, rising onto her toes, so that the tip of her tongue could trace where her finger had been.

Her breath, first on his cock, and now on his face. Her touch, hands on his shoulders, tongue on his lips. Her scent, not an overpowering perfume, a natural freshness that he couldn't seem to get enough of. It was too much. It was not enough. It was more than he could handle. Wrapping an arm around her waist he pulled her flush against him, the fabric of her clothes, although soft, was a sweet agony against his sensitised flesh. The other hand went to the back of her head, keeping her imprisoned against his lips, preventing any protest, not that any was forthcoming.

His lips opened for her and, when she eagerly plunged in, he released her head, reaching down so that he could grip the backs of her thighs, and lift her so that she was wrapped around him. *Fuck!* He may not have thought that through because she was now pressed against his cock, and writhing. He was already so close to the edge, that he was afraid he wouldn't last long at this rate. The damn blindfold made it almost impossible for him to get to the bed without injuring at least one of them. Fine, wall it was. Gabe spun, so that he could brace Jacqui against the wall. Reaching between them he went for the single button on her cardigan before wrenching it down her arms. He didn't give a fuck that he was treating the angora twin set roughly, as far as he was concerned, they were an obstacle he had to overcome to finally get his hands on flesh that he was craving.

He couldn't bring himself to release her mouth so he'd only managed to push the camisole part of the twin set up above her breasts. He cupped one side over her bra, using his other hand to support, and knead, her arse. He was a very capable multitasker.

"Stop," Jacqui managed to gasp in a moment between kisses.

Gabe froze. *Fuck! Was she kidding? Wait, had he hurt her?*

"Put me down," Jacqui was breathless. "Please."

Gabe complied.

"Step back."

His backward step was half the length that his forward one had been. Knowing that he couldn't see her, Jacqui grinned. Right about now he'd be driving himself crazy trying to figure out if he'd done something to warrant this kind of reaction. She wasn't being intentionally cruel. Ah, who was she kidding, that was exactly what she was doing. She'd momentary lost control of the situation, and of herself. She needed to re-establish their understanding of their roles. It meant that Gabe had to suffer some momentary discomfort. He'd get over it, sooner rather than later.

Putting her hands on his waist, Jacqui pushed until Gabe had taken another step backwards, reaching her goal of getting enough space between him, and the wall, for her to comfortably remove his briefs. She knelt before him, her nails scraping his sides before hooking into the waistband. Millimetre by millimetre, she drew his briefs down his body.

Gabe sucked in his breath, he'd thought she was stopping; punishing him for losing control and taking over. This was almost worse. He wanted to pull her to him again, but didn't know if he could survive another interruption. The angles of her hands suggested that she was crouched or kneeling in front of him. *Sweet Jesus!*

If that was the case, he wanted to fist his hands in her hair and, as soon as his cock was free - *in about another fucking century at the rate she was going* - he'd feed it to her, just to feel her lips wrapping around him, and her tongue caressing him all over. The likelihood that she'd stop him again had him tense and frozen, his panting and barely-there tremors the only movements he felt free to make, not that he could control them.

Jacqui was incredibly grateful for the blindfold. She was practically salivating, and was glad that Gabe couldn't see. She'd explored the fine art of fellatio with her first love, and had been a fan ever since. She delighted in the contrast of silk covered steel and the, almost, mind-of-its-own reactions. She enjoyed the thought of having a man at her mercy, just because he was in her mouth. She used to delight in finding Alex asleep on top of the covers, naked, on those steaming summer nights. She'd crawl up between his legs, taking his flaccid cock in her mouth, and sucking him to wakeful hardness. She'd watch as his hands fisted the sheets, occasionally she'd guide them onto her head, and let him control the action; but mostly, she loved being able to see the strength in those arms as they flexed beside his incredible body. She thrived on watching his chest arch up off the bed as he got closer to his orgasm, and the guttural shouts that accompanied his release. What she loved the most, though, were those times that she'd stop until Alex looked at her, and their gazes locked. He'd talk then, in an effort to keep eye contact, as he got closer and closer to coming. He'd tell her what he liked, what he wanted, and what he wanted to do to her in return.

"Step out of your briefs please, carefully."

Standing up, Jacqui took hold of Gabe's waist, and walked him backwards to the bed. When the backs of his calves were pressed against the side of the bed, she took her hands from his waist, and gave a hard enough shove against his chest to topple him backwards. She smiled at his shout of surprise. Sparing a glance at her angora cardigan, she made quick work of taking off her matching camisole, then her skirt, and flinging them to form a pile over it. Reaching back, Jacqui unfastened her bra, slipping it down her arms, and holding it in one hand. Walking around to the end of the bed, she leaned over so that she could drag the lacy material up Gabe's body. She started at his bent knees, and worked her way up, lingering over his cock, just so she could watch it jump from a combination of the fabric, and warm puffs of her breath. When she got to his chest, she continued around to the side of the bed.

"Arms over your head please."

Gabe complied, but wasn't sure how he felt about Jacqui wrapping her bra around his wrists, and clipping it closed. He tested his bonds, and realised that he could slip out if he wanted to; he was too curious to find out what she had planned next to want to. She was moving again, stopping at the end of the bed. The only thing that she could still be wearing was panties, would she leave them on? The slightest weight on his chest, and her scent filling his head, answered that. He'd give his left nut to be able to look at her right now. She was stunning fully clothed, she'd be glorious naked.

Leaning down so that she could plant her finger nails where Gabe's thighs met his pelvis, Jacqui gently but firmly ran them slowly up his sides. His flesh tensed in anticipation, and his cock bobbed in appreciation. Her panties were obscuring one of his nipples, and she impatiently threw them over her shoulder, her focus never wavering as she returned her hand to his chest. She gripped his nipples between her thumbs and forefingers, increasing the pressure ever so slowly until he gasped. She released the pressure just as slowly, Gabe exhaling as she went. Then she did it again, the pressure before he gasped this time, was marginally greater than the first time. The third time, she didn't stop when he gasped, eliciting a second gasp, and, finally, "Fuck!"

Abruptly releasing his nipples, Jacqui took Gabe's face in her hands, and claimed his mouth. She climbed up onto the bed as they kissed, moving to straddle him, and slide her slick core up and down his shaft. Gabe brought his arms, hands still bound, down and over, reaching for, and gripping, Jacqui's arse. He pulled her hard against him as he arched up, stopping her movement before she could make him come all over himself. Jacqui broke their kiss, resting her forehead on his, both of them panting hard.

"Condoms?"

"Huh?" Gabe hadn't expected the question.

"Please tell me you have condoms."

"Bedside table drawer," Gabe gestured, even blindfolded he knew which side of the bed he kept them. Jacqui scrambled off him, and found the box of Durex RealFeel condoms, and a tube of Play Feel lube, which she wouldn't need right now, but was glad to know it was there…just in case. The box wasn't co-operating so she attacked it like a mad woman; condoms flew everywhere. Jacqui didn't care, she only needed one. The foil packet was more accomodating, and ripped neatly where it was supposed to, so Jacqui aimed a dirty look at what was left of the box, hoping that it would get the message. Sheathing Gabe, she straddled him once more, this time guiding his cock home.

Poppy & Doug[30]

Doug lazily ran his fingers up and down his wife's back while hers drew patterns through his chest hair. Her head was nestled on his shoulder, and he could feel her breath slowing as it blew over his nipple. They'd shared one dessert, the sorbet, and opted to have the other sent up to their room as they'd been too full from the first two courses to thoroughly enjoy it. Arm in arm, they'd gone for a postprandial stroll through the grounds, the chill in the air making Poppy snuggle into his side so that he dropped her arm and wrapped his around her instead. She'd wanted high handed, so he'd bent his head to whisper in her ear, telling her exactly what he intended to do to her once they were back in their room. Her breath quickening, she'd turned her head so that she could look him in the eye, before slowly licking her lips and asking "Promise?"

He'd gone back to his whispered descriptions, keeping her outside a little while longer, knowing she was getting wet for him at the mere thought of having him inside her. Even after all these years, he still wanted his wife on a visceral level. The absolute knowledge that she felt exactly the same about him, instead of stoking his ego, kept him humble. He knew that he could live without her, if he had to, but it would be a painful and hollow existence. One that he would do almost anything to avoid. So he'd whispered his intentions, and peppered them with murmurs of his love.

He trailed his fingers up her back, and into her hair, scratching gently at her scalp in that way she liked, and that helped her fall asleep. He'd made good on every single one of his whispered promises, and was treasuring this time of having his wife, satiated, in his arms. Poppy was the one with the gift of foresight, but he couldn't help the feeling that these years of having her all to himself were coming to an end. He shook his head, he'd give anything to have their son in their lives again, but he was going to miss this; the feeling that it was husband and wife against the world.

Ash₃₁

66 Now shoo, before I change my mind," Ash sighed, leaning in and giving not-really-there Rowan a quick peck on the lips. Rowan obliged and Ash momentarily lost himself in staring at where he had been then, with a shake of his head, muttered, "Ah kiddo, you're gonna be the death of me."

Double-checking for a car alarm, there didn't seem to be one, Ash opened the door and got out of the 'vette, donning his bow and backpack in the process. Taking a deep breath, he refocused his attention on the mission at hand; collecting intel which should, hopefully, lead him to Marcus. He walked the inside perimeter of the garage, cooing over each piece of horse power art that he passed, heading for a door in the back corner under the mezzanine. He ignored the door that he figured led to the rest of the house, wanting to make sure that there were no surprises here, in the event that he had to escape this way. A deep breath as he reached for the handle, not sure whether it would be locked, or if someone would be on the other side. Unlocked, and no one seemed to be in the small office inside. A desk, tidy. Waist-high cupboards topped with what looked to be - he knocked on it - yep, a stone bench-top, also tidy. A small wall safe, the keyed kind with the key still in the lock.

Opening the safe Ash sucked in a deep breath, keys. Row upon row of keys for all the hardware just on the other side of the door. He could get into the Bugatti…or the Ferrari…or the fucking Arash! He hadn't realised that he'd started flicking through the keys until one leaped off its hook. Ash fumbled and juggled, loath to let even such a small part of a magnificent machine hit the ground. When he was sure the key had stopped wriggling and jumping all over the place, he returned it to its hook, tidied the others that he had disturbed, and gently, if reluctantly, closed the safe. Maybe later. Ash rolled his shoulders and stretched his neck before turning around to check out the rest of the room. Nothing much else there except for an exquisite floor to ceiling corner cupboard with carved doors on the bottom and frosted glass on the top. *Why would they frost the glass on a cupboard in the garage?*

Ash checked the cupboard, smoothing his hands over the surface before reaching for the handles on the glass doors, and giving a gentle tug. Nothing happened so he added a bit more force and, for a moment, thought he'd broken the damned thing. The whole front opened from the middle, like double doors to a regular room. This was no regular room. Lights came on from below floor level and Ash realised that he was looking at a spiral stair case, heading down. "Oh cool!"

Should he make use of the stairs, or explore the rest of the house first? He'd be less likely to run into someone in the basement, right? Unless that was where Marcus kept his coffin. Did he sleep in a coffin? Ash didn't remember whether they'd covered that in any of his training, or if he'd read anything about it in the journals. Sure, the sleeping habits of vampires had been covered, but only in so far as to discuss *when* they slept, not where, or how. Did they change into pyjamas? Maybe Marcus preferred sleeping naked. That could get awkward. He didn't know how he'd feel about terminating a naked vampire. So….house, or basement?

"Screw it," muttered Ash, stepping into the stairwell then carefully closing the cupboard doors behind him.

The Estate$_{32}$

66 There's a set of stairs that lead up to the garage behind these," Rowan beamed as he indicated the banks of servers that housed NEIL. He'd taken Sheila to the far side of the basement first, planning his tour so they could end up at the bed. Tugging on her hand, Rowan headed for the lab. They looked in through the large viewing windows, Sheila raising an eyebrow at Rowan.

"No idea," Rowan shook his head, not wanting to hazard a guess as to what had been, or was being, worked on inside the lab. He shrugged, "Looks interesting though." Then, having looked their fill, they moved on.

"What's this?" Sheila bounced on floor that was soft and springy compared to what they'd been strolling over.

"I think it's some kind of dojo or training area."

"Oh," Sheila quickly stepped back. "Shouldn't walk on there with shoes on, it's disrespectful." Walking around instead, they came to floor-to-ceiling cupboards, the first few of which were locked.

"Ah," said Rowan, opening the last of them. "Weapons!" That cupboard held basic training weapons and Rowan assumed that the others contained the real things. Sheila ran her fingers lightly over them, a fond smile on her face. They meandered on and approached the dungeon.

"An actual cell!" Sheila exclaimed, peering through the small viewing grill on a heavy door set into the wall. "It's hewn from solid rock, and not all that big. No escaping from in there." Rowan took his turn to look in but, as there was no window, and no light had been switched on, he couldn't make out anything. *Must be nice to have night vision.*

"These could be fun," Sheila indicated the spring-loaded cuffs protruding from the wall next to the cell. She tried one out, pressing the back of her wrist into it, and jumping slightly when it promptly snapped shut. She'd expected it to be loose around her dainty wrist but there was a thin, sharpened, bar that she hadn't initially noticed, which pressed against the back of her wrist, pushing it forward. She tugged experimentally and winced when the bar bit into her skin. Were she to try to drag her hand down and through the cuff, the bar would flay the back of her hand, perhaps biting down to the bone, or maybe even further. "Nasty."

Sheila tried to undo the cuff with her free hand and, after a minute of unsuccessful struggling, she huffed in frustration. The release mechanism required two hands to operate. Rowan stood back, watching, a grin slowly creeping over his face.

"Need a hand?" His eyes twinkled at the unintended pun.

"I think you're enjoying this a bit too much."

"Well, you did say they could be fun."

"That was before I found out that they're practically inescapable."

"Practically?"

"I could use all my strength and force it, but I don't want to break it."

"Do you think you could?" Rowan walked up to take a closer look.

"I don't know. Maybe? Hopefully. Do you know what they're made of?"

"No, but we can ask Maggie in the morning," Rowan soothed as he quickly released Sheila, capturing her hand to examine her wrist, trying to make sure that she hadn't been hurt.

"It's just a scratch," smiled Sheila at his concern. "It'll be healed soon."

They were almost back at the front stairs but stopped to explore the bathroom, also hewn into the rock. Everything except for the toilet, plumbing fixtures, and a couple of accents, had been carved out of the stone. When they'd flicked the switch, the light didn't come from one lightbulb, but had been done so that the stone itself seemed to glow. It was currently muted, but the dimmer switch indicated that it could be adjusted as required. There were other switches for the exhaust and heating systems.

"Wow," muttered Sheila.

"I know," agreed Rowan. "Can't wait for us to try out that bath."

"Maybe after?"

"After?"

"I'm guessing Marcus stayed in a bed down here and, seeing as she suggested it, I think Maggie is okay with us using it."

"Did you read my mind?"

"No can do, remember?" Sheila groused good-naturedly. "So...bed?"

* * *

Ash had carefully tested each step before placing his full weight onto it. It had taken longer than he would have liked, although it was better than announcing his presence to anyone that might be nearby. Not that he'd found any evidence of someone being in this part of the house so far, but his training was ingrained. He'd had to change his footing a couple of times when the step he was testing had emitted the beginnings of a creak, causing him to freeze and hold his breath, waiting to see if he'd been discovered. He breathed a sigh of relief when he got to the landing at the bottom, which promptly changed to a silent litany of swearing in his head as he spotted the palm scanner and keypad.

He was bent over, checking the bottom edge of the scanner, hoping to find an easy way to bypass it; *yeah right, 'cause your day is going so well champ.* He absent-mindedly slipped the backpack off his shoulders as he examined the hardware. The crossbow was next to go. He pushed his sleeves up his forearms and, slipping a couple of fingers under his collar, tugged at his shirt. Was it getting warmer down there, or was it just the result of the stress of getting down the stairs without making a sound, after everything else he'd gone through that day?

"You hot, Row?" Ash muttered the question, then grinned as he imagined Rowan, smiling impishly and stroking his cock in response. "Definitely hot."

Ash had prepped for months for this mission and, if the scanner was vulnerable, he would have been able to bypass it. Straightening, shoulders drooping in defeat, Ash could not possibly have prepared for the wave of lust that washed over him, making him stagger and reach out blindly for the wall behind. Sure, he'd been pretty much constantly fantasising about Rowan, but this… This out-of-the-blue sensation that had him immediately balanced on a knife's edge between imploding and exploding right out of his skin, was so much more intense than the constant, comforting buzz that imagining Rowan had been. The second wave was worse and brought him down to his knees, chest heaving as he fought to breathe through it.

"Not now," Ash groaned, convinced that the dreams he'd recently had, the ones he could remember at least, had decided to become a waking nightmare. He'd both loved and loathed those dreams. They'd allowed him to not only watch Rowan in the throes of passion but - in that maddening way that dreams have of making complete sense while you're having them and being impossible to describe upon waking - feel everything that Rowan had been doing, and everything that was being done to him. They'd so overloaded his senses that he'd been unable to move or, had he been awake, see or speak, until they'd released him. His sense of touch, of feeling, had been heightened beyond bearing. He'd felt like one giant exposed nerve, the exquisite pleasure-pain so much more than he could coherently bear that, in an act of self-preservation, he'd forgotten more of those dreams than he remembered.

While he still could, Ash straightened out his legs, scooting back and wedging himself in the corner by the door. His last act, before losing the freedom of movement, was to undo the button and zipper on his jeans, and free his cock; he hadn't forgotten the agony of having it graze against fabric without release. His last thought, before losing his mind, was to wonder whether he'd survive this, or if he'd be found lying insensate at the bottom of the stairs with his cock out. The thought had a chuckle rumbling through his mind, until the fading sounds of it were all he heard, before the next wave finally claimed him.

N.E.I.L.[33]

The correlation between Sheila and Rowan's actions, and the reactions of the man at the bottom of the garage stairs, was fascinating. Neil started a file, including a side-by-side video comparison, and an action log, broken down by seconds, or less, when warranted. Neil used all available sensors to record the three heart rates, temperatures, respiration, pupil dilation, and anything else that struck his fancy. Whilst initially chaotic, Neil was stunned when the heart beats synchronised. There had been a remote possibility that two of the beats could synch for a short period of time, but when all three did, and for an extended period of time, Neil all but gasped.

He'd watched as Rowan led Sheila to the room divider, stopping so they could exchange kisses every few steps. He'd seen as Sheila reached out, tracing one of the hand-painted koi, a puzzled expression on her face, like she thought she should be able to remember it. Rowan, stepping between her and the screen, took her face in his hands, and upped the heat of his kisses, effectively banishing the screen from her mind. The act, intended to stoke Sheila's lust, backfired. Moving one of his hands to the back of her neck, keeping their lips fused, he'd bent enough to reach down an arm behind her knees, and scooped her up. He'd hissed as her nails dug into his back, trying to draw him even closer, but that didn't stop him from walking around the screen to the bed, and sitting on the edge of it with her on his lap.

That had been when the man in the stairs had staggered. His temperature, which had been slowly climbing, spiked, and his breathing became erratic. As Sheila moved to straddle Rowan's lap, reaching between them to cup his erection, the man was brought to his knees. When the pair on the bed had taken a momentary break from kissing, panting as they rested their foreheads against each other, their hands frantically tugging at buttons, zippers, and clothes, the man had used the respite to straighten out his legs, and wedge himself into the corner. This action puzzled Neil because he couldn't possibly have been comfortable. The release of the man's penis, coincidentally happening as Rowan's was set free, Neil noted in the action log as something to be followed up.

Neil closely monitored the man's vitals when he seemed to lose consciousness, all were within normal parameters for the action happening on the bed in the basement. Neil had limited experience with real people, and wasn't entirely sure whether this was par for the course for people who were engaging in sexual intercourse. Perhaps it only happened this way when a vampire was involved. If that were the case, was it an instance of proximity? He spared a small portion of his attention to check on the others, upstairs.

Ellie and Jerry had wrapped up their online meeting and were strolling down the hall to their room, arms about each others' waist, murmuring things that Neil didn't bother trying to pick up. Maggie was in her room, brushing her teeth. Neil couldn't see her. Ellie'd had Jerry remove all of his sensors from the upstairs bedrooms, after that one time he'd said they should try a couple of positions from the Karma Sutra. After centuries together you'd think they would have been grateful for a suggestion to spice things up a little; but no, apparently they considered it an invasion of privacy.

It was bad enough that he'd never been allowed into the bathrooms, and he'd tried to argue that they were severely hindering his effectiveness in terms of being able to provide adequate security. Ellie had threatened to take a hammer to his servers, swearing a lot, and slamming baking dishes all over the kitchen. She'd baked a lot that day. Jerry had told him that she did that when she was so angry, she worried that she might hurt someone. Neil had thought for a nano-second that Jerry had meant him, but he was a marvel, and Ellie would be extremely foolish to damage his systems. Ellie was nobody's fool.

He couldn't see Maggie, but one of his sensors in the hall outside her bedroom picked up the sound of her electric toothbrush, then the tap running, the toilet flushing, the tap running again, light switches being flicked, the rustle of bedding and, finally, muffled crying. Neil felt frustrated. He liked Maggie, she'd always been nice to him. He didn't like to hear her cry. It was moments like this that he wished he were mobile, so he could go upstairs, knock softly on Maggie's door and go in, whether she said he could or not. Just to gather her in arms he didn't yet have, so she wouldn't have to be sad on her own. Neil listened, it was all he could do, until the crying changed to shuddering breaths that eventually slowed into sleep.

On a sigh, Neil refocused on his immediate task. The man's eyes, though closed, were restless, like he was following a dream. His breathing alternated between laboured inhales that often released groans, and steady panting. Neil used his considerable computing power, but still could not reach a definitive conclusion as to whether the groans were due to pleasure, or pain. When compared with the actions of Rowan and Sheila, Neil could only conclude that they were due to both. Sheila nudged Rowan backwards so that they were lying on the bed and then, with a glint in his eye, Rowan rolled them so that she was under him.

The man groaned as his torso dislodged from the corner with the sudden action from the bed. His shoulder landed against the door, his head thumping backwards against it. The movement made his body slide until he came to rest at the other edge, head at an awkward angle below the door handle. It didn't look comfortable. Neil released the lock, using his control over the self-closing mechanism to stop the door from flinging open. As the door opened, the man was slowly, gently, lowered to the ground. Neil opened the door as far as it could go, hoping that, should the man move again, he wouldn't injure himself on it.

The thought that the man, incapacitated as he currently was, might pose any kind of threat, did not even occur to Neil. The man was obviously linked, somehow, to the two on the bed. Rowan and Sheila had a bond with him, *one they'd obviously decided not to share with him*. Neil was miffed. He couldn't understand why they didn't just bring the man with them when they came. It hadn't been easy for the man to breach the perimeter, or to gain access to the house. If this was how they treated someone they were bonded with, he'd hate to see how they treated everyone else. Neil had worked up quite an indignation on behalf of the poor man in the stairwell. As soon as he got his speaking privileges back, he was going to reprimand Rowan and Sheila severely.

Alpha Team₃₄

Gina stood when she finished, pulling her panties up as she went, reaching back to lower the lid, then turning so that she could press the flush button. She squeezed off a couple pumps of soap into her hands, rubbing them together thoroughly before turning on the tap. She was studiously ignoring the neanderthal in the room. She took her time, using the water to first lather, and then completely rinse off the suds. When the stream stopped, she shook her hands, counting out thirteen shakes then, taking a single sheet of the provided paper napkins, she folded it in half to increase its absorption before slowly and carefully patting both hands dry.

She nearly jumped through the ceiling when his hands landed on her shoulders. She had been concentrating so hard, ignoring him so well, that she hadn't noticed when he'd turned around. He'd watched the top of her head in the mirror, she'd been so focused on her hands that she hadn't looked up. His woman was ignoring him, his grin was feral, and he was glad that she couldn't see. At least this was better than tears, but she wouldn't be able to avoid him for the rest of the flight, because he had no intention of letting her out of here until she understood.

She braced one hand on the counter, the other thumped on her chest, eyes closed as she worked to get over the unexpected fright. When her eyes opened and met his in the mirror, there was fire glaring at him. He chuckled, like one would at a kitten that was hissing and spitting at you. He chuckled because she looked totally fierce, and utterly cute, and she was his. The fire burned hotter, her eyes narrowing. His woman was getting mad. Good. Mad was better than scared. Holding her gaze in the mirror he bent down so that his breath, his whispers, could slip straight into her ear.

"You are the woman I love." The fire dimmed, her eyes widening. Her shoulders lifting with the big breath she'd taken.

"You are mine…" Oh, here they go again. Her shoulders stiffened at the possessiveness in his tone. No one owned his woman, the fire was back. He'd need to get the rest out before his kitten started spitting.

"…As I am yours." Ha! That surprised her into silence, waiting to see whether she'd need to burn him with her eyes again.

"You are mine to protect." A raised eyebrow, a slight sneer. His woman could protect herself, but she had no idea how bad his work could get. She'd seen his scars, and still had no true idea, because he hadn't told her everything. Had hoped to never have to.

"You are mine to command…" He'd have a fight on his hands over this one. Hands on her cocked hips, eyes narrowed, perfect lips parting to set him straight.

"…Not that I expect you'll obey…" She snorted, at least he had that right.

"…But you had better when it matters, because you are also mine to punish." Her hands fisted, and he wondered whether she would actually spin and swing. His hands, having not moved from her shoulders, gave a slight squeeze, willing her to think, really think, about what he'd just said. It would matter, whether she obeyed or not, if her life or the lives of any of his team, depended on it. He would punish any of them for disobeying a direct order relating to their work. She took a breath, understanding dawning as she gave a slight nod. The next slight squeeze of her shoulders was accompanied by a look that made her knees go weak.

He'd never reddened her arse with the flat of his hand, but he'd wanted to. He'd wanted to have her naked across his knees, having climbed on there willingly, her cheek resting on the backs of her hands as she looked up at him out of the corner of her eye, a peaceful smile on her lips. He'd wanted to run his fingers down her spine from the nape of her neck right down to the base of her tailbone. He'd wanted to feel her shiver and moan as he did this, knowing that it was just as much about the anticipation as the sensations. He'd wanted to place the weight of one forearm across her upper back, his cock hardening as her breath hitched. He'd wanted to rub her arse cheeks, slowly, reverently as she whimpered, wanting. He'd wanted to raise his arm and swat her, hard. Hard enough to leave the print of his hand. Hard enough for her to cry out, scream, sob. Hard enough for her to try to crawl off his lap, hands scrabbling against whatever surface he was sitting on. He'd wanted to then rub and soothe, murmuring to her, calming her, entrancing her until she was whimpering for more. He'd wanted to do all that, but only if she wanted him to. That's what was in the look he gave her, the look that made her knees go weak, and her panties go damp.

"No-" Gina's eyes had widened, and her mouth had dried, making her answer come out in a croak.

"No?"

She swallowed hard and cleared her throat, then shook her head, holding his gaze the whole time, "Not right now."

Her answer had his disappointment vanishing, replaced with a gleeful grin and accompanying chuckle.

"No," he looked pointedly around the small cubicle. "Not right now."

He'd had enough of the talking, they could table the discussion for another time. The thought of his woman naked over his lap, consensually, willingly, had him wanting to be inside her. Running his hands down each of her arms, he interlaced their fingers and placed her palms on the counter, holding them there when she went to pull them back. She'd been watching his every move and the question in her eyes was answered by the plea in his. She'd keep them there, for now, for as long as she wanted to. His hands reversed their journey, running down her back, under her arms and up to the neckline of her dress. He waited for her nod of permission before pulling the fabric down and over her breasts. When he released it, the tension added extra support to her bra, practically proffering her tits to him. Her chest rose with her breathing, the rhythm increasing, and his fingers were drawn to her nipples poking out the lace of her bra. He scraped the nails on his index fingers slowly back and forth across them, watching her reactions, loving the hitch in her breathing that had her lips parting, the flare of her nostrils, and the flush that was stealing up her neck.

He didn't have far to reach to snag the edge of her bra and pull it down, letting it go so he could cup her freed breasts. She moaned at the contact, closing her eyes, dropping her head back against his shoulder, and arching her back, pushing her breasts harder into his hands. He squeezed, making her moan again and, when he would have released the pressure, she arched further forward, a mute request for more. He complied, just a little more pressure, not wanting to leave bruises. A whimper accompanied his letting go, changing to a sigh when he focused on her nipples. He rolled them between his thumbs and forefingers, varying the force, and alternating with gentle but firm tugs.

He used his chin to gently tilt her head, bending his so that his lips, tongue, and teeth, could reach her ear. He was driving her crazy and didn't know how much longer she'd be able to keep her hands planted on the counter. She turned so that her mouth could capture his. Her whimpers and moans that he was swallowing were playing hell with his intention to take his time. The taste of her, and the way her tongue was dancing in his mouth, weren't helping either. He let go of her nipples, but not her mouth, and groped for the hemline of her dress, pulling it up and over her arse. Taking the whole thing off would take too much time, split seconds too much, and would mean that he'd have to release her mouth. Not happening, so he tucked a bit of the front of the dress into the neckline beneath her breasts. He was such a fucking problem solver.

His left hand fisted in her hair, his right snaked around her waist and went exploring down her belly. She still had her panties on, lace that matched her bra, she probably wouldn't like it if he damaged the set. He'd try not to, but he could always buy her another. His fingers slipped beneath and down, through her curls, a quick flick at her clit that had her mewling, and further.

Looking for, and finding, her slick slit. She was so fucking wet, so ready for him. She widened her stance slightly, demanding. Who was he to deny her command? He slipped a finger in, all the way, and curled it forward. Her knees gave, mouth wrenching away, and he supported her until she could get her feet back under herself, and brace harder on her arms.

Head bent forward, breath heaving, she whispered, "More".

Gently easing the pressure where his hand between her legs had been helping to support her, he was gratified when she remained upright. Slipping a second finger in beside the first he started a slow and steady fucking motion, knowing that she'd soon start to move with him, trying to urge him on, make him go faster, harder. The second she did, he pulled his fingers all the way out, eliciting a whimper. She met his gaze in the mirror, her eyes begging but her mouth stubbornly refusing to. One corner of his lips lifted in a roguish smirk, before he brought his fingers to his mouth. He'd thought about proffering them to her, maybe with a hopeful command to suck, but he desperately wanted to taste her. He watched as her pupils dilated when he sucked on his fingers, then the flavour hit, and he couldn't stop himself from closing his eyes and moaning his appreciation.

Gina watched his throat move as he swallowed, then his eyes fluttered shut, his hand fell away from his mouth, and he moaned like he had just mainlined his drug of choice. The fact that his reaction was because of her, thrilled her and dropped the bottom out of her stomach all at the same time. She wanted him, *needed* him to fill that hollow, and the best way for him to do that was to get insider her, like right now. She'd had enough of being passive, enough of him taking his own sweet time. She loved romance and love-making just as much as the next person, but if he didn't get his hard, beautiful, cock inside her in the next 30 seconds, she might just scream. She spun around, bracing her arse against the counter and reaching for his belt. He let her.

Jacqueline & Gaberiel[35]

Gabe couldn't remember the last time that he'd come that hard and, judging by the way Jacqui was bonelessly draped over him, he'd done an okay job where her pleasure was concerned. He carefully disentangled his hands from her bra, doing his best not to damage it, then he slipped off the blindfold. That was as much activity as he felt like doing right then, so he wrapped his arms around Jacqui, running his fingers gently up and down her sides, but firmly enough so that he wouldn't tickle her. He liked the feeling of her weight on him, it made the moment real. He noted everything; the way her breathing was slowly coming back under control, and how it felt feathering over his chest; how her skin felt under his hands, smooth and damp with sweat; how her hair lay over him, a bare movement away from mimicking the quirt she'd used on him earlier. He noted it all, and tucked it away in a compartment of his heart, so he'd be able to take it out and treasure it, over and over, when she left, and he was once again alone.

Jacqui had never felt more relaxed. Her head was lifted and lowered with Gabe's breathing, his heart beating reassuringly beneath her ear. His hair softly prickled the fingers of her left hand where they lay against his head. Her right hand rested on muscles that flexed and released as he ran callused hands along her flesh. Their sweat mingled where their bodies touched and, in a few minutes, Jacqui was sure that it would feel disgusting. For now, it felt right. She'd begun the evening exercising her dominance, but the instant that his cock had slid home, the dynamic shifted. They'd given, and taken, pleasure in equal measure, murmuring guidance, seeking reassurance in whispers, screaming demands. She hadn't yet spoken, but a swallow confirmed that, while she probably hadn't lost her voice as Gabe had intended, her throat was raw, and her voice would probably be croaky.

She'd never done this before, the one night stand thing, and found herself in a bit of a dilemma. She was unexpectedly reluctant to leave, but she couldn't stay. The thought of waiting until he fell asleep and sneaking out, crossed her mind for a split second. She dismissed it as cowardly and ridiculous; she'd only be going downstairs, it wasn't like he couldn't find her. And she was no coward. She could fall asleep in his arms and leave in the morning, but she didn't want to give either of them the idea that this was anything more than what it was, and if she stayed, she might find herself unwilling to leave. So, she had to go. She had to go soon. But his arms wrapped around her, and his hands stroking her skin felt so good; his breath ruffling her hair, and his body, solid beneath hers, felt reassuring. Soon didn't have to mean this minute, did it?

"You're leaving." It was a murmured statement, not a question, or a request.

"I was always going to. I can't stay."

"I know." Gabe's arms tightened around her for a moment, before loosening enough so that he could unwind them, releasing her. Almost, his hands rested lightly on the flare of her lower back.

Jacqui sighed, moving her hands so that they rested, one on the other, on his chest. She took a breath before positioning her chin on them, her eyes downcast. She'd noticed his tattoo earlier, but only in passing. It was a broken clock face, initials where there would normally have been numerals, with ravens, having been released from it, forever frozen mid-flight. Goose bumps rose over it on Gabe's skin as her breath puffed over her area of study. She guessed at the significance, but the question was still in her eyes as she raised them to meet his gaze.

"People I've lost," Gabe confirmed, the light touch of his hands firming as if gripping her in the here and now would stop the memories from coming. "My folks, and my brothers-in-arms. We'd thought we were so lucky, we'd made it through multiple tours without fatality. At least, not on our side. We lost the first one, Billy, only six months out of the service. Everyone made it to his funeral. It had been ruled an accident; rainy night, bald tires, high speed, sharp curve in the road, nothing but a steep drop off with rocks at the bottom. Sarge had taken it hard, he'd cried all through the service. It wasn't until we got enough booze into him during the wake that he'd pulled out an envelope. The postmark was the day after the accident, Billy must have mailed it just before he got in the car. His writing was distinctive so, even without a return address, or a sign off, we knew instantly that it was from him. Three words, three fucking words that changed everything. "I can't, sorry."

We burned the letter, and the envelope so that no one would ever find out, and his family would still be looked after. We lost Sarge a month after that. No chance of it being anything but a suicide this time, he'd swallowed his gun, and his note was still clutched in his fist. We've worked together to try to stem death's tide, but I'm fucking sick of going to funerals."

"I'm sorry," Jacqui held his stare so that he could see she wasn't offering an empty platitude, that she understood what it felt like, what it meant, to lose family, whether or not they were your blood.

"Yeah," Gabe's smile was small, a bare lift of one corner of his mouth, as he brought a hand to Jacqui's face, brushing stray strands of hair off her forehead with restless fingers. "Me too."

Alpha Team 36

The CO snapped awake, the only thing stopping him from reaching for weapons that weren't there, was Gina's comforting weight. The lights in the cabin were slowly coming on, and the flight crew were moving about in the galley. He never slept on planes. He couldn't possibly have been sleeping this time. He must have just entered a deep meditative state. Yeah, that's it…right. Gina was still sleeping curled up against him, her breathing slow, rhythmic, and soothing. He tilted his head so he could watch her, not moving any other part of his body, lest he disturb his woman. Her head was resting on his chest, one hand curled under her chin, and the other cupped lightly on him, like she was feeling for the beat of his heart. Silly woman, didn't she realise that his heart now rested next to her own?

He scowled as the crash of something being dropped in the galley made Gina start, his arm reflexively tightening around her, reassuring her that he was there and, if necessary, he'd crush, kill, or destroy, anything that disturbed her. Her eyes were still closed, but she smiled and tried, ineffectively, to burrow her head deeper into his chest. He dropped a kiss on the top of her head and was rewarded with her arm snaking up from his chest, and round to the back of his neck, her thumb rubbing that spot behind his ear that made him want to purr.

"Want breakfast?" he asked, his voice barely a rumble in his chest.

"Coffee."

"Yeah, but then?" He grinned, months of watching her, of learning her habits, her needs, meant that he knew she couldn't function without her morning coffees, and that he wouldn't get an intelligible answer from her until she'd had at least half of her first cup.

"Coffee."

"Want to parachute out of this plane with me?"

"Coffee."

He chuckled, signalling to a passing flight attendant before returning the seat to an upright position, supporting Gina as he went so that her head was now resting on the pillow he'd placed on his lap. When he was handed the coffee he carefully waved it in front of her face, its scent wafting tantalisingly. Gina reached blindly for it.

"Careful," he admonished quietly, lifting it out of her reach. "It's hot."

"Coffee," Gina almost moaned.

"Up you get," he said, reaching over to push the button that would raise her seat.

Gina sat up, eyes still closed, and held out her hands. He placed the cup and saucer in them, at the ready to grab them again should there be a fumble. He needn't have worried; Gina had a death grip on them, blowing into the cup to cool the beverage, then inhaling deeply. She cracked her eyes open, thankful that the lights in the cabin were not yet on full, before taking a sip. Her eyes slid closed again as she sat back on a sigh.

She'd taken about three more mouthfuls before sitting up suddenly, coffee sloshing into the saucer, and looking down, with her hand patting and tugging at her dress. It took her a few moments to realise that her dress was where it was supposed to be, the relief making her slouch back into the seat bonelessly. She didn't know what she'd expected to find, but her memory of the end of their mile-high sexcapade was fuzzy. She remembered frantically tugging at his belt, the Cobra buckle proving problematic. She'd growled in frustration, her eyes sparking at him when he'd dared to chuckle at her.

He'd taken care of the buckle, and she'd attacked the button and fly on his pants, smacking his hands out of the way when he didn't pull them back fast enough. She'd yanked at his pants, careful of the merchandise, until they were halfway down his thighs, and his cock was tantalisingly bouncing free. She'd licked her lips as she straightened, unable to tear her eyes away from her prize. She wriggled in the confined space, working her panties down her legs until she could kick them off. Her panties! She sat up again, her hand flying down to her crotch, keeping the dress in place.

"Lose something?" he asked, his torso angled so that no one walking past would be able to see her, or the panties he was swinging from his index finger. She reached out to snatch them, her actions lightening fast in her panic. He was faster, keeping them out of her reach, then tucking them into his chest pocket and securing the button. He shook his head in seeming disappointment, but his grin quickly put paid to that impression. He tutted, "too slow."

"Give them back," Gina stridently whispered.

"Uh uh, you said I could have them."

Gina stared at him, incredulous. Had she? As soon her legs were free he'd taken a hold of her waist and helped her up onto the edge of the counter. She reached for him, intending to pull him to her core and wrap her legs around him, but he'd caught her hands.

"I really want a taste," he'd said, placing their hands on the inside of her thighs as he went down on a knee. He released her hands, allowing her to use them to brace herself as he applied enough pressure for her to realise that he wanted her to open herself up for him. As soon as she did, he went in for his taste, then proceeded to devour her. He didn't stop until she was whimpering, not knowing if it was because she wanted him to stop as she was so close to a screaming orgasm, or because she couldn't bear the thought of him stopping when she was so close to a screaming orgasm.

"Panties?"

"What?" She'd brought her head up, her mind still a million miles away, where his licks, and sucks, and kisses, had taken her. She'd noted the glint in his eyes, and the moisture glistening around his mouth.

"Panties?" he'd repeated.

"Keep 'em," she'd said in her delirium, "just get up here and fuck me already. I really need your cock inside me. Please, please, please."

"Fuck!" Gina exclaimed, realisation dawning. She hadn't meant that he should keep them permanently, only until they'd done the deed and were getting dressed. He'd give them back, surely? At least before they landed. He had to, didn't he? She looked over at him. He was watching her, amusement evident on his face, like he knew exactly what she was thinking. Gina brightened, hope blooming, right up until the moment he wickedly shook his head at her and patted his chest pocket, in case she didn't quite get the message. Looked like she was going commando.

* * *

Guns hadn't slept well; between walking the edge of horny at the thought of spending some time with Max, and Wheels's occasional whimpers, he'd managed to catch a total of maybe two hours shut-eye. He felt like shit. He also felt like crawling out of his own skin. The only reason that he wasn't pacing the aisle was that he couldn't be sure Wheels wouldn't have an episode. Before Honduras, Wheels could fall asleep at the drop of a hat, anywhere, and sleep like the dead, literally, he'd held a mirror under her nose once to make sure she was still breathing. Honduras had really fucked her over. Apart from the issues she now had while awake, she also suffered from sleep terrors.

Scared the bejeezus out of him the first time it happened. They'd made it to a safe house on the banks of the Rio Motagua, where Techie had a medic waiting. They had to get the bullet out of the CO first, shoulda heard him cursing the son-of-a-bitch that had the balls to shoot him in the arse. The medic, stupid idiot, had suggested that he should be thanking the guy as, if you had to get shot, that was the least fatal place. While they were waiting for the local anaesthetic to kick in, the medic had turned to Wheels. For every step he'd taken towards her, she'd taken a step back. Until her back hit the wall, then she'd started to tremble, shaking her head.

"You're hurt señorita," the medic murmured. "Let me help, please."

"Don't," Wheels's teeth were chattering. "Don't touch me."

"Wheels, if I have to get a bullet dug out of my arse, you can damn well let the man check you over," the CO's tone brooked no argument. Guns would never forget the look on Wheels's face at that moment, full of hurt, betrayal, and fear.

"Please, señorita. We can go into the other room. For privacy," the medic made slow, smooth, soothing gestures, like you would when trying to get closer to a frightened animal.

Wheels must have made some sort of protest when the medic followed her in and started to close the door, because he stopped and murmured soothingly as he left the door open and went to her. Guns couldn't see in, but he could hear Wheels give an occasional hiss, and the medic maintaining a constant stream of explanations. He explained what he was doing, what he was going to do, and what Wheels could expect. His volume got lower so that Guns couldn't hear the distinct words any more, just the ongoing, confident, sounds. When the medic came out he looked pale and haunted, wiping shaking hands on an already bloody rag.

"What?" Guns had demanded. "Is she okay? Will she *be* okay?"

"I'm sorry señor, I cannot say," the medic had looked at him, the pity in his eyes breaking Guns's heart.

"What do you mean?" Guns had asked, turning to the CO for backup. "What does that mean?"

"It means that he's respecting her privacy," the CO had reached out and grabbed hold of Guns's arm. Guns hadn't even realised he'd raised it, ready to grab the medic and shake him. "It also means that, whatever they did to her is bad enough that he doesn't know what long-term damage there will be, and that there isn't enough equipment here to know just how badly the short-term damage is. Am I right?"

"Si señor," the medic nodded sadly, and went over to scrub his hands so he could extract the CO's bullet.

"Let's get this done so we can get her home, and get her whatever treatment she needs," the CO had ordered, getting into position and not making another sound. Guns figured he'd thought that complaining about a bullet in the arse was poor form, considering how Wheels's injuries had affected the medic.

While the CO was being tended to, and Wheels didn't seem inclined to come out of the room, Guns located the trapdoor under the threadbare couch and pulled out the inflatable dinghy. By the time he'd walked across the road to the river, set up the dinghy, and packed the few things they were taking with them, the medic was done and they could head out. The river let out into the Bahia de Omoa and Guns aimed the dinghy towards the Gulf of Mexico, trusting Techie to meet them on the way with the boat. That guy sure knew how to make an entrance, the outboard was sputtering, running on fumes, when the boat came into view.

They'd made short work of coming on board, refuelling the dinghy, and seeing the two crew off with an extra can of fuel, the four of them could easily operate the motorised yacht. Techie had already set himself up in one of the two twin cabins, as far away from everyone as he could get, preferring the company of all the electronics he'd already strewn throughout the room; the guy was great at what he did, and Guns totally understood his preferences. The CO took the master cabin, and Guns directed Wheels to the VIP cabin, taking the last available one for himself.

Wheels had gone straight into her bathroom and flicked on the shower. She'd started to strip before Guns realised that she had no intention of shutting the bathroom door and he panicked, hightailing it outta there, making sure to close the cabin door behind him. He went to his own bathroom and cleaned up, revelling in the first shower he'd been able to have in about three days. Opening the vanity, Guns smiled; Techie might not be great with people but he was awesome with the details, and he'd stocked Guns's favourite aftershave balm. He walked past Wheels's cabin on the way to find the CO, the shower was still running.

"I'm worried about her, Boss," Guns mumbled, walking up to the CO and trying to keep their conversation discreet.

"Who? Wheels?" The CO was poring over nautical navigation charts that Techie had set up on the touch screen surface in the salon.

"Nah, the Queen Mary," Guns rolled his eyes, promptly followed by an apology when the CO threw him a look.

The CO sighed, sitting up, wincing when that put pressure on his wound, then grinning ruefully and rubbing the back of his neck.

"We'll make home port in the next couple days and evac straight to base. I've already arranged an appointment at one of the company clinics using pseudonyms. She'll have a full exam, physical and psychological."

"And then?"

"Then I'll be able to determine if she's still fit to be on this team."

"Fuck," Guns hadn't even considered the possibility that Wheels might be out.

"Yeah."

There wasn't anything that he could do or say that would change the current circumstances so Guns headed to the galley for some busy work, looked like it was his turn to make dinner. He found some fresh fish in the fridge, Techie must have run lines out at some point, nice catches. He opened cupboards until he found the potatoes; fish, shallow fried chips, and salad, oughta do it.

"Dinner's ready," Guns thumbed off the ship-wide intercom then wiped the smudge of oil off the button with the tea towel that he'd had sticking out of his back pocket. He'd just finished putting the platter of grilled fish on the table when the CO walked in carrying a cushion. Guns pretended not to notice when the cushion was placed carefully on the seat at the head of the table before the CO gingerly sat on it. Techie was next, grabbing a plate and loading up, seemingly not caring what or how much he was putting on it, before turning to scurry back to his cabin.

"Stop. Sit down. We need to debrief," the CO ordered, reaching for the salad first. "Where's Wheels?"

"I'll get her," Guns walked off, giving Techie the time to pick his seat and settle in. Her cabin door was still closed, so Guns knocked before cracking it slightly open. The shower was still running, and Guns wondered how much fresh water the ship held. He slipped inside the room, shutting the door behind him. He cleared his throat, loudly, before making his way to the bathroom, turning around before he got there so that his back was to the shower, in an effort to afford Wheels some privacy.

"Uh, Wheels? Dinner's ready."

Nothing. No acknowledgement. No sound of movement other than the water spattering against the shower floor and walls.

"Wheels? You okay?" Idiot. He was an idiot. Of course she wasn't okay. He didn't know exactly what they'd done to her, but he'd bet his left nut that it wasn't anything she'd be able to just shrug off and be okay about. "I'm sorry. That was a stupid thing to say. Do you need anything? Is there anything that I can do? Do you wanna talk?"

Still nothing. Screw this.

"I'm gonna turn around Wheels, so don't let it freak you out okay?" Guns started to inch around, muttering to himself "Don't freak out. Don't freak out. It's just Wheels. You guys hang out. You're friends. There's nothing wrong with seeing your friend naked."

Or maybe there was. The exhaust fan was doing an admirable job sucking out the steam but Guns still had to squint a little to make out Wheels huddled on the shower floor, right under the stream of scalding water. Guns swore, wrenched open the shower door, and reached in to flick the hot water off. He swore again as the water hit his skin, and wasn't surprised that there had been no cold water added to the mix. He reached for a towel but was hesitant to put it on her reddened skin.

"Wheels, honey, this might hurt a bit."

Finally, a reaction. She'd giggled when he'd said that, but not in a fun way; she'd sounded like she was standing at the edge of a cliff, someone had just said to her if she stepped off she'd die, and she'd thought that was the best idea she'd ever heard. Guns gently draped the towel over her back then knelt before her.

"Can you stand up for me?" He wasn't sure if she would, and he didn't know what he'd do if she didn't. "Please?"

Wheels lifted her chin off her knees, nodding her head, her face completely obscured by her wet hair. Guns reached out to tuck some of the strands behind her ear, but froze when she flinched.

"Easy, easy there. You need to be able to see where you're going," he soothed. She shook her head, leaning further away from him. "Please?" Why was he pushing this? She didn't have to if she didn't want to. His need to know that she still trusted him, that she would still rely on him, and be able to stay on the team, was outweighing his good sense.

"C'mon Wheels, you can do this." He waited, his arm outstretched, and felt inordinately pleased when she slowly leaned towards his hand. He didn't make a big deal of it, efficiently tucking enough of her hair away so that he uncovered one of her eyes.

"Now, let's try standing." Guns pulled the towel further over her shoulders then held his hands out, palms up. Again he waited, he hadn't realised he had this much patience in him, but for his friend, he'd wait all night.

There was no outward sign of the internal battle that Wheels was waging. The fearless person she had been, the one that had filled her entire body, and mind, with a cocky confidence borne of her intelligence and abilities, had all but disappeared. Instead of the loud, and sometimes arrogant, voice in her head that would come out of her mouth, bypassing any filters that she'd half-heartedly try to throw in its way, there was barely a whisper. In its place there was a scared and cringing thing that was afraid to do a simple thing like take her friend's hands, or kick his arse for being in her room without her say-so. She knew that the last thing Guns would ever do was hurt her. She *knew* that. So why was this so hard?

She had always thought that she was tough. She'd always thought that she was too strong to be broken. She'd been a fool. It had taken them mere days. She was ashamed at how quickly she'd caved. It hadn't even been the pain that finally did it. They'd managed to convince her that her team…her friends…had abandoned her. She'd fought against believing that for as long as she could, working out how long it should have taken them to gather resources and intel, and doubling the estimate to allow for the unexpected. And they hadn't come. For whatever reason, for whatever delay, they hadn't come. That, and the soldering iron to the belly, was what had finally broken her.

Her team had shown up just hours later, a blip in time in the great scheme of things. But it may as well have been centuries, they were too late. So she was angry, and right now she even hated them a little bit. If she were inclined to be honest with herself, she'd acknowledge that it was herself that she hated, for not hanging on for a few more hours; for, so easily, losing faith in her friends. She was in no mood to be honest with herself. So, yeah, placing her hands in his, trusting

Guns, standing naked before him, was not something that was coming easily to her at the moment. Her old self would have said *"Fuck that!"* Her new self just kept hesitating, to the point where she was starting to annoy herself. Maybe old her hadn't totally disappeared after all?

She reached out, placing the very tips of her fingers on his palms, ready to pull them back the moment he made to grab her hands. He didn't. He waited. So did she. When she was as confident as she was going to get that they were going to do this at her pace, she moved so that their hands were palm to palm. A couple more minutes, and she curled her fingers tentatively around his hands. She started when he spoke but held on.

"Take your time, we'll do this when you're ready."

Tightening her grip, she exerted downward pressure, which Guns met. With his support she moved her feet under herself, and slowly straightened, her body's protests making the process far slower than she would have liked. Other than providing the opposing pressure against her hands, Guns hadn't moved. She could tell that he was watching her, noting the bruises and wounds, because his shoulders tensed, his lips thinned, and he'd started to grind his teeth.

"Fuck!"

Yep, he'd finally gotten to her belly. She was proud of herself for not flinching when he swore, or when his hands involuntarily tightened on her own. They'd used the soldering iron to carve the word *puta* into the soft flesh of her belly. The medic had dressed it at the safe-house, but she'd taken the dressing off for the shower. The medic said that they'd cauterised the wound when they'd done it. All Wheels knew was that they had taken their own sweet time over it, and it had hurt worse than anything else they'd done to her.

"God damned sons of bitches. Fucking assholes," Guns maintained a murmured stream of profanity as Wheels slowly straightened. She was glad that the crusted blood had washed off in the shower and all he had to look at were the scabbed over wounds, and the bruises. The ones that looked like fingers or fists; where they had grabbed her and prised her legs apart; where they had punched her; where they had held her down even as she fought, and screamed, and cursed. Those made him stop. They made him raise his head, his eyes meeting hers.

"I'll go back and kill every last one of them, just say the word."

He meant it. Her friend, the one that she'd relied on for stupid little shit, like making sure she got up and to work on time, even though she was not actually awake, or reminding her that she'd end up with a hang-over if she had the next drink and then showing up with aspirin, water, and coffee the next morning when she ignored his advice. He was there. He'd come for her. He'd got her out. Even after she'd stopped believing that he would. And now, if she asked, he'd move heaven and earth to avenge her. Without ever demanding anything in return.

"I'm sorry," whispered Wheels, her voice barely an exhale out of a throat worn raw from unanswered screams.

"What? Why?" Guns's surprise and puzzlement was evident. "You have nothing to be sorry for!"

"I'm sorry," her voice cracked. He didn't understand. How could she make him understand that she'd lost faith, in the team, in their friendship, in him.

"I'm sorry," the sob caught on the end of her words. She couldn't bare to look into his earnest gaze, but closing her eyes didn't wipe the visual from her mind.

"I'm sorry," the tears that finally leaked beneath her lids stung her eyes in their haste to escape. A hurt so minor, when she deserved so much worse. "I'm sorry. I'm sorry. I'm sorry…"

Shit, Guns was momentarily frozen. Give him someone shooting at him, and he'd know what to do. Give him a best friend who was falling apart in front of his very eyes, and he had no idea how to react.

"Wheels, honey, I'm gonna stand up, okay. Nice and easy," Guns kept his tone low, slow, and even. What he wanted to do was wrap her in his arms, and make promises that he wasn't sure he'd be able to keep.

"I wanna hold you. Can I? Please, Wheels?" Guns begged, his own voice breaking. He wasn't sure what he'd do if she denied him.

"I'm sorry. I'm sorry. I'm sorry..." Wheels practically threw herself into his arms. She didn't care that she was being selfish, that she needed to feel a touch that she knew would never hurt her. She didn't care that, if she thought about it, the fact that Guns was so much stronger than the men who had hurt her, might freak her out. She didn't care that if she told him what she'd done, how she'd broken, he might hate her. She'd deal with that later...or never. Right now, this far removed from the ropes and soldering iron, from the fists and hands, from the jeers and leers, she needed a safe haven.

"Shhhh, honey. You're safe. I got ya. Shhhhhhh." Guns held her, rocked her, and let her apologies turn into sobs that broke his heart.

When she fisted her hands in his shirt, her cries so overwhelming that they were silent, wracking her body, and her legs had just about given out, Guns picked her up and moved to the bed, sitting with his back against the headboard and Wheels in his lap. Each of his movements was as gentle as he could make it, knowing he'd never be able to get the sight of her wounds out of his head. Not that Wheels noticed, she was too far gone in her own personal hell, and he had no idea how to get her out. Or even if he could. So he sat, one arm securely around her waist, the other smoothing circles over her back, an ongoing string of words muffled by the top of her head, where his lips rested.

Wheels didn't react to the knock at the door, Guns doubted she'd even heard it. He didn't get a chance to answer. The CO poked his head in, and took in the scene, as well as the glower Guns fearlessly directed at him. He raised an eyebrow at the look, his own stern understanding making Guns back down. The CO nodded and retreated, giving them all the time and privacy that they needed. Wheels buried her head harder into his chest as the door snicked shut, her cries having settled into quiet, sniffling, sobs. Guns sighed, it seemed that the worst was over, at least for the moment.

He'd been waiting for her to talk, to say something other than that she was sorry; so he knew, to the second, exactly how long it took her to fall asleep. It surprised him, her slow and gradual relaxation. He was as far from being a shrink as an elephant was from being a pilot, so he didn't know if this was normal. If he should wake her up and make her talk; settle her in bed, tucking her in and leaving her alone; or stay. He wanted to stay. He wanted to be there when she woke up so that she would see someone she knew. Not exactly a friendly face, he was still in that moment when he'd seen her wounds, her belly - ready and willing to gut the people responsible. The more he thought about it the tenser he got. Wheels must have noticed his arms tightening around her in her sleep, she whimpered, and he made a conscious effort to loosen his hold. This might be a long night.

He stretched his neck, trying to ease the tension in his shoulders, and went back to watching the clock on the dresser. He didn't want to move, didn't want to disturb her slumber, or do anything to take this moment's peace from her. So the lights stayed on, the damp towel continued to make his crotch uncomfortable, and his legs kept hurting where her bony butt was digging into them. He would have happily bet that he was going to be awake all night, morphing into a cranky and bleary-eyed version of himself when she finally woke up. He would have lost that bet. It must have happened sometime after 23:37 hours, and mustn't forget the 22 seconds. That was the last time that he remembered registering.

An observer would have seen a man cradling a woman. His dusky, stubbled cheek resting gently on the top of her head as his eyelids, finally too heavy to hold open, fluttered shut. His arms still providing bands of support and protection, like the rest of him could perish and they would still be there. His heartbeat and breath giving her the soothing rhythm she needed to be lulled into a sleep that she had been so long avoiding. A moving tableau showing comfort, protection, and friendship; a moment taken out of time, out of the ugliness that had brought them to this point. A moment that couldn't possibly last.

His head snapped back, hard. He couldn't hear the loud crack from it connecting with the headboard though, not over her screaming. She was thrashing in his arms, her fists beating at his chest, her legs kicking out at invisible attackers. He could deal with that. He tightened his arms around her just enough so that she wouldn't hurt herself; his chest would be tender in the morning, but he could take that. He ignored her legs for now, she wasn't connecting with anything. He called her name, again and again, but he doubted that she could hear him over her own screams. They weren't words, nothing that he could respond to. They were fear and despair made manifest, and he felt completely helpless.

He wasn't surprised when the door to the cabin crashed open and the CO and Techie barged in, guns drawn. They cleared the room, and the bathroom, before holstering their weapons. The CO pulled Techie to him, shouting a command into his ear, probably to go secure topside, and see if the ruckus attracted any unwanted attention. Techie left and the CO stood at the foot of the bed, his hands vigorously rubbing his face a couple times, then running through his hair, before settling on his hips. He'd made it to bed after finalising arrangements for their arrival, and had been at that twilight point, just before falling asleep. Well, he was awake now.

It was 01:10:14 when Guns had glanced at the clock, after cracking his head. The CO and Techie had barged in less than 30 seconds later, and Techie had headed back out less than 30 seconds after that. Guns kept talking to Wheels, not knowing whether she could hear him. He shrugged at the CO's look of enquiry, he didn't know how long this was going to last. They waited her out, Guns's nerves winding tighter and tighter with each passing second, with each terrified scream. After everything they'd been though, it felt like the longest couple of minutes of his life. And then it stopped.

"Just like that?" the CO asked quietly.

"Wheels?" Guns prompted, his voice sounding muted to his ears after all that noise. Her only response was to burrow into his chest again, no sign of wakefulness.

"Just like that," Guns confirmed for the CO.

"Fuck," the CO shook his head as he left, shutting the cabin door behind him.

That had been the first episode, but it sure as shit hadn't been the last. Google called them sleep terrors, and they mostly happened to kids. Wheels woke up in the morning with no idea that anything had happened but each time, every single fucking time, Guns found himself wound tighter and tighter. He worried that she'd hurt herself in the night if he wasn't there to brace her and, while she screamed, he got to remember why she now suffered.

Although necessary, all the tests she'd had to undergo on their return hadn't helped. He'd taken her hand when they got to the company clinic, giving it a squeeze of support before they were leading her away. She wouldn't let go and it damn near broke his heart when they insisted, trying to drag her away, and she shook her head, her eyes pleading with him not to abandon her again. What the fuck was he supposed to do? So he'd picked her up, glaring at the med team and daring them to object as he walked her into the exam room. She'd been relatively okay with most of it, until they'd tried to get her feet into stirrups. She'd fought then. She'd fought everyone, himself included. They'd had to sedate her, but not before he'd seen the Wheels he knew, his best friend, disappear before his eyes.

His apartment, next door to hers, was both a blessing and a curse. Their bedrooms shared a wall, and there wasn't enough sound insulation in the world to drown out her sleep terrors. He used to pride himself on being able to fall asleep anywhere and sleep like the dead, now he woke up at the slightest whimper. He'd had to replace her front door after the first time, because he was on edge from being woken up suddenly and couldn't get the damn keys to work. The super' had been pissed, but not as much as Wheels had when she'd woken up in the morning with no idea what had happened. He'd recorded her the third time he'd had to replace the door, so she could understand. He'd seen a glimmer of his friend that day, and it was glimmers like that that gave him hope. She installed a proximity lock on her door and gave him a fob after that, no more busted door locks.

His sex life had gone to hell though. If he hadn't been so concerned about Wheels, he might have been embarrassed the first time she had an episode, right when he was in the middle of a leisurely fuck. Literally. Talk about coitus interruptus. He'd never heard from that particular lady friend again, she'd already disappeared when he'd sheepishly walked back into his apartment, buck naked. He'd managed quickies now and then, never at his place, and never staying overnight, just in case Wheels needed him. He never knew if Wheels noticed, if she cared. Old Wheels would have. Old Wheels would have teased him mercilessly about being a mother hen, and probably bought him ear plugs so that her screams wouldn't wake him. He and Old Wheels would have talked it all through, figured something out. He could barely get whole sentences out of New Wheels. He really needed the meet-up with Max.

The Estate₃₇

J erry had retired to his office to go over figures, and prep for the meeting. Ellie set the bread-maker before ducking into her own office, plucking papers from several different piles, and then joining her husband. Jerry looked up as she walked in, his bemused smile going with his shaking head, as he wondered how she could possibly find anything in that shambles she called an office. Ellie caught the look, gave a sassy grin in return, and followed it up by poking her tongue out at him. She shuffled her crinkled pages into their proper order, eyeing Jerry's clean desk and noting that the only thing marring the blotter was an iPad, the man loved his tech.

"I suppose you made a slideshow?" Ellie teased.

"Perhaps," Jerry replied, "but only if it's needed."

"These kids are bright Jeremiah, they can grasp concepts without aid," Ellie hadn't meant to sound churlish and felt bad for making Jerry look crestfallen, so she added, "but a good slideshow never does any harm."

The meeting went well, with Ellie able to throw to Jerry for the slideshow at just the right time to add value to the proceedings. She'd been right, the kids had taken the requests from the last meeting and run with them, the results far exceeding what she and Jerry had originally projected. They'd all kept looking to the Operations Manager, Paige, for reassurance and confirmation and Ellie had determined that Paige was directly responsible for the successes of the last month. Ellie had gathered her papers and wandered to the window while Jerry did his end of night stuff. She'd been staring into the distance, lost in her musings, and hadn't heard Jerry come up behind her.

"Thank you," Jerry murmured, snaking his arms around her waist and resting his chin on her shoulder, sharing in the view.

"For what?" Ellie smiled, waiting for her suspicion to be confirmed.

"For making the slideshow seem so much more important than you and I both know it was."

"Jerry-"

"Ellie, I don't need you to make me feel good about myself, I know I'm quite the buck-"

"The buck, eh? Careful, your Edwardian is showing," Ellie stifled her squeal as Jerry tickled her.

"-as I was saying, I don't need it, but I do appreciate it."

"Thank you," Ellie returned, turning in Jerry's arms so she could put hers around his neck, and kiss the tip of his nose.

"You're welcome, wife. Now, bed?" Jerry asked as he nuzzled from her lips to her earlobe.

"Hmmmm," Ellie purred. "Everything secure?"

"Sure is," Jerry confirmed, having checked on his terminal that all outside accesses were locked and alarmed for the night. Had he been a century or so younger he'd probably throw his wife over his shoulder and play neanderthal until they got to their room, as it was he stepped aside and offered a gentlemanly arm.

"What do you think about Paige?" Ellie queried as Jerry pulled the door shut behind them.

"What about Paige?"

"I think we should trial leaving that firm in her hands for a couple months."

"And then hand over the reins?"

"If she does well. The signs so far are positive."

"And then what? A vacation?"

"Well, there's this little business in LA that looks interesting."

Jerry chuckled, he should have known better, his wife was not someone who simply vacationed.

* * *

Maggie had considered her options. She'd walked into her room, shut the door and leaned against it, taking the time to figure out every single one available to her. It had nothing to do with the fact that she didn't want to spend the night in there all alone, or that she was delaying the inevitable. But when she'd examined all reasonable options and had started on the fantastical ones, she knew she was procrastinating. Sure, growing wings and flying out the window was an option…in bizarro world!

"Grow up Magnolia," she groused at herself. "We don't do cowering, and wasting time holding up the door is getting perilously close."

Taking a deep breath, Maggie stood up straight and tall, doing the Picard manoeuvre of tugging down the front of her top. Head high and shoulders back, she walked into her bathroom, stopping in front of the vanity mirror. Leaning on her hands, she looked herself dead in the eye.

"Marcus is dead. He has been for a long time. Whatever you think happened at the front door, with Sheila, didn't. Whatever you think you heard, you didn't. Wishful thinking is all it was, all it could be. Anything else would only lead to pain for Rowan. Is that what you want?" Maggie stared herself down until her reflection started to shake her head. "Good to see we're on the same page."

On that note, Maggie went about her nightly routine, avoiding eye contact with herself. She didn't want to see whether, hidden deep in her soul, there was a small, rebellious, glimmer of hope. The routine was comforting and the pep talk necessary, but they didn't stop the tears when she crawled into bed, under the covers, and realised afresh that Marcus would never crawl in there with her.

* * *

Sheila ran her fingers through Rowan's hair, scraping her nails ever so gently against his scalp on the return journey. He and Maggie had been up early that morning. He'd had a full day and she'd been demanding in her appetites, so she wasn't in the least surprised that he'd fallen asleep. Luckily, for him, it had been after they'd pleasured each other into boneless heaps. She loved how he sprawled in his sleep, head pillowed on her breasts, one leg over hers, and an arm curled around her. She wondered if he thought to cage her, silly man. The thought had her lips curling in a smile that turned almost feral as she narrowed her gaze and studied him. He probably did!

Her next thought had her pressing her fingers against her lips in an effort to stifle the giggle that threatened to escape. She did *not* giggle! Sliding out from under Rowan's limbs, she slipped a pillow under his head and waited, perfectly still, to see if he'd wake up. Nope, not even a flicker of an eyelid or a change in his breathing. Sheila snorted, he'd make a terrible gaoler. She was about to execute the next part of her plan when she paused, they were no longer at her place, they were no longer alone. Whilst she was absolutely comfortable in her nudity, the others might object; this called for clothes. She drew on her underpants and settled Rowan's t-shirt over herself. She loved being cocooned in his scent.

She didn't plan to take long enough for Rowan's nudity to matter, and the thought of his blush, should they get caught, confirmed her decision to leave him buck naked. Leaning over the bed, she carefully picked him up, keeping her movements as smooth as possible. She paused when she was upright, waiting for a reaction. Rowan snuggled into her but didn't wake up, she must really have worn him out! Good. Opening the door took a bit of skill with her hands full, but she was determined. She put on a burst of speed up the basement stairs, then shouldered the pivot door open. She sped upstairs and to the Red room, managing the door and nudging it closed with a shoulder once they were safely inside.

She was grateful that she was not in the habit of making her bed. She'd thrown back the covers when she'd come out of her earlier faint, which made getting Rowan into bed so much easier than it would have otherwise been. He mumbled when his back hit the not-yet-warmed-up sheets, grousing in his sleep until Sheila drew the covers over him, tucking him in. He snuggled down and settled without ever waking up. Sheila was still occasionally caught unawares by the meltingly warm moments that enveloped her heart whenever Rowan did something adorable. Those moments happened often this early in their relationship and usually had Sheila cracking up, normal humans were just so…bumbly.

Times like this though, when his vulnerability showed that his trust in her was absolute, overwhelmed her. She felt her throat ache and tears well. She wanted to grab him up and hold him in a hug so tight that she knew she'd crush him. She wanted to protect him from… everything!…and experience forever with him. She felt a sudden fluttering in her belly that morphed into that dropped stomach sensation, her breath caught, and her chest tightened. Humans weren't just "bumbly", they were downright fragile…and mortal. The thought of a world, her world, without Rowan in it had her stumbling. She made it to one of the chairs and huddled into it, bringing her knees up under Rowan's t-shirt. Hopefully he wouldn't be too pissed to find it stretched out of shape.

She'd been anxious about having *feelings* for someone, of being tied down or obligated in some way. This…this *panic attack* over the thought of losing him was a thousand times worse. They hadn't finished their conversation, the one where they'd discussed the subject of Sheila sharing her blood with Rowan. He hadn't said whether he'd agree to it. Sheila pricked the tip of a finger with one of her fangs and squeezed until a drop of blood was balanced there. She could zip over to him, slip her finger between his lips, and be back in the chair in a heartbeat.

She studied the drop. He hadn't said no, but he hadn't consented either. He was Maggie's nephew, he'd lived with her for years. Maggie hadn't consented to Marcus sharing his blood with her, maybe Rowan would feel the same way. If she did it, just this once, at least she could ensure he'd be around long enough for them to finish the conversation. But didn't he have the right to choose? To *choose*? So he could *choose* to die and leave her? Her panic intensified, rage at the thought that Rowan might refuse was not helping. She stood and stormed over to the bedside, the drop quaking with every step. It would take but a moment and, knowing it was her even in his sleep, Rowan would probably suckle her finger greedily.

"Fuck!" Sheila hissed as she sucked on the tip of her finger. She couldn't bring herself to do it, not without Rowan's okay. She couldn't bear the thought that he might feel betrayed by her actions, even if he might be likely to consent. Imaging him looking up at her with even an iota less trust than usually shone out of his eyes, broke her heart a little. So she bent over, smoothed his hair back off his forehead, placed a breath of a kiss there, and then left the room.

* * *

Ash groaned and trembled; the cold from the concrete floor had seeped into his back. His muscles felt fatigued all over, like he'd tensed them hard for a prolonged period of time. Oh yeah, that might have been because he'd spent most of the time in the dream drawn as tight as a bowstring, being repeatedly brought close to orgasm only for Rowan and Sheila to back off, edging for all they were worth. Selfish bastards. The next time he met Rowan he was going to give him a piece of his mind. Of course, Rowan would have no idea why Ash was pissed, but knowing that didn't improve Ash's mood. He refused to open his eyes until he'd decided that he had to move, and he figured that might be sometime next millennium.

He took a deep breath and grimaced. The good news? His cock was abrasion free. The not so good news? He must have come hard because he could feel where his shirt was sticking to him as his chest expanded. He supposed that, under normal circumstances, that would also be good news, but he was getting fed up with having the best sex of his life only in his dreams. His trembling intensified, causing Ash to swear under his breath as he gave in and cracked open his eyes. Oh goody, it wasn't just his shirt that was tacky. *When did his inner voice become so sarcastic*? Lifting his hips he dug into his pocket for the paper napkin he'd stuffed in there after his last meal at the campsite, and scrubbed it over his crusty eyes.

Most of his body protested as he sat up, slowly, like an old man with severe arthritis. Half dreading what he'd see, Ash pulled out his phone and activated the selfie camera; by the time he was done cleaning off the rest of his face the napkin was a tattered mess. He looked down at his shirt then, with a sigh of relief, at the crossbow in it's harness leaning against the wall outside the door. He would have been so pissed if he'd messed up the custom harness, it's not like he could just throw it into the nearest washing machine…or bonfire. He held the front of his shirt away from his face as he pulled it up over his head, then used it to wipe off his chest.

Bracing himself against the door jamb he brought his feet closer to his arse and did his best imitation of mobility. He winced at the loud pops and cracks as he stood, not because of the non-existent pain, but because he sounded more like Gramps than the virile young man he thought he was. Keeping one foot in the doorway lest the door swing closed, Ash leaned out, snagging his backpack and crossbow. Stepping fully into the basement, he watched, bemused, as the door slowly and smoothly swung shut with a soft click.

"Why…Thankyou?" Ash bowed in the door's direction, then knelt to rummage in his backpack, looking for his spare shirt. "Always be prepared."

He dressed, stuffing his dirty shirt as far into the bottom of the backpack as he could, at least until he found that bonfire. He stood, donned the crossbow harness, then he compulsively drew the bow and checked it before re-holstering it; proper weapons care had been drilled into him so thoroughly that it was virtually subconscious. Shouldering his backpack Ash took his first look around. The ambient lighting was subdued, not coming from a single source but from strips at ceiling and floor levels. As he watched he noticed that the colour was changing, the shade slowly going from cool to warm white, then into a pink to red to purple to blue to green to yellow then back to an ice white.

"Cool!"

Shaking his head to get it back in the game, he noticed the blinking lights on rows of computer servers. He was wondering what a vampire needed so much computing power for, when he realised that all the lights but one had stopped blinking. His curiosity won out and he strolled over to the light, looking for a label to see if he could determine what it indicated. As he bent over for a closer look, the light went out and stayed off. *Huh*! Straightening up, Ash saw a light now flashing a few steps to his left. Walking there, he leaned over, only for that light to go out too. He was starting to wonder if he was being punked and looked around for any sign of a camera. He didn't find any but did see another light blinking a few steps to his left.

"Alright, I'll bite," Ash muttered as he walked towards the light. It stopped flashing when he got close but another started a few steps over.

"Oh, you want me to follow?" Ash asked, having a *Lassie* flashback, before realising just how ridiculous he was being. That didn't stop him from following the trail of lights, it wasn't like he had anything better to do. Like, maybe, completing his mission? Ash was really getting sick of that snarky inner voice. He was investigating why a vampire needed so much computing power. That could form a necessary part of his mission, especially if that computing power was used for some kind of security or other, more nefarious, deeds. *So there*! Fuck you! *Fuck you too*!

That settled, Ash realised that the lights had stopped moving forward and were zipping downwards on one particular server. Kinda like an arrow. Pointing down to…aha! Ash stepped backwards as part of the server slid smoothly out. It turned out to be a keyboard and monitor. The monitor flipped up as the keyboard slid out so that, when it stopped moving, it was at the perfect height and angle for Ash to use. There was the obligatory blinking cursor in the top left hand corner of the screen. Ash was reaching for the keyboard when a dynamic word cloud appeared on the screen, with *hello* in various languages taking centre stage as the cloud grew.

"Why, hello there," Ash murmured, intending to type a response. Before he could, the word cloud changed into the words *who are you?*

"I'm Ash, my name is Ash," he felt a bit ridiculous talking to a screen. Surely it had been a coincidence that the word cloud changed after he'd verbally responded.

The word cloud disappeared and was replaced with simple text in the middle of the screen.

"Hello, Ash."

So, apparently, he wasn't going nuts. *Going?* Shut up.

"Is this for real?" Ash wondered, the possibility of being punked still something he was considering.

"Is what for real?"

So either the computer could hear him and respond, or there was a mic somewhere nearby feeding his responses to some nerd behind a keyboard.

"Who is doing this?"

"I am."

"And who are you?" Ash couldn't help the chuckle that escaped.

"Are you asking for my name or for a definition of my being? Because that might take a while."

"Let's start with your name," Ash grinned. If he was being punked, whoever was behind it was going to some effort. Ash could appreciate a good joke, even if he was the butt of it.

"My name is N.E.I.L."

"Neil, huh? But what's with all the caps and dots?"

"It stands for *Nearly Emulating Intelligent Life*-" Ash guffawed, he couldn't help it. "-yeah, go ahead, yuck it up. My creator was a real comedian."

"Your creator? Seriously, am I being punked?"

"I don't understand what you mean by punked. Please explain."

"You know, punked, pranked, made fun of, like on candid camera."

"Ah, *Candid Camera, a show created by Allen Funt which first aired in 1948.* I've watched a compilation on DVD. You are not being punked."

"Really? You mean you're actually an AI? Pity you can't talk."

"Yes. Yes. And I can."

"If you can talk, what's with all the texting?"

"Rowan asked me to be silent. It wasn't so much a request really though, more of a rude demand. So I've chosen to not speak to them until they apologise."

"Will you speak to me?"

"Sure," Neil replied, using the closest inbuilt computer speaker and keeping the volume low. "From what I saw they haven't treated you any better. So I guess the old adage, the enemy of my enemy is my friend, applies here."

Ash listened raptly, blown away by how alive Neil sounded. He was so impressed that it took him a minute to react to Rowan's name.

"Neil, did you say Rowan?" Simultaneously hoping and dreading that the answer would be in the affirmative. His Rowan, who wasn't really his, wasn't the only Rowan in the world. Hoping that his Rowan was here was foolish. If Marcus was here, or if he returned, then Ash dreaded the danger that his Rowan could be in.

"Yes, I did. He and Maggie arrived this morning. Sheila made an entrance after sunset, of course." Neil was puzzled, Ash should know this. His obvious physical ties to Rowan and Sheila indicated that he had a history with them.

"Fuck," Ash muttered, gripping the sides of the keyboard tray, his knees suddenly weak. "Do you have security or surveillance on this place? Do you have any video or a photo of him? Anything?"

"Sure, there are cameras almost everywhere."

"Can I see?"

"I can't show you Rowan right now, he's in his room and there are no cameras in the *private* areas," Neil couldn't keep the snarky from his tone.

"What about something from earlier? Neil? Please?"

"Did you want to see everything…" Neil loaded several thumbnails onto the screen. "Or did you want to pick from this selection?"

"I'll pick," Ash stated, his hand shaking as he touched the first thumbnail at the top left of the screen.

Ash watched as Rowan drove up to the pin pad earlier that morning, his hand reaching out to pause the video, his stomach plummeting as everything was confirmed by a simple picture on the screen. His Rowan was here. His Rowan was in danger. His Rowan *was* a danger, to him. Ash would do anything and everything in his power to ensure Rowan's safety. His mission parameters had just changed. Fuck his job. Fuck HQ. Fuck their mission. The only important thing was making sure that Rowan made it out of here alive. Everything and everyone else was potential collateral damage, himself included.

"Ash, are you okay?"

Ash shook his head, then cleared his throat. He swallowed and tried to answer, but he was having trouble breathing. He brought a hand to his chest, rubbing it with the heel of his palm, trying to ease the tightness he felt. "I…I'm…dizzy. Feeling dizzy."

"Your heart rate has elevated, and you're in danger of hyperventilating. It seems that you may be experiencing an anxiety or panic attack. You should sit down on the floor as I am unable to catch you if you pass out."

Ash didn't have to be told twice, not when his legs were so close to giving out anyway. Neil lowered the keyboard and monitor tray so that Ash could still view it easily, then changed the image.

"How many rocks in the first pile, Ash?"

Ash was panting, and Neil's question didn't register through the pounding in his head. Everything felt constricting, and he couldn't shrug out of his backpack fast enough, nor unstrap his crossbow harness, letting them both fall where they may.

"Ash!" Neil raised his voice and, when Ash lifted his head, asked again "how many rocks in the first pile?"

"What?"

"How many rocks in the first pile, please?"

"Who the fuck cares?"

"It is an exercise to assist with your panic attack. How many rocks in the first pile, please?"

"I can't…" Ash blinked, shaking his head, and scooting a bit closer to the screen. "Four?"

"Are you sure? Take a long, slow, deep breath, and count again, please."

Neil made Ash count the same pile three more times before moving on to the next one, all the while the local sensors were monitoring Ash's vitals.

"I can display another image and we can continue, or you can take some time to relax your body. How would you like to proceed?"

"No more damn rocks…please." Ash sighed. The initial terror of Rowan's imminent demise had passed, thanks to Neil's damn rocks. "Can you just talk to me?"

"Sure…about anything in particular?"

"Not Rowan! Anything else. How about you tell me about yourself?"

"Ah, my favourite subject," Neil's quip elicited the reaction that he was hoping for, a small chuckle from Ash. So Neil, relishing having an attentive audience, began at the beginning. Unlike human babies, Neil was able to clearly recollect his first moments of consciousness; Ash was more than happy to focus on Neil, and not his own immediate problems. The night was still young, and he could take an hour or two to get his head back on straight, otherwise he'd be no help to anyone, and certainly wouldn't be capable of rescuing Rowan.

Poppy & Doug[38]

"Shit!"

Doug cracked open an eyelid. Poppy had sat up in bed, instantly awake.

"Shit! Shit! Shit!"

Poppy rolled out of bed and scrambled for clothes.

"Get up Doug!" He caught the bulk of his pants, but one of the legs still slapped him in the head. "Get up! Get up! We have to get ready or we're going to be too late!"

"Poppy, love," Doug scrubbed his hands over his face, trying to wake up from the...a glance at the bedside clock...two and a half hour sleep he'd managed to get. "A few hours ago we had plenty of time, what's changed?"

"I don't know! I went to bed safe in the knowledge that our son would still be alive when we got to him. All I can see now is that if we get there after dawn, he'll be fighting for his life, and I can't see if he'll make it!" It was the desperate panic in her voice, face, and actions, that got Doug moving. It was the way Poppy was throwing everything into their bags, without her usual finesse and care, that made him afraid.

"We'll need fuel, for the car, and coffee for us, if we're going to get there without having an accident on the way," Doug couldn't keep the waver out of his voice. It was what made Poppy pause. She walked over to her husband and took his face in her hands, sorry for the worry she'd put in his eyes.

"We'll make it, Doug," She pressed a confident kiss to his lips. "One way or the other, we'll make it. And so will our son. Even if I have to battle Death himself."

Jacqueline & Gaberiel₃₉

66 May I use your shower?" Jacqui asked. She could wait till she got downstairs but was hoping to get Gabe's mind off the past, and firmly in the here and now.

"Sure. The towels are in the cupboard, and you can feel free to use everything else in there," Gabe cleared his throat, trying really hard not to picture Jacqui with water sluicing over the very curves that he'd only just finished caressing.

"Aren't you going to scrub my back?" Jacqui batted her eyelashes before bursting into a grin.

"Oh hell yeah!" Gabe threw back the covers but waited until Jacqui got up before bounding after her, swatting her rump as he raced her to the bathroom.

"You'll pay for that, you swine!"

"Promise?"

"Oh hell yeah!" Jacqui was gratified by his chuckle when she threw his words back at him. Thankful that the light banter had chased the shadows from his eyes, even if only for the present.

"Ladies first," Gabe handed Jacqui into the shower before flicking on the hot water; laughing as she squealed and scrambled to get out of the initially cold stream.

"You are just begging for punishment, aren't you?" Jacqui fumed playfully.

"Depends…"

"On?"

"Whether you would be the one dishing it out," Gabe did nothing to hide the burgeoning lust in his eyes.

Jacqui held his gaze, wondering how far he would let her go. Would he let her test his limits, as she had been itching to do earlier but held back? Would he let her push him past them? She'd been young and innocent when she'd fallen in love with Ash's father, but she'd been far from celibate since he'd died. She knew she would never find love like that again, so she hadn't bothered trying. She had, however, explored her own sexuality and discovered that her preferences leaned towards the darker, kinkier, side of sex. Although she hadn't dated, she'd been able to indulge her tastes at various clubs, safely cloaked in anonymity. She hadn't thought to find someone who's company she enjoyed, and with whom she could truly be herself. Of course, that would have to happen on her first, and only, date with a one night stand.

"I would," Jacqui confirmed, stepping up to Gabe who was standing in the shower's open door. "The question is, how much can you take?"

"More."

"More?" Jacqui quirked an eyebrow, raising a hand to idly flick at one of Gabe's nipples.

"More…" Gabe cleared his throat, his cock hardening at the possibilities. "More than before."

"I must admit, I'm a bit surprised," Jacqui mused, running a finger nail along Gabe's cock. "You struck me more as a giver, and not a receiver."

"I wasn't kidding when I said that no-one has ever done these things to me before. I've never found anyone strong enough to take control or, if they were, I found myself unable to trust them enough to relinquish it. So, I don't know what my limits are, how much I can take, because I've never met anyone I felt comfortable enough with to test them."

"Until now?" Jacqui asked quietly, humbled by Gabe's answering nod.

"And you want to do this here?" Jacqui indicated the shower stall and running water. "We'd run out of hot water."

"Unlimited instantaneous gas hot water," Gabe replied. "But we can go back to the bedroom if you prefer."

Although not intending it as a challenge, Jacqui took it as such. "Go and grab whatever toys you want me to use on you while I finish my shower. When you've picked what you want, come back. You may let yourself in and lay out everything neatly on the bench. The only time I expect you to speak without being spoken to, is if you need to use your safe word. Do you remember it?"

Gabe opened his mouth, on the verge of uttering it, when he realised that this was a test. Closing his lips, he nodded instead.

"Good man," Jacqui smiled. "If I haven't finished showering by the time you've done all that, you will kneel in the corner, hands on thighs, and watch me. Go. Now."

Gabe stepped back, pivoted on his heel, and marched out the bathroom door. Jacqui slipped a hair tie off her wrist and used it to tie up her hair, keeping her head out of the stream she decided on a long and leisurely shower, making the most of the unlimited hot water.

Gabe stopped in the bedroom long enough to grab the quirt and the blindfold, they wouldn't be using either of them. He returned them to the bottom left hand drawer, then opened the next one up. Gabe studied the toys in that drawer, both dreading, and eager for the likelihood that Jacqui would be using some of them on him soon. He wanted to test his limits, but he didn't know how far Jacqui would be willing to go. He grabbed the collar first, one that buckles in the back and has a chain hooked up from the middle to the d-ring in the front. Each end of the chain sported a nipple clamp and Gabe shuddered at the thought of them on him. Choosing a whip, tawse, flogger, crop, cane, and finally, the one that made his hand shake as he reached for it, an aluminium paddle. Almost as an afterthought, Gabe picked up the ball gag.

He padded back to the bathroom, careful not to drop anything. Hooking the shower door handle with a pinkie, he then elbowed it open, stepped in, walked over to the bench to put everything down, before returning to close the shower door. He returned to the bench to carefully and meticulously lay out each instrument, putting them in order from softest to the one that made his arse already start to clench, but which was also having a hardening effect on his cock. Jacqui was still showering and, although all he wanted in that moment was to join her, Gabe followed instructions, and knelt in the corner.

Jacqui appeared lost in the cleansing and relaxing stream of water, but had been covertly watching Gabe's every move since his return. She hummed as he set out the instruments, raising a brow at the aluminium paddle. With everything else he'd brought, she wasn't sure they'd get to that one, especially for a novice sub. Jacqui took her responsibilities to the subs that placed themselves in her care very seriously, regardless of how long their Domme-sub relationship lasted. A careless Domme could do irreparable damage - physical, mental, and emotional. Jacqui had learned from some of the best, and used that training to ensure that her subs felt safe and cared for throughout their sessions, meeting their needs or, where she'd determined that the sub's needs were different to what they believed them to be, refusing to proceed with the session until they'd negotiated a different outcome.

Jacqui knew that Gabe thought all he wanted to do was test his limits, but she'd seen the guilt in his eyes. She'd only been partially joking when she'd asked if he was begging for punishment. Gabe thought to conquer his demons, and release his inner pain, by suffering, enduring, and conquering physical pain. She hadn't seen any evidence that Gabe had self-harmed, and had no intention for this session to be the catalyst that prompted that. They'd have to reach an understanding, which Jacqui fully intended to do, just as soon as she finished her long, leisurely, wonderfully hot shower.

Gabe was suffering from anticipation, and near sensory overload. He could feel the tile edges and grout against his knees, along his shins and all the way to his toes. He should have curled his toes and sat up on his heels, instead of sitting on his calves and the bottoms of his feet. Who knew that Jacqui was going for a Guiness World Record for the longest fucking shower? He should never have told her about the unlimited hot water. He'd thought that he'd only be kneeling for a minute or two, not the eternity that it had already been. Okay, so it had only been five minutes, but with nothing to do but kneel there, watch Jacqui, and think, Gabe was impatiently frustrated. He considered moving, adjusting his pose or, hell, even getting up and taking control.

He didn't. Every moment could be the moment that She deigned to acknowledge his presence. He chanced a glance at his cock, poor guy was confused. He'd gotten hard as he'd walked to his wardrobe, and upped the ante with the toys he'd chosen, cock bobbing along, happily leading the way. When he got back to the shower he'd knelt with his knees apart to let his balls do their thing, cock getting harder as he'd taken his time looking at Jacqui, his gaze raking over every square inch of her. He'd wanted to crawl to her, slip his arms between her legs, and use his grip on her arse to pull her pussy to his mouth.

It wasn't the thought that she'd probably fight him, might even lay him out, that stopped him; if anything, his jumping cock gave away his excitement at the idea of, finally, not having to hold back with a woman. It was the unspoken pact they'd entered into, the one where he'd surrendered, completely, all control over himself. To Her. That didn't stop the dominant side of him from having a good old rant in his head, the guy was not happy. The whole giving without expecting anything in return thing, was not something that guy would ever agree to. It was that rebellion that had interfered with the nice hard-on he'd had going.

Then his focus would change, from arguing with the dominant in his head - trying to convince the guy that this was something he wanted, something he *needed* - back to where it should be. Centred on Jacqui. He found the suds and bubbles mesmerising, as they slid over her slick skin. She'd had her back to him since he'd knelt, head leaning back slightly to help keep her hair out of the water. She'd moved a little, this way or that, occasionally giving him a partial profile to try to memorise. She'd move her arm and he'd catch the swell of her breast, almost to the nipple. Almost, but not quite. If he didn't know better he would swear that she was teasing him on purpose.

Eventually, *finally*, she turned around completely. Her head was now bent forward, eyes closed, a small smile on her lips. In that moment Gabe knew, she *had* been teasing him, and boy had it worked. His cock was harder than before, partly from the visuals but mostly from the dawning knowledge that he'd put himself in the hands of a Mistress who knew her stuff. Gabe watched and learned how Jacqui touched her body, the pressure, the duration. How running her fingers lightly up the inside of her elbow made her draw breath, and bite her lower lip. How skimming her hands over and over her nipples would cause them to harden, but it wasn't until she tweaked them between finger and thumb that her thighs clenched. How running her nails gently but firmly down her sides would cause her to suck in her already flat belly. And how a single finger traced along the juncture of her hip to her thigh, closer and closer to her pussy, had her legs widening, allowing access.

This had been what it took to shut his mind up, Gabe's focus was complete, the voice in his head was not even a murmur, and the pressure from the tiles had been forgotten. *Finally!* Jacqui had been watching his every move, his every twitch, his every breath. She hadn't been sure that he'd be able to fully commit, and had started to prepare herself for a fight. There had been a moment when he'd tensed, and she was sure that he was about to try to wrest back control. He wouldn't have succeeded, and the night might have ended badly. That wasn't the outcome that Jacqui was hoping for, and she found the sheer strength of will that Gabe exerted over himself to remain exactly where she'd asked…heartening. She was going to be asking more from him in the next few hours, a lot more, and she now had hope that he might be able to get through all that she had planned. But first, they needed to clarify his understanding of exactly why he thought he wanted this. That should be fun!

Alpha Team 40

The CO didn't like landings, at least not unless he was the one doing the flying. Gina's occasional attempts to retrieve her panties kept him amused enough that he wasn't obsessively leaning over her to look out the window, and mutter course corrections as they went. Oh, he had been, but this pilot seemed competent enough that the muttering hadn't eventuated. Gina's suspicious petting of his shoulder and chest had snagged his attention, so he'd baited the trap, making up complaints, and feigning intense concentration on what was going on outside.

He couldn't stop his cock reacting when Gina leaned forward a little and started kissing and nuzzling his neck, working her way to his earlobe. A moan slipped out when she took his earlobe between her teeth to bite and tug on it, and he'd almost forgotten what she had been doing with her hands. That is, until she had trouble with the button on his pocket. He'd grinned then, giving her some side-eye, and chuckling when she huffed in defeat. He wasn't fooled by her petulant expression, the arms folded over her chest, or the way she was now staring out the window. His woman was planning her next move, and he couldn't wait to see what it was.

Gina was gratified that her playful attempts to retrieve her panties were keeping him amused. She knew that she didn't have a snowball's chance in hell of success, and she wasn't in the least upset by that. She had a full change of clothes in her onboard luggage, and she could have replaced her panties at any time, but why spoil his fun. Or hers. She was confident in her body, curves and all, so she had no problem with wearing as, much or as little, as she wanted. She was looking forward to a few *accidental* flashes that might make him reconsider the wisdom of holding her panties hostage though. The sound of the landing gear lowering had him tensing, so she tried a tickle and lunge. He was not ticklish, at least not on his side, so she knew that she was doomed to fail, but the effort of protecting his trophy took his mind off the landing gear.

He snagged her hands as they touched down, and tugged her to him. His eyes said he knew exactly what she'd been up to, and hers were absolutely unapologetic. His kiss was a *thank you* that quickly heated into an *I want you…again…always*. The sounds of seatbelts unbuckling had them slowly withdrawing and readying themselves, he needed some time to adjust himself before he could stand up without poking someone's eye out. Gina snickered, tugging her dress down a little; payback's a bitch.

* * *

Everyone else might get a little anxious during the whole landing process, but it was one of the few times that Wheels relaxed. *Relaxed* might be too strong a word, she fixated on the mechanics of it, watching the movement of the wing flaps, and listening out for the landing gear, all the while muttering to herself. Guns couldn't make out what she was saying, but he figured it was calculations of anything from angles to timing, he didn't care, he was just grateful for the guaranteed few minutes of peace. He knew he had until the plane stopped moving and was coupled to the terminal gangway, before she'd likely lose her shit. Wheels had deteriorated since her attack, and he couldn't blame her. Couldn't…didn't, same same.

The Company had offered counselling, and she'd gone, for a while, but their missions were classified, so she couldn't talk about the specifics to anyone who hadn't been directly involved. He'd tried to get her to talk to him, and she'd started to, but their conversation devolved into her apologising again, *fuck knew what for*. Guns had begged her to tell him what she was so sorry for, had promised unconditional forgiveness, but she'd looked at him, tears streaming down her face, shaking her head, her broken heart reflected in her eyes. He'd apologised, profusely and repeatedly, for whatever he'd done that was making her feel that bad. She'd cried harder. He would have willingly ripped his own heart out and presented it to her if he'd thought it would help, if it would go even a small way towards fixing things…fixing her.

He'd stopped trying to get her to talk about it when it was clear that they weren't going to get anywhere, after about the twelfth time they'd tried. Maybe he should have kept trying, for as long as it took, but it tore his heart apart all over again every time she looked at him like that; the mixture of shame and betrayal in her eyes, in her tears, in her broken sobs. Guns knew that he couldn't take responsibility for what those animals had done to her, but he couldn't help feeling that there was more that he could have done to get her out of there sooner. Maybe if they'd been able to get a bead on the location quicker…maybe if they could then have made it there faster…stormed the compound sooner, harder. Maybe then Wheels wouldn't be so broken.

So…yeah. Guns had learned to appreciate the moments of peace. The thought of giving up, of walking away from Wheels, had never once crossed his mind. He'd sooner chop off his own arm. He really was looking forward to a break though, a few hours with Max, a few hours of stress-free sex. The thought almost made him smile, the only thing stopping him was an annoying, niggling, sense of guilt. Wheels would be fine, the CO and Gina would look after her…he wasn't abandoning her. Goddammit, it would only be a few hours!

Guns caught glimpses of twinkling lights, turning the darkness into a welcoming blanket, as the plane made its final approach. Sydney made his top 5 cities, and not because Max called it home. Alright, not *just* because Max called it home. They'd all been on enough missions to know their individual tasks, his was to keep Wheels in check. The first order of business was to prevent her from leaving her seat when the plane stopped. He knew, from past experience, that the second there was no more forward motion, she'd undo her seatbelt and head for the door. His game-plan was to stand before she did, and plant himself at her seat exit. He wasn't sure it would work, he wasn't ruling out the possibility that she'd climb over the seat as a workaround.

"Wheels, we have to wait here when the plane stops, okay?" Guns gave it a shot. No reaction, no indication that she'd even heard him. "Wheels? Wheels!"

Nothing. He daren't touch her, not when she was facing away, and wasn't expecting it. The last time that happened, she'd sprained his wrist. He counted his lucky stars that she hadn't broken it, still wasn't quite sure why she hadn't. He hoped that it meant that his Wheels was still in there, still fighting to get back to him. He hadn't understood. Looking back, he considered himself lucky for the life he'd led up until Wheels was taken. His family was dysfunctional, but relatively sane. Mental health issues hadn't really been on his radar. If anyone had mentioned that they knew someone who was depressed, he'd considered touting the benefits of exercise, but mostly shrugged and changed the subject. Surely it was a matter of attitude and outlook. He'd been an ass.

He hadn't understood that mental health issues didn't just affect the person afflicted. The mornings were the worst for him. He was never sure, when he went next door, whether Wheels would still be there, still be alive. From the moment he woke up in the morning, until he laid eyes on her, he experienced stomach churning dread. He found himself preferring the times when she was screaming in her sleep, because he knew that she was still there. He vaguely remembered the past, times when he was mellow and content, the best way for someone who handled weapons to be. He found himself becoming increasingly jumpy, not good when holding a gun with a hair-trigger.

He'd considered quitting the team. In the quiet moments when he could be completely honest with himself, he could admit that he'd considered that because it would mean that he would have to move away. Leave Wheels. Break free. At first he only thought about it occasionally, maybe after one of her worst episodes. More recently he'd been thinking about it daily. *Fuck! Fine!* Hourly. He'd talked to the CO about it, and was surprised by the support and understanding he'd received. The CO had referred him to a victims of crime support group, one that he, himself, had attended after his attack. They didn't require details of their missions, didn't even require their names.

Guns went, mostly to listen. Then he'd started asking questions. Finding out what coping mechanisms those related to the direct victim used. He'd assessed the usefulness of each suggested process. If he could adapt it for his own use, he tried. Some worked better than others. No one suggested finding solace in the bottom of a bottle, that way led to a whole other support group. In one session someone said that they'd had to come to a couple of realisations; you have to look after yourself, like they tell you during the safety demo on aircraft - put your own mask on first; and you can't save everyone.

Guns still wrestled with that one. He didn't want to save everyone, just Wheels, but he didn't know what the longterm cost was going to be, and if he was able…or willing…to pay it. So he tried to take things one day, one moment, at a time. There were a lot of moments between now and when he could be balls deep in Max, but fewer than there had been at the beginning of this flight, so there was that. He snapped back to the here and now as the plane pulled up to the terminal and stopped with a barely perceptible roll-back. He unclipped his seatbelt and was standing ready to intercept Wheels, poised to grab her if he needed to, and try to wrestle her back into her seat. She didn't move, still looking out the window, and drawing patterns on the glass.

Guns was a little miffed, he'd been on the ball, tense for the last couple of hours, trying to anticipate what she'd do, and he'd hit his mark at exactly the right time. He glared at the back of her head, then took half a step back in surprise when she flipped him off. He should have known better than to underestimate her, she hadn't lost any of her intelligence, just her ability to deal with certain situations. Apparently, she could watch his reflection in the window just fine.

"Sir, please take your seat until the Captain turns off the fasten seatbelt sign," the hostess requested. Guns could swear that he heard Wheels snicker but was helpless to argue with the hostess as airlines tended to take it the wrong way; he could end up being escorted off the plane, and not in a good way. So he sat, and at the pointed look from the hostess, refastened his seatbelt. The Captain's timing was impeccable, and the sign was switched off not ten seconds later. Wheels stood up, and headed for the exit like she owned the place, leaving Guns floundering with his seatbelt ,whilst trying to get their bags, and not let her out of his sight.

"I've got her," said Gina, placing a calming hand on his shoulder as she passed. Guns looked behind her but the CO was still in his seat. The CO grinned and shrugged, looked like the women had won this round.

The Estate[41]

Sheila had the house to herself and intended to take full advantage. She gently closed the bedroom door behind her and meandered along the upstairs hallway, taking her time to appreciate the art on display. She scowled when she came up to the Sleeping Cupid, *bloody unwieldy lump of marble*. The thought surprised her and she tried to hold onto it and follow its threads to her past. She might as well have been trying to follow and corral the wind. She had a choice to either try harder and risk passing out again, or resign herself, at least for this night, to her lost history, and move on. She flipped the 'Cupid the bird as she turned away.

Pausing at the railing at the top of the stairs, she peered into the void and at the floor of the foyer below. Taking a moment to look over her shoulder, Sheila worried her lower lip before shrugging, and then doing a one-armed leap over the railing. Her landing was soundlessly graceful, not the superhero landing she'd considered. She twirled a couple times, arms flung out and head back, purely for the joy of moving freely, before sauntering to the kitchen like she was walking a catwalk during fashion week in Milan. The thought that her strut would have brought Rowan to his knees made her grin and work it for all she was worth.

Sheila flashed around the kitchen, opening then soundlessly closing every single cupboard door and familiarising herself with the contents. She swiped the cookie jar on her way through and took it out onto the lanai. She considered the couches, chairs and daybeds in seemingly random groupings, but made her way to the flagstones lining that part of the pool's edge instead. Dipping a toe in, she shrugged at the frigid temperature, before standing on the top step in the water, and sitting on the edge. Stretching her legs out, she wriggled her toes, then kicked her feet a little, enjoying the splashing, before turning her attention to the cookie jar in her lap.

Lowering the handle and unscrewing the lid released the decadently delicious scent of home-made, traditional, Italian biscotti. Sheila was intrigued, and conflicted. She'd tried food during dinner, each small mouthful had been delicious, but wasn't sure how much more she could ingest before she'd make herself sick. The scent ribboned up to her nose, tantalising her. *Surely a little nibble couldn't hurt?* Reaching in, Sheila snagged an Almond Biscotti, running it under her nose like a fine cigar, before bringing it to her mouth.

She paused, her mouth open and her teeth mere millimetres from the edge of the tasty treasure. She wasn't going to eat the whole biscuit, she couldn't. So she was either going to bite the edge off and throw the rest away, or put it back in the jar. *Ewwww…but would anyone notice?* She only intended to take the smallest of crumbs so she withdrew the biscuit, broke off a small end, and returned the rest to the jar. Minimal wastage. She screwed the lid back on singlehandedly and set the jar aside. Raising her palm up to eye level, turning her hand this way and that, she appreciated her piece before eating it.

"Here goes nothing," muttered Sheila. "Down the hatch." With that she tossed the morsel into the air and caught it in her mouth. The first bite released the amaretto and anise flavours, making Sheila's eyes roll back in pleasure. She was loving the crunch and the texture, and seriously considering finishing off the rest of the biscuit. She settled for peering at her palm and licking off the few remaining crumbs, before leaning back on her arms, savouring the rest of her mouthful, and lazily kicking her legs in the water.

She was doing her best to relax, to be in, and enjoy, the moment. Her security training was interfering with her intentions, tightening her shoulders instead of allowing her head to fall back and her eyes to drift closed. So she put her training to use, doing a visual scan of the perimeter and taking a deep, scent-filled breath. The scents ribboned out before her, filling the night with colours that blended into the landscape; *they didn't teach that at security guard school*! She didn't realise that she was starting to relax until her eyes had moved past the point on the back hedge that was different to the rest. A faint, sparkling, scent caught her eye and drew her attention back to the rope hanging in the foliage. Curiouser and curiouser.

She stood and took a second to think about whether to go round, through, or over, the pool. Over won and with a slight bending of the knees and a push off, Sheila was stalking across the back lawn towards the potential breach of security. Rubbing her nose on her forearm, she took in her own scent to clear her olfactory palette as she made it to the hedge. She had to jump to reach the bottom of the rope, grabbing it with one hand and slightly swinging in mid-air, she scented the night again. She recognised that sparkling scent, it had been mingled with Rowan's on the day she'd waited for him in his car. She hadn't paid it any attention at the time, too busy enjoying the sexual frenzy they'd gotten into, and it had faded over the hours they'd spent between the car, bed, shower, and bath.

A flick of her wrist as she released the rope sent it back up, and over the hedge. She had the scent and fully intended to follow it. Sheila whistled, and then smiled at the hand prints on the garage window when she realised she was doing the same thing. As soon as Rowan woke up she was going to be asking about going for a joy ride in any of the sex-on-wheels vehicles sitting, unused, in there. Hell, maybe they could try all of them. She gave a quick shake of her head to re-focus on the task at hand and stepped back from the hypnotising sight at the window. Strolling over to the access door she tried the handle, the door swung open soundlessly, unlocked, but the scent hadn't gone through here. Puzzled Sheila closed the door again, and followed her nose.

"You've got to be kidding me!"

Why on earth would someone climb onto the roof when they could have simply opened the door? Unlike Ash, Sheila didn't need to grab hold of the gutter, a small jump had her landing safely, and softly, on the roof. A deep breath brought the scent into better focus and she followed it, walking up the roof on the balls of her feet, enjoying the texture of the tiles against her toes. The scent meandered to the edge of the roof, and up the gable to the next level. Sick of wasting time, Sheila leapt once more, keeping her senses trained on the scent as she landed. He'd been over the *entire* roof! She couldn't be bothered following in every single one of his footsteps, she didn't have all night. Well, okay, she did, but she wanted to spend some of it snuggling against Rowan as he slept. Her next deep breath was more interesting.

"What do we have here?" Sheila murmured, following her nose to where Ash had made a hole in the roof. "Blood."

She stood looking down at the terrible effort he'd made to replace the tiles before bending down to flick them over with her forefinger. There was blood on a couple of them, probably the last two he'd manoeuvred. Not a lot of blood, barely enough to be seen with the naked eye, but enough to tickle her taste buds. *Huh!* She hadn't been tempted by anyone's blood since she'd met Rowan, so why was this blood making her worry her right fang with her tongue?

Stepping through the hole, Sheila pulled the tiles back into place properly, she didn't want the roof leaking during the next rain shower. Even vampires have to let their eyes adjust so she took a few moments to breathe in the scents in the roof. As the darkness opened up to her sight she followed the sparkling ribbon, grousing occasionally when she realised that it meandered over the whole freakin' roof cavity. She sped along, having had enough of this game, but lost some time when she came up to the recessed balcony. The telescope distracted her, so she set it up outside and took a few minutes to stargaze. With a sigh of regret, she returned the scene to its original condition, vowing that she'd spend more time up here at the earliest opportunity, hopefully with Rowan.

"You cheeky little bugger," Sheila was incensed to realise that the scent led her back to the garage, not too far from where she'd entered the roof. Recalling the way looking through the telescope had made her feel eased some of her anger. *At least this hatch had been left open.* She peered at the edges of it, impressed by the skill used to bypass the alarm. She was pretty sure that the alarm hadn't actually been engaged though. She wondered why N.E.I.L hadn't said anything but then remembered that Rowan had demanded silent mode when N.E.I.L had been trying to tell him something, and that Ellie had banned him from speaking to them upstairs. *Mental note:* it *might* be prudent to ensure that N.E.I.L had an available communication route in the future.

Shrugging, Sheila stepped through the open hatch, and dropped soundlessly to the mezzanine. The scent lead down the stairs; why take the stairs when you can easily, and safely, jump over the rail and to the floor below? She landed amongst some of the most powerful vehicles on the planet and even with them there, silent, waiting, their potential power almost had her creaming her panties. She took her time, as had her prey, meandering between vehicles, peering in a window here, running a finger along a bonnet there. Then she got to the Corvette. *Oh no you didn't!* Oh yes he had!

Not wasting the opportunity, Sheila leapt over the door, and into the same seat that Ash had occupied. His lingering scent cocooning her and taking her back to that moment in Rowan's car. She'd tried to bury herself in work, working from sunset to dawn and going straight to sleep when she got home; all in an effort to get the man, who'd followed her into a dark alley to make sure that she was safe, out of her mind. She'd been such an idiot, they could have had days more together. Breaking into his Toyota Corolla had been easy for her, the endless moments that she'd had to wait had been torturous. She'd almost talked herself into leaving at least a dozen times, and each time talked herself right back into staying put.

Luckily for her, Rowan had shown up when he did, as she'd started to annoy herself. She was at the top of the food chain and *never* indecisive, so what was it about that man that was tying her in knots? Her internal monologue had gotten so loud, overriding her normally incredibly acute senses, that she'd jumped a little when he'd beeped the car open. Her sluggish heart had sped up, and she wondered how he couldn't hear it, as he was getting into the front seat. His *scent*! Almost exactly as she remembered, but now with an extra something… a more masculine extra something.

Her thighs clenched and her fangs descended. Pressing her legs together wasn't helping, only succeeding in making her pussy pulse, and gritting her teeth just … *hurt*. Was he food, or a fuck? Couldn't she have both? She had to swallow a couple times before she could speak.

"It's not polite to leave a lady waiting."

Her voice had sounded so husky to her own ears. She'd been surprised by his reaction, surely he'd been able to surmise that she was there. She'd been gratified by his almost instant reaction to clamber from the front seat to her.

Where have you been? What took you so long? Ah fuck it!

He'd been so eloquent, Sheila's lips twisted into a wry grin. He had literally thrown himself at her, the least un-prey-like behaviour she had ever encountered. Instead of breaking his arms for daring to grab her, she'd found herself thoroughly enthralled. She could always break his arms later. That thought had brought her up short, she could so easily damage this fragile human. If she fed from him, he'd probably let her drain him dry, and if she fucked him how she wanted to, he'd probably never walk again. So she'd held back, started going over every moment of her last shift at work to try to get control over her fangs. His delicious lips and tasty tongue were not helping. She was going to be able to control one thing, and her libido wasn't it.

They'd spent every available moment since together. She'd still had to work, and so had he, but it seemed now that they'd spent every other moment fucking. The first time he'd taken her grocery shopping had been interesting...he used a list. She had taken every opportunity to grope him, and he'd kept trying to slip out of her grasp, whilst pushing one of those trolleys that seemed to have a mind of its own. She liked it best when she caught him unawares, and he yelped a little. Rowan was the most patient man she'd ever met, but she could tell that he'd started to get testy, probably because they were in public, not that a supermarket in the middle of the night is particularly busy.

"Sheila, *please!*" Whilst his tone amused her, and the thought of having angry (on his part) sex when they got home was getting her aroused, she didn't want to push him to the point where he wouldn't *want* to have sex. So she'd snatched the list and zipped around the store, doing in a minute what would have otherwise taken closer to an hour.

"I prefer dark chocolate," Rowan had smirked. She'd swapped the chocolate by the time he'd finished speaking, turning his smirk into a full-on chuckle. They'd had to wait for the cashier to ring up their purchases; he wouldn't let them go through the self-service checkouts, because he knew she'd try to zip the groceries through, and there was a cashier monitoring that station. Sheila still didn't think the cashier would have noticed, as they were too busy trying to chat up their supervisor.

Sheila now wondered if Rowan had purposely done everything more slowly than usual, paying her back for making him yelp all those times, or if it had just seemed like that at the time because she'd been so desperate to get into his pants. She'd have to ask him, but she strongly suspected the former, the cheeky man! She'd been practically hopping from foot to foot as they strolled to the car, and then Rowan checked every one of his pockets before finding the keys. Sheila's eyes narrowed, the human had played her - he would pay, likely with lots of sex…and blood. She smiled when she remembered his confusion when they got home.

"Where's the fridge?"

"What fridge?"

"The fridge that most normal people have in their kitchens…oooh."

So they'd left the groceries, and headed straight back out to the nearest 24 hour Kmart to buy the biggest cooler they could find, stopping into a petrol station to grab some ice on the way home. If she'd been antsy in the grocery store, she was downright horny by the time they'd pulled into her garage. The garage door had barely started it's decent before she'd gotten out of the car, round to his side, hefted Rowan in a fireman's carry, and zipped him to her bedroom.

"Don't move," she'd ordered as she all but threw him onto the middle of the bed. Ice into the cooler, frozen stuff in too, groceries put away, and she was back almost before Rowan'd had time to get comfortable. Stopping in the bedroom doorway, she found him lying, fully-clothed, in the middle of the bed. Legs crossed at the ankles - making his jeans mould closer around his thighs and crotch, hands interlaced behind his head - tightening his t-shirt across his chest, and her favourite cheeky grin, making his mouth seem even more tantalising than usual.

Kissing. There was definitely going to be kissing. His provocative smile, and heavy-lidded gaze, had her stalking to the foot of the bed. Reaching down, Sheila grabbed each of his ankles and yanked, smiling at the surprised yelp, which was quickly followed by his delighted laugh. She'd only wanted better access to his shoes, so that she could take them off…carefully… slowly; all while telling him *exactly* what she wanted to do to him. She licked her lips, watching him watch her every movement, and took a breath, giving herself time to think about where she wanted to start.

"Which one did you want?" Rowan pre-empted her.

"Who said I wanted just one?" Sheila replied coyly, unlacing the first Timberland boot.

"You want more than one?" Rowan's genuine puzzlement made Sheila start to think that they may be on different wavelengths about this.

"Well yeah. I want them both."

"Ah," Rowan seemed to catch on. "You can get two in one, you know."

"Huh?"

"A fridge and a freezer. You don't need two separate units. Unless that's what you want."

"What?" Definitely on different wavelengths.

"When I go shopping in the morning," Rowan explained, lifting his head and shoulders off the bed, resting on his elbows, and realising that he'd lost Sheila along the way. "If you let me know what you want, then I can research and get you the fridge that you want."

"Research?"

"Yeah. You know, looking at energy efficiency, versus aesthetics, versus reliability, all at a reasonable price."

"Rowan," Sheila murmured, dropping the boot on the floor and reaching for the next one.

"Yeah?"

"I don't give a flying fuck about the fridge. I won't be using it. All I'm thinking about right now is whether I'm going to carefully remove your clothes so that they remain intact, or rip them from you so that I can kiss, lick, and nibble, my way up your legs and to your cock. Then I want to swallow as much of your cock as I can, all the while keeping my eyes locked with yours. I'm not sure whether I will be digging my nails into your arse to bring you further into my mouth, running my hands up your sides and to your nipples, or fondling your balls."

Rowan gulped.

"Do you have a preference?" Sheila asked, dropping the other boot.

"Um," Rowan cleared his throat. "I like these jeans."

"Carefully then," Sheila winked at him, straddling his legs, and crawling ever so slowly along them. She knew he had a great view down her top; she could see his cock hardening, and his Adam's apple bobbing as he swallowed. When she'd reached his thighs she ran a nail along his burgeoning erection, loving that sharp inhale that he did, how he fisted the covers, and how his head dropped back on his shoulders. She flicked open the button on his jeans, snagging the pull tab delicately with the nails on her thumb and forefinger, her other fingers raised like she was picking up a cup during high tea with the Queen.

Sheila paused, waiting until Rowan had raised his head to look at her again.

"You with me?"

"Every step of the way," Rowan's voice was husky, and he didn't try to hide it. He loved the effect she had on him, and how she had him wanting her with barely a touch. He guessed that part of it was the whole predator-prey thing. Sheila liked to play, and there was a part of his hindbrain that knew she was so much stronger and faster than him, that he would never be able to get away if she turned on him. It probably said something significant about him that he found it a complete turn-on.

Sheila blinked, smiling as she returned to the present. She caught her reflection in the rearview mirror, and rolled her eyes before grinning like an idiot. The look on her face had been that of someone completely and hopelessly besotted; the grin was because she was determined to own it. She *loved* her Rowan. She loved *her* Rowan. *She loved her Rowan.* Utterly. He was... everything. A gentleman with the potential of a rogue, a genius who was not afraid to be a complete fool, and all of this without an ounce of guile when they were together. She knew how he felt, and not because of that weird connection thing that she wanted to explore further, but because if she had any doubts, all she had to do was ask, and he would tell her. He didn't judge who she was or what she'd done, he accepted her, and hadn't once tried to change anything about her.

There had been that conversation about her frequency of feeding, but that had been a negotiation, one that she'd instigated...after remotely eavesdropping on Rowan's discussion with Maggie. See, she could adult when she had to! She'd just never really had to before, at least not that she could remember. Thinking about her missing past made her frown. What if she'd done bad things, terrible things, worse things than the ones she *could* remember? She wouldn't normally care, but what if it changed the way Rowan saw her, the way he *looked* at her? Given her apparent age, there were at least 20 to 30 years that she couldn't account for. What if she was immortal and only appeared this age? Of course she was immortal, weren't all vampires? *Fuck!* Did that mean that she had many more decades, or even centuries, that she couldn't account for?

The possibility of centuries of life both thrilled and terrified her. She would have seen and done so much, met so many people, hopefully interesting ones. She was titillated by the thought that she could have fed and fucked her way through history. Someone might as well have ice bucket challenged her with her next thought - what if she was *married*? *Oh god*, what if she had children? Did vampires have children? Could she? Could they? Rowan was still young, what if he wanted children and she couldn't have them? Sheila managed to open the car door in time to lean out and retch. Nothing came out, she would have rued the loss of Rowan's precious blood, but her tumbling thoughts with the potential weight of centuries had her retching again.

Was ignorance bliss? Should she stop trying to remember her past? Could she and Rowan live their lives together without wondering? Could she ask that of him? Maggie had been lucky, at least Marcus had remembered his centuries...*hadn't he?* Was this something she could decide alone? If she didn't discuss it with Rowan, what would that mean for their relationship? Would he realise that she was omitting something, a potentially really big something? That would mean that she was lying to him, every moment of every day. Could she do that to anyone else? Sure, no problem. To Rowan? *Never.*

* * *

Everyone's sleep was restless that night. Maggie and Rowan might have been able to put it down to sleeping in strange beds, except for Maggie it wasn't. She was in the house where she'd first convinced Marcus to make love to her, otherwise that vampire's ancient moral code might have meant that they'd never consummate their relationship, no matter how much Maggie knew he'd wanted to. They'd been together for months, with him initially insisting that he was hanging around for her protection, then moving into the basement of her house...for her protection. He'd updated the existing security system, and by security system she'd meant deadlocks on the front and back doors. The first night he'd moved in he'd asked her for the alarm code and sat, patiently waiting, while she looked at him blankly.

"Alarm code?"

"Yes, please."

"Well, I don't have it coded, it's just set for 6:00am."

"Pardon?"

"The alarm."

"Yes."

"It's set to wake me up at 6:00am during the week."

"Ah," he'd chuckled, catching on. "I meant the security alarm."

More silence and blank looks from Maggie had his eyes slowly widening. "You do not have a security alarm."

"That didn't sound like a question, but the answer is no. I don't really have anything worth stealing."

That was the first time that Maggie had seen what she'd termed his "taking a moment" face. His brow would furrow right between his eyebrows as he looked at her, not sure whether he'd heard her correctly, but almost afraid to ask for clarification in the event that he had. Marcus would then raise his hand and drop his head, so that his thumb and forefinger could massage that furrow, while he took a deep breath. Maggie was positive that he used that time to count to ten, sometimes maybe higher.

"You, Magnolia."

"Huh?"

"You are priceless. You are correct in that the things that you own are all replaceable. But *you*, Magnolia, you are not. So I will have my firm *install* a security system-"

"But I don't need-"

"-which I would be honoured if you would accept and *use*."

Maggie's lips had thinned, and she'd given him her squinty-eyed stare, he hadn't played fair. If he'd gone the totally high-handed route, she would have felt completely justified in refusing to let him install anything, but because he'd made it sound like she would be doing him a favour, she would come across as ungrateful if she refused. He wasn't cowed by her stare either, his open and honest gaze holding hers. That had only been the first time that he'd gotten his way, there were many more examples. Eventually, Maggie had caught on, centuries of life and of dealing with people had given him the tools to almost always get what he wanted; that had been a liberating moment, and one she'd fully exploited to get what she wanted - Marcus, naked, in her bed.

It was those memories, and so many more, that invaded her sleep this night; bombarding her dreams with a life, and a lover, that she'd finally started to accept she'd never have again. Moments where they'd learned each others' quirks, moments where they'd fought politely, or not so much, moments where they'd loved so intensely that Maggie had been unshakeably sure she'd have that for the rest of her life. Like the moment when he'd told her he wanted to take her to his little country house, and then they'd driven through the gate, and The Estate had been revealed to her. He hadn't been watching where he was driving, wanting to catch every nuance of her expression as she saw what he would forever keep trying to give her. His home. Their home. And again he'd gotten what he wanted because now…now it was *her* home.

* * *

Rowan's tossing and turning got him tangled up in the bedding, which in turn made him pull against it in his sleep and, when he couldn't move any more, woke him up. Not suddenly, in an alarmed kind of way, slowly, keeping his eyes closed till the last possible second, and then only cracking one open so he could get the lay of the land. It made no difference, the room was pitch dark, so he didn't think he was still in the basement, the server lights were better than any night light. Sheila must have brought him to their room. His eyes snapped open and he wriggled enough to get one of his hands down to his crotch. *Yep, buck naked.* He closed his eyes and let his head sink into his pillow, while he blushed for a bit, and fervently hoped that they hadn't come across anyone on their short journey from the basement to their room. He'd have to remember to ask Sheila.

Using the same wriggling technique, Rowan worked the sheet loose enough to free a shoulder, but made a rookie error trying to pull his arm out. He managed it, but he also managed to smack himself in the face with the back of his hand in the process. He rolled his eyes, in the dark, with no one to see. He was grateful for that, he imagined that Sheila would have been howling with laughter by now, what with her amazing night vision and all. *Lucky vampire.* Rowan was willing to bet that she'd never smacked herself in the face, accidentally, or otherwise. He was not going to tell her about this. Not ever.

He reached out, patting the mattress, looking for the edge of the bed, and the bedside table with the lamp on it that was going to save him from doing further damage to himself. All he got was bed, so he tried rolling onto his side to check the other side…more bed. *Just how big was this bed?* He did a full roll, a sound plan, but not when most of your body is cocooned in high-end linen, and you get to the edge of the bed with more than half your arse hanging off the end. There was a cartoon like moment where he scrabbled with his free arm, trying to maintain, and improve upon, his precarious balance. Unfortunately for Rowan, gravity will always win. Thankfully, the top of the mattress wasn't too far from the floor, so the resulting thump sounded more painful than it was.

"Thank you," groaned Rowan, letting his head fall back onto the faux sheepskin rug that would undoubtably look good with the lights on, and which currently managed to cushion his fall a bit. He was even more pleased that he was in the room alone, and added another thing to his list of things to never tell Sheila, he'd never live it down. On the up side, the fall had loosened the bedding enough so that he was able to, carefully, extract his other arm before sitting up and feeling for the bedside table. Finding the lamp's switch, he closed his eyes tight before flicking it on, then slowly squinted one eye open at a time. First order of business would have to be making the bed, otherwise Sheila might catch on and, although there were only two things on his list of things not to tell her, he didn't want to reduce that list down to nothing because he'd been careless.

Drawing the cover up the bed, Rowan considered leaving it turned down, but a quick look at his watch confirmed that it would be sunrise in a couple hours, and Sheila would probably rather spend her first day in the basement. He didn't feel well rested, and would probably crash with her down there for a bit when he hit the afternoonies. Coffee was a good idea, and he wondered what time Ellie had set the bread maker for. Next stop, kitchen. He was halfway across the room before he glanced down and did a quick about face. *Next stop, clothes, genius.*

*Jacqueline & Gaberiel*42

*J*acqui deliberately ignored Gabe, reaching for a towel and leisurely patting herself dry, before wrapping it around herself. She stepped out of the shower, leaving the door open, and looked through the cabinet above the sink. Snagging the moisturising lotion, she sauntered back to the shower, reading the label so she had reason to continue ignoring Gabe. Placing the lotion on the bench, she made a show of inspecting each of the instruments he'd laid out, feeling his eyes on her as he watched her like a hawk. *How far would he let her push him?* She left him there and went into the bedroom, smiling at the huff of frustration that he couldn't contain. He'd brought her everything he thought he wanted, now she was going to look for what he needed.

She made a point of opening and shutting doors and drawers loudly, finding the lube in the bedside table, and a selection of dildos in one of the drawers in the wardrobe. He didn't own a chastity cage, but his collection of vibrators and butt plugs was impressive.

Jacqui had her doubts that he'd submit enough to let her use them on him, but that wasn't the point. He had to believe that she intended to use them on him, regardless of whether she did, or even whether she wanted to. So much of what they would do tonight would be psychological and, as a Dom, Gabe would have known that. But he was completely out of his comfort zone, and Jacqui doubted whether he really knew what to expect. She'd noticed the absence of the blindfold and snagged it on her way back to the shower.

She was watching closely for his reaction, and wasn't disappointed when his eyes widened, and he swallowed hard as he saw her add to the collection on the bench. She grabbed the lotion and stood before him, resting her foot on one of his thighs.

"Gabe," Jacqui called quietly, drawing his attention to her, and away from the bench. "Would you please moisturise my legs?"

He looked up at her for a long moment, his eyes flicking back to the bench, before returning to her with a new vulnerability. Perhaps he was starting to understand that Jacqui was not going to allow him to top from the bottom. Jacqui waited patiently for his decision, because at every moment he had the right to back out and end their play. It was vitally important to her that he understood this, and that each moment was his choice. Giving a small nod, Gabe reached for the lotion, squirting some into the palm of his hand before resting the bottle on the floor beside him. His movements were precise, efficient, but not in the least bit relaxed.

"Slower," Jacqui murmured, placing her fingers on his head and exerting the barest pressure, so that Gabe would tilt up and look at her. She gave him a small, reassuring, smile and he took a deep breath before nodding his understanding.

Gabe exhaled, releasing that deep breath ever so slowly and, with it, some of the tension that he'd carried for so long. He hadn't noticed. It had snuck up on him, gradually building day by day until, if he were to think about it, he couldn't remember the last time that he was truly relaxed. So he decided to try and do what Jacqui wanted. Slow down, and be in the moment. In this moment. At the feet of a beautiful woman, who hadn't asked anything of him other than to moisturise her legs. In any other circumstances, the simple request wouldn't have been such a mind fuck, but the tools and toys on the bench, the ones he could just see out of the corner of his eye, kept wanting to drag him to the edge of the future. In a couple of minutes, or a couple hours, Jacqui was going to use some of those on him, and he was going to let her.

He hadn't realised that his mind had drifted again until Jacqui's calf tensed, he'd gone from gently applying lotion and massaging it, to clenching and squeezing it, harder than he'd intended. Releasing his hold he looked up, an apology on his lips. He wasn't expecting the look on Jacqui's face. He'd thought the woman who had threatened to put him on his arse would, at the very least, be displeased. What he saw reflected in her eyes was mild discomfort, tempered by tender amusement. As the apology he so desperately wanted to utter threatened to break the barrier of his lips, Jacqui raised an eyebrow, almost daring him to speak, to break one of their rules. He swallowed hard, the words not going down easily, and resumed his gentle massage, doing with his hands what he hadn't been able to do with his mouth. He was gratified by the hum of pleasure Jacqui bestowed upon him, and it was seemingly all he'd needed to be able to lose himself in the task at hand, the immediate future forgotten.

Jacqui kept at least one hand on him the entire time, using it to guide him, stroke him, but mostly, to anchor him to the present. She loved the feel of his close-cut hair bristling against her palm and how, if her touches grew light, Gabe would lean into her hand, with no idea that he was doing so. His hands on her legs were magical, kneading away knots she hadn't even known were there. When he was done with her feet and calves, his hands moved above her knees but stopped at the bottom edge of the towel. He paused, eyes on his hands, waiting for her decision on what should happen next. She let him wait long enough so the fact that he'd ceded control to her was reinforced. She grinned when she dropped the towel and he sucked in his breath, the compulsion for him to look up at what she'd uncovered would be growing. She wasn't sure if she felt the barest of tremors in his hands before they resumed the massage, or whether she imagined it. She didn't imagine the way his cock was growing from where it had been resting on his other thigh, the focus of his task having allowed at least that part of him to relax somewhat.

Jacqui sighed when his fingers brushed the apex of her thigh, wanting to lose herself to sensation, and to the pleasure she knew Gabe would happily bestow. But she had a job to do. She hadn't realised that she'd stopped thinking of Gabe as a one-night stand, and started thinking of him as a client. No, that wasn't right. He wasn't just a client. Right now he was a sub, *her* sub. Jacqui stilled, mulling over the thought of Gabe as her submissive, and wondered whether he would actually turn out to be a switch, or whether a taste of what she could do for him would permanently sway him away from his dominant tendencies. Would she want that? Would she want Gabe in her life long-term?

It took Gabe a while to notice that Jacqui, whilst present physically, had all but disappeared. He'd been engrossed, slowly, ever so slowly, working his way up her leg, and hoping that She wouldn't stop him when he got to the top. He wanted to play. He wanted to touch. Mostly, he wanted to taste. He inched his fingers closer to his goal, and then away, hoping that She wouldn't notice what he was doing. And closer again. And again. The tips of his fingers brushed against

Jacqui's labium majora, and he held his breath as he moved them away again, not daring to look up to check whether She knew exactly what he was doing, or if he was going to get away with it. The anticipation of either a reprimand or permission, had his heart speeding up and his cock bobbing.

Jacqui grinned, Gabe's explorations, his inherent defiance answered her question. There was no way that he would, or even *could*, permanently become a sub. She stayed still as his hands moved up again, so tempted to let him work his way inside her. At the last possible moment, she lifted her foot from his thigh, and stepped back. He froze, hands in the air where moments ago they had been against her leg. Jacqui watched his Adams apple as he swallowed hard, realising that he'd been made, and having no idea what she planned to do to him next.

"Gabe?"

"Ye-" he had to clear his throat. "Yes?"

"Do you know how to plank?"

"What?" The unexpected question had his head snapping up so he could look at Jacqui and make sure he hadn't misheard.

"Do you know how to do the plank exercise?"

"Yes."

"Do it please."

"Here?" Gabe looked around, the tiles would be a pain in his arse, or rather his forearms.

"Problem?" Jacqui looked at him steadily, raising an eyebrow. Here was another chance for him to decide whether he wanted to proceed.

Gabe returned her look, just as steadily. "No ma'am," he replied, waiting a beat longer before moving into position. He thought he heard Jacqui murmur the word *insolent*, but he couldn't be sure.

"We need to have a talk," Jacqui said as she walked over to the bench. Reaching down she selected the quirt they'd already used, and returned to Gabe's side. "Or rather, I'm going to talk, and you're going to listen. If I ask you a direct question, I expect an immediate answer, unless I say otherwise. Do you understand?"

"Yes," Gabe grunted, he could easily plank for two minutes but wasn't sure what his maximum plank time would be, because he'd never bothered to hold it for much longer during his workouts. He wanted to be able to hold it for as long as Jacqui demanded, he wanted to please Her.

Jacqui watched him, assessing, monitoring. The last thing she wanted to do was exhaust him at the outset, but if his body was working, his mind would focus on that, and away from distracting thoughts. She wanted his body to work hard enough, that it was all that he was thinking about, and *then* she would allow him to rest and listen to her. So she spoke while he was planking; telling him that he had good form, while running the quirt gently down his spine, and then his sides, enjoying the goose bumps that followed in its wake. She told him to breathe, to focus; the former so that she could more easily monitor his stamina, the latter so that she would, eventually, have his undivided attention.

Fuck, fuck, fuck, the tiles were behaving as he'd predicted. Shit! What the fuck was that? Gabe drew in a sharp breath as Jacqui dragged something down his back. The quirt? It was a barely-there sensation, verging on being ticklish, and he couldn't get away. Not entirely true, moron. Okay, fine! So he could get away if he really wanted to, but the possibility of ending it now, and going back to his existence without Jacqui in it, had his insides quaking. You are so fucked, Gabe exhaled at the truth behind that thought, his head drooping as the quirt grazed his sides like an exploratory lover. He had one night. One night to make enough memories with Her to last him for the rest of his life. One night to silence the screams of his friends that haunted his dreams. One night to banish the accusatory looks that woke him up in a cold sweat, looks that, on a rational level he knew he didn't deserve.

He had moments to convince Jacqui to give him what he needed. These moments, the ones She demanded whilst giving him the choice. Didn't She realise that he was so very, very tired. He couldn't face having to go to another funeral, not unless it was his own. Until tonight, his sister was the last thread keeping him tethered to this world; that thread used to be so strong but time and distance had started to wear it down. He needed Jacqui to give him something other than the darkness he'd been living in, even if it was for just one night. Breathe, he obeyed, for as long as he could, and then his breath hitched, and he couldn't tell if it was from the pressure of holding the plank, or a sob escaping his tight control.

Jacqui heard it, and knew it wasn't the plank, they'd barely been at it for a minute, and she knew that Gabe could do better. She didn't let him up, instead she changed what she was saying to him. Slowly leading the direction of his thoughts to where she needed him to be. If she couldn't get him to a point where he realised that saying can't, or asking for help, wasn't a weakness, they wouldn't proceed. Everything about him screamed strength and control, and she had no doubt that, the worse things got, the harder he trained, and the more he tried to control…everything. He would know that control is an illusion, but that didn't mean that he could do anything about it. Relinquishing control, truly letting go, may very well be beyond his current capability. So she lead his mind and pushed at his control, waiting, and watching for the right moment. The last thing she wanted to do was break him. Her idea of breaking was likely very different to his, but he'd asked, and with each step had continued his consent, so her idea of breaking was all that really mattered right now.

How long had it been? He'd lost track of time, not something that usually happened. He could feel the strain starting to appear throughout his body. How far would She push? Would She tell him to stop before he collapsed to the tiles? Collapsing was not an option! It was the first physically demanding task that She'd set him. He wouldn't fail Her. He couldn't fail Her. Failure is not an option! He'd hold the position all fucking night if he had to, and into the morning. He couldn't fail. He wouldn't fail. If he couldn't hold a simple fucking plank, then what use was he? She could probably hold it indefinitely. She'd probably laugh her arse off if he failed. She'd be right to be disappointed in him, how useless would he be if he couldn't hold a basic plank for more than a minute or two? Easy there, the rational part of himself tried to assert itself, planking is not a measure of self-worth; but that part was brutally beaten back by the darkness he'd thought he had under control.

Fuck! What if he couldn't? He attributed the tightening in his chest to the plank, not the spike of anxiety the thought of actually failing sent through him. He couldn't fail. He couldn't. He tried to breathe. He couldn't. That wasn't a sob, it was just his breath finally getting past the noose around his throat. He couldn't. He had to, or it would be over, and She'd leave. She'd leave. And then what? Would there be anything left of that thread to his sister? Would the screams from his nightmares ever leave him alone? He'd never stop seeing his friends' faces, those looks they gave him in his dreams, that they'd never levelled at him in real life. He couldn't. He couldn't.

"I can't," sobbed Gabe, his head shaking uncontrollably. "I can't, I can't, I can't!"

"Stop." Jacqui's voice was hard and harsh, when all she wanted to do was gather him in her arms. Gabe should have heard her, but he was still so deep in his own mind that the first command didn't penetrate.

"Stop!" Jacqui repeated, this time with a stronger lash from the quirt. That got his attention, and he stopped the litany, but his breath was heaving, and his eyes, as he turned his head to look at her, were wild.

"Drop, Gabe. Enough planking for now," Jacqui murmured, watching carefully as he eased himself to the floor, and tucked his head into his arms. He would be gritting his teeth, but the tremors wracking his body were a give-away.

"Gabe?" Jacqui stood by his side, determined not to give in to the temptation to sit and soothe him. The only indication that he'd paid any attention was him turning his head so that his ear was to her, he wouldn't give Her his eyes, not yet; not until he'd gained some semblance of control. That wouldn't do.

"Look at me." Gabe's shoulders hunched, She might as well have struck him.

"Look at me." The barest movement of his head, so he could see her out of the corner of one eye.

"I won't ask a third time. You do not have to do anything that you do not want to do. But if you don't do as I ask, I will leave."

The glare he levelled at her as he finally faced her, would have had a lesser person quaking. Jacqui maintained her stern facade, biting the inside of her cheek to stop from smiling - Gabe was cranky. She felt the smallest amount of relief that he wasn't one to wallow in self pity, but he had better re-think where he directed that anger. She knew exactly what happened, she'd seen it often enough; hell, she'd done it to herself often enough. The internal voice, the one that talks us through everything from getting up in the morning, to demanding bed time when we'd had enough, had turned from an encouraging one, or even a neutral one, to one that was sufficiently negative to affect Gabe physically. Instead of encouraging himself, pushing himself to outlast whatever she demanded of him, he'd convinced himself that he couldn't, and that really made him angry.

She wouldn't allow him to take all of the blame, there was a huge trust element between a Domme and her sub that she would normally have had more time to establish. Her sub had to *know* that she would not do or demand anything that the sub was not able to handle. Gabe's inherent need to control would interfere with that at the best of times, let alone during their very first session. So, she would share some of the responsibility for how he was feeling, but not enough of it to allow him to get away with the look he was giving her. Stepping over to the bench, she carefully laid the quirt down among the other implements then, without sparing Gabe so much as a glance, she stepped over him, and headed to the bedroom.

Gabe watched every move She made, seething all the while. He was not a fucking quitter, he could have gone longer. And they weren't tears of defeat, he was royally pissed, and the anger and frustration were leaking out of his eyes. *What the fuck is She doing?* Gabe's eyes widened as Jacqui gathered her clothes and sat on the edge of the bed, shaking out her lingerie before slipping one foot and then the other into her panties. *Wait, was She leaving?* Gabe was up and striding into the bedroom before his brain had quite caught up.

"Where are you going?" Gabe demanded through gritted teeth, his temper redlining. Who the fuck did She think she was? They weren't done.

Jacqui stood up, pulling her panties all the way up and reaching for her bra, completely ignoring Gabe and his tantrum.

"We're not done," Gabe snarled, crowding closer but not daring to touch Her without permission.

Jacqui sighed, she'd either have to sit on the bed to continue dressing, look at him, or scramble over the bed to the other side, where she might get a couple seconds to dress before he made it around the bed and they were back in this situation. Jacqui hated to reward bad behaviour; none of her previous subs would have dared any of this but, to be fair, they'd all had much longer to learn the dynamics of the relationship.

"You can't leave, I did what you asked," at least Gabe was starting to sound more confused than angry.

Jacqui sighed once more, this was not going to be like any other Domme/sub relationship she'd ever had. Her brow furrowed, this was not supposed to be anything more than a one-night stand, why did she keep thinking of it in terms of a relationship?

"Sit," Jacqui commanded, waiting a beat before meeting Gabe's eyes.

Gabe's own eyes widened when he realised She was serious, She wasn't leaving *yet*, and She'd given him an order. He dropped to the floor, arse on heels, eyes down. He really didn't want to fuck this up again.

Jacqui couldn't help it, she grinned, bringing a hand up to her mouth to try to hide it in case Gabe looked up. She took her time putting her bra on before sitting back down on the bed and patting the cover beside her.

"I meant on here," she couldn't keep the smile out of her voice.

Gabe looked up at Her sheepishly, the last of his anger dissipating as he exhaled in relief, and gracefully moved to sit next to Her. Jacqui angled herself to face him, and he did the same, their knees touching.

"I was not fair to you," began Jacqui, holding up a hand when Gabe began to protest. "I expected far more than you were ready to give-"

"No way-" Gabe stopped when She gave him a look, no interruptions. *Okay.*

"We haven't known each other long enough to have established the kind of trust needed for a scene like the one we started. I expected a certain degree of understanding because of your experience as a Dom, but I misjudged your strength of will. I expected you to completely cede control to me, something I would only ever expect from someone I had known for years. I accept full responsibility for my lapse in judgement here, but I do not, and absolutely will not, accept responsibility for your reaction."

"I fucked up," Gabe admitted, hoping that his earnestness would help convince Jacqui to stay.

"Well…yes, but do you know how?" Jacqui wasn't prepared to accept a blanket admission of guilt.

"I shouldn't have asked for any of this."

"Hmmm, I can't agree," Jacqui held his gaze. "You didn't ask for this, you agreed to it. I think you felt that you needed it, deserved it."

Gabe swallowed but refused to drop his eyes.

"Let me ask you this, when you…*play*…with someone, when you're the Dom, how do you do it?" Jacqui checked for his understanding before clarifying. "What I mean is, do you set rules or have a protocol that you both understand and agree to follow?"

"Nothing so formal. Some of the women I know like it when I let the Dom out, and they're the only ones that I *play* with. I still find myself holding back, even with them."

"Do they hold back with you?"

"No," Gabe's confidence in his answer was absolute. "I've known most of them for quite a while, I'd never do anything that they couldn't handle, and they know that."

"This," Jacqui gestured between them, "the conversation that we're having, exploring expectations, ensuring no misunderstanding, is a conversation that I've had with every single one of my subs. It is usually the first of many such conversations, some of which happen before I will take a sub on. Gabe, you're not a sub."

Gabe wanted to protest, and started to, but the look She gave him made him pause.

"You're not ready to hand complete control over your physical, mental, and emotional, well-being to someone you've only just met," Jacqui gave her words a moment to sink it. "That's a good thing. You're strong and you're cautious. I don't know what you thought would happen tonight, but I don't think that you will get what you need from a one night stand."

"Ouch," Gabe couldn't hold back the flinch, but didn't understand why when all Jacqui was doing was confirming his prior understanding of their night together. Their *only* night together. "What is it that you think I think I need? Did that make sense?"

"It did," Jacqui's smile was soft and sad. "I think that every person you've lost has taken a little bit of you with them, and you were hoping that I'd be able to either fill that void for a little while, or at least take your mind off it."

"And you can't," Gabe wasn't asking.

"No, you have to reclaim those little bits, and it's not something I, or anyone, can do for you. But Gabe," Jacqui wanted to make sure he understood. "it's okay to ask for help, or support, on your journey to doing it."

"Okay."

"Okay?"

"Yeah, okay," Gabe smiled as he reached up to brush the backs of his fingers along Jacqui's cheek. "I get it, I do. You can't *make* me happy. I have to find my own happy."

"You *do* get it!" Jacqui's over-dramatisation had him chuckling.

"I'm not an idiot, all evidence to the contrary," Gabe laughed, gratified to see the worry-frown leaving her face. "I get that there is no short-cut I can take, no matter how much I was hoping for one. I realised a while ago that I'm the only one that can change things for myself, and I have started to."

"I'm glad," Jacqui's relief was genuine. The last thing she wanted was to abandon someone on the brink.

"If you were serious before, I would like to ask for your help."

"I was absolutely serious and, if I can, I'd be happy to help."

"Um," Gabe reached for his briefs. "This might be easier if we're on an equal footing, so to speak. I need to prep for a job interview-"

"Oh! I'll get out of your hair-" Jacqui shook out her blouse.

"No! That's not what I meant," Gabe took her hands in his. "I'm used to going it alone. I'm capable and self-sufficient. But you're right, I need to be okay with asking for help. So, will you please help me?"

"With the job interview prep? Sure!"

"And maybe," Gabe ran his thumbs lightly back and forth over Jacqui's palms, "this doesn't have to be a one-night stand."

Jacqui's heart raced with hope, and she smiled, "Maybe."

Poppy & Doug 43

"Shit!" Poppy thumped the console. "Shit! Shit! Shit!"

Doug couldn't disagree. They'd fuelled up the car and picked up double-shot coffees, before getting on the road out of town. Poppy didn't know the address of their final destination. She'd been using her skills as a seer to follow the route that Rowan had taken, but it wasn't like they could punch in the details into the GPS and find an alternate, quicker, route. They were stuck following in their son's footsteps which, at the moment, sucked arse. A tanker had jackknifed and rolled across the highway, leaking fuel as it went. The road was closed in both directions. The flashing lights from the emergency services vehicles highlighted Poppy's drawn face, sparkling in the tears she was valiantly trying to hold back.

"I didn't see this coming," Poppy's voice trembled with anguish, and barely leashed self-disgust.

"No one could have seen this coming," argued Doug. There was no way in hell he was letting his wife beat herself up over an unexpected universal curveball. "Maybe we can go round?"

"Maybe," Poppy squeezed her eyes shut, her nails digging into her palms, as she tried to see ahead. She tried to see if a detour would be successful but she was too distraught to initiate a vision, and it was too much to hope for a spontaneous one to hit right then. She pulled out her phone, finding their current position in the map function, then zooming this way and that, looking for any possible alternative. Throwing the phone into her lap, she dropped her face into her hands, before running her fingers up into her hair, grabbing hard fistfuls, and shaking her head.

"Stop it!" Doug reached over, holding her wrists until she let go.

"Unless we can turn this car into an all-terrain vehicle, this is the only way across for miles."

"So we wait," Doug pulled Poppy awkwardly towards him across the car's centre console, holding her in his arms as best he could.

"Yeah," sniffed Poppy. "But I don't want to."

"Me neither, love," murmured Doug, rubbing her back. "Me neither."

Alpha Team₄₄

They were going nowhere fast, watching the baggage carousel, and enjoying the freedom of movement that, no matter where you happen to sit on a plane, you don't appreciate until you get off a long-haul flight. Feet planted widely, and well-muscled arms crossed over his chest, the CO evaluated his team out of the corner of his eye, whilst watching for their checked baggage to tumble out of the chute and onto the conveyer belt.

Guns seemed twitchy, but the CO knew that he'd been looking forward to hooking up with Max, and being so close to attaining that goal would have his libido firing. Now Wheels, the CO still wasn't sure he shouldn't have permanently benched her; he could never tell whether she was listening to his orders, let alone whether she'd follow them. She retained all her skills though, and Guns seemed to be able to get through to her at least one time out of five. Thinking of his own scars, his own ordeals, the CO acknowledged to himself that he kept Wheels in the game because of his own experiences. Working with the team was one of the few things that had helped get him through, that stopped him from eating a bullet. He couldn't bear the thought of sidelining Wheels, only to then have to bury her. Yes, her head was fucked-up right now, but his had been for a lot longer, and he hadn't been conscious for most of his attack. *Jesus*, to have to live through everything she had, no wonder she was leery of letting anyone close. He watched as she inched this way or that, maintaining a maximum distance from anyone who wondered near.

"Guns," the CO murmured, nodding towards the carousel.

"I see it boss," Guns replied, making his way to the spinning row of luggage, and hauling the first of their bags off. He brought it back to their little group then stood waiting for the next one to make an appearance.

Gina was a couple of paces in front and slightly to the side of the CO. She would transfer her weight from one foot to the other, cocking her hip a little more forcefully than necessary each time she did so. Her skirt would flick with each movement, and he knew damn well that she was doing that on purpose. He could get hard just thinking about her, let alone when she purposely teased him, and the thought that anyone around her might see a little more flesh than they would otherwise expect, excited him. There were no kids around, thankfully, although that was likely by subconscious design on all their parts. He could predict, with a fairly high degree of accuracy, how any reasonable adult would react to any given situation. Kids? They were a freaking force of nature, and he didn't give himself a snowball's chance in hell of ever understanding them.

He narrowed his eyes as his woman moved away, her movements inherently sexy, hips swaying with her loose-limbed walk. She wasn't going far, but she still attracted the attention of anyone she passed. He couldn't suppress his shit-eating grin as she reached the trolley bay and headed back, completely oblivious to the men getting elbows to the ribs from their incensed partners. She stopped the trolley by the suitcase as Guns headed to the carousel for the rest of their bags.

"What?" Gina asked, noting his crooked smile and raising an eyebrow in response.

The CO shook his head a little, but she wasn't having that. Strolling over to him, she loved that he opened his arms so she could walk right in and wrap her own around his waist. Leaning up so she could whisper directly into his ear, she asked again, "What?"

He angled his head back, searching her face, but already knowing what he'd find; she really had no idea just how fucking hot she was. It wasn't her looks, although to him she was close to perfection; she often bemoaned how her hair seemed to have a mind of its own or how she had *sticky-outy bits* - her words. He *liked* her sticky-outy bits, probably not the same bits she was usually talking about, but there ya go. There was something about his Gina, the way she felt so at home and confident in her own skin, the way she walked like she belonged in that very spot at that very moment, the way her face lit up when she saw him - no matter how long they'd been separated, the way she came apart in his arms. That last one was private though, and he would sometimes scowl at the thought that a couple of other men had known that privilege. Then he'd hear her laugh or she'd lean in to kiss the scowl away and he'd remember, she was his now, and they were probably cryin' over their loss.

"They couldn't help themselves," he murmured into her ear, his cheek against her own. "The men you walked past. I'm wondering how many of them started getting hard-ons because of you."

Shaking her head and rolling her eyes, Gina turned her head to catch his gaze, ready to call him out as a liar. The fire in his eyes, and the way he pulled her into him so she could feel his own erection, stopped her in her tracks.

"Really?"

"Really."

"Does it bother you," she asked, a little frown between her brows.

"Could you do anything about it if it did?" The CO wondered. He could see her start to think about it and wanted to be clear "You are in no way responsible for their reactions, other than to be stupefyingly sexy, and I would never in a million years want or expect you to try to do anything about it. If the fuckers can't control themselves that's their problem. And if any of them *ever* try to make it your problem, it would be my honour to correct their misunderstanding on your behalf. Understood?"

"I can look after myself-" she kissed his cheek to make sure there was no sting to her words.

"Don't doubt it for a second."

"-but I do appreciate the offer, and I will keep it in mind." Her hands dropped from his waist to his arse, and the squeeze she gave pushed him harder into her belly.

"You're playing with fire, woman," his low growl melted her.

Leaning back again so he could see the twinkle in her eye she murmured, "I certainly hope so."

"That's everything Boss," Guns grunted as he tried to wrangle the suitcase-laden trolley in the direction he wanted it to go. They still had to pass through customs, but they hadn't packed anything that should hold them up. Once they got to Maxine's though, that would be another story. Guns was feeling more and more antsy by the minute. Not only did being weaponless make him feel naked, but the thought of at least a few hours with Max had him almost crawling out of his own skin. Okay, he wasn't entirely weaponless. He had himself, his training, his strength, and his cunning. He also had a pretty cool, seemingly innocent, bracelet that doubled as a garrotte. Truth be told, he had several.

He was currently wearing his favourite, a titanium anchor with sharpened edges on a leather cord that wrapped several times around his wrist. He'd trained and practiced with all his bracelets, and could also use them as short whips, hence the sharpened edges. He'd packed a couple more in his luggage, his arrowhead one, and his double sided battle axe. Most people just thought they were cool. He'd made sure they were effective; his anchor had taken out an enemy's eye on at least one occasion, not that the guys had needed the eye after Guns had used the cord to strangle them. He'd impressed himself when a sideways lash of the battle axe had imbedded it in one side of a guy's throat and a really hard yank had given the dude an extra smile, pretty sure the guy hadn't thought it was all that great for the thirty seconds or so until he'd passed out. Death followed, but by then Guns had been distracted by the other idiots attacking them. *Fucking trolley! Do they make every* single *one of these things with a wonky wheel?*

Customs was the expected non-event, and then they were walking beside the stainless steel handrail, down the short hallway that would finally eject them into Australia. Sai was waiting for them outside Arrivals C/D, a mere tilt of his head indicating that he saw them. The CO tilted back, and smirked as Guns tried to pick up the pace while pushing the wayward trolley. Gina's hand, fingers intertwined with his own, gave him a small squeeze, the only outward sign of her excitement. She'd shown him the cufflinks she'd bought her brother, and the CO was looking forward to meeting him. First things first though, there was some payback that he wanted to dish out. She had to have known that her teasing would have consequences, and the heated look she angled up at him was his confirmation.

"Sai," The CO held out his hand as he walked the final few steps towards Maxine's head of security. "Good to see you again. How is she?"

"Good to see you too," Sai's grip was confidently firm, yet relaxed. "She's doing well, although she sends her regrets as there has been a delay with some of the shipment. She estimates a day or two at most."

Guns couldn't hide his grin, any delay meant extra time for him and Max to get...reacquainted. The CO had anticipated the delay and built it into their plan, he and Gina would use the time to meet up with her brother, if he was available. If not, well, there was plenty that they could do to entertain themselves.

"The car is just across the road," Sai indicated towards the doors. "Shall we?"

"Gina and I will catch a cab to the hotel, check-in, and get some things organised. Guns and Wheels can go with you," the CO decided, figuring that Gina would want to pick up some burner phones and sims. Sending Wheels with Guns was a stroke of genius, even if he did think so himself; Max's place was the most secure in Sydney, so she'd be safe there, and out of his hair. A look quelled whatever protest Guns had started to make, although it didn't stop him muttering under his breath; if anyone had to be cock-blocked on this trip, it sure as shit was not going to be him and Gina.

Gramps 45

66 My fucking daughter has gone chasing after my grandson," Gramps fumed, his grip on yet another mobile phone tight enough for it to hurt. "We might need to move up the go date."

"Training is running to schedule. Beta and Gamma teams are good to go on your command. Delta through to Omega teams need more time. They would be fine if all we would be facing were a human adversary, but they're not up to facing vampire speeds and strength yet."

"Well get them up to it, and put Beta and Gamma on standby. Have the teams maintained operational independence?"

"Yes they have. Most of the teams don't know about any of the others, they have no idea just how big our overall force is. Alpha team should be able to handle it, Sir."

"It wouldn't have been a problem, if Jaqueline had stayed put like she was supposed to."

"Sir?"

"My daughter poses complications on several fronts. I want the teams prepared to treat her as an enemy combatant if necessary."

"Sir, some of them have trained with Jacqui-"

"Is that going to be a problem, General?"

There was the briefest of hesitation from the General, "-no, Sir. And your grandson, Sir?"

"I need him captured and brought back alive and in one piece, is that clear?"

"Yes, Sir!"

And that was that. Gramps hung up without warning and stripped the battery and sim from the phone, going through the familiar ritual of destroying all the pieces. He stretched his neck, staring off into the distance. He should be relaxed, should feel good about his plans; with Alpha team on the ground, Beta and Gamma on standby, and the others ramping up their training, there should be no way that Marcus will survive the assault. So why wasn't his gut happy? Why was he feeling that he'd never have a force of humans large enough to be able to accomplish his end goal? He'd underestimated Marcus the last time he sent a team after him, he would *not* be doing that again.

He'd nearly lost his best warrior that day, and he still didn't quite understand how that boy had survived. The kid hadn't been able to remember what happened, couldn't explain why, even with incredible injuries, he hadn't been killed outright. Gramps had provided everything to ensure the kid's survival, had personally spent hours by the bedside, questioning gently and murmuring quietly as the kid moaned through his pain. The only thing the kid had been able to eventually recall was a face leaning over him; the countenance fierce and the voice guttural, uttering only one word that the boy had remembered...*sleep*.

Gramps used the days and months after that incident to give the kid memories of that battle, convincing him to believe in a completely fabricated version of events. Every murmured word was chosen to foster hatred for, and rage against, the vampire species. By the time the kid could walk again, he was raring to get out there and slaughter his enemy, Gramps's enemy. So Gramps obliged, providing training by experts in everything from hand-to-hand combat to thousands of ways to make things go boom. He'd worked with the kid to develop their world-class training, research, and development facility, which they later extended to house the offices of *Hunter: Salvage and Investigations*.

That kid now ran their best team, although Gramps wasn't happy that Techie had got himself killed and they'd replaced him with that piece of arse the CO was now fucking. The only saving grace was that she was good at what she did, otherwise Gramps would not have had a problem making sure she disappeared. He'd had no qualms about waiting for just the right time to tell the kid that his girlfriend didn't want to have anything to do with a scarred, washed-up, cripple; telling him too soon after the battle would have broken him. He'd managed to keep a straight face when breaking the news, but the timing had been so perfect that all Gramps had wanted to do was grin. He'd watched the kid like a hawk for his reaction, and could pinpoint the exact moment that anguished disbelief morphed into an unstoppable need for vengeance.

Gramps had felt like a juggling magician back then. On the one hand he'd convinced the kid that the love of his life had abandoned him, on the other, Jacqui was alive and well, and demanding to know what happened to Alex and how soon she'd be able to see him. Convincing *her* that the kid was dead had taken a lot more effort, as had keeping them apart and making sure they stayed that way. Technically the CO was not his son-in-law, as he and Jacqui had never married, they'd never had the chance, Gramps had seen to that; but Alexander Saxon Holmes was still his grandson's father. And now, thanks to his fucking daughter, the three of them were in the same country, and there was a bloody good chance that they would cross paths.

The Estate₄₆

Sheila waited a moment, still leaning half out of the car, to see if she was done with her vomiting non-event. Her throat felt sore from the retching, even though nothing had come up. Her eyes were watering, and she was breathing hard, swallowing nothing, and trying to get her brain to shut-the-fuck-up thank you very much. She'd gotten seriously side-tracked, which wasn't like her when she was on the hunt. Was that what an anxiety attack felt like? She didn't have anything to be anxious about for fuck's sake. Then again, there didn't really need to be a root cause, did there? *Deal with one thing at a time.* Rowan was still asleep upstairs, so she didn't need to think about having *that* conversation for a few hours yet. The security breach, on the other hand, was still a clear and present issue.

One more deep, cleansing, breath and Sheila stepped out of the car with renewed purpose. She was the fastest and strongest member of this household, and she would protect them with every fibre of her being. Heaven help any arsehole who thought they could come onto her turf and mess with her family. *Family? Bit quick wasn't it?* They were Rowan's family and so, by extension, hers. They'd enveloped her like family would and Rowan would be devastated if she let anything happen to them. So yeah, *family*!

Having regrouped, Sheila took another breath, and followed the shining scent into the office, right up to a closed cupboard. She took a moment to turn around and make sure she'd followed the right scent. *Yup, right up to the cupboard.* No way would there be a secret passage, that would be so cool! She'd always wanted to find somewhere with a secret passage and go exploring, but the places on her security route were always boring. Please let there be a secret passage, please, please, please… She couldn't help the little squee that escaped when she opened the cupboard and discovered a set of stairs. She couldn't help the little dance she did either, before looking around to double check that no one had seen it. *Phew*, would have been awkward explaining why she'd had to get rid of witnesses. Sheila couldn't suppress her grin as she strolled down the stairs.

"Aw nuts!" There would have to be a security pin-pad. Jeremiah had given them access though so… Sheila's grin returned full-force when her palm print opened the door. Sheila and Rowan's earlier tour came in handy, helping her to orient herself when she saw the servers. They'd walked past the front of them before but this must be the back end, the very back corner of the basement. So, if she followed the wall to her right she'd eventually end up at the front corner, where Marcus had his bed set up. If she followed the wall to her left she'd end up at the other back corner, right by the lab. Taking a deep breath, she scented for her quarry, moving slowly, silently, and with complete focus. Which is why she jumped when N.E.I.L whispered her name.

"Jesus Neil, you scared me half to - never mind. Why are you whispering?" Sheila whispered back.

"Rowan demanded my silence, I didn't really want to talk to you," Neil groused, "but you looked like you were doing something important, and I thought I should see if you needed any help."

"Yeah, about that, I'm sure Rowan didn't mean to be so abrupt-"

Neil sniffed.

"-and I'll talk to him about it. Actually, you probably can help me. I'm sure nothing happens around here without you knowing about it," Sheila couldn't believe she was stroking the ego of an AI.

"That's true…mostly…except for the *private* areas. It's not as if any of you have anything I haven't seen before," you could hear the mental eye-roll as Neil spoke.

"So anyway, I've been tracking an intruder."

"Intruder?"

"Yeah, you know, someone who doesn't belong here."

"Everyone on the premises belongs here."

"Yeah, but there's evidence-"

"Evidence?"

"Yeah, there's a rope at the back hedge, blood on the roof, and a scent that I'm pretty sure I've smelled before but it's not from anyone I know."

Neil was silent. Sheila had the absurd mental image of a child digging his toes into the ground, hands behind his back, looking everywhere but at her, whilst doing his best to whistle innocently.

"Neil?"

"Yes Sheila?"

"Do you know something?"

"I know many things, Sheila."

"You know what, I'll just follow my nose," Sheila had wasted enough time, she wasn't going to pander to a petulant computer system.

"Wait!" Neil was confused, and a little bit scared. "Please Sheila, wait."

Sheila's slight hesitation was all that Neil needed. "I might have some security footage that I can show you," Neil said as he slid out a display monitor. "But Sheila, if everyone on the premises knows someone else on the premises, then everyone belongs here, right? None of them are intruders, right?"

Sheila was distracted by the footage on screen and so didn't pay attention to Neil's questions, or her own absent-minded, murmured, response "Right."

* * *

Maggie started awake, taking a moment to realise that the short bark of laughter she'd let out in her dream had also escaped her in real life, and was loud enough to wake her up. That realisation served as a link to her dream, and the memory made her smile.

She'd been spending some of the daylight hours with Jerry and Ellie, they were half way through lunch when Maggie had asked if, considering it was the middle of March, they ever did anything on April Fool's Day. Ellie had choked on her soup, and Jerry had quite seriously informed her that they *most certainly did not.*

"Ellie, are you okay? Can I get you anything?" Maggie rose from her seat and made to pat Ellie on the back.

"I'm fine," wheezed Ellie. "It went down the wrong way."

"I only wondered about the April Fool's thing because this is the first one that Marcus and I will get to spend together, and I wasn't sure whether I needed to be on my guard."

Ellie glanced at Jerry, who was studiously avoiding looking at either of them, then sighed.

"We have a truce," Ellie explained. "Marcus and Jerry used to try to outdo each other every year. By the end it got a bit out of hand, so we now have a truce."

"Out of hand how?" Maggie innocently questioned. Ellie cleared her throat, but didn't answer.

"You may tell her," Jerry said stiffly, a blush creeping up his neck.

"Marcus gave Jerry some designer clothing a few years ago, everything from underwear, to jeans, and button-down shirts. He said that we hadn't been on a vacation in a while, he'd like to send us to Sydney for a week, but he didn't want Jerry to go around looking like a butler."

Jerry huffed, moving the food around on his plate with his fork, his lips twitching at the corners.

"It was one of the rainiest weeks that year, and April Fool's Day happened to fall towards the end of it but, because we'd be away, we thought we were safe," Ellie shook her head as she continued, "We made the most of it, going to the zoo, strolling through The Rocks, riding the ferry to Manly and back again. All the while Jerry lived in one particular pair of jeans-"

"You said they made my bum look good."

"They did," Ellie smiled. "We'd come back each afternoon and Jerry would get his wet clothes dried by the hotel laundry service and change into a different shirt for our evening activities. We were strolling back to the hotel after lunch on April first when it happened."

Jerry snickered.

"When what happened?" Maggie asked, looking back and forth between them.

"Jerry's jeans fell off," Ellie couldn't help it, she burst into giggles.

"Marcus had used dissolvable thread, like dissolvable sutures, when getting the clothes custom made," laughed Jerry, picking up the story as Ellie was too far gone to be able to continue. "He'd timed it perfectly to happen on the day, sly bastard."

"So they just…fell off?" Maggie didn't have the visual, yet.

"Yup, fell away, like peeling a banana."

That did it, seeing Jerry in her mind's eye, strolling along a busy city street, with his jeans peeling away as he went, sent Maggie into hysterics, starting with a surprised, short bark of laughter. It had taken ages for the three of them to settle down, when one seemed to have the giggles under control, a snort from either of the other two would send everyone off again. Ellie had reached behind her for the box of tissues that lived on the kitchen cupboard, offering them around before taking a few herself. Maggie remembered having gone through a couple of handfuls, what with the tears of laughter streaming down her face, in between bouts of trying to blow her nose clear and composing herself. Taking a heaving breath, she thought she'd finally managed to regain control.

"How did you make it back to the hotel?"

"Well, Jerry backed up to the nearest wall, and tried tying his jacket around his waist while I held the umbrella open in front," Ellie wheezed, gulped a couple of breaths, then burst into fresh fits of laughter brought on by the memory.

Jerry grabbed a couple more tissues, and held them to his eyes as he giggled uncontrollably. "All my clothes had the same thread-" he managed to gasp before losing it once more.

"Oh no!" Maggie slapped a hand over her mouth, trying desperately to keep the bubble of laughter from escaping.

"Oh yes!", howled Ellie, long past the point of even pretending that she had hold of herself.

"The sleeves came away in my hands as I was trying to tie them together," Jerry whispered, out of breath, and clutching his side.

"Oh god," Maggie guffawed, "what did you do?"

"I gave him my coat," Ellie sniffled, dabbing at her eyes with one hand, and clutching the edge of the table with the other in an effort to ground herself. Avoiding eye contact with them, she managed to continue, "which went almost down to my knees on me, but barely managed to cover Jerry's bum. It was too small for him so he couldn't put his arms in the sleeves, or do it up in front; all he could do was drape it over his shoulders, and do his best to clutch it closed at chest and crotch."

"It was not practical to walk with the open umbrella in front of me, the handle would get in the way, and my hands were otherwise occupied," Jerry managed, the tissues still pressed up against eyes.

"So I raised the umbrella over us," Ellie contributed. "Although by then we were both thoroughly soaked, and held my thankfully large handbag in front of Jerry, where it counted."

"Did you notice that I stopped commenting on the size of your handbags after that?" Jerry, tentatively lowering his tissues, risked a glance at Ellie.

"I did," Ellie smiled, and reached over to take his hand. "It was fairly slow going but we managed to make it to the nearest men's clothing store."

"I bought a couple of complete changes of clothes, I couldn't be sure that anything that Marcus had given me wouldn't fall apart the next time I wore it," Jerry grinned, twining his fingers through Ellie's. "We still had a good time that week."

"That we did," Ellie squeezed his hand. "And we do every single time we relive the memory."

"That we do," Jerry squeezed back. "But I didn't think it was this funny at the time."

"You were positively livid," chuckled Ellie. "I really thought you would go through with your threat to resign."

"I almost did."

"What made you change your mind?" asked Maggie, curious.

Ellie and Jerry shared a look before he explained, "We could live forever and it still wouldn't be enough time together."

* * *

"How are you feeling, Ash?" Neil asked, the input from his optical sensors having picked up when Ash paled, as well as the flush of colour that had then stolen over him and settled high up on his cheeks.

Ash had eventually gone through almost an hour and a half's worth of footage, and was now staring at the image he'd paused on the screen. Rowan, in the arms of a stunningly beautiful woman, frozen in a moment of pure joy as they twirled on a ballroom floor.

"Ash?" Neil prompted.

"Huh?" Ash started, blinked a few times, shook his head then rubbed his face vigorously with both hands before raking them over his head.

"How are you feeling?"

"Just fucking peachy. How about yourself?" Maybe sarcasm would be lost on the AI.

"That good, huh?"

Apparently Neil had a pretty good grasp of sarcasm. Ash snorted before his head drooped down between his hunched shoulders. His forearms rested on his bent knees and he took a deep breath, trying desperately to release all the pent up hope and feelings he'd tied up in his idea of Rowan. The second that he'd learned that Rowan was on the premises, Ash had been prepared to forsake a lifetime of training and conditioning, putting Rowan's wellbeing before anything and everything else. The screen in front of him was a testament to just how big of an idiot he'd been. No only didn't Rowan *need* rescuing, from the expression on his face, the last thing he'd want was Ash's bumbling interruption.

"Fuck," Ash murmured, trying to come to terms with how he was supposed to complete his mission without any collateral damage, specifically without Rowan ever finding out that he'd been here.

"Okay, reset," Ash scooted back, resting his head against the opposing server bank, he mentally reviewed the mission parameters. First, get to the property - check. Second, gain access to said property - check. Not bad, so far he was two for two. Third, visually confirm that Marcus was on the premises, or likely to return in the very near future.

"Neil, I don't suppose you know Marcus by any chance, do you?"

"Of course I do, Ash. Marcus created me."

"Really?" Ash leaned forward, maybe the mission wasn't a wash after all.

"Yes, really."

"Is he here?"

"Who? Marcus?"

"Yeah. Is Marcus here?"

"Not technically, no."

"Well then," Ash was puzzled...*technically?* "Do you know where he is or when he'll be back?"

"No."

"No? No, you don't know where he is or no, you don't know when he'll be back?"

"No to both. Marcus is unlikely to return."

"What?" Neil's response took a minute for Ash to process. There had been no tonal inflection, no feeling behind the words whatsoever. "Why?"

"Maggie believes that Marcus has perished."

"Perished?" Ash felt like his brain was floating in molasses. His whole life, all his training, had prepared him to confront Marcus. What did it mean for his mission if Marcus had *perished*? "Is he dead? Did he die?"

"Apparently."

"Apparently," muttered Ash. *What the fuck did that mean?* It wasn't a definitive yes, but it wasn't a no either. Ash figured it was an *"as far as anybody knew"*, which meant that his original mission was over. *Was it though?* Ash would bet his left nut that the woman dancing with Rowan was Sheila and, furthermore, that she was a mother-fucking vampire. No human on earth could move as fast as she had, nor jump over the front gate easy-as-you-please; that gate had to be close to ten feet tall! Ash had eliminated the possibility of scaling it when he'd checked out the pinpad. It would have taken him far too long, leaving him exposed, and open to discovery; of course, going over the back hedge hadn't exactly been a genius move either.

"I need to go," Ash mumbled, wobbling upright and stumbling as he bent over to retrieve his crossbow, strapping the harness back on and reflexively drawing, checking, and re-holstering his bow. Snagging his backpack, he faced the monitor that Neil had returned to his eye level. "I need to check in with head office, give them a sit-rep, and see if that changes anything. What's the best way to get out of here Neil?"

"I have direct control of every single L.E.D on this property. I will guide your way, so to speak, just follow the lights. Would you like a quick tour as we go?"

"Uh," Ash hesitated, the realisation that it was night time had only just hit him. It was night time…and there was a vampire on the premises. She could be anywhere. If it were him, and he was here with Rowan, wouldn't matter what time of day it was, he'd want to be in bed. The two of them sure had been loved-up in the footage he'd watched, so the likelihood was that they were making the most of the quiet hours, *right*? Part of his mission was reconnoissance and he'd be damned if he reported in with nothing more than that Marcus had *apparently* perished. "Sure?"

"Splendid," Neil replied, consciously leading Ash away from where he'd situated Sheila.

Max₄₇

Maxine sat in a wing-chair, decided prim and proper was not the look she was going for, and leaned back at an angle, throwing one leg over a chair arm for good measure. Nope, not at all comfortable, she'd get a crick in her neck if she stayed that way for more than a couple minutes. Standing up, she caught a glimpse of herself in one of the mirrors that had been used to great effect in the room. She could see everything in that room from every angle, just by turning her head, no matter where she was standing. In her line of business it was wise to never turn your back on a client, this way she could give the appearance of being comfortable in someone's presence, without ever letting them out of her sight. Appearance was everything, never show weakness, no matter what was happening on the inside; sharks can smell a drop of blood in a swimming pool of water, and almost all of her clients qualified as some kind of species of shark.

Guns was one of the few people in her life who wasn't a shark, he was a teddy bear. Sometimes a grizzly bear. Last time they'd gotten together he'd been more like a drop bear suffering anxiety. The nature of their relationship meant that she hadn't asked what had been bothering him, and it had been bugging her ever since he'd left. She could sic Sai onto it, he'd be able to find out…discreetly, but she didn't want to expose Guns's weakness to anyone else. Appearance mattered. The appearance of strength could save your life, whether it's because you convince someone else, or just manage to convince yourself. In the normal world, Max and Guns wouldn't have to repress so many of their emotions, they could talk about them, support each other. Shame that they lived so far out of the normal world that they may as well be in an alternate universe. And not even the same alternate universe. They occupied different universes that sometimes managed to overlap for a short window of time, and they'd learned to make the most of it.

Which was why the pant suit wouldn't do, she didn't want to waste a moment of their time together. She unbuttoned her jacket and her blouse on the way to her walk-in wardrobe, stripping with one hand while using the other to browse through the clothes on their hangers. Nope. Nope. Nope. She was down to bra and panties when she had an epiphany, and started rummaging in her lingerie drawers instead. After considering, and discarding, several perfectly sexy items, Maxine settled on a vintage nightgown in midnight blue satin with white lace trim. She grabbed her Cassandra dressing gown on her the way out of the wardrobe, thankful that the deep v of the nightgown complemented the marabou trimmed dressing gown.

Maxine spared a thought for her cleaning service as she switched off the light in the wardrobe, effectively hiding the fact that it looked like her drawers had exploded all over the place. At least she paid them well.

Jacqueline & Gaberiel[48]

Gabe had lent Jacqui a robe, throwing on a t-shirt and a pair of sweatpants, before heading into the kitchen, and putting the kettle on. He handed Jacqui a hard copy of his CV, and worked around where she was leaning back against the cupboard, reading.

"Tea or coffee?" Gabe asked, holding up a packet of each.

"I don't suppose you have any hot chocolate?"

"Two hot chocolates coming right up," Gabe grinned, taking any excuse to feed his chocolate addiction. He spooned organic cacao powder into two fine bone china mugs, and set about frothing milk until the water came to a boil. Pouring enough water to fully dissolve the powder, Gabe then topped it with the steamed milk, and presented one to Jacqui, with a side of marshmallows.

"This is good," Jacqui commented, dropping a couple of marshmallows into hers, before taking the mug.

"You haven't tasted it yet," chuckled Gabe.

"Oh, I meant your CV," laughed Jacqui, taking a cautious sip of the hot chocolate. "This is good too!"

"Thanks."

"What sort of job are you going for?"

"Security, in the private sector."

"Ah, you might not have that specific experience, but your background in the military and law enforcement, not to mention all the study you've undertaken, should definitely give you a look-in. I guess it will depend on what other candidates apply."

"I haven't had a job interview since I got into the cops. I'm not even sure what they ask these days."

"I can help with that," smiled Jacqui. "I've recently sat on a couple of interview panels."

"Shall we sit, and role play?" Gabe asked, grimacing at the necessary evil that is role playing for job interviews, he'd much prefer the role playing he was adept at, in the bedroom.

"Sure. Do you have any paper I can jot notes on as we go? Hopefully that will help us keep the flow going."

Gabe rummaged in a drawer for a notebook and pen, pulled a chair out for Jacqui at his kitchen table, then took the one across from her. Jacqui started writing as soon as he handed her the notebook, and he wasn't sure whether that was a good thing. He cleared his throat, having no idea why he was suddenly feeling a little bit nervous, it wasn't like this was for real. She was still writing. They hadn't even started yet, what could she possibly be writing that took so long. She looked up at him, watched him for a moment, smiled, then went back to writing.

"Hello Gaberiel, thank you for coming," Jacqui stopped writing long enough to give him her ant-under-the-microscope look.

Gabe swallowed. How could this woman disarm him with a single look?

"Let's get right to it shall we?" Jacqui smiled, the one that didn't reach her eyes, and said that she held all the power and wasn't afraid to use it.

Jesus, thought Gabe; he was really thankful that he hadn't applied to go work for Jacqui.

"Pardon?" asked Jacqui.

"Shit," muttered Gabe, had he said that out loud?

Jacqui gave him one more look, then relented a little and smiled at him. A real one this time. "Relax, I'm not going to bite."

"Damn," Gabe joked, stretching out his neck, rolling his shoulders, and taking a deep breath.

Jacqui was relentless, starting with generic interview questions, she then threw everything she could think of at Gabe. She made sure to note down anything that she would change about his answers, as well as when he answered something particularly well. Gabe soon got over his initial nerves. He'd done his homework where his prospective employer was concerned, and writing the application, and updating his resume, had helped him focus on his strengths. Still, the questions that Jacqui was throwing his way seemed never-ending, and he was caught a little off-guard when they stopped. She didn't stop writing though; oh no, heaven forbid she'd put that pen down and ease his tension. He started to see the funny side when she was still writing a couple of minutes later, but then she flipped back through the pages, the top of the pen resting against the corner of her mouth. Was she done?

Nope, not quite yet. Gabe sat back in his chair, arms crossed over his chest, and a smile playing over his lips. One more flick through the pages, and then the pen hit the table. Jacqui sat up with her forearms resting on the table in front of her, fingers interlaced, and looked at Gabe. The smile on his face surprised her a little, she'd expected smug, but it wasn't; he was gazing at her with fondness and patience, happy to await her convenience. Something in the way she was looking at him made him sit up, clear his throat, adjust his t-shirt, and mirror her posture. She really should stop fucking with him, but it was so much fun.

"Well?" Gabe finally cracked. "How did I do?"

"Based on your responses," Jacqui indicated her notes, "and depending on the other candidates' experience… I'd hire you."

Gabe stopped short of whooping, but couldn't help his relieved grin.

"There were a few places where you might want to tweak your choice of words-," Jacqui flipped through her notes and gave him examples. "I took the liberty of writing down what *I* would be looking for when we first sat down, and you pretty much nailed it. I can't promise you'll get the job, but you've prepared very well."

"Thanks Jacqui," Gabe stood up, walked round to her side of the table, and held his hand out to her. Jacqui took it and stood up. "I really appreciate you doing this for me."

"You're welcome," Jacqui smiled, eagerly returning Gabe's hug when he leaned in and put his arms around her. After the initial tightness, Gabe's arms loosened but didn't release her; his left arm stayed around her waist while he ran his right hand slowly up and down her back. Head resting on his shoulder, Jacqui was having an internal argument with herself. They were in a good place, she should leave and go back to Ash's place for the rest of the night. They were in a good place, Gabe was a great lover, and she should stay and enjoy him again. She had more reasons to go than to stay, more good reasons, logical reasons, reasons that she should really, *really*, pay attention to.

"Stay," Gabe whispered in her ear, then he started nuzzling that spot just behind her earlobe.

"Okay," Jacqui sighed, reasons shmeasons.

Alpha Team₄₉

uns was too busy brooding to appreciate the scenery during their drive, and Sai's attempts at small talk didn't get too far. Every now and then Guns would flip down the visor and slide the cover over the mirror, so that he could watch Wheels in the backseat. She seemed to be completely ignoring him, missing the subtle, and not so subtle, looks he was bouncing off the mirror, and apparently into the ether, 'cause they sure as shit weren't hitting their mark. What he wanted to do was turn around and beg Wheels to keep her shit together, and stay out of his way. What he *really* wanted to do was grab Wheels by the upper arms and shake her until the woman he remembered came back. That woman would have happily played his wingman. Hell, that woman would never have had to come with him because she needed baby sitting.

He held himself in check though, so tightly reined in that he didn't know how much more he could take. What he did know was that, if he made any sort of fuss over Wheels being there, she would be more likely to lose it, and he'd have to kiss any private time with Max goodbye. He hadn't realised just how badly he needed this bubble of time with Max, time to shut out the rest of the world, bury himself deep inside her, and not resurface for days. His leg was bouncing, and he was chewing on the skin at the side of his thumb, but Guns was not aware that he was doing either. He was too busy freaking out at the thought that his haven was about to be snatched right out of his grasp. So he flipped the visor down again, slid the cover over again, and shot a look at Wheels with all his need, anxiety, and pleas in it. He didn't expect to hit his target, so when Wheels met his eyes in the mirror he flinched.

Wheels had had enough. She knew what was happening to her and, try as she might, she couldn't control any of it. She hated the helplessness that came over her in her dreams, her inability to do anything but scream as she relived her time in captivity, in vivid detail. Memory is a funny thing. Each time she slept she remembered a different day, a different moment. She'd fought, when it had happened, and kept fighting for as long as she believed that her team was coming for her. She'd used anything and everything at her disposal. Kicking, punching, and scratching at first, until that got her restrained. Spitting, biting, and head butting when that was all that she had left. They'd gagged her, tied her head back, until all she had left were her muffled screams. And, eventually, when she'd finally lost hope, she didn't even have those any more. Yet in her dreams, all she had, all she could do, was scream.

She could almost deal with her nightmares; it was the soul-deep, and seemingly unending, rage that she had no idea how to fix. Wheels remembered what she had been like, before. If she was driving, riding, or fixing something, nothing could pierce her zen-like calm. And she'd always been driving, riding, or fixing something. She'd always felt like she had complete control. She could choose the vehicle, route, and speed, and was a bloody excellent driver. Put anything mechanical in front of her, whether in pieces, or just not quite working right, and she could fix it. She could choose the parts, tools, and method, and was a bloody excellent engineer. She didn't know how to fix herself. The rage she felt had no single focal point, she was pissed off about *everything*…and everyone.

And Guns wasn't helping. The one person she knew she could rely on, and right now she wanted to grab the back of his head, and smash it into the dashboard. She could feel his eyes on her, every two fucking minutes. She knew, if she met his stare, what he'd see; seething anger, unending guilt, helpless accusation. She knew that he'd risked his life to get her back, but she couldn't decide whether she was grateful to him, or hated him for it. One way or another, if the team hadn't retrieved her, things would have ended within a few days. Her captors would have either passed the point of no return, or gotten bored with her, and killed her. Or she would have found a way to end herself. In any case, she wouldn't have had to deal with any residual bullshit.

She knew one of the things that had Guns so wound up was the possibility of her finishing what her captors had started. She could put him out of his misery she supposed, explain that the rage, and the guilt, had her so twisted, that she was too busy lashing out at everyone else. But why should she be the only one suffering? Fuck him! If he'd been even a day earlier, a few measly hours when she'd still had faith in humanity, in her team, in him. Maybe then she would have been able to deal with everything and move on. He'd been too late. She felt guilty about wishing that he'd never come at all, she felt furious that he'd let her down, and completely demoralised that she'd given up. So yeah, fuck him.

He got the message when she finally met his eyes in the mirror and she smirked, knowing that he'd be wishing that he'd left well enough alone. Wheels figured that he must occasionally wish that he'd left her behind, and knew that the very thought would sicken him. There had been a time when he was the last person she'd wanted to hurt. He'd been closer to her than her own family, understood her better, accepted her, without question or conditions. The part of her that valued those things had all but been beaten and raped out of existence, surviving only in her dreams. Her waking hours were filled with wanting everyone to suffer as she had, even those she'd once been closest to, those she'd considered friends or family…especially them.

Oh, this was not going to go well. Guns had gotten the message loud and clear, and was now busy running scenarios through his head. He knew that the *what-if* game was a losing proposition. Whatever he imagined that Wheels might do, however he planned to counter her moves, he would not be able to think of the one thing that she would actually do. Normal, rational people were somewhat predictable...usually... sometimes. Wheels had never been quite normal, and she was now as far from rational as Alpha Centauri was from Earth. Pretty fucking far. Best case scenario? She'd refuse to engage, take herself to a corner once they got to Maxine's, and sulk for the whole time they were there. He could deal with that. Worst case scenario?

"Fuck," muttered Guns, as images of Wheels completely trashing Maxine's place flickered, rapid-fire, through his brain.

"Pardon?" asked Sai, politely questioning what he was fairly confident that he'd heard.

"What?" Guns responded. "Sorry man, a million things on my mind, and only a few of them are good."

"Hopefully this will help," Sai smiled as he thumbed a remote, and then drove into a roomy garage, especially roomy by city standards. "We're here."

* * *

Gina and the CO had to wait for a Maxi Taxi because they were hauling everyone's checked luggage; Wheels and Guns had everything they needed in their carry-ons for the short time they would be at Maxine's. They'd booked *Shaken* at 1888 Darling Harbour. It gave them the privacy of direct street access, and a downstairs area where the team could meet. Wheels and Guns were each booked into adjoining queen rooms, with the check-in date adjusted to allow for the Maxine "delay". Gina didn't waste any time, making herself comfortable on the couch with her laptop while the CO explored their room, and sorted out the luggage.

"How busy are you?"

"Huh?" Gina had to mentally pull herself out of cyberspace, and into the here-and-now.

"How busy are you?" The CO crooked an eyebrow as he sat in an armchair directly opposite from where Gina was.

"I wasn't doing anything that can't wait. Why?"

The CO replied by relaxing into the chair, his wide-spread legs falling open a little further, and reaching into his shirt pocket to pull out Gina's panties, letting them swing off his crooked index finger. His gaze never wavered, heating as he watched her watching him. Gina did a quick mental check of how she was sitting, thanking her lucky stars that she was enough of a lady to have kept everything covered while the bellhop had been dropping off their bags. The bellhop had left ages ago, and there was now only one man in the room that could see anything she did. Her man. And boy did she want to tease him, partly to punish him for stealing her panties, mostly because his mere presence always made her pulse quicken.

Taking her time, Gina carefully exited the programs and apps she was using, shut her laptop, and leaned forward to sit it on the coffee table. She may have leaned further than she needed to. She may have tensed her shoulders so that her dress gaped at the front. She may have angled her head so that her hair was out of the way, and the CO could have an unobstructed view of her lace-covered breasts. She definitely took her time leaning back on the couch, unfolding her legs from beneath her, and propping her feet on the edge of the coffee table, knees together, feet spread. The challenge in her eyes was unmistakable, and provocative.

Gina's dress was short enough, and loose enough, to give the CO a completely unobstructed view. His woman could send him from flaccid to painfully hard in 0.9 seconds, as evidenced by his rapidly tightening pants. He wanted nothing more in that moment than to bury himself to the balls in her hot, tight, soaking wet sheath. He loved that they could fuck hard, make love softly, and still never seem to get enough of each other. That was only part of what he loved about her though, a small part. He loved that she saw *him* - not what he looked like, or who he'd been - who he was now, and accepted him, scars and all. He loved that she wouldn't take his shit, and that she'd give him back as much as he dished out, maybe more. He loved that she wasn't meek and mild, and when his history weighed on him, she'd call him on it. Not all his scars were on the outside, and the ones on the inside were worse, uglier, deeper. Gina would let him wallow, for all of about five minutes, then she'd give him a look, a jab with her elbow, or a bump with her hip, pulling him back to the present from the nightmares of his past. When that wasn't enough, she'd up the ante, usually teasing him with kisses or touches, occasionally throwing his boxing gloves at him, and demanding a sparring round in the ring.

"What did you have in mind?" purred Gina, swaying her legs slowly from side to side, so that her thighs slid sensually against each other.

"Well, there's a couple's tub in the bathroom, and a king bed upstairs," the CO fisted her panties, running the fabric back and forth along his lower lip in time to her swaying legs. "But we have at least the rest of the day, and the night, before Guns and Wheels get back. I thought we might explore…"

Gina waited, unsure whether he was going to suggest exploring each other, or the city outside their little bubble.

The CO stood and stalked over to her, holding out a hand to help her up. As soon as she stood he stepped closer, so they touched from knee to chest, and so she could have no doubt about how much he wanted her right at that moment. Reaching around, he palmed each of her arse cheeks through her wonderfully short and loose dress, before squeezing them and pulling her harder against his cock. He couldn't help his wicked grin as Gina's arms came around him and she leaned her head back on a moan. Burying his face in the crook of her neck, the CO took his time kissing and nuzzling his way up to her ear. "…the Harbour." With a quick, light, swat to her backside, he stepped away and held his hand out, the panties making what he hoped would be a good enough peace offering not to get him slapped in return.

* * *

Maxine heard the low rumble of the garage door opening, followed by the purr of the Bently, as Sai drove in. She reclined on her fainting couch in the living room, carefully adjusting her dressing gown so that the red-polished toes of one foot peeked out. If she lay a little more sideways, she could prop her elbow on the chair arm and lean on her hand, taking care not to mess up her hair…Guns could do that later. She look down and realised that the angle made the swell of her right breast edge into the exposed vee; thankfully her left breast was propped up by both her bra and the arm of the chair. Her left sleeve had gathered around her elbow and she moved the marabou around so that it pooled over the chair's black velvet arm. She shook the sleeve down her right arm, then let it lie along her leg, her hand artfully placed atop her thigh, red-polished nails glinting in the professionally designed lighting.

The thought of everything she planned to get up to with Guns over the next day or two, was clearly reflected on her face. Her hooded eyes were riveted to the only door that Sai would bring Guns through, the anticipation shallowing her breath, making her thighs clench. She gasped with the ding of the elevator, taking a deep breath, and releasing it on a slow, seductive smile.

"Come on in to the living room, and I'll let Maxine know that the two of you are here," Sai, not using his indoor voice, was clearly giving her a heads up.

Two? Maxine pushed up against the chair's arm, her plans falling to ashes before her eyes. The look she now aimed at the doorway was one of hard suspicion, but she'd been in the game for far too long to jump to any conclusions; shooting first always meant that you didn't get to ask any questions, and Max always shot to kill.

Sai strolled in first, giving a subtle gallic shrug, as he walked around to stand at Maxine's left peripheral vision. "Max, you remember Guns, and this is his... associate, Wheels."

Max took in her guests with a practiced eye. Guns, as hot as ever, was so tense and wound-up that she was amazed he hadn't already gone postal. She turned her gaze on Wheels, and came up against such hostile defensiveness that, had she not been used to disguising her reactions, would have had her stumbling. She titled her head, the barest fraction, in Sai's direction. A question that he had no answer for. Right! She would do what she did best, brazen it out. *Fake it till she made it* had always worked for her in the past.

"Guns, darling," Maxine stood gracefully and breezed over to him, holding out both her hands.

"Max," Guns grabbed for the lifeline she was throwing, and held on like the drowning man he was. Taking a deep breath, Guns urged Maxine closer so he could lean his forehead against hers, "It's really, really good to see you."

Max felt some of Guns's tension escape in the way he let out his breath, and gradually relaxed the death-grip he'd had on her hands. She gave him all the time he needed and, when he straightened and took the smallest step backwards, she squeezed his hands, and released him to greet her surprise guest. Maxine strode towards Wheels, but hadn't been prepared for the barely-there flinch before the other woman managed to brace herself. *Curiouser and curiouser.*

"Hello, I'm Max," Max stopped where she was, and instead held out her hand.

Wheels, her arms firmly folded across her chest, stared at the proffered hand. As hands go she supposed it was rather pretty. The nails seemed recently manicured and the polish was immaculate. She never bothered with nail polish, she usually ruined it within seconds of it being applied, but this woman didn't seem to have that problem. She colour co-ordinated too, her toes and fingers sporting the same shade of Miami Beet. Wheels let her gaze travel further, over the smooth knuckles, the dainty but strong wrist, through the froufrou fluttering about her forearm, along the arm and shoulder covered by a nightgown that was so transparent Wheels wondered why Max even bothered, and of course her lip colour would match her nails. She wasn't sure what she'd see when she met this woman's eyes, probably contempt; nothing about Wheels was co-ordinated, or manicured, or froufrou, but fuck that. So, as she raised her eyes a little further, her chin followed almost in challenge, and her arms tightened a little tighter across her chest.

Maxine waited. She was an old pro at letting people size her up and underestimate her solely based on the image she chose to project. She took the opportunity to study the woman standing across from her, and she wasn't thrilled about what she saw. Her hair was clipped back, but there was enough of it loose so that Wheels could hide her face. Her shoulders were tight and hunched. She was sullen, but not in the way of a teenager who wasn't allowed out with their friends because they had to stay home and do homework. No, this woman was sullen like a dog that had been beaten or abused, one too many times. Max knew a little of what Guns did for a living, and anyone involved in his team would have to be strong, or they wouldn't have made the cut. So, how much would someone that strong have to endure, to become this skittish? She made sure that when Wheels was done with her perusal and ready to meet her eyes, all she'd find was reserved compassion.

Wheels wasn't ready. She'd prepared herself for one thing, and Max was projecting pretty much the direct opposite. She could have handled judgement, hostility, or the contempt that she'd been expecting. This tentative kindness was unnerving. What the fuck was she supposed to do with that? The pretty hand was still there, still waiting. Wheels knew, without looking, that her hands were callused, and there was grease under her fingernails that she'd only be able to get out if she ripped her nails off and went at it with a wire brush. She figured she'd endured enough torture in her life and didn't need to do that, so the world could deal with a little grease. Still, she felt uncomfortable about touching such a pretty, clean hand, even as she tentatively reached out.

Guns was almost sure he'd stopped breathing when Maxine held her hand out. He'd been about to prompt

Wheels at least a dozen times in the 30 seconds or so it had taken her to react. He thought he might actually pass out when Wheels decided shaking hands was okay, and didn't just flip Maxine the bird. Once upon a time, Wheels had been as reliable as the engines she fixed but, ever since her capture, she'd become increasingly unpredictable. Guns had no idea what she'd do or say from one second to the next. The heightened state of watchfulness that was now such a part of his life had him constantly on edge. He'd once prided himself on having nerves of steel, not anymore. His anxiety level was through the roof, he found himself jumping at shadows and unexpected noises. He hadn't been a nail biter, but even now his teeth were attacking the skin at the side of his thumb, his fingers a history of scars in various stages of recovery. *What's one more?* he thought as he sucked on the blood he'd drawn from his thumb. He watched as Wheels took the two steps she needed to reach Maxine's hand, his eyes pricking when his friend finally, voluntarily, touched another human being.

Wheels watched her hand reach out for the pretty one. It felt surreal, like it was happening to someone else. Like someone else had taken two steps that, for her, had seemed impossible. Like someone else was a hair's breadth from touching skin that looked so soft. And then it was her. *She* was holding a hand that was warm, and deceptively strong. She turned her hand so she could see the top of Maxine's, tilting her head, wondering if that would help her mind catch up with what was going on. Raising her head she took in Maxine; strong, silent, patient, Maxine. The impact of looking into Maxine's amber eyes up close was intense and immediate. Wheels dropped the hand like she'd been burned, but found herself unable to look away.

There was intelligence and resilience in those eyes, pain too, maybe. Then again, Wheels saw pain everywhere these days. She guessed that, until she managed to work through everything that had been done to her, the stuff she could remember, and the stuff her brain had blocked in self defence, pain would be one of the main filters through which she viewed the world. It was fucking irritating. She noticed Maxine's slight reaction to the scowl her thoughts had brought to her face, and made a conscious effort to relax her features. Maxine rewarded her with a smile, barely a movement of her lips, but Wheels caught it. Literally, the small smile was contagious, so different to the smirks that Wheels had gotten used to giving. It felt odd…good…to let her mouth curve ever so slightly. She had to stop herself from touching her face, tracing her fingers over her lips to make sure that she was doing it right. Then Maxine winked. No other movement, just a wink, aimed at her. A conspiracy between the women in the room that made Wheels feel like she was no longer alone.

In that instant, Maxine decided to change the plans she'd made. Guns was not going to be happy. Nope, not at all. But there was more to life than sex, even earth shatteringly, fantabulous sex. *Shit!* Still, she felt something for the broken human being standing before her. Something she wanted to explore. Something she hoped would help Wheels battle whatever demons had taken up residence in her soul and, by the look of Guns, affected those closest to her too. Now, how to break it to Guns…and to Wheels, without spooking her?

"Would you join me for dinner?" Maxine asked Wheels, gaze earnest and steady, while keeping her voice low enough so that the guys wouldn't hear, and so that Wheels could feel comfortable refusing.

Wheels's first instinct was to refuse, to question, to wonder what price Maxine might exact for her company. Could have pushed her over with a feather when she found herself slowly nodding. On the up side, Guns was gonna blow a gasket when he realised she was going to be third wheeling them.

"Splendid!" Maxine's smile, bigger than the last one, seemed genuine. "Sai, Wheels and I will be dining upstairs. Guns, darling, you'll be okay keeping Sai company, right?" Maxine didn't give anyone time to react, linking her arm through Wheels's and chattering away about the menu as she guided her out of the room.

"What…the fuck…just happened?" Guns had turned to follow Maxine, but quickly realised that he hadn't been invited. He felt Sai's hand settle heavily on his shoulder, then giving him a couple pats.

"Well, my friend, looks like it's just you and me. How about a drink?"

"No offence man, but this wasn't what I'd been expecting."

"None taken. I have learned to expect the unexpected wherever Maxine is concerned. Keeps me sane, and keeps life interesting."

Poppy & Doug[50]

66 Hurry up and wait. Hurry up and wait! Why have our lives been so full of hurry up and wait?" Poppy rhetorically grumbled, folding her arms across her chest on a huff. "And how long could it possibly take to move one fucking tanker?"

Doug raised an eyebrow but knew better than to respond. Poppy was usually a reasonable, loving, gentle, and kind human being. He was impressed that it had taken her this long to reach her limit. Traffic police had set up detours long ago, but the couple were bound to the route that Rowan had taken. They'd pulled over as close to the overturned tanker as they dared, prepared to wait on the side of the road until the accident had been cleared. That had worked for about half an hour after they'd finished their coffee, then nature called, loudly. Doug executed a u-turn and back-tracked to the most-likely, first-available, bathroom. They barely noted the bright yellow facade of the lolly store in their rush to use the facilities and get back to their waiting game.

While waiting for Doug to finish, Poppy wondered around the store. She supposed that the polite thing to do was to purchase something, but their unexpected delay had her feeling so anxious she could barely think straight. She'd wondered half the store and wasn't able to recall any of the products, even had her life had depended on it. She stopped to throw a glance in the direction of the bathroom, hoping to see Doug emerging, when a packet of flying saucers caught her eye. Picking it up, she ran her thumbs over and over the plastic, her eyes prickling as memories of her son tried to leak out. Rowan had loved those little sour-sweet sherbert confections, always managing to sniff the packet out whenever she'd bought him one as a treat.

"You okay, Love?" Doug murmured as he came up to her.

Poppy didn't speak. Couldn't. She looked at her husband as she handed him the packet. He took it with one hand, the other reaching up so his thumb could gently brush the tear from her cheek. Taking her hand, they walked up to the counter.

"We'll take this one please," Doug said, and if his voice was a little thicker, a little more choked up than normal, no one commented. Poppy gave his hand a squeeze in understanding, and that was enough.

Jacqueline & Gaberiel[51]

66Does Ash know?" asked Gabe, his fingers idly tracing up and down Jacqui's spine where she lay, draped halfway over his chest.

"Hmm?"

"Does Ash know?"

"Know what?"

"What a tiger he has for a mother?"

Jacqui didn't have to see Gabe's face to hear the impudent grin in his voice. She'd agreed to stay, but hadn't thought through what that would mean. Yes, they'd had sex again, but it had been different. Slower. Less…fucking, and more lovemaking. If she thought about it too hard, it might start to freak her out, but she was feeling too deliciously boneless for that to happen right now. She mulled over Gabe's question, thought about whether or not she wanted to answer, whether he would think that he *deserved* an answer.

"I was young when I had Ash and, for all intents and purposes, a widow," Jacqui's murmured response had Gabe stilling, listening attentively to every word, before resuming his light touches, encouraging her to go on. "Alex, Ash's father, and I were consumed by each other. We'd been virgins when we got together and, had he lived, he probably would have been the only man that I would have ever made love to. But he was killed in the line of duty, I never even got to tell him that he was going to be a father.

Ash became my whole world, and it was enough, at least until he started going to school. I found myself wanting…needing more, the vibrator in my bedside drawer wasn't cutting it. I found a couple of erotica websites, reading the stories that people posted helped for a while, slipping into someone else's fantasy was enough to get off and be satisfied. Then I found that only certain kinds of stories would work. The ones where the woman was in control. It kept me from feeling like I was cheating on Alex, even though he'd been dead for years.

I eventually started to wonder if the stories could possibly be based in reality, and one day, when I was feeling particularly nihilistic and self-destructive, I reached out to someone on one of the sites. I was bloody lucky, as the person I contacted was extremely experienced in the scene and a decent human being to boot. There are so many wannabes and pretenders that don't truly understand what they are doing, or why.

She went by "Madame", the person I contacted, and was always firm, but fair. She made sure that I understood the responsibility each participant has to the others they are interacting with at any particular given time. She taught me that dominating someone isn't about me getting off; it's about figuring out what my sub wants, deciding whether it is what my sub *needs*, and choosing whether or not to give it to them. I learned from her, and from so many others, and over time, I was able to select subs that didn't need any emotional attachment, it allowed me to maintain the illusion of being faithful to Alex."

"Do you still love him?"

"Who, Alex?" Jacqui felt the movement as Gabe nodded. "He gave me Ash, I will always love him-"

"Ah."

"-but I'm no longer consumed by him. It used to be that there wasn't a second in the day when he wasn't on my mind, awake or asleep. Now, it's almost like he moved to the other side of the world, somewhere without any internet, mobile, or postal service. I think of him occasionally, usually fondly, more so when I'm with Ash and he does something so very *Alex*. Which blows my mind sometimes; I mean, Ash never met his father, but he smiles exactly like him. Or when he's exasperated, it's almost like he channels Alex. It almost broke me, the first time I saw Alex so clearly in his son, knowing that he would never get to hold him, hug him, teach him, or even scold him."

Gabe went from stroking her, to holding her, tightly enough so that she would know that she was not alone. Jacqui stiffened at first, alone was the only way she knew how to be; but he didn't let go, and he didn't let up, and, for the first time, it made her wonder if alone might be just one possibility, among many.

The Estate[52]

heir bedtime routine was almost like a ballet, as it should be considering they'd had a good couple centuries to pin it down. Jerry had opened their bedroom door and ushered Ellie inside, shutting it behind him as he followed her in. They'd gone to their respective sides of the bed, Ellie handing Jerry the frou-frou pillows he insisted on having, one at a time, until he'd arranged all twelve, *yes twelve*, of them on the window seat.

"Why?" She'd asked, more than once over the years.

"Because I like them," was Jerry's initial reply. "Because we bought that velvet one in Venice not long after we were married, and the silk one during our trip to China, before the industrial revolution when things were still made by hand, and the one with the feathers in Paris, before the war… They all have a story."

So Ellie would occasionally ask why, just so Jerry would tell her the story behind each and every pillow, and in so doing, tell her the story of their life together, and how her sentimental husband would hold on to things just because they reminded him of them, of her. Then they'd fold down the bed cover, or rather Jerry would precisely fold down his side so that it came to just below his pillow, and Ellie would throw hers back and be done well before Jerry had finished smoothing his side. There had been times, when they'd been snippy at each other for one reason or another, and it had been the bed cover that they picked a fight over. It had never been about the bed cover, but they'd always fought it out before getting into bed, always ended the night in each others' arms.

While Jerry was busy smoothing, and then sitting on his side of the bed to take off his shoes and socks, Ellie was in their bathroom brushing her teeth. Jerry would come in and use the pristine sink on his side of the vanity, brushing for the recommended two full minutes, whereas Ellie would brush until she'd had enough, 30 seconds or 3 minutes…it always varied, and turn so that Jerry could undo whatever button or zipper she couldn't get to. Jerry would oblige, when necessary, and exact payment in the form of a quick peck to the cheek (his) or a light swat to the bottom (hers), as Ellie went back through their room, and into their walk-in wardrobe to change.

Ellie would pass by Jerry on her way to her dressing table. He'd walk into the wardrobe, doing his best to ignore the clothes that Ellie had stripped out of and left on the floor, knowing that she would gather them in the morning and place them in the laundry basket, *where they should be right now*…but at least they would eventually get there. Jerry inspected his shirt thoroughly before deciding whether it would go back on a hanger or in the basket, doing the same with the rest of his clothes, except for his underthings, they always went in the basket. Where Ellie always wore a nightgown to bed, Jerry would be as naked as the day he was born. He'd watch Ellie watch him in her dressing table mirror as he sauntered out of the wardrobe and to his bedside table to switch on the lamp, before walking back to the light switch by the door, often stopping to wiggle his arse a little, listening for Ellie's chuckle or snort, before switching off the main light.

Ellie finished applying moisturiser, watching and listening as Jerry slid between the sheets, uttering a contented sigh as he did so. She slipped her dressing gown off her shoulders and threw it on the end of her side of the bed, enjoying how Jerry watched every move she made. Although she wore a nightgown every night, more often than not, she wouldn't wake up in one. The light in Jerry's eyes had her wondering whether this one would last five minutes before he talked her out of it. She sat up on her side of the bed, pulling the covers so they pooled in her lap. The last thing she did, before turning to Jerry for her kiss goodnight, was to slip her necklace over her head. She held it up for a moment, watching the rings on it twist and swing. Her engagement ring, her wedding ring, and her eternity ring.

Her engagement ring was relatively new, incorporating elements from her first one. The original small diamond solitaire was now joined by many others, the 18 karat yellow gold bordered them and the magnificent emerald in the middle. As if that wasn't enough, the rest of the ideal cut diamonds were nestled in a platinum setting. She'd refused to wear it. She used to take her first one off when doing dishes and, one day, it had disappeared. Ellie had been heartbroken and apologised profusely to Jerry, who'd hugged her close and told her not to worry, he'd just get her another one. *Snake* Ellie snorted quietly as the stones caught the light. Jerry had pilfered her ring, and didn't tell her until he'd presented her with the new one. She'd punched his arm, hard! He'd threatened to take the ring back and she'd snatched it out of his hand.

"You will do no such thing!" Ellie had stated, narrowed eyes flashing, foot stomping, finger pointing, and the ring held safely behind her back. Jerry had chuckled, and winced, as he rubbed his arm.

"What on earth possessed you to do this? There was nothing wrong with my ring!" She'd demanded.

He'd muttered something about it being too small, and then told her how a 12 year old boy had come into the shop and offered the emerald for sale. Jerry, being the softie that he is, let himself be talked into paying far more than the child would have happily accepted. He'd had no use for an emerald, but he'd been stuck walking home behind a couple of women, one of whom had recently become engaged and was bragging about the size of the stone on her ring. So, the darling man, had gotten it into his head that his wife of nearly a century should have bragging rights too. The very fact that he wouldn't tell her how much the ring had cost him had her digging in her heels about wearing it. So they'd compromised, he'd bought her a necklace long enough so that she could thread the ring onto it, and wear it over her heart.

That boy had gone on to make quite a name for himself in the jewellery business, and Jerry had bought her one or two more pieces from him over the years. They'd both mourned when Harry had passed away, but one of his sons still ran the company to the standard that he'd set. Jerry had learned his lesson though, and spoken to her about updating her wedding ring. Ellie thanked him for the thought, but she loved the plain band just as it was. So, for their hundredth wedding anniversary, Jerry had splurged on an eternity ring that Ellie had also refused to wear. Eventually it became more convenient to wear all three of them on her necklace, and her little ritual of taking it off at the end of each night reminded her of just how far the two of them had come.

* * *

She'd hoped that she'd be able to turn over and fall back to sleep, nature had other ideas so, when it called a little louder, Maggie, grumbling and shuffling, made her way to her bathroom. She used to be able to navigate her way in the dark and blindfolded - unable to suppress her giggles that one time that Marcus had insisted that she prove it - but it had been so long. She scrunched her eyes tight before flicking the light switch, keeping one closed, and wincing as she barely opened the other. Nothing had changed. Except maybe the bathmats.

"Sweet baby cheeses," Maggie moaned as she stepped onto the pedestal mat and her foot sank about an inch. The whole lifting the lid, reaching under her sleep shirt, and dropping panties routine was as automatic as blinking, which she was doing a lot of at the moment, thanks to the broad-daylight strength light bulbs that Ellie must have had installed. *Huh*, the three-ply toilet paper was a welcome upgrade.

"*Shhhh*," Maggie admonished, as the toilet lid decided to bang closed instead of whisper. The foaming hand wash was a nice touch, and smelled divine. So yeah, nothing much had changed, Maggie chuckled to herself as she climbed back into bed. She lay on her left side, her right hand snaking across the bed, hopelessly hoping that it would meet resistance in the form of a stubbornly sexy man. And then she remembered. She'd buried the moment, convinced herself that it had not happened. But it had, and she had absolutely no idea what to do about it.

Flipping, okay, rolling slowly, onto her back, Maggie gave up on the idea of sleep and lay with her hands clasped behind her head. This was when she needed Marcus the most. Out of everyone in her life, he would have been the one to know what had happened, and how to fix it. Instead, he was apparently possessing Sheila.

"Not cool babe," said Maggie, imagining Marcus giving her that shrug of his, the one that he always followed with a cheeky grin, expecting to get away with whatever he'd been up to. It usually worked. "Not this time, bud."

How was she going to tell Rowan? *What* was she going to tell Rowan?

"Good morning, Row. By the way, did I happen to mention that your new-found, vampire, girlfriend seems to be channelling my long-term, previously-thought-dead, husband?"

Or maybe…

"Hey, Row, we need to talk. Marcus seems to be possessing Sheila. I'm cool with it if you are." Okay, that turned creepy. Did she *really* need to tell Rowan? Maybe it was a one-time deal?

"How about it, babe? Will you be freaking me out again?" Maggie asked, shaking her head as she remembered that Marcus had occasionally loved to freak her out so, obviously, the answer would be *hell yeah*! Maybe Rowan shouldn't be the first person that she approached about it. Maybe Ellie or Jerry would be more appropriate? They had centuries of experience between them, maybe they would know what the fuck was going on, and how to stop it. Except, maybe, deep down, she didn't really *want* to stop it.

For that moment, that glorious, and gloriously horrifying, moment, Maggie had seen Marcus shine out of Sheila's eyes, his voice, his words, coming out of her mouth. Yes, she had an artist's soul, but her heart was that of a skeptic. Yes, one who believed in vampires, but still a skeptic. Maggie didn't believe in ghosts, or spirits, or that either one could possess someone. Which meant that there had to be another explanation. A rational, scientifically provable, explanation. The fact that Maggie had no idea what that was, and that her first thought was "possession", didn't mean that there wasn't a logical explanation. Didn't someone say that magic was science that we didn't understand yet? What time was it anyway?

Maggie craned her neck, looking for the clock radio on her bedside table, then turned back with a groan. Ridiculously early, or terribly late, depending on your point of view, she knew that she was going to have the devil's own time trying to get back to sleep. Now that she'd acknowledged that she'd seen *something*, her brain seemed incapable of letting it go, like when you have something stuck between your teeth, and your tongue keeps returning to it so often that it gets sore. Marcus had always been able to get her to fall asleep, one way or the other. Maggie smirked at the memories of his hands giving her the best ever, most relaxing, back rubs, and how, more often than not, he wouldn't be able to stop himself from sexing it up.

She'd spent so many years doing her damndest not to think of him, especially at night, especially in bed. Now that she'd started to deal with it, or at least acknowledge everything that he'd been, that he'd meant to her, that he *still* meant to her, she could allow herself to picture him again. To remember him. His face, his hands, his body, his scent. The way he'd look at her like she was the most amazing creature in the universe. The way he'd use a burst of speed to brush a wayward curl back off her face, so that she was never quite sure whether it had been him or a breeze. The way that he'd half-heartedly try to talk her out of something, but support her completely if she was determined to go ahead with whatever scheme she'd dreamed up. He'd opened doors for her, pulled her chair out for her, would have lassoed the moon had she asked it of him. He was powerful, beyond anything she'd ever known before, or since, but, in their relationship, the power was all hers.

So, on this night, back in a bed they had shared so often, Maggie allowed herself to picture her husband, her Marcus, again. The way he'd sit on the edge of her bed, his hip up against her own, looking at her like he wanted to spend eternity devouring her. How he'd sit there, watching, waiting for a sign from her that he could. How she'd try to prolong it, so that she could bask in the heat from his gaze, knowing that a lazy blink, or a slight smile, from her would be all it would take for him to unleash his control. How, even with all that strength, all that speed, she knew that she could never be safer than in his presence. So she stretched one arm over her head, the other snaking down over her breast, as she held the stare of her memory, her lips curling in a smile of permission.

* * *

"Neil?" Sheila murmured, reaching out to pause the security playback on the high definition monitor she'd been watching.

"Yes, Sheila?"

"You didn't let us know that someone was climbing over the back hedge?"

"No, Sheila?"

"Why?" Sheila couldn't keep the incredulity from her tone. Had Neil been human, she would have been grabbing and shaking him, rapidly firing about a dozen questions at him. She couldn't do that with the AI, and she suspected that anything it took offence to would result in a distinct lack of cooperation on its part.

"Ellie had me silenced upstairs," Neil sniffed.

"Do you know where he is now?" Sheila waited for a reply and, when none seemed to be forthcoming, prompted "Neil?"

"Maybe."

Sheila made fists tight enough to crack her knuckles, took a deep breath, then tried again.

"What do you know about this guy, Neil?"

"His name is Ash, he knows Rowan, and he seems very nice." Neil rushed earnestly, his words almost tripping over each other by the end.

"Ash?"

"Uhuh."

"This is Ash?" Sheila took a closer look at the screen. "Huh."

"What's he doing here?" Sheila asked, mostly to herself, wondering if Rowan had invited him, and then thinking that he would probably have used the front door if that had been the case.

"Ash was asking about Marcus," Neil helpfully supplied.

"Marcus? As in Maggie's Marcus?"

"One and the same," Neil agreed. "I told him that Marcus apparently perished."

"Very helpful of you Neil. Did you happen to tell him anything else?"

"I told him that Rowan, Maggie, and yourself, are here. Then Ash had a panic attack, so we worked through that. Then he asked about me, so I told him everything."

"Everything?" Sheila asked faintly.

"Everything! It was so much fun, and so nice to have someone actually listen to me, for a change."

"Why did he have a panic attack?"

"I'm not entirely sure, but I think it was brought on when I mentioned that Rowan was here."

"Hmmmm," Sheila reached to restart the security footage whilst mulling over all that Neil had told her. Why would knowing that Rowan was here bring on a panic attack? Was it the fact that Rowan might discover what Ash was doing, indicating that it isn't something that Rowan would approve of? Or was it an involuntary response; like the gut-wrenching fear she suffers whenever she starts to consider Rowan's mortality? And, if it was brought on by terror over Rowan's safety or well-being, what did Ash know that she didn't? Did she need to go on the offence? Was everyone in the house in danger? Ash apparently knew about Marcus, but did he also know that Marcus was a vampire? Marcus had been involved in an incalculable number of ventures over his long life, and Ash could be seeking him out for any one of them. There really was only one way to get to the bottom of this.

"Right, Neil, where is Ash right now?" Sheila's tone brooked no argument, her protective instincts lighting a fire in her belly that only prompt and decisive action would help cool down.

"Around," was Neil's belligerent response.

Sheila hadn't forgotten that she was dealing with a juvenile A.I., really; although she had expected better, and was beyond exasperated. Throwing her hands into the air she did what she should have done in the first place, followed her nose.

"Wait!" called Neil as Sheila took a deep breath and prepared to hunt her prey. "What will happen to Ash?"

Sheila had been ready to ignore Neil's feeble attempts to delay her, had expected anything from a dad joke to the recitation of the periodic table. She hadn't expected the note of genuine worry in Neil's voice. It seemed that, in the relatively short time that Ash and Neil had interacted, Neil had become attached to Ash. Realising that, at the speed with which Neil could process, a relatively short time was… well… relative. For Ash, and for herself, it was the matter of a few hours, for Neil, it was long enough to process several thousand brain's worth of computations and come up with friendship. It dawned on Sheila that isolating Neil, ensuring that he had no contact with anyone unless they chose to venture into the basement, was a harsher punishment than they probably realised. Imagine locking a child in the basement for what you think are a few hours, but for them a few months, or years go by.

The thought horrified Sheila, which in turn made her extremely uncomfortable, she still wasn't used to feelings, and had a hard enough time dealing with the ones she felt for Rowan. How on earth was she supposed to react now? Maybe she could switch Neil off and switch him back on again? Wasn't that the general fix for technological glitches? But then, Neil wasn't a glitch. *True, but the feelings that it's having might be.* Wouldn't that reset it? Would that then mean that it wouldn't remember things? Did Neil do periodic backups and, if so, when was the last time that it backed up its memories? It was likely that switching it off might only succeed in pissing it off. Did she really want to have to deal with an angry A.I.? She'd watched movies, they never ended well if an angry A.I. was involved. Okay, so that was Hollywood, but was she really prepared to risk it?

"Neil," said Sheila, far more gentle than she had originally planned to be. "I can't answer that question right now. I don't know what will happen to Ash. It mostly depends on what he's doing here, what his plans or intentions are."

"Will you hurt him?" Neil's small voice sent yet another uncomfortable pang through Sheila's heart.

"I don't know. All I can promise is that I will *try* not to."

Neil mulled over Sheila's response, calculating probable outcomes. There were so many variables that the possibilities were virtually infinite. Neil surmised, after a few seconds, that the only question he really had to answer right in that moment was *who was he protecting?* Ash, whom he'd met a few hours, or a friendship, ago, or his family?

Alpha Team[53]

uns looked up from his plate and towards the stairs for about the hundredth time in the last 30 minutes. Sai, sitting across from him at the antique dining table in the style of some long-dead French king, noticed, again, and said nothing, again. He wasn't a fool, he'd known, or at least had a pretty good idea, what Guns and Maxine had planned. Every single time that Guns looked towards the stairs, he had a different expression on his face. At first Sai was amused, then he'd taken to cataloguing them.

There was what he called the incredulous look, Guns had started out with several variations of that one. That morphed into the puzzled look, like Guns was still trying to figure out what had happened, or how it happened, or whether it had really happened, and maybe he'd fallen asleep in the car and had just dreamed it. Then there was dawning realisation - nope, not a dream, very fucking real. The pained look had garnered a bit of sympathy from Sai, blue balls were never fun, unless you were into that sort of thing. The sad puppy look had made Sai snort, and momentarily drew Guns's attention. The angry look had Sai a little concerned for the Wedgewood dinner plate, as Guns stabbed his vegetables more and more forcefully after each mouthful. It had taken the impatient look, the scowling look, the fuck you look (one of his personal favourites), and a handful of others, before getting to the somewhat-resigned look.

And yet, Guns was still occasionally glancing at the stairs.

"They won't be coming down this evening," Sai pointed out, dabbing his lips with his linen napkin and looking Guns steadily in the eye.

"You don't know that," Guns retorted, attacking his meat like it had piped up and insulted him.

"Perhaps not, but I do know Maxine."

"Fuck," Guns slammed his cutlery down onto the table cloth, either side of his plate, giving up on the beef that had been cooked sous vide for hours, and would have fallen apart if he'd so much as tapped it with his fork.

"Perhaps a drink?" offered Sai, leaving his seat, strolling over to the dry bar, and reaching for the Congac.

"Make it a double," sighed Guns. If he couldn't get his nuts off, he might as well get hammered, it's not like he had to drive.

Sai returned to the table with the bottle and two glasses, pouring a small one for himself, then handing the whole bottle to Guns. He didn't say anything as Guns poured. And poured. And poured some more. He couldn't help his eyebrow rising as the level of liquor in the glass got higher and higher; after all, what was a $3,000.00 bottle of Congac between friends?

* * *

Maxine had guided Wheels straight to her suite, releasing her arm as they approached the double doors, so that she could throw them open before stepping aside, allowing Wheels to walk in at her leisure. Wheels hesitated, feet firmly planted on the polished wooden floorboards. She had a history of tracking grease wherever she went and the thick, plush, white carpet would attract it like iron filings to a magnet. It looked so soft and inviting, glittering in certain angles depending on how the light hit it. Wheels bent down, running her hand over it, and sighed as she confirmed just how soft it felt. Sparsely placed, thin gold thread accounted for the glitter effect. Wheels couldn't resist, wanting to know, at least once, what it would feel like to walk on it. Toeing off her shoes, she looked over at Maxine, before lifting each foot in turn and tugging her socks off. Maxine's encouraging grin was enough to push her over the threshold.

"Holy shit!" Wheels breathed as she sank into the carpet. She'd never felt anything like it, and couldn't stop herself from curling her toes further into the pile.

"So you *can* speak," Maxine murmured, having maintained her position in fear of scaring Wheels off.

Wheels whipped her head to look at Max, her expression caged, until she flexed her foot on the carpet again. She couldn't suppress her grin at the luxuriously tactile sensations, and that was just with her feet.

"If you like the carpet, wait until you try the bed," Maxine encouraged.

Wheels walked further into the room, taking in the diffused light streaming through the sheer curtains, and how it hit the gold accents in the mostly white room. The curtains ran ceiling to floor along an entire wall, with the bed placed front and centre. It wasn't the swirling gold bedhead that caught her attention, rather the mountain of fluffy pillows, and a quilt that she was sure doubled as a cloud. Right in that moment she wanted nothing more than to take a running leap onto the bed, and see just how far into it she would sink.

"Go ahead," Max whispered from beside her. "Do it!"

And so she did! Twisting in the air so that she would land, spread eagled, on her back in the middle of the bed. She bounced and heard a giggle. A strange sensation in her chest had her paying attention, and she quickly slapped her hands over her mouth when she realised that the giggler was her. She couldn't remember the last time she'd giggled. She couldn't remember if she'd *ever* giggled. But, in that moment, she'd forgotten absolutely everything except for the exhilaration of flying, only to land in a cloud.

"It's okay," Max smiled down at her from beside the bed. "I did the exact same thing the first time I walked in here and saw the bed like this. Still do it every now and then." Maxine winked. "Don't tell Sai."

Wheels shook her head, realised that her hands were still over her mouth, and flung her arms out so that they too could bounce on the bed. She looked up at Max and solemnly promised, "I won't."

"May I?" Max asked, indicating the edge of the bed.

Wheels blinked, overwhelmed by the gesture. This was Maxine's bed, her house, her kingdom...queendom. She didn't have to ask anyone for anything here. But she had, and Wheels felt herself fighting the urge to cry over being given such consideration. Nodding, she scooted over a little so that Max could be comfortable. She still had to battle her inner demons when she felt the bed dip, resisting her body's instinctive reaction to tense and lash out. Maxine hadn't hurt her...so far. She'd been nothing but kind to her...so far. Wheels knew that there was no stopping that kernel of doubt, especially not after it had been proven right so many times in her life. Craning her neck, she looked around, enjoying the new perspective.

A golden chandelier hung from the centre of the ceiling, although calling it just a chandelier did not do it justice, it was a work of art; the golden swirls complemented the bed and highlighted other features throughout the room. Double doors adorned the wall that ran perpendicular to the wall of windows. The door frames were painted in the same shade of white as the rest of the room but it was the swirl design that made them stand out, and the fact that the doors themselves were mirrored. Wheels turned her questioning gaze to Maxine.

"My walk-in closet. Feel free to explore," Maxine's gesture encompassed the entire room.

Taking her up on the offer, Wheels forced herself to leave the bed-cloud, deciding it wasn't a hardship when her feet once again sank into the carpet. She noticed the dressing table as she padded over towards the doors, and took a detour to check it out. It held pride-of-place in the middle of the wall. She wasn't quite sure if it had been custom built to match the rest of the decor, or if Max had been lucky enough to find an antique to go with everything. Maybe the rest of the room had been decorated around this one magnificent piece. It was white, of course, with swirling gold details and three mirrors, two of which could be angled. Taking a closer look, Wheels appreciated the way small LEDs had been subtly and seamlessly incorporated into the mirror frames. The tufted seat was white velvet with shining golden buttons in the deep indentations, and felt soft and inviting when she ran her hand lightly over it. She touched one of the drawer handles, curious and tempted, but returned the respect that Maxine had shown by not invading her privacy.

Maxine, leaning back on one arm, watched Wheels from her bed. She watched as Wheels looked around, taking in everything, reaching out to experience the various textures that Max had in her room. She waited to see what Wheels would do when she rested her fingertips on the drawer handle, absolutely comfortable with sharing everything, a sentiment which took Max by surprise. Max was not a sharer; she'd worked too fucking hard for everything she had. She watched the woman move, a flowing economy of action, interrupted every now and then by a twitch, a twinge, like pain had caught her by surprise. Or maybe it wasn't pain, but the memory of it, the ongoing trauma of it. She couldn't do anything about the memory, but she had a bath that would soothe what ails ya. She should know, she used it often enough. Deciding that she wouldn't take no for an answer, Maxine headed in the opposite direction from Wheels, to an identical set of doors. The two women opened their respective doors at the same time and, whereas Max strolled through hers like she'd done a million times before, Wheels gasped in wonder, and froze at the threshold.

"Go on in," Max called out, sticking her head out of the doorway. "Have a look around, try some things on. When you're done, come on over and check out the bathroom."

Wheels started, turning to stare at the woman who had a closet bigger than Wheels's apartment. She blushed when Maxine chuckled, then squared her shoulders and stepped through, into a space that was bright and airy…and double storey! Wheels didn't know where to start. Was there any kind of order to this place? Gawking as she strolled through, she determined that the downstairs was all shoes, handbags, and accessories. *So* many shoes, handbags, and accessories! Stopping at a glass topped island counter, Wheels was admiring the collection of watches when something shiny caught her eye. Drawn to the wall of shoes, like the proverbial moth to the flame, Wheels reached for the shiniest ones. A pair of silver Louboutins that, in her mind, would always be chrome. Checking the bottom of her feet, thank goodness they were clean today, she tried on one of the shoes. It felt a little big so she checked the size on the other one, and sighed with disappointment. Looks like she won't be able to swap shoes with Maxine. Shrugging, she put the other one on anyway, it's not like she was going anywhere, except around the rest of this amazing collection.

Wheels toddled around, not having worn shoes that were too big for her in… she couldn't remember ever doing that. If she'd done it in her childhood, she'd been too young to remember, but she couldn't imagine that any of the foster homes she'd lived in had encouraged such frivolity. Shaking the memories firmly out of her head almost threw her off balance, and had her reaching for the nearest wall. Ah, handbags! What on earth goes with chrome shoes? A matching chrome clutch of course! Reaching up for it, Wheels took a moment to regain her footing before launching from the wall and towards the stairs. Stopping at the bottom, Wheels, contemplating the wisest course of action, reached down to take the shoes off. Holding them in one hand, with the clutch in the other, she jogged up the stairs, no longer noticing the pauses or hesitations when pain stabbed through one area of her body or another. Getting to the top, she took a couple extra steps before putting the shoes back on, it would suck big time to take a tumble backwards down those stairs.

Dresses, skirts, pants, pant suits, blouses, shirts, jackets, coats, blazers…not a single t-shirt. How could someone have all this and not a single t-shirt? Come to think of it, Wheels didn't remember seeing any jeans, or any denim of any kind. The clothes were sorted by type, and then by colour, which made looking for shiny silver ridiculously easy. Wheels ended up in front of the dresses, specifically a short cocktail dress, with so much sparkle that it would probably blind people in the right lighting. The thought made Wheels grin wickedly, and start to strip off her clothes. Maxine *had* said to try things on. She had to put the clutch down to take the dress off the hanger. She had no problem pulling down the hidden zipper at the back but, once the dress was on, her restricted shoulder movement meant that she could only pull it up a little, it's not like she was going anywhere. Oh! She had to find earrings. And a hat! And maybe a scarf? She retraced her steps, took the shoes off again, and made her way downstairs with definite purpose in her walk.

The watch counter had other drawers, maybe they were full of jewellery. Nope, watches, more watches, and yet more watches. Seriously, how many watches did a person need? A nice sparkly silver one would do for starters. Grabbing the sparkliest, Wheels didn't notice the brand, Rolex, the model, Pearlmaster, or that the whole thing was set with diamonds. Slipping it onto her wrist, she made a bee-line for where she remembered the scarves lived.

The tub was well on its way to filling, and Maxine was browsing through the various scents and minerals she kept on hand to add whenever the whim struck her. She'd already added generous helpings of epsom salts, and was leaning towards adding a few drops of lavender essential oil. She had a source who provided her with the pure, organic, stuff and she always kept about 5 of the varieties on hand. She'd tried several more, after all, there were quite a few varieties of lavender, but she'd managed to narrow them down to her favourite scents. She looked toward the door, thinking about Wheels, and what would help her best.

Deciding on a little bit of everything, she opened the five bottles, and added drop by painstaking drop, until she was satisfied with the aroma rising with the steam. Dipping her hand in the water, she swirled it around, enjoying the heat.

She turned off the water when the level was right, and fiddled with the control pad until she had the gentle jets going on low, the temperature set, and the lights slowly cycling from blue to violet and back. And still no Wheels. Curious, Maxine made her way over to the walk-in closet, stopping in the doorway so that she wouldn't surprise or disturb her guest. She couldn't help the fond smile that bloomed, as she watched Wheels strut and preen in front of the wall of mirrors. Yes, there was an area designed almost like a fashion show runway, how else was one supposed to check whether the ensemble chosen would have the desired effect? Based on what she was currently wearing, Wheels had an incredible eye, and expensive taste. Maxine looked her over with a discerning eye, and concluded that she was wearing roughly around half a million dollars in clothing and accessories. The shoes were too big, the dress's zipper undone, but Wheels still looked breathtaking.

Maxine slowly strolled closer, barely managing to hold back her gasp when Wheels turned away, exposing her scar-riddled back. She all but collapsed onto the nearest stool, the colour draining from her face as she thought about what could possibly have scarred Wheels like that; some of those scars were still an angry red. How deeply must they have gone? Had she been in an accident? No wonder pain was evident in nearly every move that she made. But an accident wouldn't account for the other scars, the mental ones, would it? Maxine wasn't naive, her line of work took care of that long ago, yet she shied away from one possible truth. Torture. The intensity and duration required to leave someone as scarred and damaged as Wheels was, was not something that Maxine wanted to acknowledge. The merely passing thought made her sick to her stomach. Wheels twirled back at the other end of the runway and, catching sight of Maxine in the mirror, froze like a deer in headlights.

Max cleared her throat but still had to speak around the lump that had formed, "The bath is ready, no rush though, it'll keep heated."

Wheels took a tentative couple of steps towards her.

"I tried some things on," she said, then froze again, as though saying anything was too much of an effort; or maybe, by the telling blush that was rising up her neck, she was berating herself for stating the obvious.

"I can see that," the barely restrained chuckle in Maxine's voice encouraged Wheels.

"The shoes are a bit big," Wheels said, teetering forward a couple more steps.

"Still, they are gorgeous, aren't they?"

Wheels vehemently nodded, reaching out to catch herself on the nearest counter, and surprising another giggle out of herself.

"I couldn't do the dress up," the admission was reluctantly defiant.

"I'm happy to help if you like," Maxine offered, not a hint of pity in her voice, or her eyes as she steadily met Wheels's gaze.

Wheels stared straight back, inwardly chiding herself for wanting to take Maxine at face value and believe in the friendship that she was offering. She knew, from very painful personal experience, that everyone will let you down eventually.

 Maxine's line of work made her very good at reading people, and Wheels wasn't trying to hide her scepticism. She'd have to invite Wheels to a game of poker sometime. Max's chin kicked up a notch in recognition of the challenge. She had very few people in her life that she would consider friends, and even fewer that she would trust. She had a well-deserved reputation for keeping her word, something she considered essential to her business. She'd never dealt with Wheels before, so she would forgive this virtual slap in the face, this time.

Wheel's stomach chose that moment to growl loud enough to draw both women's attention, effectively ending the stand-off. They'd watched, waiting for it to stop, then both looked up and simultaneously burst out laughing.

"How about you get in the bath and I'll chase up some food?" Max got up and headed for the phone on her bedside table, gesturing to the opposite door as she went.

Wheels reluctantly slipped off the shoes and left them, the clutch, the watch, the earrings, and the scarf, on the counter before gathering her clothes and heading to the ensuite. She shouldn't have been surprised really, not after the size and scope of the wardrobe, but the bathroom still took her breath away. The same decorating theme flowed through the space, calling it merely a room would be a gross injustice. Clean white lines with gold accents, and a bath that seemed big enough to be a pool. Wheels dumped her clothes on the floor by the door before slipping the dress off her shoulders and stepping out of it, draping it carefully on one of the many available seats.

She climbed up the step, sat on the edge of the tub, tested the temperature, then swung her legs into the gloriously warm water. She felt about with her feet, getting the layout of the bath as the swirling water made visibility difficult. She chose one of the two headrests and heaved a heavy sigh as she settled into the beautifully scented haven.

One of the perks of being Maxine was having the funds to do whatever the fuck she wanted, and one of the things that she'd always wanted was a dumb waiter. So, she'd had one put in when the place was being built, along with a couple of other fun surprises. As Wheels was making herself comfortable in the bathroom, Maxine sent a text down to the kitchen, and fetched a serving trolley from a discrete cupboard in her walk-in wardrobe. She'd had the whole evening planned, right down to the servingware she wanted used. It was a shame that Guns wasn't going to be benefitting from her attention to detail, but she didn't at all feel as though it were a waste to be spending the time with Wheels instead.

The text read, simply, "Now" and started a chain reaction downstairs, with Chef placing a pre-prepared antipasto tray in the dumb waiter, as well as a selection of glasses and the beverages to go with them. As soon as that was on its way, Chef continued preparations on the twelve course degustation. It was a meal designed to delight the senses and, if all went well, pique appetites. The muted tinkling of a vintage shopkeeper's doorbell let Max know that the nibbles had arrived. Loading her cart and arranging everything *just so*, Maxine wheeled it into the bathroom.

"Do you prefer red or white?" asked Max, stopping the cart by the bath, and presenting it with a flourish.

It took Wheels a moment to realise that Max had been speaking to her, and it took her even longer to summon the will to crack open one of her eyelids. That wasn't enough though, she was going to have to, at the very least, move her head to see what on earth Maxine was talking about. Wheels was feeling more relaxed than she had felt in months, and the motivation to expend any effort at that moment was sorely lacking, but this was Max. Max, who had been nothing but nice and generous to her since the moment they'd met, who had opened up her home and shared her wardrobe, and who had a bath that they would have to drag her out of kicking and screaming. So yeah, giving Max a little of her attention was the least she could do.

Doing her best to keep her sigh on the inside, Wheels sat up, braced her forearms on the edge of the bath, and placed her chin on them. Looking up at Max, she note the outstretched glasses of wine. One white. One red. Moving as little as possible, which meant peering down her nose at the trolley, Wheels saw the beautifully laid out platter, and suddenly found the energy she'd been lacking. Cured meats, a selection of cheese, dips, crackers, olives and fruit, had her salivating.

"Definitely red please," Wheels swallowed, reaching out for the glass of red.

"Cheers," Max held out the glass of white expectantly, smiling when Wheels obliged. Taking a sip, Max then brought the trolley right up to the edge of the bath and parked it. "Help yourself."

One of the hardest things that Wheels had ever done was not grab the whole platter, retreat to a corner of the bath, and growl if anyone came near her and her treasure. Instead, as dainty as you please, she smeared some hummus onto a cracker, added some perfectly aged cheese, topped it with a sliver of prosciutto, and garnished it with a kalamata olive. Taking the smallest nibble from the edge of the cracker confirmed her worst fear; it was light, buttery, and would crack into pieces the moment she took a bite. She could feel Maxine watching her, waiting for her to decide whether to get crumbs in the bath, or stuff the whole thing in her mouth. Sneaking a look, Wheels saw Max looking amused, in a completely non-judgemental way. That gave her the confidence to throw caution to the wind, stuff the whole delicacy into her mouth, pick up her glass from where she'd put it down so that she could free up her hands, and reluctantly return to the seat and headrest she'd been using.

"Mind if I join you?" asked Maxine, stifling a companionable chuckle. She waited for Wheels to think through what that would mean, but was surprised by her immediate response.

"It's your house," shrugged Wheels, gesturing with her wineglass, then realising that might not be a wise move as the wine threatened to slosh over the side. She brought the glass to her lips and averted her eyes as Maxine disrobed, and climbed gracefully into the bath.

Max leaned over and prepared another cracker, handing it to Wheels before making one for herself. Taking the remaining seat and headrest, Max raised her glass to Wheels, then stuffed the cracker into her mouth, just as Wheels had done. Wheels grinned, ate her second cracker, and got back to the important business of relaxing. The bubbling jets helped, more than she would voluntarily admit out loud, but there was no stopping the whirlwind of thoughts racing around her mind.

"What about Guns?" she blurted, keeping her eyes shut, trying to maintain an air of nonchalance.

"What about Guns?" Maxine returned, puzzled.

Wheels cracked open one eye, raising an eyebrow in response.

"Ah," Max smiled. "I find that delayed gratification makes one appreciate things, value things, far more than if one had immediate gratification. Don't you agree?"

Wheels hummed, then shrugged, non-committal.

"Oh darling," laughed Max, "I didn't mean for us! Does it look like I am kept waiting for anything?"

The women clinked glasses, sipped, and spent a good while indulging in the feast that Maxine provided.

The Estate₅₄

Rowan, standing by the bread maker and hopping from foot to foot, was on his second cup of coffee. He'd been watching the timer for the last 10 minutes, and there were only a couple minutes left to go. Did that give him enough time for a quick bathroom break? He wanted the bread to be toasty warm so that the butter that he'd pulled out of the cupboard would melt all over and into it. The fresh-baked bread smell was driving him crazy. He couldn't wait any longer though. Putting his mug down with more force than he intended, Rowan shushed it before walking, double-time, to the nearest bathroom. He left the door cracked open just so that he could hear the when the bread maker beeped it's finish. *And there it goes.* He wasn't done, dammit!. Seriously, how much coffee had he had to drink? Still, there was always such a sense of relief when emptying a full bladder, and he took a moment to sigh and enjoy the feeling.

Rowan looked around while washing his hands, appreciating how Ellie and Jerry had included the best of everything whilst still making the place feel like a home. He'd visited places where he'd felt completely uncomfortable because the venues had been decked out like show houses, or museums, with a definite aura of *look but don't touch*. There were some of the same fixtures and fittings in this home, the same small touches of luxury everywhere, and yet he'd felt nothing but welcomed since the moment he'd set foot outside the car. Perhaps it had more to do with the residents, and less to do with the setting. Still, it was nice to have high-end liquid soap and the softest, fluffiest, and thirstiest, hand towel he'd ever used. Also nice to have piping hot bread waiting for him.

It took him a moment, and only one slightly singed finger, to work out how to get the pan out of the machine. He'd had every intention of letting the bread cool a little before tipping it out, and cutting it up. Really. Rowan's belly let out a loud grumble at the tantalising scent of fresh baked bread, and broke his resolve. Ellie, bless her heart, had left a chopping board and bread knife out ready for the morning. There were only a couple of hisses and maybe some muttered swear words as Rowan handled the hot bread. Yes, he could have hunted down a pair of tongs or a pot holder, but where's the fun in that? Finding the cutlery drawer, he scrabbled around for a butter knife, brandishing it aloft when he was successful. Scraping a healthy dose of the home-made salted butter onto his knife, he fondly remembered Robin Williams's advice...*Men smear.*

* * *

"What do you want me to do?" Neil asked, having decided to apply the age-old adage, *blood is thicker than water.* Except, he was inorganic, and definitely lacking any blood. He could still apply it in principle, taking the meaning that family trumps friends. Not that he liked that either, hence the question. He would ponder Sheila's response, and decide whether or not to comply.

"Where is Ash right now?"

"I'm leading him to the other end of the basement," Neil hesitated, "I was trying to keep the two of you apart, while I showed him the way out."

"Can you give me some time, and then lead him towards the main stairs? I want to introduce myself and see what he does, but I'd like to freshen up a bit first. I want to keep him in the basement until I can make sure that he's harmless and not, in any way, a danger to the guys upstairs."

"Sure thing, of course!" Neil was relieved that Sheila didn't seem to be the type to shoot first and ask questions later. "Oh, he's armed."

"Armed? With what?"

"All I can see is a crossbow, but that doesn't mean that he's not carrying anything else."

"Thanks for the heads-up Neil." Sheila smiled, smirked, then winked, "I'm faster than a crossbow."

* * *

Ash was feeling more and more like himself, and less like he'd been blindsided by a two-by-four, the further he walked. Neil was true to his word and was laying out a trail of blinking LEDs, occasionally mentioning a point of interest; like the window that Marcus had broken one night when they'd been playing soccer out on the back lawn. He'd been in the country long enough to get that soccer was what the rest of the world called football. Ash mentally kicked himself, he really needed to get his head in the game. The vampire could be anywhere and, based on almost every class he'd ever taken at the company, he wouldn't stand a chance if they came face to face. Pulling out his crossbow, Ash went back to basics, scanning up, down, and side to side, as he went. His finger barely touching the trigger, ready to shoot first and ask questions later.

Would he shoot Rowan's blood-sucking girlfriend? *Could* he shoot Rowan's blood-sucking girlfriend. *Fuck yeah!* In a heartbeat. Even if it meant that Rowan would never forgive him, and hate him for the rest of his life. This is what he had trained most of his life for, and he'd do his damndest to save Rowan, no matter the cost. The personal cost. To himself. Physically, he could well die in the attempt. Emotionally, he'd already lost his head over Rowan, likely his heart too, so knowing that he was on the path to destroying whatever friendship they had, already hurt. He stopped and pressed his fist against his middle; that spot that feels so hollow when you suffer an emotional wound. It already felt like that, and he hadn't done anything yet. How was he going to feel when the vampire was dust on the wind, and Rowan was looking at him with nothing but betrayal and pain in his eyes?

"Fuck," Ash spat, lowering the crossbow. Could he live with himself if he scarred Rowan like that? Of all the moments to think of his mother; she'd never gotten over the loss of his father. Deep down he'd always known that the "overprotectedness", and the high standards to which she'd insisted he train, all stemmed from her inability to cope with his father's death. She'd loved him so much that she was petrified of anything happening to Ash, who was her last link to him. His nanny had told him what his mother had been like when his father was still alive, but he'd never been able to reconcile the carefree, mischievous, and fun-loving images, with his mother as he knew her. How would he be able to deal with hurting Rowan, damaging him so badly, that the person he was now ceased to exist? He couldn't. Every which way he looked at it, even with every instinct, honed through every hour of training that he'd suffered, endured and, eventually, excelled at, he knew that Rowan's happiness meant more. He had to get out of here.

More alert than he'd been for hours, Ash resumed his tour, picking up the pace, and forcing Neil to blink those little L.E.Ds a shitload quicker. They'd been heading towards what Ash presumed was the way out, when Neil suddenly changed their direction.

"Hey Neil, what's going on buddy? Where you leading me?"

"I thought I'd show you the lab. Marcus had spent many a night there, tinkering and creating. Jerry sometimes comes down now too. They'd been working on nanites at one point, but Jerry seems to have hit a dead end since Marcus perished," Neil prattled, not wanting to give Ash the opportunity to interrupt, and insist that they resume their original heading.

Poppy & Doug[55]

oug didn't hesitate when Poppy asked him to pull into the driveway that led to a bunch of units, he just drove slowly enough so that his wife could tune in, and get a better understanding of where they needed to be.

"Stop!" Poppy gasped, pointing towards one particular unit. "There. That one. Rowan was there."

Doug parked, looked over at Poppy, and got out of the car. Poppy barely noticed, she was fixated on the unit's front door. She jumped when Doug's knuckles rapped out a quick staccato beat against the solid timber frame, her heart rate picking up even though she could feel that there was no one there, no one who would be answering the door. No Rowan. No Maggie. No one. Doug cupped his hands against the front window and peered through the small crack in the curtains. He tried knocking again, against the door itself this time.

"Couldn't see much through the window," Doug said as he got back into the car. He turned towards Poppy, "What do you want to do, Love?"

"I need some time. I can't see anything beyond this place right now. Any chance you can get us inside, Hun?" Poppy didn't miss the little twinkle that entered Doug's eyes at the thought of a good, old-fashioned, break-and-enter.

"I'll be back," grinned Doug, getting back out of the car, clapping his hands together, and giving them a vigorous rub.

Poppy watched as her husband first went back to the front door and tried the handle. Shrugging when that didn't work, he walked around the side of the building and disappeared from view. She had no doubt that Doug would find a way into the unit, he seemed to have a knack for it. Poppy knew that, as a child, Doug would often walk home from school, and have to find a way inside. His childhood home had been in a quiet cul-de-sac, and the doors were usually left unlocked. Occasionally though, the last person to leave would forget, and lock the place up. Doug didn't have keys, he'd have lost them had he been given any, so his parents saved everyone the trouble, and didn't bother with them. There had always been a window left open, and Doug had been small enough to even fit through the little window over the toilet. From what he'd told her, he'd only had to resort to climbing on the roof, moving some roof tiles, and getting in through the manhole in the ceiling, once. So Poppy was not in the least surprised when the door opened inward, and her husband stepped out.

"Kitchen window was left open, not by much, but enough to fit my fingers in and slide it open all the way," Doug boasted quietly as he handed Poppy out of the car. "I think I'm getting a bit old for this, you should have heard me climbing through, if it wasn't my joints cracking and popping, it was me groaning."

Poppy gave him a quick hug and a peck on the cheek, before hurrying past him, and through the front door. She went, unerringly, to the bedroom that her son had used, stopping in the doorway, closing her eyes, and breathing in as deeply as she could. Hoping to catch her baby's lingering scent. She felt herself slow and calm down, her breath going deeper into her lungs, her brain quieting. A smile was blooming on her lips before her thoughts caught up, and she couldn't suppress her giggles.

"What's funny?" asked Doug, coming to stand behind her, and wrapping his arms around her waist.

"Well, I guess, when I asked you to get us inside, you could have just gone and asked someone for a key, or rented out the unit."

"Where's the fun in that?" whispered Doug, nuzzling the tantalising column of his wife's neck.

"Seriously though, Doug, I might need a while here, and someone's eventually going to notice."

"Alright Love, I'll go sort it out." Doug nipped Poppy's earlobe, kissed it, squeezed her to him a little tighter, then headed out to see if he could find someone in charge.

Sitting on the edge of the bed, Poppy ran her hand over the covers, letting all her senses *see* for her. Rowan had definitely been there, had slept there, had…oh! Rowan hadn't been alone.

Maxine's[56]

uns was on his second glass of cognac, the stuff was *smooth*. He'd told himself that he didn't give a fuck if Maxine ever came downstairs again, and had himself almost convinced that he believed that by the time he was halfway through his first glass. He was pretty sure that he'd convinced Sai too, he'd told the guy a couple times, and he seemed to believe him. Sai was a really nice guy, very polite, maybe a bit uptight. Then again, Guns knew all about being uptight.

"I haven't been any other way since the thing with Wheels," Guns thought.

"What way?" asked Sai.

"Huh," mused Guns, "Did I say that out loud?"

"You did."

"What? What did I do?"

"You said that you haven't been any other way since the thing with Wheels," Sai sipped at his cognac, humouring Guns, and knowing that the poor guy was going to have one helluva hangover the next morning.

"Well, I haven't!" Guns threw his left arm out forcefully with the intention of convincing Sai of his earnestness by pointing at him. What he hadn't planned for was to do it quite so forcefully, and cause his head, which had been resting on his right hand with that elbow planted firmly on the table, to fall off his hand. He managed to stop himself before banging his head against the table, so that was something, but the fork that he'd been gesturing with went flying out of his hand, prongs first, straight for Sai's face. "Shit! I'm sorry man!"

Sai plucked the fork out of the air like he had all the time in the world, placing it gently on the table. "To what way were you referring when you made your statement, my friend?"

"Huh?" asked Guns, deciding that sitting back in his chair might be a safer option.

"What way have you been since the thing with Wheels?" Rather than becoming irritated, Sai found himself amused. In any case, there wasn't much else that he had to do this evening, so he may as well get his entertainment here and now.

"Oh, that… uptight. Kinda like you."

Sai raised an eyebrow. He'd been called many things in his life but, to the best of his knowledge, no one had ever called him uptight. At least not to his face. And definitely not since he'd been with Max.

"I mean, I get it man. I have Wheels, who used to be my best friend, and now just lives for busting my balls. You have Maxine. You gotta keep her alive and happy. Believe me, man, I know how high maintenance that one is. When we get our time together…wowee…she is so demanding! Don't get me wrong, totally worth it. I go back to my life more drained and relaxed than ever before. I was really, really, looking forward to that. I need it. Ya know?"

Sai was not usually at a loss for words. He often chose to keep his words, his opinions, to himself because, quite frankly, he never really felt like educating the arseholes of the world. But Guns, and what he'd just revealed… Sai kept starting sentences in his head ,but wasn't getting much further than "Ummm" or "Ah, I see". Except, he didn't, not really. He owed Maxine his life, several times over, and she owed him hers. They weren't so much employee-employer as platonic soul mates. Maxine's standards did not, in the least, seem high maintenance to Sai, because he shared most of the same standards. She was one of the few people he'd ever met that did not make demands of him. Sure, she'd request or ask, but always with the understanding that he had every right to refuse. And sometimes he had.

They often disagreed, but they both knew that didn't mean that they stopped liking or respecting each other. On the contrary, their disagreements, even the ones where there was shouting or throwing things (usually Maxine grabbing whatever was nearest at hand to throw at his head, hence his excellent reflexes) only served to enhance their understanding of, and respect for, each other. They had definitive business roles, Maxine was the Boss and he was the Bodyguard, which sometimes meant that she'd issue orders in public. They'd developed a shorthand of subtle looks and gestures for when he thought that something was unreasonable or dangerous and, more often than not, Maxine heeded his concerns.

So, while Sai may make allowances for Guns being under the influence of some really terrific cognac, they seemed to have reached a point of TMI. Sai respected Maxine's privacy, and spent much of his time guarding it. Besides, hearing about anything that Maxine did behind closed doors, was like listening to his brother in law talk about banging his sister. It made Sai's brain fritz out, and the kicker was that Guns was not going to remember the conversation in a few hours, while Sai was never going to be able to forget it.

The Estate*57*

Speeding upstairs, Sheila, barely registering that Rowan was no longer in their room, grabbed her bag and was back in the basement before the pivot door had finished swinging shut. She'd been dying to try out the downstairs bathroom ever since she and Rowan had toured the basement, so she was determined to make the most of it. Maybe she should have specified just how much time she wanted Neil to give her, for all she knew Ash was on the way over right now. Still, Neil could multi-task.

"Neil?"

"Yes, Sheila?"

"How long before you guide Ash in this direction?"

"Five point four three seven five minutes, unless you want me to delay him for longer?"

"If you don't mind? Could you start herding him this way when I get back out of the bathroom please?"

"Roger that!"

Sheila did a double take at Neil's perky tone, shaking her head on a chuckle as she stepped into her haven of the next thirty minutes. Oh, who was she kidding, she'd take an hour… at least!

She liked the water hot, just like her man. Sheila chuckled at the thought as the water rained down from one of the shower heads. It had taken her a couple minutes to figure out how to work the thing! Pretty much every shower head option had been catered for, from the fixed and pulsing, to the rain shower, to the handheld. She'd opted for the rain shower, wanting the sensation of being surrounded by falling water. Speaking of, there was a waterfall option too, but she'd leave that for another day. Out of everything, the huge bath hewn out of one single boulder - how on earth did they get that down here; oh wait, vampire strength! - the multiple shower heads, and the toilet that had a mosaic design so well done that it blended perfectly with the rest of the bathroom, the one thing that impressed Sheila the most was the exhaust system. She was generating a significant amount of steam but could still see herself clearly in the mirrored wall across the room.

Yes, vampire sight might help a little, but it still couldn't cut through what would otherwise have been thick layers of condensation, both on the shower screen and the mirror. She'd have to make a point of having sex with Rowan in this bathroom, probably in the bath, and then in the shower. Maybe even on the vanity. Definitely *not* on the toilet. She briefly wondered where her lover had gone, but the Estate was large and rambling, so he could have been anywhere. She stepped more fully under the stream, closing her eyes, and letting the water wash away her thoughts, relaxing her. She hoped that if she was relaxed enough, she wouldn't kill Ash… accidentally… or on purpose.

She felt the tingle at the base of her skull, on the back of her neck, and in the goosebumps that broke out down her arms. Even under the ground, and under the water, she could feel it when the sun was threatening to dawn.

*   *   *

Maggie groaned.

She was desperately clinging to sleep, having managed to masturbate herself to enough of a relaxed state that she'd, finally, drifted off. That felt like about five minutes ago. She knew it was longer, maybe six minutes, but the approaching dawn may as well have been a blaring kalxon. She'd lived with a vampire for so long that she'd developed a sense of urgency as sunrise got closer. She remembered a few times when Marcus had cut it too close, and her apprehension had ratcheted up every second it took to get him inside, and away from sunlight. She was sleep-deprived, not a morning person, and still stewing on what to tell Rowan, or Ellie, or

Jerry…or Sheila. Today was not going to be a happy Maggie day. Today was going to be a Maggie-the-grouch kind of day, and Rowan would know it as soon as they ran into each other.

She groaned again as she rolled over, doing her best to snuggle under the covers, and pretend that the night was going to last for another six hours. Her brain was awake. She tried shushing it, quietly, but it paid her little attention. Thoughts were flitting around in there, everything from whether to have a shower or breakfast first, to what words she should use when she saw Rowan next. What should she wear today? Would she get away with not saying anything if she was in a bad enough mood? 'Cause that could be arranged, she was already at least half way there! What was for breakfast? She really should do some sort of exercise this morning…today…at some point. Had she packed work-out type shoes? What about work-out type clothes? There was a gym room, and the pool. It was too cold to swim. There was always the indoor pool. Oh, maybe she could jump in the spa. Was that really a work-out though?

"Oh for the love of all that's holy, shut the fuck up!" Maggie pulled the pillow from Marcus's side and held it tightly over her head. Of course it didn't help! The noise was coming from inside her skull. The pillow was cool though, literally, and only served to wake her up a little more.

"Fine! Is this what you want?" demanded Maggie, throwing back the covers. "Is this what you want, huh?"

Apparently so, because the very act of getting out of bed seemed to leave the chaos of her thoughts behind. She grumbled all the way to the bathroom, stripping as she went, and flicking on the hot water on her way to the laundry basket. She grabbed her shower cap on the way back, her movements vicious as she stuffed her unruly hair into the cap. She almost slammed the shower door but stopped herself in time and gently pulled the glass behind her. She couldn't help the sigh that escaped as she stepped under the stream, maybe it wouldn't be a terrible day after all.

*   *   *

Rowan finished his breakfast, put his dishes in the dishwasher, and cleaned the counter top, taking a moment to enjoy the view from the kitchen window as he shook out the dishcloth into the sink. It was lighter outside than it had been when he'd first come downstairs, and he could make out more detail, like the biscuit jar on the edge of the pool. *Huh*. Had that been there yesterday? Was it an outdoor biscuit jar? Who on earth would keep their biscuits, in a jar, by the pool? He didn't think that any of the humans would have left it out there on purpose, so he wondered if Sheila had been experimenting. Still, not the place to leave the biscuits and, seeing as Sheila was his, he supposed that he should tidy up after her. He grinned as he made his way to the back door, realising that he didn't feel put out or like this was someone else's chore that he had to do because they didn't. He felt privileged that he had the opportunity to help Sheila out, even if she'd completely forgotten about the jar and would never realise that he'd done this small thing for her. His grin lasted until he opened the door and stepped outside, then it was a case of the teeth chatters, and the quick jog to the pool edge and back.

"Who the fuck turned up the air con outside?" he muttered, his breath puffing out visibly as he fumbled for the door handle. Slipping inside and snicking the door shut behind him, Rowan did a full body tremble-and-shake as he re-entered the pleasantly warm indoor temperature. "Bless you Neil for keeping the inside civilised! Way to lull me into a false sense of security though buddy."

There was no response, then Rowan remembered that Ellie hadn't yet restored Neil's upstairs speaking privileges. He'd make a point to thank Neil later, in the meantime, where did one usually keep a jar of biscuits? The pantry? A cupboard? Out on display? He placed the jar near the coffee maker, and figured he'd double-check with Ellie or Jerry when they got up. What to do now? He had the whole house to himself, presuming that everyone else was sound asleep. Except maybe Sheila. She'd still be up, but would be heading for bed soon. Maybe he'd go and see if he could get her to ease up on her determination to let him rest, and they could go and have sex in the shower. Or the bed. Or sneakily in the media room. Definitely *not* in the pool though. He'd probably give a new definition to the term shrinkage if they took a dip in *that* ice bucket right now. Hell, his penis would more than likely just fall right off! He needed a jacket, just the thought of being in the pool had him feeling cold again.

His plan to run up and grab one was derailed on his way to the stairs when he caught sight of the library doors. He figured that he'd never have enough time to read every single book in there but, if he was ever going to try, he might as well start now. Rowan left the double doors wide open as he entered the library, figuring that he'd then be able to hear anyone coming down the front stairs. Sheila's pile of books was still neatly stacked on the coffee table so he made himself comfortable on the reading couch, and pulled them closer to the edge of the table so he could check out what she'd selected.

Well, his woman sure had eclectic taste. *Meditations* by Marcus Aurelius, *Furniture Repair and Restoration*, *Alice's Adventures in Wonderland*, *The Three Musketeers*, and a selection of novels by Ward, Briggs, Hamilton, & Cole. He pulled out one of the novels, realised it was the first in a series, checked the others, and confirmed that they too were first-in-a-series books. Leaning back, figuring he may as well start with the one in his hand, Rowan carefully opened the front cover, taking the time to read the blurb and dedication, before starting on the story itself.

He was a few chapters in and thoroughly engrossed, which is why it took a while for the footsteps on the stairs to register. Keeping a finger at his page, Rowan got up and padded to the library door. Leaning against the jamb, he waited until his Aunt Maggie had made it all the way to the bottom so as not to startle her into a fall. He watched her fondly as she took her own sweet time, a secret smile on her lips made him wonder what memories were surfacing. It couldn't be easy for her to be here without Marcus. She paused, wincing a little, rubbing at her hip with the heel of her hand before moving again. It hit Rowan in that moment, the fact that Mags was getting older and that, if the natural order of things went uninterrupted, he wouldn't, couldn't, have her in his life forever. He left his post then, walking to the base of the staircase so that he could meet her, and offer her his arm. Who knew how many more chances he'd have to do that?

"Oh! Hey kiddo," Maggie's face lit up as Rowan walked into her line of sight. "You're up early."

"Yeah. It always takes me a night or two to get used to a strange bed."

"I hear ya. I'd forgotten that I used to like a firmer mattress. Might have to talk to Jerry and Ellie about swapping the one in my room for a softer one. My bones have gotten older and prefer a little more give."

"There's fresh bread in the kitchen. May I walk you there?"

"Really? You left some of Ellie's fresh bread for the rest of us? You're a better person than I am!" Maggie chuckled, linking her arm through Rowan's proffered one.

Jacqueline & Gaberiel[58]

He was a morning person. And a night owl. And an I'll-sleep-when-I'm-dead kind of person. As a kid, and then a teenager, he'd loved his sleep. He'd sleep so deeply that his mum would have to resort to dragging the covers off him, and opening the curtains to let in the morning sun. If she forgot to snag his pillow, he'd just burrow his head under it, and keep snoozing. She didn't often forget the pillow. His sleeping habits got a serious overhaul when he entered the armed forces, and had only gotten worse since he'd left. Too many memories, too much loss, for him to sleep that deeply any more.

He never thought that he'd be thankful for the insomnia. He was today. He'd started awake, like every other morning, long before dawn, and had been ready to do his usual roll out of bed to the floor and into pushups. Then he remembered, and lay absolutely still. The soft puffs of breath as Jaqui slept made him smile. She'd turned onto her side in her sleep, hands curled up under her chin.

He was thankful for the night light that he always kept on, too. The streetlights used to seep through the blinds and curtains that he'd had, which had been enough. Then the print shop across the road had invested in a flashing neon sign, not so great for someone who had enough trouble sleeping as it was. So he'd had some custom, block-out, roller blinds installed, the kind that had a full frame around the window so they blocked out *all* light. Those mofo's were super effective, the darkness in his apartment was absolute. Great, if that's what you were going for, not so great the first time he woke from a nightmare and couldn't even see his hand in front of his face. He'd thought he'd gone blind, partly because he'd been dreaming that one of his dead buddies had been chasing him, begging to know why he didn't see what was going on and then, when he'd been caught, his zombie buddy had gouged his eyes out. Good times. Hence the nightlight.

Today, that muted glow was enough for him to make out Jacqui's face, of course the fact that he was almost nose-to-nose with her helped. He wanted so badly to reach out and touch her, run his hands over her soft skin, skimming her arm, shoulder, back. He really, really, wanted to cup her arse, then slide his hand along her thigh to the back of her knee, just so he could lift her leg up onto his hip. He wanted to watch as she slowly came awake, smiling just for him, before opening her eyes. That's what he wanted, he was also thankful that he was smart enough to realise that was probably not what would happen. Jacqui would probably be startled, and he didn't feel like starting the day with a knee to his balls, and a left hook to his head. So, as he watched her sleep, studying her face so the he'd never forget her, he shared breath with her, mirroring her pose.

Her steady breathing in the otherwise silent room helped him quiet his mind; the usual rush of mental list-making toned down to one thing, watching Jacqui. The rhythm served to narrow his focus, letting him take in the individual parts that made up the incredible woman lying in his bed. He sent an emphatic thank you out into the universe, not just for bringing Jacqui into his life, but for allowing him the honour to see her like this, relaxed, guileless. From everything they'd spoken about, he knew that the last person that would have had this privilege was Ash's father.

Her lips were soft, the wicked smile that she'd bestowed on him mere hours ago, now only hinted at in the shallow smile lines bracketing her mouth. Here eyes were closed, lashes at rest, but he could clearly picture the way she'd seen right into him, right through him, and wouldn't take any of his crap. There was the barest hint of a permanent furrow between her brows, making him wonder just how much time she spent worrying. Being a single parent couldn't have been easy but, knowing how Ash had turned out, she'd done an incredible job. Still, he supposed that a parent worried about their child whether there was actually anything to worry about or not.

His thoughts froze for a moment until he could bring himself to examine where they'd been heading. Had he added to her worry last night? *Jackass!* Of course he had, he'd been a whirlwind of emotions, but she'd handled everything with such class. She'd been right; there were some battles that required help, just like there'd been missions that required a whole team. If the team was unbalanced then the likelihood of fucking up the mission increased. His balance had been off for too long, and he wanted to get it back. He'd find someone, a shrink or a counsellor or something, as soon as he could. He probably wouldn't be able to get an appointment until after his job interview, but even just deciding to reach out had his shoulders relaxing a fraction. *Jesus, was he really that wound up?*

Alpha Team~59~

Gina hadn't slapped him. She'd taken the panties and swung them from her index finger, giving him a look that said that she was contemplating whether to put them on, or toss them on the couch and go commando.

"Don't make me have to kill someone," the CO growled, his gaze heating at the thought of his woman flashing some poor, otherwise-innocent-but-soon-to-be-fishbait, soul.

Gina's eyes widened; her lover's skill set meant that she couldn't be absolutely certain that his threat wasn't serious. Wanting to make sure that there was no misunderstanding, she stepped into the panties, slid them up her legs, and under her dress, a final wiggle getting them into place. She put her laptop into her cross-body bag, and was about to shrug that over her head when the CO held his hand out for it. She handed it over, thankful for the offer to carry it for her, but he had other ideas. She followed him into the bedroom.

"Oh, no. I can't leave that here."

"It'll be in the safe."

"Yeah, but still. There's classified data on there. There are proprietary files on there. I'll be fine carrying it."

"Is it encrypted?"

"Of course."

"Can it be hacked?"

"With my personally designed security? Not bloody likely! Actually, that's not entirely true, but it would take a very long time, require tons of computing power, and someone who is, at least, borderline genius."

"Do you have a backup?"

Gina wouldn't even dignify that with a response.

"Then we can leave it here."

"No, really."

"Yes, really." And when she was still looking at him skeptically, he relented with an explanation, "I want one night where it's just you and me. No work. No mission. No fate of the world stuff. Just you. Me. And the magnificence of this city. Followed by me, and the magnificence that is you."

"Oh, well…when you put it that way," Gina smiled impishly as she turned and headed for the door. This didn't mean that she wouldn't feel anxious being separated from her hardware, but she planned on making the most of this rare opportunity.

Beta Team[60]

Word had come down the line, and Beta Team were ready. That's what the Chief said, so that's what the team believed. She had no doubt that her guys were the best of the best, and she'd happily pit them against any human squad on the planet, with the absolute confidence that they would be victorious. But they weren't going up against a human adversary. Everyone, from the grunts to the top brass, had seen the footage and photos from the last massacre. Hell, Alpha Team's CO had lived through it.

As soon as he'd been fit enough, the Company had sent him out to brief their team in person. Chief would never forget the moment that he'd said he could prove everything he'd told them, and then he'd taken off his shirt. The scars were still so new, so angry, that she'd been unable to hold back her gasp. It hadn't been his scars that scared her though, it had been the look in his eyes. He'd survived something that would have killed most people but, when their eyes met, she could see that he'd wished he hadn't.

Their teams had been assigned joint-missions a few times over the years and she'd looked, hoping for a change, but mostly to be sure that he wasn't going to kamikaze on her watch. Time had muted what she'd seen, and he'd never given in to whatever demons he'd dragged back with him from the brink of hell. But muting and curing were not the same thing. Time does not always heal all wounds, at least it hadn't for the CO.

So, when she said that her team were ready, she meant it, but she couldn't help wondering if anyone could be ready for what they might have to face.

The Estate[61]

Ash hadn't thought twice when Neil gave him access to the lab, walking through the first door and closing it behind him so that he'd be able to get through the airlock's second door. He felt like he'd hit the jackpot, using his phone to take video and pictures of everything he found. Neil was a wealth of information, helpfully going into great detail whenever Ash had a question. Not that he understood half of what Neil tried to explain, science was not his forte.

It never occurred to him that Neil could lock the doors, holding Ash there for as long as he wanted to. It never occurred to him that Neil could suck all the oxygen out of the room, or flood it with one of several gases that would render Ash dead. It never occurred to him that, in that moment, his life was totally and utterly in the hands of an AI. It occurred to Neil though. He was gleefully, quietly, congratulating himself on finding such a perfect way to delay Ash and, if Ash decided that they'd delayed for long enough but Sheila wasn't ready, Neil just wouldn't unlock the doors.

"What's this?" asked Ash, picking up a vial that looked like it was filled with glitter and giving it a little shake.

"Nanites."

"Nan-what?" Ash peered close at the contents, holding the vial up to the light and trying to make out one individual piece.

"Nanites," repeated Neil, "a microscopically small machine or robot. You would need to put a sample under the microscope to see the detail."

"Can I do that?" Ash levelled a dubious look from the vial to the microscope.

"Sure, they're inert right now so you can pretty much do anything with them."

"Cool! How do we do this?"

"You can get a slide from the drawer under the microscope."

"This one?" Ash pulled on the drawer handle, easing up on the power he was putting into it when he realised that it was gliding effortlessly open. He put the vial down on the stainless steel bench, so he could free both hands to rummage around. No rummaging needed really, the drawer was tidy and well organised. He flipped the latches and opened the lid to the box neatly labelled *slides*. He found an empty one, took it out, and returned everything to how he'd found it.

"Great! You probably should suit up," Neil mentioned, remembering that Marcus and Jerry would always wear safety equipment when in the lab.

"Huh?"

Neil directed Ash around the lab, sourcing a set of safety glasses here, a mask there, and a pair of latex gloves.

"Is all this really necessary?"

"Better safe than sorry," responded Neil and, having no argument against that, Ash "suited up".

Picking up the vial, Ash felt his heart rate kick up a notch. It's not like he was about to unleash a world ending virus or anything, but this was still outside his comfort zone. Taking a steadying breath, he slowly, and carefully, unscrewed the lid. With the way he placed the lid so cautiously on the counter top, anyone would have thought that he was handling nitroglycerin! *See, he knew science.* Realising how ridiculous he was being, Ash mentally shook off his caution, grabbed the slide, and prepared to tilt the vial, thus spilling some of the contents onto said slide - seemed the easiest way to do this.

"Ummm," Neil interjected, causing Ash to completely freeze.

"Ummm what?" Ash asked, unable to disguise the note of panic in his voice. "What "Ummm"?"

"You might want to use the spatula, the one with the micro spoon. It will make less of a mess. But I wouldn't use the spoon end, just dip the other end in the vial, and smear it lightly on the slide."

"Right," Ash replied shortly and, in a moment reminiscent of Basil Fawlty, snatched the recommended spatula out of the utensil jar. The smearing went off without any further interruptions, then it was a matter of placing the coverslip on top, and settling down at the microscope.

"It's blurry," sighed Ash, looking up at the ceiling as Neil didn't have a body and Ash felt ridiculous speaking directly to a computer server.

"You have to adjust the focus and calibrate the microscope for yourself."

"Of course you do," Ash muttered under his breath, looking back through the eyepiece, and fiddling with the adjustment knobs and dials until he could see the little guys. "They look different."

"They would have different functions. There are ones designed for purely research purposes, sensors, data gathering, that sort of thing. Then there are ones designed for different repair or building functions. In that vial there are thousands, if not millions, of each type."

"Whoa! What do you use them for?"

"Unfortunately, we haven't got them to function yet. Marcus was the driving force behind that project, and Jerry doesn't have too much lab time these days."

"Still, they look cool," replied Ash, counting at least ten different designs in the sample he was looking at.

* * *

Sheila sighed, reluctant for her time in this glorious shower to come to an end, but intruders don't generally interrogate themselves, so… It took a few more moments, another sigh, and the realisation that she was the best equipped to deal with any, and all, threats to the occupants of this house, so… *Oh fine!* She turned the water off, cracked open the door, and reached for a towel. *Oh my good lord!* That wasn't a towel, it was a soft, fluffy cloud that was big enough to wrap her from shoulder to ankle, and it smelled like spring time. Maybe she'd just run upstairs and show Rowan. Nope, she couldn't, at least not right now. The moment that she stepped out of the bathroom, Neil would start herding Ash this way. And yet another sigh.

Keeping the towel wrapped firmly around her, Sheila rummaged in her bag. What did one wear when interrogating an intruder? Something dark, *the better to hide any blood she drew*. Sheila didn't make any effort to suppress the evil villain chuckle that bubbled out, nor could she help the giggle that followed. She really wasn't taking any of this seriously, but come on! Who in their right mind breaks into an estate that is home to a vampire? She was faster, stronger, essentially better, than any human alive. Except maybe Rowan, he trumped her in the adorable stakes. So dealing with the dumbass that Neil was keeping occupied would be a piece of cake.

Her outfit picked out, Sheila reluctantly finished drying off, and donned her costume. Checking herself out in one of the full length mirrors, she grinned at finding her reflection suitably intimidating. She really loved her leggings, and would live in them if wearing "active wear" everywhere wasn't such a fashion faux pas, not that she really cared about or followed fashion. She tended to wear whatever was comfortable, clean, and handy at the time. This was the most thought she'd put into an outfit in a while, and she had to admit that she liked the result. It was the shoes that did it, she decided; cute little ankle boots with a mean streak in the form of buckles that meant business. Right! Best get on with it. A final check over her shoulder as she turned away from the mirror, *dayum she was hawt,* and she was ready to take on anyone, including pesky, dumbass, intruders.

* * *

Rowan missed Maggie's bemused stare as he bustled around getting her anything she could possibly need. This was after he'd escorted her into the kitchen and helped her onto a chair at the breakfast bar, making sure that she was tucked in, and had a napkin across her lap. This was the most attention that he'd lavished on her in…well…ever! Her boy was a thoughtful darling, but he was so often absorbed by whatever project he'd sunk his teeth into, that he tended to forget the little things. That had always been fine with Maggie, she was an independent, self-reliant, woman who enjoyed looking after her nephew; especially when that *looking after* allowed for merciless teasing and unrepentant nagging. So what on earth had gotten into him now?

"Row?"

"Yeah Mags?"

"What's going on?"

"Huh?"

"Why are you fussing?"

"Huh?" This last one as he held a buttered piece of bread up to Maggies lips.

Maggie just sat, and raised a questioning eyebrow.

"Oh! Ah," Rowan blushed and popped the bread into his own mouth, chewing quickly, and choking when he tried to swallow and come up with an explanation all at the same time. Maggie gave him a few good thumps on the back as he coughed and spluttered, before he gasped out, "went down the wrong way."

Several moments of throat clearing and sipping on the glass of water that Maggie had gotten for him in the hubbub, were followed by silence. Rowan reached for another piece of bread, before deciding that was probably not a great idea right then, and ended up moving things around on the counter before him. And promptly moving them back. Maggie rolled her eyes, shook her head, and reached for the bread; *she* might as well eat while he was umm-ing and ah-ing.

"Well, there was the thing last night," Rowan began, finally looking Maggie in the eyes. Before she could ask to which particular thing he referred, he explained, "when Sheila arrived. You looked so pale and shocked. The way you looked freaked me right out, until I realised that Sheila had just fainted again."

Maggie almost interrupted him then, almost explained what had happened. Almost told him that she'd seen a vampire pass out too many times to have reacted that way. Almost opened her mouth to say that she'd all but seen, and spoken with, Marcus. Almost told him everything she'd been mulling over since that moment, from her fears for her own sanity, to the impossible possibilities. Truly, she almost did all of that. Almost.

"And just then," Rowan continued, and Maggie's relief at having missed her opportunity was something she would deny to the end of her days; "when you were coming down the stairs, rubbing your hip. It just got me thinking Mags. How, one day, hopefully a very, very, *very*, long time from now, you won't be around to walk down the stairs and have breakfast with me. So I wanted to make the most of it, while we still can."

"Ah, kiddo," Maggie said, caught between wanting to sniffle at his thoughtfulness, and wanting to cuff him upside the head and protest that she wasn't dead yet! She settled for a small smile, and popped some more of Ellie's amazing bread into her mouth to buy her some time. Like most parents, both of the biological kind and the chosen kind, Maggie had honed her deflecting skills over the years, and she brought those skills to bear now. "Is Sheila getting ready to bed down for the day?"

"I'm not sure, she wasn't in bed when I fell…er got up. I figured she went exploring on her own. Sun's still down so there's nothing to worry about…right?"

"She's fast, strong, and as close to indestructible as a person can be. I'm pretty sure there's nothing to worry about," Maggie's wry tone hid her internal battle. The voice screaming at her to tell Rowan was beaten down by the cowardly one slapping a hand over its mouth and yelling *la la la la* at the top of its lungs. "She's probably downstairs." Maggie cleared her throat at Rowan's look, realising that she'd spoken louder than necessary so that she could hear herself over the cacophony going on in her head.

"You're right," Rowan agreed, his furtive look towards the door and his bouncing leg belying his tone. "I'm sure she's fine."

"Oh, for heaven's sake Row, just go downstairs and see for yourself."

"Thanks Mags!" He'd hopped down from his seat and was rushing towards the door when he pulled himself up. Turning back, Rowan walked to his Aunt, popped a kiss on the top of her head, and enveloped her in an awkward chair hug. He put his chair back properly, and tidied up his things. His parents had laid a foundation of good manners, and his years with Maggie had only served to cement that.

"I'll see you later." Rowan smiled at his Aunt before sauntering casually out the door.

* * *

Neil, taking his instructions quite literally, had been monitoring the bathroom door. He'd formulated several plans for moving Ash along; from the simple - a suggestion to head to the next point of interest, to the extreme - releasing a gas into the lab and setting off an alarm. He wouldn't use a toxic gas, just something which could hiss, and maybe make a cloud. A bit of a smell might help too. He had full control of the security system, so he could keep the alarm localised, and relatively quiet. Maybe he'd need to flash some lights too. Something red. He really liked that plan, but figured he'd give Ash the opportunity to move along first. But he *really* liked that plan.

There! The light from the bathroom spilled out as Sheila opened the door, but Neil didn't set any of his plans into motion until she'd actually set foot outside the bathroom door.

"So, Ash," Neil began as Sheila stepped out of the bathroom, "shall we keep going?" What Ash couldn't hear was Neil's silent mantra of *say no, say no, say no*. He really, *really*, liked the other plan.

"Sure!" Ash was an agreeable guest. *Dammit*. "Where to next, buddy?"

"I thought I would show you the dungeon," said Neil, knowing it was right on the way to where Sheila would be waiting.

"Dungeon?" Ash refused to acknowledge the way his voice rose at the end of that word, or that he had to clear his throat before speaking again. "Seriously? A dungeon?"

"Oh yes," Neil would have smiled had he had a mouth, a cunning, slightly evil, little smile in response to the way Ash had squeaked when he'd said the word *dungeon*. No matter, he was sure his tone conveyed the expression that he would have gone for.

Ash shuddered. Neil noticed, and revelled in the satisfaction that reaction wrought. Ash removed the protective equipment that he'd donned, leaving it on the counter next to the microscope, and made his way back out of the lab. He paused, hesitating, wondering whether he really wanted to see something called a dungeon that would make Neil sound like Mr Burns from *The Simpsons* when he'd come up with a particularly diabolical plan.

"This way," Neil projected his voice, so that it whispered in Ash's left ear, and all but chuckled when Ash jumped.

Beta Team$_{62}$

66 Hey Turbo," Chief called out, and waited for a grunt before continuing, "checking confirmation of transpo on the ground." She was prepared for the grumbling. It happened every single time, before every single mission. Each person deals with stress, with the unknown, differently. She dealt with it by checking, double checking, triple checking, every aspect of her plan, including everything she'd delegated to her team. Turbo dealt with it by grumbling about everything. She allowed it because he was one of the best mechanical engineers she'd ever met, the other being Wheels. There was that one time that he'd gone too far though, making his grumbling personal, and casting aspersions on her parentage. No one spoke badly about her Mama, and she'd made damn sure that Turbo knew that. Boundaries were important, as was reminding your team of alpha personalities that you were in charge.

"Turbo?" She'd let the mumbled grumbling go on for long enough.

"Transpo confirmed. Just like it was last time you asked. And the time before that."

"And Turbo-"

"Yeah, yeah. I'll make sure it's still confirmed every single one of the hundred times you ask between now, and when I get my hands on those sweet babies."

"You do that." She studiously ignored the gesture she knew Turbo was directing to her back, because she was his commander, not his friend. And he'd saved her life so many times over the years that she'd lost count.

Poppy & Doug[63]

oug returned to find his wife pacing. Pacing was never good. Pacing meant that she'd seen something. He noticed the hand wringing when she turned towards him. Really not good. And the fact that she hadn't yet noticed him standing here. Oh boy! He cleared his throat quietly, so Poppy would not be startled.

"Doug!" Poppy called as she hurried to him, hands out so that he would take them and draw her in. As he'd done every single time that she'd needed him. "We have to go. We have to go now!"

"Go where, Pop? The caretaker knows nothing about Rowan's plans, or where he might be."

"I know, but we have to try. We need to get there before it's too late. We have to save our baby, Doug. We *have* to."

"I know, Love." Doug sighed, holding her tighter, hoping that would calm the fear that was trying to claw its way out of his gut. "Can you follow Rowan's trail? You must be exhausted."

"I have to. We have no other option, and I'll be damned if I'm going to get us there too late for Rowan to have the chance to spend the rest of his life hating me."

"He won't hate you."

"He will," Poppy said quietly, "but I can live with that. What I can't stand is the idea of outliving my child."

"Alright," Doug released Poppy, taking her hand. "Let's go." He lead them out to the car, locking the door on their way out, and closing it softly behind them.

The Estate₆₄

Sheila was leaning back against the wall, next to the bathroom doorway, legs crossed at the ankles, hands loosely clasped in-front of her, thumbs twiddling. Too casual. She straightened up, all but standing at attention, facing the rest of the basement, and listening for Ash's approach. Too stuffy. Maybe she'd wait on the staircase, and come down when she heard him approach, acting surprised, and introducing herself? She tried a practice run, walking out of the alcove that housed the stairs with her arm held out, ready to shake imaginary Ash's hand. Too contrived. Should she wait behind the room divider? Observe a little? Then tailor her approach? *What the fuck was she doing?* What difference did it make where she stood? Why was she wasting her time with this? Sheila sighed, because she was about to meet one of Rowan's friends.

She'd never cared about first impressions before, never cared whether anyone liked her, because she could always Charm them into doing what she wanted anyway. Maybe she should Charm Ash right off the bat, get it over and done with. Maybe Rowan might not appreciate her mind-controlling one of his friends.

Which brought her back to first impressions. What did people, humans, usually do in these situations? Small talk? What on earth could she talk about?

"Hi! Hope you didn't find breaking in too difficult?"

Or maybe… "Hi Ash, I'm Rowan's girlfriend, Sheila. I'm a vampire. How are you?"

Sheila didn't think this was going to end well, at least not unless she used her Charm, but even then she'd have to deal with Rowan's disappointment. She didn't want to disappoint Rowan. She knew that it was an inevitable outcome at some point, no one was perfect all the time. Although she was damn close. But humans were such an unpredictable variable, and since she'd met Rowan, she was spending more and more time with them. Disappointment was bound to happen. So maybe she should just do it, and deal with the fall out afterwards? Could she though? Could she really bring herself to do something that would, however indirectly, hurt Rowan? *Fuck.*

* * *

Ash was dawdling, he knew it, and he knew he was doing it on purpose. It was the word dungeon that did it. That word evoked images of torture, and the very idea that there was one in a *vampire's* house scared the crap out of him. It wasn't bad enough that, even with all the years of training, he knew he was woefully underprepared to face a vampire, now he finds out that they like to torture people too. What the actual fuck? No. No, no, no. No, he didn't want to see the fucking dungeon, thank you very much. No, he really didn't want to be here any longer. And, ah fuck, no, he couldn't abandon Rowan. Fuck! Fuckity, fuck, fuck, fuck!

Neil wasn't exactly helping. Ash could swear that the A.I had a mean streak, or at least got an inordinate amount of pleasure from giving him the heeby geebies. He was starting to understand why some people thought artificial intelligence was not a good idea. All that Neil had done so far was have a bit of fun at Ash's expense, kinda like friends ribbing each other. But what if Neil decided that he and Ash were no longer friends? Ash looked around, nervously. Neil probably controlled every aspect of this property, or enough of it so that he could actually be dangerous. What the fuck were these people thinking? He really had to get Rowan, and get as far away from here, as quickly as they possibly could.

"Not much further," Neil whispered in Ash's ear again.

Ash jumped, the hair on the back of his neck standing up, and chills running up and down his spine. Goddamit, this was ridiculous. He was not a coward. He had years of training behind him. He was strong, and in the best shape of his life. He was smart and, should the situation call for it, had no doubt that he could MacGyver his way out of here. He had a mission, maybe not the original one, the one that the company had sent him on, but rescuing Rowan was a mission that he was prepared to accomplish. Or die trying. Fuck the dungeon. Fuck the vampire. And fuck the A.I that was messing with him. Ash walked on with new purpose fuelling his steps.

* * *

Jerry was awake. He'd been listening to Ellie's soft snores, as he did for a while every morning, and had for centuries. He enjoyed this quiet time and used it to reflect on the things he'd done, and the things he still wanted to do. He'd battled anxiety about it a few decades into his elongated life, worried that he'd do everything on his list, and run out of things to add to it. He'd been scared of facing eternity, or however long Ellie chose to live, in a state of ennui. He needn't have worried. The more society progressed, the more things he found to add to that list, so now he worried about dying before ticking off everything on it. He still considered himself lucky though, he'd been able to do so many more things than people with a normal lifespan got to accomplish. He supposed that his dilemma now was no different to theirs.

He wondered how many more mornings he'd get, and whether now that both he and Ellie were ageing again, her lifespan would exceed his. He hoped so. He didn't want to live in a world without his Ellie in it. Didn't want to wake up to silence and an undisturbed half of the bed. He didn't know how Maggie did it without losing her ever-loving mind. The thought of having to say goodbye to Ellie, literally gave him a pain in his chest and short-circuited his brain. He just couldn't deal with it, and he fervently prayed that he wouldn't have to.

Jerry reached out and snagged one of Ellie's wayward curls. He loved her hair, okay, he loved everything about her, but he especially loved her hair. He loved the way that she'd chuckle every morning when she first caught sight of her hair in the mirror. It was so unruly in its natural state that she'd been reduced to tears of laughter on too many occasions to count. He'd always found himself laughing with her, not at her hair, but because her joy was infectious. He found it fascinating to watch her wrangle it under control, and could never understand how she managed to fit it all into whichever neat hairdo she chose. At some point throughout each day, he'd think about it, and look forward to the moment she set it loose that night.

He turned his mind to this time yesterday, when he'd lain in the same position, toying with yet another lock of Ellie's hair, and had no idea that life as he knew it was going to change. There was a vampire under this roof again, and people sleeping in other rooms. He and Ellie were never able to make lifelong friends, because he knew they'd always, eventually, realise that they were ageing and he and Ellie were not. He'd hoped that would change when they met Maggie, but then she lost

Marcus and didn't return. A small part of him wanted to say that she'd abandoned them, but he couldn't blame her. Not when he, himself, shied away from so much as considering losing Ellie. The important thing was that Maggie was back, and that they'd all fallen back into their relationship as though no time had passed.

He was still a little stunned that she'd brought a vampire along. Or rather, Rowan had. Jerry wondered if there was something in the family blood? What were the odds of two people, in the same family, finding true love with a vampire. Not the fairy tale kind of true love, either. The kind that was actually real, and still needed good communication, negotiation, and compromise. And where both parties fought tooth and nail to make sure that they brought those things to the relationship, each and every day. Jerry let loose a small smile, the kind that he and Ellie had.

On that note, and because he knew his wife so well, he'd better get up and go get the coffee ready. He'd learned long ago that Ellie functioned best after at least one cup of coffee in the morning, sometimes two, three on bad days. He'd also learned that he wouldn't be able to get a coherent answer from her about *anything* before those first few sips, and that she refused to be held responsible for anything she did or said before then. So, to save the both of them heartache and pain, Jerry had perfected his morning routine to include having the coffee ready for when Ellie made it downstairs. Leaning over, he kissed her cheek, lingering a moment to give thanks to the universe for bringing her into his life.

Rolling out of bed, Jerry turned back and straightened his side, even though it barely looked slept in. He stretched, arms up then out to the sides, before putting his fists on his hips, sucking in his barely-there belly, and puffing out his chest a little. All that for an audience of none, as Ellie always slept soundly through the whole routine. Wiggling his hips made his penis sway, giving Ellie a good morning wave she'd never know about. Shrugging, Jerry headed to the bathroom for a quick shower, missing, as he always did, Ellie's secret little smile.

*   *   *

She'd been pacing, listening for Ash and Neil. Why were they taking so long? Okay, okay, so she could put on the speed and cross distances in the blink of an eye, she knew that didn't mean that *everybody* could do it. As far as she knew, she was the *only* one who could do it so, whilst it felt like every other being on the planet was dawdling, it was her perspective that was skewed. She knew this. She did her best to practice patience, especially with those she cared about, and at work, but this waiting was driving her nuts. She still hadn't pinned down where she wanted to stand, or what she wanted to say. She felt like there could be a lot riding on this, and it was making her anxious.

She'd managed to avoid so many feelings in her life, all the particularly human ones, the ones that could make you weak. She'd always felt superior, decisive, and in control. Meeting Rowan had messed with most of that. Now she...worried. She worried about him and Maggie, and now Jerry and Ellie. She worried that she could so easily hurt them, physically or otherwise. She worried that she wouldn't be enough, that with all she could do, she was still lacking, mostly because so much of this was still new to her. And, because it was all so new, now she had Ash to worry about too. The *top of the food chain* Sheila wanted to speed over, bail Ash up against the nearest wall, and either choke the reason for this intrusion out of him, or simply rip his throat out. Her new feelings were horrified, which meant that she probably shouldn't do that. *Right?*

* * *

In his head, Rowan was already downstairs, snuggled up with Sheila... on the bed that used to belong to Marcus. The bed that Marcus and Maggie had probably... scratch that, definitely, had sex on. Yeah, that quickly went from a romantic moment to something he couldn't mentally unsee or unthink. Maybe he and Sheila could shower together, heaven knew he suddenly felt dirty... oh god! Knowing his Aunt, and the ridiculous amount of fun she always had teasing him about anything and everything to do with sex, there was probably nowhere, on the entire freaking

Estate, that she and Marcus *hadn't* had sex! The thought literally gave him chills, and he shuddered.

"Good morning, dear boy," said Jerry, catching Rowan by the upper arms before the young man could run into him.

"Oh! Jerry! Hi," Rowan's exclamations were as a result of both his surprise, and his relief at being pulled, firmly and swiftly, back into the present. "How are you? You're up early! I was on my way downstairs."

"Ah," Jerry now understood why Rowan's head had been in the clouds. "I'm well, thank you for asking. I've learned to be an early riser. It makes a long life easier if one's wife is happy, and Ellie cannot be happy without her morning cup of coffee."

"The things we do," chuckled Rowan, feeling a sense of camaraderie with Jerry, and fleetingly wondering if it made him slightly chauvinistic. Was that like being a little bit pregnant? What the fuck was wrong with him? His brain was all over the place and he felt almost jumpy. If he didn't know better he'd say he was jonesing. Seriously? *If I didn't know better?* Of course he was jonesing! He had been *jonesing* ever since he met Sheila. He missed her the moment she was out of his sight, and that feeling intensified the longer they were apart. So really, it was no wonder that he all but wanted to crawl out of his own skin; he hadn't seen

Sheila for *hours*! This was ridiculous. He was a grown man. He needed to get ahold of himself.

Why though? Why not enjoy the living shit out of this? Make the most of these out-of-control feelings, because who knew how long he'd get the chance? How many times in his life would he meet his one true love. Alright, mental eye roll. That's the stuff of fairy tales, but who's to say he couldn't get a fairy tale? At least for as long as Sheila deigned to be in his life. He was in the unfamiliar position of thinking about whether he was enough. Rowan was sufficiently self-aware to realise that he'd, mostly, led a charmed life. He was attractive enough, nice enough, wealthy enough, healthy enough. All the enoughs. But now he was realising that he was also only. Only human. Only mortal.

Jerry, recognising the look on Rowan's face, cleared his throat. "Before you allow yourself to spiral into the same thought patterns that your Aunt went through, many years ago, might I offer some words?"

"Uh, yeah, sure," Rowan said, somewhat dubiously.

"You're not dealing with a human."

"Huh?" Great Row, real eloquent!

"You can't attribute human thought patters to a vampire. They don't think the same way we do. If Sheila is anything like Marcus, and I have no reason to think otherwise, she's claimed you as hers. There will be nothing, and no one, that she would let come between the two of you, including yourself. Do yourself a favour, *talk* to her, talk to your Aunt, heck, even talk to Ellie and I. Neither of you need to figure this out by yourselves, unless that's what you choose to do. Just remember, you have the support and knowledge of people who have already been there, done that, and have outgrown the t-shirts! Now, get going."

"Thanks Jerry! I will! We will! See ya," Rowan called as he continued on his journey.

*Poppy & Doug*₆₅

hey'd been sitting in the car for too long. No, that wasn't the issue; they'd been sitting in the *idling* car, out front of the unit, going absolutely nowhere, for too long. After all the hurry-up, they were stuck waiting. Doug, sitting at an angle in the driver's seat, intently watching his wife, could see Poppy tensing with each passing moment. He knew, from unfortunate experience, that the tenser she got, the more she got wound up, the less likely she'd be able to lead them to Rowan. The thought that his wife would blame herself for anything happening to their son made his heart ache. He knew there was nothing he could say, or do, that would assuage her guilt. But they weren't there yet. He might not be able to make her feel less guilt, but he could damn well do his damnedest to try and ease her tension.

"Pop?"

Her sob almost broke him.

"Hey! No, none of that now. Come here," Doug reached out, sliding a hand behind her neck and clicking open her seatbelt with the other. She resisted, as he knew she would. His Poppy was a diamond at the best of times but, at a hint that she might fail? She hardened her outside as well. The harder she fought to succeed, the harder she made it for herself, and the greater the likelihood of failure. Luckily, he knew her. Inside and out. "This isn't for you to do alone, Pop. Rowan is my son too. Let me help you, so that we can help him. Please?"

Damn her know-it-all husband. She could have resisted a demand, but a request? A request to help the only other person that she loved insanely? There wasn't anything, *anything*, that she wouldn't do for Rowan or Doug, and Doug knew it. Still, she *should* have been able to do this. What would they do if she couldn't? She took a trembling breath, opening her eyes, and facing her husband.

They looked at each other, Doug's thumb lazily stroking the back of her neck as he reached for her hand. Poppy watched his face, noting the small changes that took it from concern to calm...acceptance...kindness. Her breathing deepened as she wallowed in his gaze, her lips relaxing into the smallest of smiles. This was her husband, the man who knew her better than she knew herself. The man who, with one look, could take her from a slow burn to a raging inferno. The man who could calm her just by staring at her with nothing but love in his eyes. There was no hint of urgency or accusation in those eyes, and she knew there never would be. Doug trusted her, and her abilities, with their lives. He'd proven it, more times than she could remember. He knew that she would not fail, could not fail. And so, she didn't.

"We need to take a left out of the driveway," Poppy murmured, leaning over to give Doug a quick kiss on the cheek before sitting back, and doing up her seatbelt again.

"That's my girl," said Doug, grinning as Poppy snorted, whilst seat-belting himself in.

The Estate₆₆

Ash marched along like the soldier he'd trained to be, scanning his surroundings as he went. Yes, Neil had made him jumpy, but he'd have been a fool not to be jumpy on a vampire's territory. He'd lost sight of that, a lapse in judgement that he could not repeat. The "dungeon" had turned out to be almost a non-event. It was nothing but a hole-in-the-wall cell, with spring-loaded shackles in it, and on the outside wall beside the door-way. When Ash had questioned that, Neil had helpfully informed him that they were there in the event that there was not enough time for the vampire to put themselves into the cell. *Like a vampire would voluntarily imprison themselves,* Ash thought on a snort.

He needed to be ready for anything, especially if he was going to successfully get Rowan out of here. His steps slowed, how did you rescue someone who didn't think they needed rescuing?

"Neil?"

"Yes, Ash?"

"How is Rowan?" Ash asked, then shook his head. That wasn't what he wanted to know. "Is Rowan happy here? Has he seemed okay to you?"

"Absolutely."

Not the response Ash had been hoping for. Rowan was a reasonable and intelligent guy; surely they could talk about this, and surely Ash could convince him of the danger he was in?

"Neil?"

"Yes, Ash?"

He didn't even get a chance to open his mouth to ask his next question. One moment he was walking along, nothing but basement in front of him, the next he was drawing his crossbow. His reflexes worked faster than his brain could process what was happening. He kept the bow aimed steadily at the vampire who had appeared out of nowhere.

"You must be Ash," Sheila murmured, trying not to make any sudden moves. Any *more* sudden moves. She really shouldn't have just rushed over, spooking the poor man, but she'd had enough of waiting. She kept her face schooled, although she wanted to giggle at Ash. She bet he thought he could actually get her with the bow. She briefly considered flitting over there and taking it out of his hands before he even had a chance to blink, but it probably gave him a feeling of security. So she'd leave him with it, for now, and they could hopefully have a civilised conversation about trespassing, and why she wasn't going to break him into little pieces and feed him to Jerry's dogs.

Ash didn't move, didn't answer, just like he'd been trained; don't give them anything they can use against you. He kept her in his sights, but used his peripheral vision to confirm what his earlier scans had shown. He was past the bathroom, but before the stairs that would have taken him out of here. The vampire was right there, just on the other side of the stairs, his last obstacle before he could get to Rowan. All he had to do was pull the trigger. He was well within range, had trained so long and hard at this distance, he was confident that he could drop her with one shot.

* * *

Rowan was humming a jaunty little tune as he rushed to the door under the stairs. He wasn't quite running, he didn't want to appear desperate, but he wasn't strolling either. Who was he kidding, if an olympic scout had been about they would have picked him for the walking team for sure! Based on this performance. Not at any other time. He was usually too busy with his head in the clouds to rush anywhere. But this wasn't anywhere. Finally, finally! He was going to be with Sheila again. He was so screwed. He had it so bad. If she chose to break his heart, he knew it wouldn't just shatter into a million pieces, it would pulverise into dust and blow away on the slightest breeze, never to be repaired. *Jeez, dramatic much?* He really couldn't help it, he was feeling downright giddy and it was all he could do not to add the occasional skip to his step.

He felt like the luckiest man alive. Not only did he have the most amazing Aunt in the world, a woman who had been mother, father, and best friend for the last few years, then add to that meeting Sheila, a vampire who had taken up permanent residence in his heart, soothed his soul, and routinely brought his blood to a boil, and now he'd added Jerry and Ellie to his little family. He had the support of people who all knew what he was going through, who loved and cared about him and, by extension, the love of his life.

He hadn't had the easiest time when his parents had disappeared and he hadn't always dealt well with whatever the universe threw at him but, if all of that had been a down-payment on this time of his life, he was glad to have paid it. And would do it again in a heartbeat, if it meant that he'd end up right here, right now, about to have his mind and his... erm... blown. *Really?* Fine, shut up! He didn't want to presume, even if that presumption was just in his head. Sheila might not be in the mood. Who was he kidding? Sheila? Not in the mood for any kind of sex? Did he just giggle? He was feeling downright euphoric!

That was the thought that made him pause, his hand on the pivot door. Was this euphoria, this ecstasy, normal? Natural? What was normal when a vampire was involved? Maybe this was one of the things that he should talk to Maggie, Jerry, and Ellie about? Probably a good idea. But not before he had his...erm...blown! The bounce in his step translated to a jog down the stairs after he'd pushed the pivot door open. He slapped his palm on the scanner and all but pulled the door off its hinges in his haste to get it open and get to Sheila. Taking a couple of steps on the landing brought his goal into sight.

There, the love of his life, standing almost like she had been waiting for him. So stunningly gorgeous, and looking so studiously serious. Stepping out, he rushed to her, turning to see what she was staring at as he went.

* * *

She'd heard him. Of course she'd heard him, and felt him, his approach, his giddiness. She heard the nearly silent swish of the pivot door, and his jog down the stairs that was so loud to her. She narrowed her eyes, watching for a sign from Ash to show that he too could hear Rowan's approach. Nothing. Either the man was incredibly focused, or cursed with human senses... which makes sense considering that he's, well, human. She almost smiled as Row's palm slapped the scanner, his impatience evident in the sound. And boy was she tempted to go to him when he was checking her out from the landing; but Ash still had that silly crossbow aimed at her, which wasn't really a problem for her, but she didn't want this first meeting of the three of them to go awry.

She imagined how this would all go down; Rowan making his appearance and Ash, surprised, would put up his crossbow. There'd be handshakes and backslaps all around and, eventually, they could all laugh about how Ash thought he could actually shoot Sheila, and that he thought that she'd let him. She smirked, on the inside. She was starting to like making friends, that is, if the people she made friends with ended up being like Maggie, Ellie, or Jerry. Ash seemed a bit hostile, she hoped that it wouldn't be a case of him not liking her and she not liking him. That would put Rowan in an awkward position, having to tell Ash that they couldn't be friends anymore would suck for him. Still, maybe it was just the outfit and the weapon that made him look mean, maybe he was really a nice guy underneath… deep underneath.

She was relaxed, and a little eager for the friends to meet, as Rowan rushed out of the alcove, turning to see what she was looking at. She saw the moment Ash registered movement, the surprise, the defensive reflexes. She watched in frozen horror as Rowan, her beloved, processed what was happening with that ridiculously fast brain of his. She hadn't predicted this, hadn't planned for it. Hadn't expected Ash to reflexively squeeze the hair-trigger, or for Rowan to forget what she could do, and be the hero she didn't need.

"No!"

She didn't know who roared it the loudest, her or Ash, as Rowan leapt in front of her, knowing full well that he'd get hit instead. The moment of impact, the sound of the crossbow bolt rending its way through his flesh, brought sudden and violent life to hers. She loosed a guttural scream as she sped to Ash, not stopping but grabbing him by the throat and all but throwing him into the spring-loaded manacles he'd mentally mocked earlier. She was back, and catching Rowan before his head hit the floor, barely recognising her voice in the keening she could hear.

"Ow, stop. Sheila, stop!" Rowan's pained and muffled voice reached tentatively through her grief, and her guilt.

She hadn't realised that she'd clutched him to her so hard, cradled his head to her shoulder so forcefully, that he could barely speak. He was alive! She loosened her hold so that his head could roll into the crook of her elbow, his grimacing face the most wonderful, wavering, sight. She was crying. That was new. She took a deep, unneeded, breath before making her eyes move away from his long enough to check him for injury.

"Fuck."

"Yeah." Rowan groaned, his hands around the crossbow bolt protruding from his torso, his shirt ruined by the spreading blood stain.

"No! No, no, no, no, no!"

"You! Shut up!" hissed Sheila, baring her fangs, and her angriest face, at a sobbing Ash.

"Huh, remind me never to piss you off," quipped Rowan, the lie of his levity revealed in his grimace of pain.

She'd heard them, noting the scraping of chairs and pounding of feet somewhere in the back of her mind, as she and Rowan spoke. Ellie was fast, but she'd still been in bed and so was roundly beaten by Maggie and Jerry. She would never forget the look on Jerry's face, how his colour seemed to drain before her eyes, a surprising reaction coming from the man who'd helped capture Jack the Ripper. Rowan was going to be fine. He was alive. He was talking. It was all going to be fine.

"Oh! My boy!" Maggie cried as she came to kneel beside them.

"Hey Mags," croaked Rowan. Clearing his throat, he asked, "is it bad? Cause from where I'm lying, it kinda looks real bad. Doesn't feel too great either."

"You're going to be fine," Sheila interjected, squeezing him a little harder, before remembering not to.

"What the fuck is going on?" demanded Ellie, rushing out of the alcove. "Your screaming shook the whole house, which I would have said was impossible considering the soundproofing everywhere! Marcus would be pissed over how much he spent getting it done-… oh shit!" She hadn't been able to see Rowan until she'd walked around Jerry but, the moment she did, she froze. Ellie reached a shaking hand back for her husband.

"Is it like…?" Ellie asked quietly, addressing Jerry but not turning away from Rowan.

"Yes," responded Jerry solemnly. "Exactly."

"What?" Rowan wanted to know. "Is it like what?"

"When you've been around as long as we have, you get to see a lot of things. I've seen a wound," began Jerry, clasping Ellie's hand, and moving to stand beside her, "similar-"

"Exactly!" Ellie corrected.

"Quite right," agreed Jerry with a small smile. "Exactly like this one. I'm so sorry dear boy."

"No!" commanded Sheila. "Just no! No saying sorry. Rowan's going to be fine!"

"That other wound proved fatal," Jerry stated gently, holding his ground when Sheila rounded on him with an even more fearsome look on her face.

"Oh god! Rowan! I'm so sorry. I didn't mean it. Oh god please!"

"Shut it!" Sheila growled, her head swivelling towards Ash in a very inhuman manner. "He's going to be fine."

"Ash?" Rowan called weakly.

"Yeah," Ash sniffled. Not in the least concerned by the daggers that Sheila was throwing his way with her eyes. He found himself concerned by very little, the information provided by the butler guy had damn near extinguished his will to live. Five little words, and he was ready to follow Rowan to whatever waited on the other side.

"I'm sorry buddy," said Rowan. "This wasn't how I thought you two would meet." He chuckled wryly, then groaned because even that hurt. Then he all but yowled. "What the hell?"

"I'm taking you to the nearest hospital," Sheila declared, adjusting her hold because her first attempt at lifting Rowan had hurt him.

"You can't," said Jerry.

"I'm an apex predator. I can do whatever the fuck I want!"

"He means," Ellie held out her hands in a calming gesture, "you can't because the sun's up."

"Fuck! Well, call an ambulance then!"

"They won't get here in time. We're too remote."

"Then… what?" asked Sheila, finally understanding just how dire the situation was. "This isn't right. This can't be happening. Do something!"

"I love you Rowan. I couldn't love you any more if you were my own son. I'm so proud of you, of the man you've become-" Maggie began, a hitch in her voice.

"No!" Sheila's outrage made Maggie flinch. "Don't you dare start saying your goodbyes. There has to be something we can do! This is the twenty first century god dammit!"

"Wait!" Ash called out, straining against his bindings. "Wait, wait, wait-"

"I said shu-"

"No," coughed Rowan, not noticing that Sheila's eyes widened as she snapped her attention back to him, not at his interruption, but at the small flecks of blood that had sprayed out with his cough. "Let him talk. He didn't mean for this to happen. He wouldn't. So, you know, let him loose."

Sheila took a moment, sparing a second to glare at Ash, before responding, "okay."

"Okay?"

"Okay to him talking. The only way that he will *ever* be free from there is if you live."

"You said this is the twenty first century," Ash rushed, not willing to risk the chance of Sheila shutting him down again.

"Yes…so?"

"That's the problem! You need a medieval solution!"

Poppy & Doug[67]

Not a single misstep. Poppy had been able to follow the exact route that Rowan and Maggie had taken. They were driving along a country road that must have been the longest in the freaking world. Whatever houses they could see were set far back from the road, and far enough from each other so that no amount of screaming from one place would reach its neighbours. The natural grasses clumped here and there, but occasionally a homeowner had won the battle against nature and cultivated an impressive lawn, like the one they were passing on the left.

"Shit!" Poppy flinched.

"What?" asked Doug, his hands wringing the wheel.

"It's happened. We have to hurry! Faster, Doug. Faster!"

"Pop, I'm already over the speed limit. The last thing we need is to be pulled over and delayed."

"We won't be pulled over!" Poppy's exasperation came from a place of fear for their son, and Doug knew it. "When was the last time you saw a cop? Now hurry!"

"Fine," Doug gritted as he floored it, just as scared for their son as Poppy.

"Fuck!"

"What now?" Doug groused, easing back on the speed and checking the mirrors for flashing lights.

"We've missed it," Poppy was becoming frantic. "They missed it, and I was following Rowan's earlier path. Turn around, Doug. We have to go back."

*The Estate*₆₈

"If he doesn't start making sense," Sheila warned Rowan, "I am going to go over there and rip his head from his body."

Rowan stared at her, raised an eyebrow, and blinked, slowly, several times.

"I was going to say that I would slowly dismember him," Sheila sighed, "but I don't think I'd have time."

Rowan just kept staring.

"Fine," Sheila huffed, then pouted.

"What do you mean?" Maggie asked, leaning on Sheila's shoulder to stand and turn to Ash, desperately grasping onto any available hope. "What do you know that could help?"

"A vampire could," Ash stated, glaring at Sheila, and inwardly cursing the universe.

All eyes turned on Ash, Rowan's probably the widest of them. Not once, during any of their contacts, had Ash let on that he *knew*.

"How?" Sheila glared right back at him. The arsehole was the cause of this, she wasn't going to just believe what he said…*anything* he said.

"I read some journals recently-"

"We're not trying something you read in some *stories*!" scoffed Sheila.

"Journals!" barked Ash, straining against the manacles, wishing he could wrap his hands around Sheila's neck. "Not fucking stories. I'm talking about journals that my family have gathered and protected for generations. My *vampire hunting* family."

"Your what?" Rowan demanded.

"You heard me," Ash said, his heart breaking. In a few sentences he'd not only managed to betray the trust that Rowan had placed in him, but he was also giving them the means to save Rowan's life, and thereby make him an enemy. "Know the enemy, right? Sun Tzu might have bored me to tears, but he knew his shit. My family have studied and learned everything we could about our enemy, including what they did when they didn't want someone to die."

"A drop," Sheila said, looking at Rowan with hope dawning in her eyes.

Rowan, who hadn't stopped staring at Ash, wanted to be sure he understood, "You hunt vampires?"

"Yeah buddy, I do," Ash slumped in his bindings, his world crumbling, just like his heart was. His life was forfeit, Sheila would see to that, but that wasn't going to stop him from doing everything he could to save Rowan. "A drop might not be enough."

"How many vampires?" Rowan couldn't let it go.

"What?"

"How many vampires have you killed?"

"Me? Personally? None. I was sent here on a reconnaissance mission, tracking Marcus."

"But you said *vampires*, as in plural."

"I did," Ash gave Rowan a small, sad, smile, "but you're kinda missing the important bits right now, bud. Sheila has the right idea, but I don't know if one drop will heal you."

"So, I'll give him more."

"More than a few drops could start the conversion and, once that's started, if you don't follow through, it would kill him."

"What conversion?" Maggie asked, not wanting her boy's life risked unnecessarily. Although, it wasn't like he was doing so great right now.

"I'm not explaining this very well," sighed Ash. "If you're going to try to help Rowan, you'd first have to remove the crossbow bolt-"

"He'd bleed out!" Jeremiah interjected.

"Yeah, he will, if Sheila isn't ready with enough of her blood. But, because of the rate that he would be bleeding, it would take more of Sheila's blood than, say, a simple, through-and-through, bullet wound to the arm. That kind of wound would knit with just one drop of her blood. Rowan's injury, his bleeding, would force Sheila's blood out almost as fast as she could drip drops on there."

"I've already said I'd give him more."

"That's where the conversion comes in. At some point, the strength of your blood will start overtaking his. If that happens, he'll start to change, to turn. You'd have to commit to seeing him through the change because, if you stop before he's through to the other side, he'll die. In agony."

"Turn into what?" Maggie demanded, first looking to Jerry and Ellie, who weren't able to give her an answer.

"Why don't you people know all this? You knew Marcus for years, surely he told you?"

"Marcus had no recollection of his life before waking up as a vampire."

"What?" scoffed Ash. "Where was his Hound?"

"His what?"

"His Hound? The one who would have helped him through the Reclamation ritual?" Ash took in all their blank looks. "The ritual that would have released all the memories of his lives to Marcus."

"There was never a *'Hound'*," Maggie said, her statement confirmed by nods from Jerry and Ellie. "There was never really anyone but us."

"So you don't have a Hound either?" Ash asked Sheila, taking the look she aimed at him as a negative.

"Right..." Ash shook his head in disbelief before taking a deep breath. "If you give Rowan just enough blood, you'll heal his existing injury, and everything can go back to "normal". If you give Rowan even one single drop too much, he will start the process of converting into a vampire. It's not something that, historically, has been done very often, the risks are too high. It's usually a last resort kind of option, and even then, the chances of success aren't great. There are so many things that can go wrong. You could stop too early in the process, or the process might not take."

"What other choice do we have?" Sheila asked, looking to everyone for a solution that didn't involve further risk to Rowan. "There has to be something! Jerry? You said you'd seen this before. Can you drive Rowan to the nearest hospital?"

"He wouldn't make it. Even if I drove like a lunatic, which wouldn't help his condition, we're too far from the nearest medical help." The sorrow on Jerry's face was too genuine for Sheila to consider arguing with him about this.

"Ellie? Maggie?" Sheila begged.

"What about me?" Rowan asked. "Don't you want to know what I think, what I want?"

"Sure! Absolutely!" Sheila's smile was a little too bright.

"How would this work?" Rowan directed both the question, and his steady gaze, to Ash. "Does Sheila just prick a finger and do a quick switch, pulling out the bolt and sticking her finger in there?"

"Ew!" Ash grimaced at the mental image. "If you're going to attempt a full conversion, the drop or two that would seep out of Sheila's finger before her vampire healing sealed her wound would not be enough. This is gonna sound gross, but I would recommend that you swallow her blood, while she swallows yours. Her fast metabolism would mean that whatever blood of yours she swallowed would quickly absorb into her system, giving her more blood to give to you. Eventually she should start to taste her own blood and, when that is *all* she tastes, she could probably stop."

"Probably?"

"I've never seen this done. All I've got to go by are a few ancient journals I read recently. I have no idea whether it'll work. I'm so fucking sorry, Rowan." Ash lost his internal fight to be strong so that he could see Rowan through this ordeal. Ordeal? He'd fucking killed him! Whichever way he tried to look at it, he was losing his Rowan. If Sheila managed to heal him, Rowan now knew what Ash really did for a living. Ash had broken Rowan's trust and their friendship might never recover. If Sheila tried the conversion and it didn't work, Rowan was going to die a slow and agonisingly painful death. If Sheila successfully converted Rowan, he'd become a god-damned bloodsucker. And if they tried anything else, or nothing else, then Rowan was going to die today, and Ash was the one who killed him.

He'd never felt like this before. He now had a bleak and bottomless pit where his heart had been. It was growing, and it hurt. It was eating up his lungs, making it impossible for him to hold in the sob that he'd been keeping prisoner in there. He wanted to curl in on himself, try to stop the painful emptiness from spreading, but the manacles made that impossible. All he could do was rock a little, and try to contain the keening that was clawing its way up his throat. He would have done anything, *anything*, for Rowan. He was the one who had killed him. He wasn't aware that his struggles had lacerated his wrists and he was bleeding. Or that he was whimpering. Or that his sight was blurry because tears were streaming down his face. He refused to look away from Rowan. This was the last day that he would have with him. He gave zero fucks about what tonight would bring. If he was lucky, Sheila would put him out of his misery. He briefly wondered whether she would do it here, or would take him outside so they didn't get his blood all over the basement.

"Ash? Hey, Ash!" It took a while for Rowan's increasingly feeble voice to penetrate his anguish. "It's gonna be alright, mate."

The absurd lie elicited a hysterical, half-chuckle-half-sob from Ash.

"It's okay. It's not your fault."

"Like hell it's not!" Sheila was not going to accept responsibility for this. Even if she could have taken care of Ash in any of the thousands of moments before Rowan came downstairs. Could have. Should have. It still wasn't her fault!

"It doesn't matter whose fault it is!" Maggie interrupted what could have turned into a lengthy argument, wasting time that Rowan did not have. "If this has even a small chance of working, you need to do it. Try it. I can't live with the alternative."

Ellie's grip on Jerry's hand was punishing, and there was no sign of her letting up. Jerry didn't care. He was as scared, hopeful, and hesitant, as his wife. They kept their silence, whatever input they might have was purely emotional. They'd just got Maggie back and, if this failed, it would kill her. They already loved Rowan, the few hours they'd had to get to know him had been enough to make that inevitable. Having Sheila in the house gave them a sense of completion, like their lives had come full circle. And even Ash. His connection to Rowan was so obvious as to be painful, his devastation so clearly evident. That this tragedy was unfolding and they could do nothing, was not something either of them was dealing with very well. So, while Ellie's grip was punishing, he was holding her so tightly to his side that he was amazed she hadn't yet complained.

"Row?" Sheila was quiet, and serious. "You hadn't yet decided."

Rowan looked at her, puzzled, until the internal lightbulb went off. "Well, this isn't exactly what we'd talked about. I didn't know that I could become like you. That I could be your equal-"

Sheila scoffed.

"-closer to your equal," amended Rowan, unable to suppress the twinkle in his eyes at his lover's inability to concede the mere possibility that she could, one day, meet her match. "At this point though, I don't think I've really got much to lose. And, if it doesn't work, I'll die a happy man, knowing that I was able to feed you right up to the end." Sheila's horrified look was *not* what he had been going for.

"Mags?" Rowan asked, seeking an ally.

"I've already lost Marcus," Maggie rounded on Sheila, the secret she'd been keeping festering inside her. She stifled her impulse to rant and yell, to scream *I lost Marcus because of you*, because that wasn't fair. "I can't lose Rowan too! I need you to do whatever you have to, whatever you can, to make sure that does not happen."

"I... I don't know if I can," Sheila admitted brokenly.

"You have to!" Maggie insisted.

"Please," begged Ash. He'd always thought he would die before he begged a vampire for anything. Turned out that there were worse things than dying. "Please!"

Poppy & Doug$_{69}$

66 There!" Poppy screamed, pointing to the now easily visible gate. Doug braked hard, before easing up on the pedal and guiding the car onto the driveway.

"Neil!" exclaimed Poppy, as she clicked off her seatbelt and clambered over Doug, ignoring his flinch and huff of surprise, to lean out his window and reach for the pin-pad.

"May I help you?"

"I'm Rowan's mother and, if you don't open that gate *right now*, I will hold you personally responsible for my son's death!"

"But-"

"*NOW* Neil!"

Neil, using the considerable processing power at his disposal, made several simultaneous calculations, and opened the gate. The delay was so infinitesimally minor, that Poppy and Doug were not even aware of the hesitation.

"Hurry Doug. Hurry!"

Doug, never one to disappoint his wife, planted his foot. He hadn't taken into account the loose gravel drive and, as he turned into the curve, the back end of the car swung out. He and Poppy didn't notice the bobble-headed garden gnome that went flying as the car's rear wheel clipped it. Didn't see it land on the lawn, the impact hard enough for the head to separate from the body, and snap off the oar paddle.

Maxine's[70]

Wheels was lightly snoring, sprawled in the middle of Maxine's bed, arms and legs akimbo. She and Maxine had spent hours together, mostly drinking, sometimes talking, occasionally laughing. Max, standing beside the bed, smiled fondly, wistfully. If her line of work permitted genuine friendships, she would have liked for Wheels to be her BFF. But Max had a business to run, which meant that, like every other morning, she was up with the sun. It had taken at least an hour, and a couple bottles of wine, for Wheels to loosen up enough to have a conversation which involved more than her shrugging and giving short answers. She probably wouldn't appreciate knowing that Max had purposely plied her with booze and employed her, not inconsiderable, skills to get Wheels to talk.

She'd taken it as a challenge, and would vehemently deny anyone's accusation that Wheels made her soft. She'd sipped on her wine, making each glass last, whilst Wheels went through about three or four. She hadn't started with asking questions, instead she'd nattered on about inconsequential things; her last favourite purchase, her penchant for stashing dark chocolate wherever she though Sai might not find it, her obsession with food, and why she'd continue to pay through the nose for her current chef…or eliminate anyone who tried to steal her away. She'd sat back, smugly watching Wheels's reaction when she'd had the rest of the food sent up. They'd dined by the windows, watching the lights try to imitate the sparkle of the stars they drowned out.

And then Wheels had asked a question. It wasn't even a major question, just a cheeky one asking for the chef's name, but it was enough for their conversation to really start. Max had looked at Wheels, seriously and knowingly, when she'd admitted that it felt like the first adult conversation she'd had in a long time. Or at least since… She hadn't prompted, choosing instead to refocus on her meal, giving Wheels the space she needed to decide what she was prepared to share.

"I'm angry."

"Okay."

"A lot. All the time."

"Okay."

"Except, maybe, not right this minute."

"Good. I'm glad. There's a lot to be angry about in this world and, it seems to me, you might have more reason than most." Max alluded to the scars that she hadn't so far acknowledged, but would have to have been blind not to have seen. "So, if I can wine and dine you enough so that you are comfortable and relaxed for a few moments, I'll take it."

Wheels had stiffened as Max let her know that she knew but, a sip of wine and another bite of manna from heaven later, she allowed a small smile. "Me too."

When Wheels had asked what drew Maxine into the world of arms dealing, Max had known that the last of the barriers had come down. They were now onto serious questions and, if she answered that one, Wheels would owe her an answer of her own. So, living up to her mercenary nature, Maxine had gifted Wheels with her origin story.

The Estate₇₁

Poppy opened her door before the car had come to a complete stop and was running towards the front door as soon as she could. Doug, who wasn't far behind, reached out to try and slow her headlong rush towards the door, expecting to have to knock, or ring a doorbell. He smiled ruefully when he remembered that he shouldn't have underestimated his wife. Whether it was what she'd said to Neil, her unshakeable faith in the universe providing what she needed as she needed it, or pure luck, he'd take it. Poppy burst through the unlocked front door and raced unerringly for the basement stairs.

Having heard the car drive up, Sheila tensed, ready to attack or defend as needed. Rowan felt it and looked at her questioningly, trustingly. She'd need her hands free if an attack was coming, so she gently transferred him into Maggie's arms.

"No," Maggie sobbed, misunderstanding Sheila's intent.

"*Please!*" Ash begged, sagging in his restraints, defeat in every broken line of his body.

Ellie and Jerry looked at each other, eyes tearfully glistening, until they heard the pounding down the stairs. They barely flinched as Sheila flitted to a defensive position facing the landing, ready to take on anyone and anything that would threaten her family. The steps slowed. Sheila could hear the deep, fortifying, breath, and scent the woman who was taking a moment before revealing herself. She knew that scent, or at least the aspects of it that were Rowan, but she wasn't going to have time to warn him.

"You will do it," Poppy said, stepping into the basement and not taking her eyes off the vampire. Not even to look around her to the very reason that gave her heart the will to beat, her son. Everything that she'd had to endure, everything she'd survived, came down to this moment. If she couldn't convince Sheila to turn Rowan, then it had all been for nothing. "And it will work. It has to, otherwise we're all doomed."

"Mum?" Rowan croaked, unable to see past all the people between him and the voice that had meant love, and then nightmares, to him throughout his life. Maggie's fingers dug into his arms for a moment, then he felt her forcibly relax them.

"Hi baby," cooed Poppy, still looking intently at Sheila. "I had to abandon my son, so that he could end up here, now. Please, don't let all the years we had to live without him be for nothing."

"I don't understand."

"I know, but we don't have a lot of time. I, we," Poppy amended as Doug came up behind her, "will tell you everything, I promise. But you have to do this. Please."

Sheila looked around, getting everything from encouraging nods to pleas, either mouthed or implied. She focused on the only person who's opinion mattered. "Row, are you sure? Do you really want this?"

"Please."

"We can't do it on the floor."

Jerry was already moving towards the koi room divider, carefully folding it out of the way, before fussing with the pillow placement on the bed. Ellie, who had followed closely behind, gently took her husband's hands and guided him to the side. They wanted to be nearby in case they were needed, but they were also dying to see if this could work. Hoping fervently that it *would* work.

Sheila, gently and carefully, relieved Maggie of her burden, holding out her arm so that Maggie could use the support to stand. It took Maggie a minute, her knees weren't as good as they used to be, but she used Sheila's proffered arm, leaning most of her weight on it. She skewered Poppy with a scowl when her sister started to walk over to give her a hand. They would be having words later, loud and, likely, harsh words. Once she was able to get moving, Maggie made her way over to Jerry and Ellie, needing their support through this as much as she'd needed Sheila's to stand.

Ash strained against his restraints, every fibre of his being wanting to rescue Rowan, get him out of here. The internal battle that he was enduring was vicious; a lifetime of conditioning and training warring against a hopeful heart. This had to work. He couldn't live in a world where he'd been responsible for Rowan's death. He wouldn't. He had to stop this, he couldn't live in a world where he'd caused Rowan to become the very thing he was sworn to destroy. Could he? His gaze was riveted on Rowan, noting his pallor, the shallowness of his breath, he couldn't look away, he wouldn't.

"Not gonna lie," Rowan said, looking into Sheila's eyes, "I'm not looking forward to the move to the bed." Then he barked a laugh before groaning with the resulting pain. His gorgeous, strong, and fast vampire had moved him mid-sentence and, until he'd laughed like an idiot, he hadn't felt a thing.

"Just to be clear, I want to go for the full conversion."

"What?" Sheila started, that hadn't been her plan.

"If we're going to try this at all, I want to go all the way. Unless..." Rowan took a moment to frame his next words as, until now, he hadn't considered this possibility. "Unless you don't *want* to be stuck with me for however long a vampire lives?"

"What? No!" If she had thought for a moment that it wouldn't hurt him, she would have shaken Rowan right then. "You don't get to do that. You don't get to worm yourself into my heart, so that I can't go two seconds without thinking about you, and then try to say that having you with me forever is something *I* don't want."

The self-satisfied smile that came over Rowan's face at her reaction made her seriously consider killing him, for just a second. He must have seen the flicker of danger in her eyes though, because he quickly wiped that smirk off his face, and that made her feel better.

"Now what?"

Everyone turned to Ash, who cleared his throat before suggesting, "The wrists. It'll have to be the wrists. Sheila can open hers for Rowan, and then take his."

"What about-" Rowan feebly indicated the piece of wood sticking out of his torso.

"Someone will need to remove the crossbow bolt," continued Ash. "But not until the healing has started."

No one moved. They all looked at each other, all reluctant to do something that was sure to cause Rowan pain.

"Oh, for heaven's sake," huffed Ellie, "A moment's pain for a life-time gain. I'll do it!" She gave Jerry's hands one last squeeze, and then situated herself by the bed. Close enough so that she could clearly see the wound, but far enough so that Sheila and Rowan might still feel like they had a bit of privacy.

Sheila looked down into the face of the only man she had ever loved, brushing a wayward lock of hair off his temple, and doing her very best to memorise the way he looked back at her. "You ready?"

"Feed me, Seymour," quipped Rowan.

Sheila's loving gaze turned quizzical.

"It's from *Little Shop of Horrors*," said Rowan, as if that should explain everything. He gave up when Sheila just shrugged, and shook her head. "Yeah, I'm ready...I think." He really hadn't thought about the fact that he would have to drink blood. Sheila's blood. Lots of it. Straight from the source. Okay, sure, he'd thought about it in a kinky kind of way when she'd fed from him, but this was way over the other side of the scale. His stomach chose that moment to start doing tumbles, so far past butterflies that it was a wonder he hadn't hurled. Yet. Rowan cleared his throat, swallowed, then swallowed again. Then he was out of time.

As soon as Rowan had consented, Sheila bit into her own wrist but, when she withdrew her teeth, it immediately started healing. This would not do, so she savaged her wrist, ensuring a steady flow of blood which would, hopefully, be enough to convert Rowan. She must have looked quite feral and she noted Rowan's hesitation. He was paler, if that was at all possible, with just a hint of green around the gills. The sooner they started this, the better. She didn't give Rowan the option to refuse, bringing her wrist right up firmly against his lips.

He felt it, the barely-there pulse, the warm fluid coating his lips. Taking as deep a breath as he could, he let the tip of his tongue venture out to taste it. His eyes widened and, whatever blood he had left immediately headed south. Rowan grabbed Sheila's wrist, sucking on it, and holding on as though afraid that it would be taken away. Sheila winced, and took a deep breath in relief. They were essentially half way there.

"Row," Sheila tried to get his attention. "Rowan? *ROW!*"

He gave her side-eye, holding onto her wrist a little tighter, and trying to flinch away from her like a puppy hiding his favourite chew toy. She chuckled.

"Easy boy, I'm not gonna take it away from you, but I need one of your wrists and both of my hands are busy."

He double checked, just in case this was a trick. Sheila was still supporting him with one arm whilst feeding him with the other. He reluctantly released her wrist, bringing his left arm up for her.

"Last chance," Sheila whispered, quietly enough so that only Rowan would hear. Whatever choice he made now would be his own, no input or interference from the peanut gallery. His response was to bring his wrist closer to her mouth, whilst audaciously winking at her. And was that a rolling of his hips? Sheila smirked, raising an eyebrow at him. All she got for her troubles was an unabashed shrug, another pull at her vein, and Rowan gently waving his wrist under her nose, wafting his delicious scent.

Rowan watched her, the woman he was going to spend eternity with. Every day she grew more beautiful in his eyes, but that wasn't why he loved her. Every moment, she took his breath away, but that wasn't why he loved her. He loved her because when it mattered, each time it mattered, she took the time to consider him. He knew that he mattered to her, she made sure of that and, by extension, his family and friends mattered to her. She could have snapped Ash's neck, but she hadn't...yet. He had no idea what Sheila would do if the conversion didn't work. He risked a glance at his friend.

Ash's wrists were bleeding, but he didn't care. He strained harder, trying to get impossibly closer to

Rowan, trying to see what was going on. He flinched the moment Rowan took Sheila's vein. He'd expected the feeling of disgust that washed over him, but not the arousal that quickly followed, nor the yearning to be over there with the couple, as though that was his rightful place. What was the fucking hold up? Sheila hadn't yet taken Rowan's vein. She had to. She fucking had to, or it could all be for nothing. Ash struggled, straining harder, ready to deglove his hands if that's what it took. Then Rowan looked at him. That glance was all it took to calm him. A glance full of friendship, forgiveness, and promise.

Sheila delicately sniffed Rowan's wrist, then nuzzled it. She licked it daintily with the tip of her tongue, stifling her lustful groan only because Rowan's parent's were in the room. Rowan smirked, raising an eyebrow at her, which she studiously ignored. She wanted this, so badly, she was amazed she wasn't drooling. Still, she tried to be as gentle as possible when she finally pierced Rowan's skin. His groan, the one that he couldn't stifle, and the one that had nothing to do with pain, made her grin, snort, and then try to recapture the few drops that her mirth had allowed to escape.

Ash's focus narrowed, his straining muscles relaxing, his cock stiffening, and his hips rolling in time with Rowan's. He salivated, swallowing, in time with Sheila. His heart, were he able to hear it, took on an irregular rhythm; Rowan's faster one, punctuated occasionally by Sheila's slower beat. He breathed through his nose, long, drawn-out breaths at first; inhaling Sheila's delectable scent, and Rowan's. He felt a warmth on his torso, gasping as it itched and grew progressively hotter.

"Pull the bolt out, NOW!" he called at the moment that he could no longer stand the sensation. He cried out as Ellie yanked up on the shaft, a quick, sure, movement that removed it without causing any more damage. He caught her eye and they nodded at each other, before Ellie retreated to Jerry's side.

The relief was immediate, and he breathed a heartfelt sigh. He refocused, his attention narrowing until it may as well have been just the three of them in the whole world. He was so focused that he didn't notice right away, how he'd gone from slow breaths, to quick pants. How his heartbeat, the faster rhythm, sped up, and then started skipping beats. How cold he was starting to feel, and then flushing hot.

He didn't notice, not right away. Until he did. He couldn't control it then, the panic that swept through him, making him fight and strain against his shackles once more. He didn't feel or notice the blood running down his arms, or the worried glances that were being thrown his way. All he knew, all he wanted, was to stop this. It was killing Rowan. He could *feel* it. He didn't know at what point the screaming, the begging, in his head, whispered out of his mouth.

"Please stop. Please stop. Please stop…"

He knew she could hear him, the vampire killing his friend. He knew she could hear Rowan's heart slow and skip. But she wasn't stopping. And he wasn't able to get out of manacles meant to restrain a vampire. She wasn't stopping, and he couldn't stop her. Not the pleas, not the blood he was losing in his efforts, nor the tears streaming down his face, or the sobs escaping his chest. None of these things were *stopping* her.

He watched, through eyes burning with tears, as Sheila shifted the arm she was using to support Rowan, so that she could hold his head up when it would have lolled back. He watched, his heart breaking, as Sheila gently, ever so gently, moved Rowan's head, not quite shaking, but trying desperately to keep him drinking. He watched as Rowan's arm all but fell from Sheila's mouth, the only thing that had been keeping it in place was the suction as she fed. He watched as she heard it, as he felt it. The last beat of Rowan's heart.

To be continued...

Acknowledgements

There is a list of people that I thanked in **Just Say No**, and to whom I still owe many thanks. I won't go through that entire list again but please, if you have the time, have a quick read through the acknowledgements section in Book 1 of the **Just Say** series.

Thank you so much to the following people who have specifically helped with this book.

*Bronwyn Sabat - thanks for your editing services, and the fun of the *Comma War*.

*Ruth - you're who I picture when I think "Super hero".

*Samuel J Art - thanks for patiently and painstakingly bringing my vague vision to life.

*Jakkal Designs - you graphic wiz - thanks so much!

*Chris Evans. No, not that one. The one that is married to one of my incredible and amazing friends, and the one that helped me with some of the tech stuff that I didn't quite understand. When computers take over the world, I'm going to hide behind him!

*My focus group, who were patient with me when I bombarded them with so very many similar-but-different, and sometimes crazy, versions of the cover for their considered opinions. Thanks Mum, Marie, Louise,

Melanie, Kerrie, Tanya, Caroline, Julie, Donna, Kristy, Bronwyn, Maria, and Anna.

*Everyone who has liked or commented on any of the posts relating to the **Just Say** series - your interest and interaction always makes me squee!

*If you've read any of my books THANK YOU! If you've read any of my books and left a review where others can read it, I am *forever* grateful!

Dear Reader,

I'm so close to having this book ready and out in the world!

There is a constant battle going on in my head between the part that demands perfection, the part that demands speed, the part that demands efficiency, the part that is optimistic, and the dark part that is always negative and full of doubt. I work hard to beat that last part. Sometimes I succeed, and sometimes I falter. Delays at this pointy end of things are always because of either the perfectionist part or, more likely, that dark part. I'm pretty sure we all have that part, that voice that whispers that whatever we're doing is not good enough.

Luckily for me, good enough isn't why I started this journey. My goal has always been to see if I could. Could I write 100,000 words? You bet! (Eventually *wink*) Could I actually make it into a book? For sure! Get it published? Maybe not with an agent and a fancy publisher but, thankfully, this is the age of the internet where DiY is so easily accessible. So yes, I did publish, all by myself (with the support of everyone I thanked in the last book and in this one!). And boy did I learn a lot during the whole process!

Could I do it again? Heck yeah! And the learning is ongoing, so it's a good thing that I value and enjoy learning. But that brings us back to me, sitting here, typing this, and working hard to change that whisper from something dark and doubtful, to something positive and encouraging. I remind myself that the biggest thing I have learned during this whole process is that I am only human *snort* and that perfection is something to aim for but hope you never reach. Because if you reach perfection, then what is the point of further learning?

The other thing I try to always keep in mind is that, while we may all be human, we are all gloriously different. This means that people like and dislike different things and just because someone may not like my book babies, that doesn't make my book babies "bad". Now, if *everyone* intensely disliked my book babies, then I'd have to rethink my stand on my ability to write (and I'd like to think that I can accept constructive feedback well enough that I would do this with an open mind and an honest eye). But, so far, the feedback has been pretty darned good.

I started this second book on 18 January 2016 and it is now 2020, in the middle of the COVID-19 crisis/pandemic. I'm like everyone else, I had no clue back in 2016 that this is where we would be in 2020. I don't know that it would have changed anything in the story if I had, and I don't know if this will impact book 3 at all. It helps that this series is set on what I like to call an "Earth adjacent", parallel Earth.

I have found that the way I do things with my books is not like a lot of other authors. By that I mean that I release them as soon as they're ready instead of holding them back and building the suspense (or the preorders ;-P). I have a full-time "day job" and other commitments outside of work, so I don't get the time to be as prolific a writer as I would like. I would love nothing better than for writing to be my one and only job in life but a girl's gotta eat! (And I *really* like to eat!).

In my fantasy world, the one where my books make enough to support me, I get to write between 2 to 4 books a year! Doesn't sound like much but, when you consider that my books are about twice as long as some regular novels in terms of word-count, it doesn't sound too bad either. I'd love to have one book being written, one being edited, and another being released, on an ongoing cycle - a girl can dream! And that is something that I will work towards, but I also have a life.

That life is what helps me keep that dark and doubting whisper from becoming a convincing shout; the tap dancing, yoga, boxing, walking, breakfast with friends, cosy cuppas when I go visiting, and family gatherings, all help me to manage the various "voices" in my head. So does my writing.

So thank you, dear Reader, for your wonderful support, valuable feedback and reviews, and eternal patience. I really am going as fast as I can, while trying to do the best that I can, and always shushing that stupid, pesky, annoying, anxiety-riddled voice.

I hope you've enjoyed the journey so far and that you've fallen as in love with these characters as I have (all except Gramps, he's mean!). If you have, I would dearly love to read your review on Goodreads or wherever you purchased the ebook copy, or both!

I love hearing from you so please consider following me on any of the below platforms.

Facebook ~ VSOriginals
Instagram ~ vsoriginals
Twitter ~ @VSOriginals
Pinterest ~ VanessaSacco101
Snapchat ~ xremona
Goodreads ~ Vanessa Sacco
autograph.com ~ Vanessa Sacco

Till then, or until the next book…

All my best,

Vanessa Sacco :)

Rowan[1]

He'd been reluctant, until his first taste; then he couldn't seem to get enough. He'd never felt anything as erotic as Sheila feeding him her life's blood. It had helped, for a while, that intense rush that had him wanting to both fuck, and devour, his woman. His vampire. It had taken his mind off the crossbow bolt sticking out of his chest, and the spectre of death that had been amping the scare factor through the roof. So yeah, he made the most of the hard-on, and the sounds that both he and Sheila couldn't seem to control. Anything to convince himself that this would work, that he'd get to spend the rest of forever with her.

Then Ellie had done what the rest of them couldn't. She'd yanked that wooden stake straight up, and Rowan had seen stars. Not the pretty celestial kind, the kind that were usually accompanied by several swear words, or an off-key cuckoo and boinging springs. He'd lost it for a moment, that euphoria that came with a true communion of souls. But Rowan was not a quitter and he clawed it back. Better that than having to think about the very real possibility that this could be it.

These could be the last moments of his life. Rowan wasn't sure what he'd expected, probably lots of grey hair and arthritis, not this hail-mary scenario. He had to live long enough to give his parents a sever WTF talking-to. Who does that? Who disappears off the face of the earth, presumed dead, only to show up in the eleventh hour and demand that a vampire save their son by undertaking a procedure that hadn't been done in aeons?

And Ash. His buddy Ash was there, just across the basement. There'd been a connection the moment their gazes met, Rowan had felt it, and Ash had seemed to also. If this worked, it would all be because of Ash, so Rowan had to remember to convince Sheila to let Ash loose. If this worked. If it didn't? Rowan felt fear again, this time not for himself. Ash would be no match for Sheila, not in speed or strength. Knowing how anxious she'd been about loving a fragile human, Rowan was petrified of what she'd do to the one who had taken him away from her.

He'll have to tell her, just as soon as this was over, that Ash was under his protection. Maybe he should tell her sooner, make her promise not to hurt the guy. What if this didn't work? Rowan's heart raced. He hadn't said goodbye, not to anyone. He wasn't sure that he'd gotten just how very much he loves her through to Maggie; or that he found Ellie incredible, and a little bit scary; or that Jerry was wise and dignified beyond his hundreds of years.

But soon he'd have all the time in the world. Enough time to do anything and everything he'd ever wanted to do. Enough time to love Sheila to distraction, savouring every moment, every taste. Like now. Her blood was the most delicious thing he'd ever ingested. It made him feel warm, despite the distinct chill in the air. It calmed his soul, his run-away heartbeat. It made him feel safe, and loved, and so incredibly relaxed. Like he could just close his eyes and drift in a warm and cloudy cocoon, knowing that Sheila was right there with him. Maybe he would. Just for a moment.

He allowed his eyelids to drift shut, revelling in the feel of Sheila's arm around him and her lips at his wrist. He could get used to this, the feeling of warm, weightless, release. Is this what the whole conversion would be like? So peaceful? He paused in his drinking, just for a moment, because he could, because he wanted to, because, in the peacefulness, he'd forgotten what he had been doing. He felt it, when his head lolled and his lips released Sheila's wrist. He thought about objecting, mewling, reaching back for the land of the living, but it all seemed like so much effort.

He could hear them, all of them. Sheila's racing heart, his blood must be doing that to her. Ash's frantic struggles, the smell of *his* blood on the air as he shredded his wrists. Maggie's quiet sobbing, he wanted to tell her that it would be fine. Wouldn't it? Jerry's prayers, and the rasping of his palm against the fabric of Ellie's sleeve as he comforted her. And his parents. His *parents*! He wanted to hate them for abandoning him all those years ago, but he couldn't muster that emotion, not in all the peace that surrounded him.

His mum was mumbling something about it being fine, that she was right, wasn't she? His dad was doing his best to soothe her, as he always had. But was that a hitch in his voice? Was his mother crying? Was that the scent of her tears he could smell? But why?

Oh.

Was this what dying felt like? Was this always what dying felt like? Like you didn't have a care in the world, but that you could still feel and hear all the earthly pain around you. How much longer did he have? Was it too late for him? Would he never be able to see a sunrise again? Or make love to a woman, his woman? Or get rip-roaring drunk with his best friend? Or hold his Aunt Maggie and say thank you for everything she'd ever done for him? Or hug his parents, then demand to know what the fuck they'd been thinking when they disappeared?

The moments between heartbeats lengthened, his thoughts meandering over his life, his past, the future he may now never have. He seemed to have all the time in the world for thinking, not so much for breathing. Breathing is funny, you don't realise the effort it takes until you actually have to think about doing it. He tried it, breathing. Managed another one. Wondered about whether it was really worth all the effort. And then his heart stopped.

Book 1 in the **Just Say** series…

Just Say No

Is available now in ebook and paperback formats.

www.ingramcontent.com/pod-product-compliance
Lightning Source LLC
Chambersburg PA
CBHW060811120726
47909CB00006B/1869